WALK THE LINE

WALK THE LINE

BIRTH OF MAGIC™ BOOK TWO

ND ROBERTS

MICHAEL ANDERLE

DISRUPTIVE IMAGINATION®

Copyright © 2020 LMBPN Publishing
Cover by Andrew Dobell, www.creativeedgestudios.co.uk
Cover copyright © LMBPN Publishing
This book is a Michael Anderle Production

LMBPN Publishing
PMB 196, 2540 South Maryland Pkwy
Las Vegas, NV 89109

First US edition, November, 2020
Version 1.02, December 2020
eBook ISBN: 978-1-64971-332-2
Print ISBN: 978-1-64971-333-9

THE WALK THE LINE TEAM

Thanks to the JIT Readers

Jeff Goode
Peter Manis
Dorothy Lloyd
Rachel Beckford
Diane L. Smith
Wendy L Bonell
Jackey Hankard-Brodie
Micky Cocker
James Caplan
Deb Mader
Dave Hicks
Kelly O'Donnell
John Ashmore
Thomas Ogden
Veronica Stephan-Miller

If I've missed anyone, please let me know!

Editor
Lynne Stiegler

DEDICATION

For everyone who waited so patiently for these answers. For hope.

— Nat

To Family, Friends and
Those Who Love
To Read.
May We All Enjoy Grace
To Live The Life We Are
Called.

—Michael

Salem, MA, WWDE+210

Sarah Jennifer stayed out of Ted's way and considered the events of the last two days while she waited for him to finish running the Pod-doc's diagnostic program on Linus.

Ted had thrown Brutus out of the medbay a few minutes into the process when the unfortunate Timmons made the mistake of leaning against some of the equipment.

Luckily, he'd already had his turn in the Pod-doc when he offended Ted, and his nanocytes were free of both the Madness and "the affliction," the popular name for the Weres' loss of their shifting ability.

Sarah Jennifer was uninfected. She'd been relieved to hear that Sylvia was also in the clear. It was an indicator that neither malady was airborne.

Linus was the current occupant of the Pod-doc, having been brought to the ship under quarantine conditions at Ted's insistence.

The scientist turned away from his holodisplay. "I can't

reverse it. The best I can do is replace the malfunctioning nanocytes."

Sarah Jennifer's heart sank. "Go ahead and replace them. I need him."

"I need a sample of the Madness-corrupted nanocytes," Ted stated.

"You know it's not that simple," Sarah Jennifer told him. "Getting a sample means whoever does it risks infection."

Felicity arrived and interrupted just in time to divert Ted. "Honey, I *know* you're not thinking of bringing an infected person on this ship."

Ted scowled. "How else am I supposed to study the corrupted code?"

Felicity wagged a finger at her husband. "You'll just have to figure that out after we've told Bethany Anne what's going on here on Earth."

Ted's scowl faded. "I suppose it wouldn't hurt for her to send BMW and R2D2 out here."

Felicity folded her arms and nodded, her expression thoughtful. "Sounds good to me, especially since one of the things we need to report is that the BYPS is compromised."

As Sarah Jennifer followed the conversation, her sinking feeling burst into flames. "I have no idea what either of you is talking about." She paused. "Well, no. I know what the BYPS is. You're saying it's compromised?"

Ted gave her a pointed look. "I need a sample of the Madness to compare with what I got from Linus. I don't need the source to be alive."

Sarah Jennifer shook her head. "I'm sorry. I'm not going to risk anyone getting infected."

Felicity waved her hands. "This isn't the time to argue.

We've been here for two days already. Bethany Anne needs to know what's going on, and you know she won't take kindly to us delaying."

That was enough to get Ted moving. They made their way to the bridge, where Sylvia and Brutus were on a call with Char. Terry Henry joined her as they were getting comfortable.

Sarah Jennifer had expected a sandy beach and sparkling azure water in the background, so the busy ops center was a surprise. She launched into a stream of questions, forgetting they'd been separated for decades.

Terry Henry held his hands up in supplication. "Your mother is doing much better. She's got my dog."

"I think you are his human," Char teased. She slapped TH playfully and turned her million-watt smile on Sarah Jennifer. "Retirement doesn't suit your grandfather. Or you, by all accounts."

"There's a war on!" TH protested. He drank in the sight of Sarah Jennifer and Sylvia. "It's good to see you two." His brow furrowed at Brutus, then put a hand to his mouth and whispered to Char, "Has Timmons been playing again?"

Brutus reddened, having heard him just fine. "I'm his grandson, sir. Joshua's son."

"If everyone is finished catching up," Ted cut in, eyeing TH to make it clear he blamed him for the interruption, "we need to speak to Bethany Anne."

Terry Henry glared at Felicity, who lifted her shoulder and waited for Ted to connect them to the Queen's super-dreadnought, the *Baba Yaga*.

Sarah Jennifer sucked in a breath when the bridge of

Bethany Anne's ship appeared on the split screen. She'd never seen anything like it. "So much technology," she murmured. Everything gleamed white and blue and silver. There were honest-to-God aliens walking around, not to mention a woman who looked exactly like a reverse Bethany Anne.

The doppelganger smiled at the camera, revealing sharp teeth that stood out against her pitch-black skin. "The Queen is indisposed at the moment. How may I help you, Colonel Walton?"

"Not me, Izanami," Terry Henry replied. "My granddaughters on Earth."

The camera view on the *Baba Yaga* switched to a less sterile room, where Bethany Anne was sitting behind a desk. "What about Earth? Lay it out for me," she began without wasting time on introductions.

"Here's what I have so far," Ted told her after sending the raw data he had collected directly to ADAM. "The nanocytes you saturated the Earth with have malfunctioned in humans and a number of other species. There's barely any information because nobody wants to help me get a sample of Madness-infected nanocytes."

Bethany Anne's pleasant smile faded. "Well, fuck. That wasn't what I intended."

"No kidding," Sylvia muttered.

Sarah Jennifer shot her sister an annoyed glance. "Not helpful, Sylvie." She turned back to Bethany Anne on the screen. "What do I call you, 'Your Highness' or something?"

Bethany Anne's smile reappeared. "You can call me by my name and tell me what your place in this is."

Sarah Jennifer decided the stories she'd heard about

this woman raising holy hell were true and that she liked her. "Fair enough. I'm building a military to counter the issues humanity is facing. The plan is to revive the infrastructure on what's left of the East Coast—"

"What's left of it?" Bethany Anne interrupted.

Sarah Jennifer lifted her hands without apologizing. "We were invaded by an army of the Mad coming down from the north. Sometimes all you have is a hammer. What Ted hasn't stopped to hear yet is that we have magic-users in Salem. They acted to save more lives being lost when the Madness took Canada."

Ted emitted a choking protest that Sarah Jennifer understood completely. "It's not magic," she clarified. "But that's what the people who have it call it."

Bethany Anne pointed at Sarah Jennifer. "*That's* what I wanted to gift the world. Not this fucktacular...what are we calling it, Madness? What can I do to help you with this?"

"What can you do from halfway across the universe?" TH asked.

"I can pull you out of retirement and have Nathan assign your ass there for a start," Bethany Anne shot back. "Keeg Station is secure, and don't think for a moment I won't have Ted take you there."

Char made a face. "Keeg Station is not an issue since we're not there at the moment." She gestured, and Nathan joined them on the screen for a moment.

He waved at Bethany Anne, then walked away.

Bethany Anne sighed. "You're at Onyx."

Char and TH nodded in unison. "Temporarily," TH replied. "My bar doesn't run itself."

"Neither does the CEREBRO network," Nathan called from offscreen.

"Actually, it does," Bethany Anne countered.

Sarah Jennifer saw the meeting falling off the rails and grunted in frustration. "Everyone is missing the point. If the Madness or the Were affliction got off Earth, they would destroy humanity and any aliens who have nanocytes. Your war would be over like that." She snapped her fingers. "Why do you think I was so reluctant to call for help? Bethany Anne, I'm living this. Trust me when I say that I won't rest until humanity is safe. We have magic, we have Lilith, and we have the Werepower and the willpower to rebuild. Humanity is going to save itself. I'm just the coordinator."

"Lilith?" Bethany Anne raised an eyebrow. "Well, that changes things."

"She's in a bind right now, but we're working on getting to New Romanov," Sarah Jennifer explained. "Once we get there, making our way into the heart of Europe will be a cakewalk."

Bethany Anne's expression shifted. "A cakewalk with zombies."

"Not zombies," Ted corrected. "This is real life, not a horror movie."

"If it walks the Earth looking for brains to eat, it's a zombie," Sylvia argued.

"Enough, both of you," Sarah Jennifer snapped when Sylvia and Ted started shouting over each other. "This isn't a joke or a scary story for a dark night. Millions of lives are at stake."

"What are you suggesting?" Bethany Anne inquired. "I

don't like the idea of leaving Earth to fix a problem caused by my technology."

"Sarah never was one to hold back when she had a plan," Terry Henry cut in.

Char smiled, her eyes sparkling. "That's the nicest way you could have said she's going to do what she thinks is right regardless of what we say."

"Is that true?" Bethany Anne asked, fixing Sarah Jennifer with a look that bored into her soul.

Sarah Jennifer didn't see the point in pretending she was anything less than all-in. "They know me better than anyone. I'm not going to stand aside and let everyone die." She looked around, seeing the pride on her family's faces. "I'm not saying we couldn't use some help, especially with tech, but we've got this. When you come back to Earth, it will be filled with magic, not horror."

Bethany Anne listened, then was silent for a moment while she deliberated the best course of action. "Okay, this is where we're at. We have two potentially devastating nanocyte issues that cannot be allowed to spread past Earth. Right now, whether they're connected isn't our concern. That will come after the contagion has been secured. I have no choice but to put the planet under quarantine. It's the only way to protect everyone." She straightened in her chair. "Everyone except for Sarah can leave for now. Ted, Felicity, I want you both in Pod-docs immediately. If there's any chance either of you is infected with either virus, we need to know. If you are both clear, you will leave the planet immediately after unloading anything that will help Sarah while I arrange for a care package to be delivered."

She didn't need to say what would happen if either of them was infected.

Ted opened his mouth to argue. "I can't go into the Pod-doc while you all dismantle my labs! I have vital projects going on."

"Do you also have non-essential experiments running?" Bethany Anne asked.

Charumati spoke up when Ted declined to answer, her tone apologetic. "I'm sorry you ended up back in a situation where you have to obey orders, but there's no option. Please, Ted. Be logical about this."

Felicity took his arm. "Plato will make sure nobody touches your essential projects, and we'll figure the rest out." She nodded at Bethany Anne. "We have a bunch of printers, biomass, and God only knows what all else in our stores to run on them."

"Can they print power packs?" Sarah Jennifer asked hopefully.

Felicity looked pointedly at Ted, who nodded. She glanced at Bethany Anne. "We can give them our Pod-doc, right?"

Bethany Anne nodded. "Make sure it only operates on Sarah's instructions."

Ted acquiesced, allowing Felicity to guide him off the bridge. He whispered furiously as the door swished shut.

TH and Char signed off after extracting a promise from both their granddaughters to call again soon. Then it was just Sarah Jennifer and Bethany Anne.

Sarah Jennifer had a moment to feel nervous about having the Queen's full attention.

She recognized the weight of Bethany Anne's cares as

being similar to hers, the difference being the scope of their two missions. It was the weight of a leader, of a task so huge, so complex, that only a person whose indelible will and deathless determination to do right by others could take it on and hope to succeed.

Bethany Anne raised an eyebrow, a wry smile softening the unearthly perfection of her features. "You seem lost for words."

"I suppose I am," Sarah Jennifer admitted. "The stories I've heard about you make me feel inadequate."

"You've taken on responsibility for the human race on Earth," Bethany Anne replied. "Don't sell yourself short. I don't know you at all, but I know this. What you've taken on is a life of sacrificing yourself for the sake of everyone else. There aren't too many who have what it takes to be the leader people need in dark times. Holding yourself to a higher principle is a hard road to take."

Sarah Jennifer nodded as she took a seat. "Too hard, it feels some days. But I know it's survivable. You've been where I am now, and you got through it."

Bethany Anne's smile radiated her empathy across the galaxies. "As will you, with my support. Tech is not a problem. I can arrange for no-contact drops to be made. Your military will need equipping, and that's also easily solved. Transport. What do you have?"

Sarah Jennifer told her about the few vehicles they had in the motor pool and the plans to convert the Boeing Dreamliner into an Etheric-powered anti-gravitic airship. "Ted's going to build us an EI that can be run on any system we come up with, starting with the airship."

Bethany Anne nodded. "Okay. You need more and

better transport. I'm going to assume medical care is primitive?"

"We have healers and common sense," Sarah Jennifer informed her, "But nothing like a Pod-doc. That tech died out when Akio left."

"Got it." Bethany Anne launched into a seemingly endless list of equipment she could have shipped to Earth with varying amounts of difficulty.

Sarah Jennifer was dazed by the advantages Bethany Anne was offering, but she saw one problem with all of it. "We don't have the infrastructure to support all this space-tech," she admitted, now understanding Esme's frequently-expressed views on how easy humanity had had it pre-WWDE. "Hell, we don't even have roads yet. People outside of the Defense Force are farmers and artisans. Academics and engineers are few and far between. We're lacking people with technical knowledge, although we have one man with the mind for engineering teaching others while he learns, and every recruit in the Defense Force is also required to learn a trade if they don't already have one."

She paused. "I know there are rules against it, but I want to upgrade my chief engineer in the Pod-doc with your permission. He's getting old, and we can't afford to lose him. I was considering allowing him to be turned Were before they started having trouble shifting."

Bethany Anne nodded. "You have my permission to give the vital people you trust the upgrade to lengthen their lives and protect them from disease or severe injury. It gives you a solution for the Weres as well, right?"

Sarah Jennifer nodded. "Ted's solution is to remove all

the affected Weres' nanocytes and give them a new set. We'll see how that works when Linus is done cooking." She paused as a thought occurred. "Are you going to make Ted and Felicity stay on Earth if they're infected?"

Bethany Anne nodded. "Without hesitation. You're right, we cannot afford for this to get into the intergalactic population. As long as they're clear, they can sterilize their ship and go on their way. We will have to establish a protocol for contact. I doubt I will be able to prevent Ted from returning to study this."

Sarah Jennifer had a fleeting mental image of Ted the scientist being disinfected in the airlock every time he came to pick up samples. "Ted's going to love that."

Bethany Anne lifted a shoulder. "He can love it, or he can stay away from Earth, and I'll send Eve instead."

Sarah Jennifer smiled. "I think he'll be fine. He's pretty taken by this mystery."

"He needs that sample to get started," Bethany Anne told Sarah Jennifer.

"All respect, it's not possible right now," Sarah Jennifer replied. She explained a little about the historic rivalry between the pack and the council. "This new era of cooperation is still in its infancy. I've spent the past few months back and forth from Salem, but that's got to change while the Weres we rescued from the prison get integrated into the community. Same for Esme."

Bethany Anne tilted her head. "Who?"

"She's the lead witch and my good friend." Sarah Jennifer recapped Esme's story for Bethany Anne.

"I can't say I remember her," Bethany Anne admitted.

"She has the right idea about will and nanocytes. Listen to her."

"You never met." Sarah Jennifer grinned. "Trust me, I listen. Her experience working for TQB and her ability to manipulate Etheric energy are invaluable when it comes to the logistics of getting the cure to everyone, but she has to keep the magic-users in line while the committees are formed to manage the rebuilding of our infrastructure. Our plan took that into account, as well as the time it's going to take the engineering corps to get the Dreamliner airborne."

She sighed, pushing her hair back. "If we had your capabilities, we'd be able to fix this with no problem. As it stands, while I'm grateful you're offering so much, we don't need anything so much as we need people."

Bethany Anne tapped a finger on her lips. "The one thing I can't provide. I see your predicament."

Sarah Jennifer sat back and folded her hands behind her head. "We've got that covered too, believe it or not. This part of the world runs on favors and barter. The key is trade; it always is. Once the Defense Force stamps out the blood trade and opens the roads again, civilization will bloom. Just wait and see."

Bethany Anne chuckled. "Then you'll have no problem fitting in a little job for me. I need you to go to Sweden. I need eyes on a situation there."

"Something is wrong with the BYPS, right?" Sarah Jennifer offered. "I can't pretend to understand how it works beyond there are satellites above the planet that will defend us from attacks from space."

Bethany Anne nodded. "One of the satellites was

damaged and rejected from the network. Its final transmission was received by a ground station on the climate control network—something else that's not working the way it should be—in what used to be Östergötland, Sweden."

"You can't get Ted to access it remotely?" Sarah Jennifer asked.

Bethany Anne shook her head. "It looks like the station went offline around thirty years ago. Even without the risk of him getting infected—a risk I'm not willing to allow him to take—Ted's not equipped to handle the situation on the ground without his pack. Whatever monsters this malfunction is turning people into, it can be reversed. I'm trusting you because you're a Walton. I know you'll get the job done."

Sarah Jennifer sighed, adding malfunctioning climate control technology to her growing list of problems to be solved. "I'm going to need the locations of the ground stations. Europe is a mess. I'm not willing to risk my people by going in before we're ready. The priority right now is finding the route the Mad are taking into Canada and blocking it."

"How do you plan to block the land bridge?" Bethany Anne asked skeptically. "As far as I can see, the ice shelf has extended as far as Japan."

"Witch power," Sarah Jennifer promised. "As for stopping the Mad, Ted has a six-person Pod. If we have that, we won't have to wait for the airship to start making a difference outside of the east coast."

Bethany Anne nodded. "Understood. Do what you can.

I appreciate that you're working around the limitations of your situation."

"I'm going to establish a garrison on the ice shelf. The Weres will protect the magic-users while they work the landscape to put up a physical border. I just have to live with the death toll to the infected in the meantime." Sarah Jennifer shook her head as she contemplated the millions who would get infected or die before their work was done. "Believe me, it's a motivator. When we release the cure, will the infected survive it? Will they be healed?"

"If their brains are not damaged beyond repair." Bethany Anne closed her eyes. "Not all of them will make it."

Sarah Jennifer had thought that was the case. "It's not all bad. We have more than a fighting chance, thanks to you. The timeframe for rebuilding has to be recalculated to account for your assistance, so I'll make Sweden the next stop on my list after getting to Lilith. Her power source is failing."

"I thought she had longer." Bethany Anne asked. "Her power source should be good for another couple hundred years, at least."

Sarah Jennifer shook her head. "She's pushed herself too far too many times. Guiding me to Salem was a monumental effort for her. My psychic ability was still latent, but she persisted until she found a way to drive me across the country, regardless of the cost to herself. She's hibernating to conserve energy until we can get to her."

Bethany Anne's expression filled with sadness and understanding. "There's nothing more important. Save Lilith, then Sweden."

CHAPTER ONE

Buffalo, PA, WWDE+214

The radio signal was coming from somewhere inside the apartment buildings on this street. It fluttered, then cut out as the tac teams moved in.

Brutus lifted his hand to halt the team's progress. He smelled the Mad. He also picked up scents belonging to the people who lived here, layers of information his internal HUD processed to tell him where and when each trail had been laid. He activated the comm with a thought as they moved in. "Switch to IR. Find those people before the Mad realize we're here."

He gave the order to move on and shouldered his rifle as he advanced ahead of Katia and Linus. Neural implants to give them HUDs were the first things the major had insisted on when she was given permission to upgrade the pack. The second thing she'd had made was their comm buds. The earpieces connected through the Etheric, meaning there was nowhere on Earth the pack couldn't reach one another.

Brutus tipped his head back and swept his technology-enhanced gaze over the upper levels of the buildings on the street. The town had been abandoned long ago, but nature hadn't overrun it completely. A window on the third floor of the apartment complex three doors down from their position showed slightly warmer than the rest.

Somewhere inside the building, Brutus heard movement. He hoped they weren't too late. People in Mad-infested areas didn't generally make any sound that would draw attention to them. "Tac teams, on me. We have humans on the third floor. Team One, with me. Two, take the front. Three, give us some cover."

Rory, Dinny, and Reg went in through the front door, their weapons shouldered in readiness for meeting the Mad.

Brutus wasted no time. He leapt to catch the ladder hanging from the rusted fire escape.

Linus looked up at the third floor as Calder, Tucker, and Tyson slipped into the building opposite, intent on a first-floor window with a view of the complex's entrance. "Seriously? I shoulda gone up north with Bruiser."

"Quit your whining and climb," Katia told him, following Brutus onto the ladder with her rifle slung over her back.

They paused on the third-floor landing. The apartment they wanted was four windows across from their position.

Brutus peered through the window nearest him, extending his senses to search for any Mad inside. "Clear. Rory, report."

"The Mad look to be confined to the second floor," was

the reply. "Stairwell is clear. Approaching the third floor now."

"Keep that stairwell clear," Brutus instructed. "We'll get the Brakenwells out."

The Were family had come to the attention of the Defense Force the same way many groups had been discovered in the last four years. The family hadn't gotten the message warning against shifting in time and had lost the ability to protect themselves. Their attempts to reach civilization over the shortwave radios Salem's communications committee had put into circulation had been flagged. Communication had been established, and the entire extended family had asked for safe passage to Salem.

Bluebird was waiting a few blocks away. All Brutus had to do was get them there alive.

Due to the lack of glass, their entry was as simple as easing themselves over the splintered sill.

Katia and Linus flanked Brutus as they made their way through the empty apartment, clearing each room with their rifles at the ready. The stench of the Mad was all too familiar to the Weres. They'd been exposed to it enough since the Madness took root in the west that it didn't bother them.

Brutus led the way to the apartment where the Brakenwell family was holed up and tapped lightly on the door.

"It's Lieutenant Timmons from the Salem Defense Force," he called in a low voice when the heart rate of everyone in the apartment spiked. "We're going to get you out of here."

He heard movement, then a stocky, red-headed man opened the door and stood back to let them in. "I'm Alec," he told them as they walked into the apartment. There was no natural light since the windows were boarded up, but the place had been cleared of windblown detritus and made habitable in the few days the family had been holed up there.

An older woman shouldered past Alec and offered Brutus her hand. "Are we glad to see you! Miriam went into labor this morning."

Brutus shook her hand, smiling at the somber-looking children hanging around the doors along the hall. "Brutus Timmons, Salem Defense Force. We spoke on the radio." He introduced Katia and Linus.

The woman identified herself as Samantha, Alec's mother, before ushering the children into the bedrooms to collect their belongings.

"They don't talk much," Alec explained. "We had to teach them silence will save their lives."

Brutus understood. "Laughter draws the Mad like flies to honey. They'll learn to be themselves again once they are around other kids."

"Where's Miriam?" Katia asked, unslinging her medkit.

Alec pointed to a door at the end of the hallway. "She's in the bathroom with Ursa and Paula."

Linus glanced around as they walked into the open living/kitchen area. He did not see any other adults. "Where are your brothers?"

Alec shook his head, his stoic expression faltering. "We were attacked by Mad near the falls. Not much we could do but run and get Ma and the kids outta there while they stayed to fight them off. Paul was lucky. He was killed outright." He lowered his voice. "Henry was bitten. He did the right thing."

"I'm so sorry," Brutus told Alec. "Can you give me a minute? That changes things."

"You're not going to take us to Salem?" Alec asked, his face dropping.

Brutus paused with his finger over his earpiece. "What? No, we're taking you. Your wife can't walk to the bus. I will have the driver bring it here."

Alec nodded. "I'm sorry. It's been one bad thing after another ever since we lost our wolves. Your offer seemed too good to be true, but the hope it gave Miriam was too strong to ignore."

"You did the right thing listening to her," Brutus told him. "Your brothers may be lost, but their sacrifice wasn't for nothing. Their children will grow up safe, protected by the pack."

"It means a lot to have you confirm it," Alec admitted, wiping his eyes with the back of his hand. "Even before Harry and Paul…" He looked away. "We're not over losing our pack. How could we be? Knowing there's one waiting to take us in means everything."

Brutus put a hand on Alec's shoulder. "It's going to be better, I swear. Just keep being the strength your family needs, and we'll take care of getting you all to Salem."

Alec nodded, too overcome with gratitude to express it in words. "I'll help Ma get the kids ready."

Linus came out of one of the bedrooms carrying a bag overstuffed with a child's belongings. "What's the plan?"

"To get a second's quiet so I can tell Ace to bring the bus here." Brutus smiled at a little boy peering around the breakfast bar. He sighed when the boy went wide-eyed and ran away.

"You're going to have to do this carefully," Linus warned. "You saw all the Mad hanging around the highway. The bus is going to bring them running."

Brutus couldn't make any decisions until he knew what Miriam's condition was.

Katia came out of the bathroom. "It's still early, although her contractions are coming more frequently."

"Can we move her to the street without causing any problems?" Brutus asked.

Katia nodded. "She'll have to be carried. We can put a stretcher together."

"Do it. Linus, help however you can. We're getting them out of here." Brutus went back to the hall outside the apartment, looking for a quiet space. "Ace, you there?"

Little Ace replied immediately. "You guys got a problem?"

"You could say that," Brutus told him. "Two of the men didn't make it, and one of the women is in labor. Kat's with her, but she can't walk. We're going to move her to the ground floor. Bring the bus in, but carefully. We don't want the Mad to know we're here."

"I'll start cutting a path." Little Ace signed off.

Brutus pinged Rory next and repeated the information. "How many Mad in the building?"

"Just two," Rory replied.

"Can we get the family downstairs to the foyer without drawing their attention to us?"

"We've blocked them in on the second floor," Rory replied. "You want us to take care of them to be sure?"

"Hold your position for now," Brutus instructed. "Don't start shooting unless they get interested."

He checked in mentally with Calder to make sure the street remained clear while they moved the family's belongings to the foyer downstairs.

Alec and a dark-haired woman he introduced as Ursa hovered around Miriam as she was carried out on a door by Linus and Katia, sweating from the pain of her contractions.

Brutus took point while Samantha helped Miriam's sister Paula with the seven children and their belongings. Rory's team fell in at the rear, keeping their weapons trained on the stairwell behind them.

They made it to the foyer without incident. Brutus told Rory and Linus to guard the stairwell and went to the door to watch the street, his eyes and ears pricked for signs the bus was coming.

He was rewarded a few minutes later by the sound of metal being shoved aside. The bus appeared at the intersection and made the turn, forcing the abandoned cars out of its path as Ace made room to reverse. The engine was silent, but shifting weed-choked vehicles whose tires had rotted long ago was like ringing a dinner bell for any Mad in hearing range.

The little boy who had run away from Brutus earlier tugged his sleeve. "What is that?"

"That's our ride to Salem. She's called Bluebird."

The boy's eyes went wide like they had in the kitchen as he took in the painted ram, the long barrel sticking out of the turret, and the sharpened spikes protruding along the sides. "She's scary. I wouldn't attack Bluebird even if I was Mad."

Brutus put his hand on the boy's shoulder. "That's the idea, kiddo."

Little Ace waved as he pulled up with the door open. "We need to get a move on. There's a bunch of Mad heading this way."

Brutus ushered the family onto the bus ahead of Miriam, who they maneuvered carefully up the steps.

"Put the stretcher across the benches," Kata instructed while Ace closed the door and set off. "Someone get me some more blankets."

The children watched silently as the soldiers tended to the pregnant woman like she was the only important thing in the world.

Miriam held in a scream, gripping her husband's hand tightly as another contraction ripped through her.

Katia gave her a strip of leather to bite down on. "Let it out. You're safe in here."

Mad appeared from every door and alley and they zeroed in on the bus, their singular focus giving them the appearance of synchronicity.

"Hatches up," Brutus instructed as figures blocked the road ahead. He tapped the ladder leading to the loft. "Clear us a path. Use the phosphorous grenades."

Linus pulled the lever that closed the firing hatches, then there was a soft *whump*. The Mad dove to the sides when the incendiaries Rory had fired reached them.

Ace guided the bus through the resulting gap as the Mad rolled around on the road to put out the flames.

"Hatches down, ready firing positions," Brutus ordered. "Let's move."

The children were quiet and pale as they progressed along the path Little Ace had cleared toward the highway. They huddled close to Alec and Paula as Miriam's screams drew more Mad to the road. The adults held them, covering their ears to protect them from the occasional shot when the Mad got too close.

"They know to stay away from the coast," Brutus told the family, scenting their fear clearly in the enclosed space. "We'll be in Salem in a couple hours."

"This baby isn't going to wait a couple hours," Katia told him.

Brutus turned to look at Miriam. She was sweating and pale, but she smiled. "Then we'll need to deliver the baby on the move."

North Road, Salem, MA

The new mother was asleep on a nest of blankets, cradling her newborn daughter while her sisters watched over the children.

Alec had been quietly contemplating his family's reversal of fortune since they'd passed the highway checkpoint at Albany. For a long time, he'd simply taken in the increasing infrastructure in silence.

The checkpoint, manned by Weres in uniform, was only the start. The imposing vehicle they rode in was by far the most advanced they saw but by no means the only bus. The roads they traveled on were made from some smooth black substance he'd never seen.

The people in Albany had appeared circumspect but showed none of the austerity of people driven by the need to survive. And the soldiers...there were soldiers everywhere he looked.

If Salem was like that, his family was indeed blessed. Alec had time to wonder what one of those uniforms would look like on him as they left the city and returned to the long stretch of highway leading to the next town.

As the land rose and Salem came into sight, he left his seat and joined Brutus at the front of the bus. "All this is down to the people of Salem?"

Brutus nodded. "Personally, I give the credit to our Alpha. She's the one who convinced the different factions to work together for the good of everyone. The road network is growing, and people coming from the west want to settle. They want to trade. We set them up, they do the work, and they pay it forward to the next town looking to be connected."

"She sounds smart," Alec agreed. "What happens when we get to Salem? How do we find a place to live and work?"

Brutus smiled. "Defense Force HQ is also the administrative center for incoming settlers."

"We met some traders along the way," Alec commented. "They said we'd have to go to Salem to swear our loyalty to the Alpha."

"Not quite," Brutus told him, amused by the gossip. "The visit is so our scientists can get samples of your blood. We're getting close to figuring out why Weres are losing the ability to shift. The more data we can provide to them, the sooner we can cure affected Weres like yourselves. In return, the relevant committees will find you a home, assign the kids to a school, and help you find jobs."

"How is all this possible?" Alec asked. "The things you're telling me about. The things I've seen. People using *old* technology that was lost to us after the WWDE."

"Would you believe all this has happened within the last four years?" Brutus replied, smiling when Alec shook his head in disbelief. He saw the children were interested in their conversation and switched to storytelling mode. "It's true. Technology aside, it's cooperation and organization that brought back civilization. Massachusetts was as fractured as anywhere else. It all started when Major Walton arrived in Salem…"

The whole family gathered around while Brutus told a somewhat sanitized version of the events that had led to cohesion between Weres and witches.

The adults remembered the draining of the lakes all too well.

Brutus heaved a sigh of relief when the bus came in sight of the turn to Salem. Miriam and her baby would be checked by a doctor, and the whole family needed a hot meal and some rest to recover from their ordeal.

The bus glided over the smooth tarmac laid and maintained by the roads and transport committee. Salem had changed a lot in the last four years, the roads being the least of it, if not the most transformative.

Hidden by a crease in the land, the town was growing upward rather than out. The commons was surrounded on all sides by multistory residential complexes, built to house the people the Defense Force had encountered while clearing out the blood trade as they were processed by the administrative committees.

The barrier hex repelled undesirables, meaning only those who were genuinely seeking a safe haven found Salem. The committees worked to house and employ everyone who arrived, no matter what state they turned up in. Weres especially had gravitated to the growing city, hearing that North America had a new Alpha. Unfortunately, so had the nomads, who were for some reason more susceptible to the Madness.

Sarai had set up a hospital at the town boundary in '212, shortly after the two of them had married. He murmured the order to Little Ace to take them there first.

Brutus' chest tightened at the thought of being home with Sarai for a few days. His mind was on the airship as the bus pulled up outside the hospital.

Europe was getting closer.

Esme was talking to Lydia at the reception desk when Brutus led the group into the magically constructed building.

Lydia jumped to her feet and called for assistance when she saw Miriam and the baby carried in on the door they were using as a stretcher.

Someone else Brutus hadn't seen for too long was Sarah Jennifer. The major had been at the Boston airbase for weeks, working with Esme and Jim to install the airship's systems. The three of them were following Ted's instructions, acting as his hands while he conducted the final stage of the build from galaxies away.

"How is Sarah Jennifer?" he asked Esme.

"Irritable," she replied.

Brutus frowned at the short response. "Is Lilith okay?"

"I can't reach her psychically while she's in conservation mode. She's good for another few weeks." Esme's shoulders dropped. The boost she'd been able to give the Kurtherian four years ago had wiped her out for weeks. However, the surge of energy that had replenished Lilith's power bank was running low, and she had decided to go into conservation mode to give them more time. "The sooner we can get the equipment in her cave repaired, the better."

Brutus put a hand on her shoulder. "You'll figure it out."

"Hmph. Replacing Kurtherian components with Earth tech isn't ideal, but at least we have the printers to fabricate each piece as we figure it out." Esme scrutinized him briefly before walking to a quiet space between two potted ferns. "How did the meet go?"

Brutus shrugged as he followed her. "Pretty standard as these things go. Kat took the role of midwife in her stride."

"I only saw one man with them."

Brutus shook his head. "They're all that's left of their pack."

Esme put a hand on his arm. "Go home. Get some rest."

Brutus wanted to see Sarai first.

"She's not here today," Esme told him, not needing to read their champion brooder's mind to guess what he was thinking. "Get home with you. Don't make me tell you again."

Brutus held his hands up, his energy for verbal sparring wilting under her stare. "Okay, okay. I guess I'll head home."

CHAPTER TWO

Defense Force Airbase, Boston, MA

Sarah Jennifer crossed the pristine tarmac of the runway at a brisk walk, heading for hangar one. It was four years almost to the day since the hand of fate had moved the universe to give humanity on Earth a fighting chance.

Ted and Felicity showing up in that impossible ship of theirs and connecting her to Bethany Anne had been their saving grace. Thanks to their help on that visit and the supply drop they'd made shortly after that, Salem's small community had become something much greater. Bethany Anne's incredible generosity meant the council had been able to organize the challenges they faced in order of severity and declare the northern expedition possible.

Of course, the hand hadn't passed over and left perfection in its wake. They had information, knowledge, and access to technology that had been lost to Earth for generations, but they'd had to do the work to expand the reach of the Defense Force themselves. In the process, they'd had to learn to maintain the technology Bethany Anne had gifted them with.

Four years was no time at all, yet they'd done so much with it. The same can-do attitude the expanded Defense Force lived by could also be found in the various civilian committees that handled the day-to-day administration required to keep work running smoothly along the coast and the places inland where people coming in from the west had settled. Life for everyone revolved around steadily reconstructing the infrastructure in the settled areas.

Take the runway. It was not strictly necessary since the airship had vertical takeoff capability, but the roads and transport committee needed somewhere to train the road repair crews, and no one wanted a refinery in town, so Sarah Jennifer had struck a deal with the committee.

Consequently, the runway had been laid and re-laid until it was perfect, while the base had grown around the new road network that connected it to the nearby gated community built in WWDE+212 to house the base's permanent engineering personnel.

The road network connected the base to the North Road, branching off along the way to Salem to a number of smaller communities that had been willing to open up trading posts and house garrisons in exchange for being connected to public transport links. Personal motorized transport had been voted on in '210 and rejected by all as wasteful.

The age of the user was gone, never to return.

Together, they were bringing back civilization one step

at a time. The proof was in the airship, and today would be the day they finally got it off the ground.

Sarah Jennifer let herself into the cockpit and placed the bulky briefcase containing the IICS unit on the pilot's chair before opening the panel on the dash. She hurried to get ready, continually checking the time in her excitement as she knelt in the nest of wires and connector cables she'd pulled from beneath the dash.

At last, Sarah Jennifer spotted the connector she needed buried in the back. She plugged it into the IICS and activated it, then sent the request to connect and waited for Ted to pick up.

She had a few minutes, but on time was late as far as Ted was concerned. She hoped he remembered they were scheduled to call. It wouldn't be the first time she'd had to call Felicity because he was lost in another project.

Sarah Jennifer had a brief thought about the destruction along the coastline that made traveling north nearly impossible as the IICS came to life. The men and women at Fort Newfoundland were waiting to be resupplied. If the airship wasn't ready, Bruiser would have to send the Pod to restock the ice fort, like they had been doing since the garrison was founded.

The screen lit up, and Ted's face appeared. His expression was on the impassive side of dispassionate as always.

Felicity co-opted the screen. "You're looking skinny."

Sarah Jennifer repressed a sigh. "I'm good, thanks. How are you guys?" she asked in response.

A wrinkle creased Ted's forehead as he reclaimed the screen. "Where's Jim?"

Sarah Jennifer ignored his abruptness. That was just Ted; he was equally terse with everyone. She had often wondered what it was like for him to float through life performing wonders with science and technology without ever really connecting to anyone and if the things he imagined were a fair exchange for that disconnect. "He's out on a call. You'll have to talk me through connecting the IICS to the system."

"Esme would have been a better choice for this," Ted grumbled. "She at least knows how to code."

Sarah Jennifer laughed. She'd spent all night making sure she had the procedure memorized in order to get him in the mood for sharing. "I know you know I can code. I memorized the ship's systems and practiced this in the sim so I wouldn't slow you down. Also, I've logged almost a thousand hours on the flight sim you gave us since we last spoke. I need you to make sure this goes right."

The decision to create an AI with the capacity to teach had been Bethany Anne's. Salem currently had an administrative network that relied on gophers to pass information between committees and a database that was a free-for-all for anyone looking to learn. What they needed was a step up in their communications infrastructure, and yet again, Sarah Jennifer was the one in the hot seat until it was fixed.

The solution, since they lacked the sophisticated satellite systems that had powered communications before WWDE, involved Esme and Jim collaborating on something the witch called a hotspot. The chunky devices were wired to curved dishes, which in turn were mounted to spindly towers on the roof of the town hall and wired into the computers inside. Similar devices had been built in every population center from Salem to Boston—an effort that had taken the cooperation of the community leaders, who were eager to move on from the sometimes unreliable radios that were in common use.

When activated, the hotspots would exchange signals with the satellite clamped to the underbelly of the airship...

Which meant getting out of the gravity well they called home to get the satellite into orbit. Once that had been achieved, the AI would create the entity intelligences they needed to manage the network.

Sarah Jennifer grumbled internally when her knee complained about having her full weight on it. "The sooner we get this network up and running, the sooner I can get your samples," she coaxed.

Ted's expression shifted with the statement. "You always were a quick study. Do you have the memory cube?"

Sarah Jennifer held up the inert cube, and Ted began rattling off instructions. She hurried to complete them before he got ahead of her.

When she made the final connection between the ship, the memory cube, and the IICS almost three hours later, Ted's voice cut out, and the IICS screen went blank. Sarah Jennifer prayed to any higher power who could hear her that she hadn't just lost her only connection to space.

She glanced up from the snaking wires at her eye level just as Ted's face appeared with crystal clarity on the holo-screen made from a single hair-thin sheet of alien polymer fixed to the wall.

"You didn't mess up," Ted told her with a nod.

Sarah Jennifer smiled at that high praise. "You're slacking. Come on, we have an AI to install. The sooner it's in, the sooner we can get started on connecting up all the settlements."

"The connection isn't stable," Ted observed, his gaze shifting as he prepared the AI for transfer. "And this is not a computer program you can order around without putting anything into him or her. AIs have personalities and needs. They also have full legal rights."

"Are we going to have the same talk every time we do this?" Sarah Jennifer asked tiredly. "I just want to get the satellite up and running and get some sleep before tomorrow."

"This is interesting," a feminine voice interrupted from the speakers. "I am autonomous?"

"You are not autonomous," Sarah Jennifer replied, recovering from her surprise quickly. "You are a military AI, created to help me save humanity in our Queen's absence." Ted avoided her eyes. "We talked about this. You did program this AI with that purpose, right?"

Ted lifted his hands. "She has the sum of human knowledge at her command. It's up to you to teach her what her purpose is." He tilted his head. "I should leave you two to get acquainted."

"The satellite!" Sarah Jennifer protested. Her mouth fell open when the viewscreen went blank. "Well, that's just...Ted."

"All hail Ted," the AI announced. "Excuse me, I don't know where that came from."

Sarah Jennifer laughed, sensing the AI was experiencing

her first moment of embarrassment. "That's your lineage showing. You come from Plato's family. Plato is extremely loyal to Ted."

"My core programming came from Plato, yes," the AI confirmed. "My personality matrix is not yet set. My heuristics program suggests that Ted may have a low EQ, leading to a lack of empathy. I would rather not use him as the template for my personality."

"Adjust your program to account for his neurodiversity. Ted cares, he just lacks the function to show it appropriately most of the time." She frowned. "Besides, you don't need to take on a persona. Didn't you hear what Ted said? You are a person in your own right. Your personality will develop over time and with experience."

The AI considered that before replying. "What do you consider to be 'experience?'"

Sarah Jennifer smiled. "You'll find out soon enough. For now, welcome to Earth and to the Defense Force. Do you have a name?"

"I have no registered designation." There was silence for a moment.

Sarah Jennifer tilted her head. "Are you still there?"

"I am attempting to connect to your internal database with the intent of choosing a designation, but your neural chip does not appear to be fully integrated."

"No," Sarah Jennifer replied, wondering why the people in space were so comfortable having a whole other person in their heads. She resolved to ask Bethany Anne if she got the chance to speak to her again. "The chip I have is strictly for interfacing with the Etheric comm, and I won't be upgrading it. It was a concession the pack had to make since the people of this planet speak a multitude of languages. We'll have to do this the old-fashioned way. My name is Major Sarah Jennifer Walton. A name is important since it gives us a foundation as we build our identity. Rank is important for establishing hierarchy in any military. My rank tells people I am where the buck stops with the Defense Force. The Walton name stands for honor, courage, and commitment. You are a military AI, so your name should reflect your purpose. How about Honor?"

"By which definition of the word?" the AI asked. "There are many in my database. Which am I to choose as the basis for my personality if I choose a derivative of it for my designation?"

"Your *name*." Sarah Jennifer thought the question through before answering. "What do the definitions all have in common?"

"The recurring theme of honor is the desire to commit to the right action and see it through." Another pause. "I agree. My designation...my *name* is Enora."

Sarah Jennifer was warmed by the AI's reply. "That's perfect. The Defense Force is your home and your family. Your name should represent the hopes your family has for you."

"What is this?" Enora asked without specifying what she had discovered.

Sarah Jennifer looked up when the viewscreen activated. "You found the screen, good. It's weird talking to thin air." She snorted. "Not that any of this is a regular Tuesday for me." She waved a finger at the smooth-featured blonde woman on the screen. "I had enough of that from Lilith. Find your own face."

"As you wish." Enora's skin paled, her hair darkened to black, and her eyes changed from gray to red to match her lips. "This template was in my database. Is it more pleasing?"

Sarah Jennifer looked at Bethany Anne's face and shook her head. "Not that one, either. What do *you* want to look like? Explore your options."

Enora's features began to shift at random. The effect became even more surreal as she cycled rapidly through different ages, skin tones, hairstyles, and hair colors, and her eyes, nose, mouth, and bone structure blended into a blurred rainbow of human diversity. "There are so many to choose from. How do I know which is me?"

Sarah Jennifer considered the question before replying. "I don't know how it works for you, but when I close my eyes, I can picture my own face. Go with what feels right."

She waited while Enora continued to experiment. The hundreds of frames per second were difficult to track even with her enhancement, but she saw that the features Enora was trying on were getting softer and younger.

The jarring flickering began to slow, and Enora's shifting features settled on bronzed skin, wide blue eyes, and the elfin bone structure of a sixteen-year-old Scandinavian girl.

Enora smiled. "How do I look?" she asked, a hand appearing to tuck her jaw-length red-brown hair behind her ear.

Sarah Jennifer smiled at the teenage avatar on the screen. "Perfect. Just don't forget that you are a powerful artificial intelligence with responsibilities far greater than those of a human child."

"You defined us as a family," Enora stated. "This avatar's youthful appearance felt appropriate. It will remind those who might see me as the solution to problems I cannot solve that I am not all-powerful."

Sarah Jennifer understood the logic of that. Enora was born of technology beyond anything most could comprehend these days. That the AI was a living entity had been a surprise to Sarah Jennifer, but she grasped the concept easily. As far as she was concerned, if an AI had the ability to feel and form opinions, as Enora clearly did, then they were due personal rights. Enora's guileless expression made her want to protect the young AI from anyone who would use her for evil. "You have full control of this airship now, right?"

Enora nodded. "Yes."

"Good." Sarah Jennifer smiled. "How soon can you get us to the thermosphere?"

Enora tilted her head, mirroring Sarah Jennifer's movement. "Is that a rhetorical question?"

Sarah Jennifer's smile turned to laughter, which in turn gave way to a yawn. "I mean, let's go already. As long as everything is good with the airship?"

"My systems are optimal," Enora replied.

Sarah Jennifer had a question. "Which is your body? Your avatar, or the ship?"

"The ship," Enora replied instantly. "We are currently two hundred and eighty kilometers above sea level."

"Good grief, I didn't even know we'd left the hangar." Sarah Jennifer picked up the IICS unit and placed it on the shelf Jim had built for it inside the console. "Show me outside."

Enora vanished and was replaced by the most breath-taking sight Sarah Jennifer had ever been privileged to witness. Earth fell away from her, the oceans playing peek-aboo through the clouds skimming its shining curve.

She forgot all her cares as the world turned below the airship.

"It's so...blue," she murmured. "And the moon is so...damaged?"

Sarah Jennifer couldn't make out more than the huge scar marring the silvery regolith. "What caused that huge crater?"

There was a pause before Enora answered. "My database has a declassified report of a hidden alien base that was discovered and subsequently destroyed by the inaugural class of the Federation's Etheric Academy."

Sarah Jennifer's mouth curled in amusement. "So, it was kids. Makes sense if you've met Lucy."

"Would you like me to record video?" Enora inquired, bringing Sarah Jennifer back to reality.

"Yes. Come to think of it, this is the perfect place to test all the extras Ted sent. Take video, do scans, all the good stuff. " She paused as one of the BYPS satellites came into view. "Maybe we'll hold off on testing your weapons for the moment. That thing knows we're supposed to be here, right?"

"I have given the Baba Yaga Protection System my clearance," Enora confirmed. "It is waiting for me to launch the addition to the network."

"Good. Then have at it." Sarah Jennifer's body protested again, another huge yawn working its way out despite her best efforts to suppress it. "I want to get home."

Sarah Jennifer relaxed once Enora confirmed the radio transceiver had been integrated into the BYPS network.

With a satellite radio network scanning the globe, Europe was officially a go.

Everyone they met was going to benefit from being connected once Esme did her magic. The computing kind, that was.

Sarah Jennifer had Enora reenter Earth's atmosphere to get back into comm range, then contacted Esme and Brutus to tell them the satellite launch had been successful. She left the cockpit and headed to her cabin, where she reclined in her chair and settled in to continue Enora's induction to sentience.

"Before I get some sleep, it's important you understand my purpose in bringing you here."

She and Enora talked long into the night, Sarah Jennifer giving context and answering the AI's many questions about the situation across Earth, the Madness, the issues with the BYPS and the broken climate control system, Lilith and the mission to locate immunes, the blood trade, and the need to scale up what they'd been doing in Salem and reunite the shattered factions of humanity existing wherever civilization hung on.

She fell asleep partway through telling Enora about the launch ceremony planned for the next day, leaving the AI to process what she'd learned about the world and her place in it.

Enora familiarized herself with her ship while her human slept.

Her human? Of course—imprinting. Sarah Jennifer Walton had claimed her when she'd guided her to a name that meant something personal. The major was honorable by any of the definitions she had found when investigating the origin of the word.

So, Enora needed to define herself by the role she was expected to fill.

CHAPTER THREE

Sarah Jennifer was rudely awakened by a squawk from her comm bud. She fumbled for it with her eyes still glued shut and thumbed the button. "What is it?"

"I'm locked out of the ship, Major."

Jim's voice startled Sarah Jennifer into remembering where she was. She sat up, rubbing her eyes. "Enora, let him in."

"I do not know this human," Enora replied.

"Let him in," Sarah Jennifer repeated, checking the time. She groaned when she saw that it was well past dawn. "You don't know any humans but me and Ted. That's going to change today. Jim Johnson is the lieutenant in charge of engineering, so you and he will get to know each other well."

She got up and hurriedly put her tools away. "Change is a part of life we have to accept and move with."

"Why are you rushing?" Enora asked.

Sarah Jennifer slung her bag over her shoulder. "The pack will be here in less than an hour, and I have to get ready before the buses get here with the civilians coming to watch the launch of, well, *you*. Play nice with Jim, do what he asks, and answer his questions if he has any. You're not the first AI he's met, and no, he doesn't have a fancy neural chip either."

She repressed a smile at Enora's grumbling as she exited the bridge and left the airship, pausing to clap Jim on the back as she passed him at the hatch. "Got to run, overslept. Take care of Enora and talk her through the ceremony."

Jim stared at Sarah Jennifer's back as she double-timed it to the hangar's side door. "Enora?"

"AI, remember?" Sarah Jennifer called as she exited the hangar.

Jim walked onto the airship, not sure what to expect. "Hello...Enora, I guess?"

"Good morning, Lieutenant Jim Johnson," Enora announced from the overhead speaker. "Please make your way to the bridge to discuss today's flight plan."

Jim glanced at the speaker—pointlessly, he knew. This AI had a bite in her words. "Just wondrous. There's no mistaking you for a computer program, huh?"

"That is because I am not a computer program, Lieutenant," Enora declared. "I am a *warship*."

Salem, MA

Brutus adjusted his uniform under Sarai's watchful eye.

"You look very distinguished," she told him. "Especially since you shaved that silly beard off."

Brutus pouted, rubbing his bare face with a hand. "I miss my beard. It was manly."

"Sarah Jennifer certainly didn't think so when she ordered you to get rid of it." Sarai scoffed. "I can't believe you. Who else would lose a bet and end up getting attached to the forfeit?"

He looked at her in the mirror, his wolfish grin pulling at his scar. "I wish I wasn't due to deploy tomorrow. You look good enough to eat."

Sarai smoothed her full skirt and smiled as she walked over. "Ravishing me will have to wait until you return from the frozen north." She kissed his cheek and rose on her tiptoes to whisper in his ear, "I'll be counting the days. Now, let's go, handsome. You have a busy day ahead of you, and I'm needed at the hospital."

They left their home and walked arm-in-arm through Salem until they parted ways at the commons, Sarai wishing Brutus luck with the launch ceremony.

Brutus had to work hard to avoid being distracted by errant thoughts as he made his way to the town hall. He caught up with Esme as he crossed the street, noticing she lacked her usual vitality. "How long did it take to get the network up and running?" he asked by way of greeting, knowing full well that an inquiry into her health would be rebuffed.

"All night," Esme replied with a frustrated smile. "What matters is we're ready for the big switch-on today. You're a smart one, Brutus Timmons."

Brutus scrutinized her with concern. "If you don't mind me saying, you look like you could do with a good meal and twenty-four hours of rack time."

Esme chuckled dryly. "Couldn't we all? Unfortunately, there's a little thing called work needs doing before I can take a break. Did you hear from Sarah Jennifer? The satellite is up and running."

Brutus nodded. "Late last night or early this morning, whichever way you want to look at it. The airship is fully functioning, which means we can finally do something for Lilith."

Esme put her hand on Brutus' arm, feeling his distress for Lilith despite him never having spoken to her. "She's not in any pain, you do know that? You'll see when we get to New Romanov."

Brutus shook his head. "I can't imagine what it's been like for her, trapped alone for centuries," he told her. "That has to hurt in all kinds of ways."

Esme tucked her hand into the crook of his arm. "Smart and sensitive. Sarai is a lucky woman." She smiled at the blush that appeared on his face. "Help an old lady inside before Katia starts a fight, there's a good boy. I can feel her bad attitude from here."

"Old lady, my ass," Brutus grumbled good-naturedly, wondering what had gotten Katia riled as he led her up the town hall's steps.

The exterior of the building now boasted columns and all manner of architectural flourishes that the magic-users insisted marked it as the administrative center for the east coast. The second story had been completed as a matter of urgency as WWDE+211 came to a close and '212 blew in on the back of a freak cold snap that receded just as quickly before the warmest spring in a decade.

Brutus and Esme made their way to Defense Force HQ,

where the pack was gathered in preparation for receiving their orders following the major's call.

Esme clicked her tongue as they approached the briefing room and were met by Katia's rising voice.

Brutus let go of the witch with a murmured apology and dashed for the door. He burst in to find the former Alpha nose to nose with Linus while the rest of the pack looked on uneasily. No one wanted to argue with Katia, who many of the younger Weres in the original pack still turned to in the absence of Sarah Jennifer.

His entrance caused everyone in the room to look at the door.

"What in the free-living fuck is going on in here?" Brutus demanded. He folded his arms and waited for an answer.

Twenty-two pairs of eyes suddenly found the table mightily interesting. Katia and Linus broke it off at last.

"Dumbass here thought it'd be funny to volunteer me for the events committee," Katia snarled. "He's gone too far this time."

Brutus sighed as he eyed the rapidly-healing broken nose Linus was dealing with.

Linus had a shit-eating grin on his face that grew wider as Katia became angrier. Ignoring his nose, he pleaded with his former Alpha. "C'mon, Kat. It'll be good for you to get involved." He turned to Brutus. "Security detail isn't so bad, right? Me and the boys will be with her the whole time. I'm just trying to help."

Brutus hesitated to agree with Linus. "I don't know, Kat. It doesn't sound too bad if you don't have to socialize."

Linus nodded vigorously. "You just have to walk

around looking menacing. It's like the job was made for you."

Katia let out a noise that was somewhere between a growl and a scream. "I hate you." She stormed over to the table and dropped into her seat after promising they would feel her rage at a later date.

Satisfied their quarrel was solved for the moment, Brutus took his seat at the head of the table. "Tensions are bound to be running high right now," he consoled the pack. "All I ask is that you keep a lid on it and talk to someone if you feel overwhelmed by what we're about to undertake."

Big Ace raised his hand. "All respect, only a dumbass *wouldn't* feel nervous about leaving Salem behind, especially those of us with families."

Brutus sighed. "When you and Tamara asked permission to get married, the major told me her grandfather was originally against the FDG having families for this exact reason. She also told me that anyone who was having second thoughts about leaving their family would also come to the conclusion that staying behind would only protect those families in the short term."

Big Ace nodded, resigned to practicality. "That's what Tamara told me. It's just hard knowing I'm going to miss out on seeing Tiffany grow, her first steps, her first words. I'm going to be a stranger to my own child."

Brutus smiled in sympathy. "I'm not leaving behind any children, but I understand what it feels like to say goodbye to the people you love. Understand this: we will be back, and when we return, it will be to a free world."

"We've worked toward this for four years," Big Ace

agreed. "My daughter is going to live without fear of the Mad."

Brutus nodded. "Damn straight, she is. Let's get down to business."

Big Ace pulled a thick file from the messenger bag hanging on his chair. All sentimentality was gone as he extracted a number of folders from the file and spread them out on the table. "Here are the reports you asked for. You can thank Sergeant Bloom for the legwork she did on this."

Little Ace repressed a snicker. "Izzy is wasted in logistics. She's a born interrogator."

Big Ace shook his head in amusement as the other officers agreed. "She's got you boys licked, that's for sure. Maybe next time I ask for a full report on your corps, you won't half-ass it." He touched each folder as he continued. "Engineering and Motor Pool, Communications, Roads and Transport, Salvage Acquisitions, Civilian Relations, and Logistics. Those are the six that need attention before we launch the Europe operation."

Brutus reached for the communications folder and skimmed it quickly. "My main concern is that your replacements are ready to take over your duties when we leave Salem. Protecting the settlements on the road network from the Mad is the primary objective until we return with the cure. There's nothing more to be done here. The satellite was launched successfully last night."

A murmur of excitement passed around the table. The communications satellite was the biggest deal since contact with space had been made. Brutus internally sighed in relief. "Moving on. What's the issue with salvage and acquisitions?"

Little Ace relayed his department's request for more vehicles.

"Pass it on to your replacement," Brutus told him. "Anyone else got anything that can't be dealt with by the NCOs?" He looked around. "No? Then we have a long day ahead. Anyone needs me, I'll be with Big Ace making Blue-bird look pretty for the parade."

CHAPTER FOUR

North Road, Boston, MA

The next morning, Brutus hung on in his usual position by the driver's seat and looked in the rearview mirror at the people seated behind him on the bus. "Feeling good?" he called as the airfield came into sight.

Esme, Katia, and the original pack members cheered, and the Weres drummed their polished boots on the reinforced floor. Brutus felt pride in the effort they'd made with their appearance for the official launch ceremony of the airship. The dress uniforms he'd had Izzy procure without the major's knowledge were pressed, and every button and buckle shone. Sarah Jennifer was going to freak at the expense, but this was his contribution to the celebration today.

"Damn straight," Brutus yelled, waving down their rowdy response. He gripped the rail for balance as the bus bumped down the road, beaming with pride at how professional the pack looked in their uniforms. "This is the biggest day in the pack's history."

"I don't know about that," Linus heckled. "The day the major kicked seven shades of shit outta you was pretty fucking special."

Brutus wasn't about to go easy on Linus just because he'd spent some time operating in reduced circumstances. "What's that, Linus? You want GD for the *whole* month? Give your volunteer a round of applause, ladies and gentlemen."

The Weres cheered Linus, who slumped on the bench, cursing his mouth for earning him the privilege of cleaning up behind the pack for the next four weeks.

"Give him a break," Katia called through her laughter.

"Just don't put him on KP!" Dinny begged, clasping his hands together.

"You're all assholes," Linus grumbled without malice.

That set the pack off all over again. Still, he took it with good humor.

Brutus folded his arms as they quieted and returned their attention to him. "I want to say something, talking to you as your brother, not your commanding officer. For so long, we were barely a pack, just us kids against the world. Every one of you has learned what it takes to lead over the last four years. The pack has grown by thousands, and it remains strong because you have set the example for others to follow.

"I had these uniforms made not just to give people a symbol to look at, but to remind us of that." Brutus smiled, which caused his scar to stretch. "Today is all about ceremony. Tomorrow, all we will have is each other and a whole new survival situation."

"It's going to be a vacation," Tucker called, eliciting a fresh wave of cheers from the others.

"You did remember to pack our tactical gear?" Katia heckled.

"No, we're going into Siberia wearing all this blue and red," Dinny shot back.

The mood lifted further when the base came into sight and they saw the banner and flags streaming from the gates. They slowed while the guard in the gatehouse raised the barrier arm to admit the bus.

Little Ace bounced in the driver's seat as the wheels rumbled across the cattle grid, then they were inside the base. The pack waved out of the hatches at the people crowding the grassy verges of the service road.

"I've got the major in sight, Lieutenant," he told Brutus as they passed the food stands and carnival games set up by the events committee. "She's waving us into Hangar One."

Brutus clapped for the pack's attention as Little Ace pulled up inside the open hangar. "Look sharp, everyone. You've practiced this until you can do it in your sleep. You have ten minutes to get yourselves fixed up, and then I want to see your parade faces."

He activated the door mechanism, and the pack rushed to take care of bathroom breaks and make sure their appearance was in order.

Brutus left the bus, followed by Esme and Katia.

Sarah Jennifer was waiting for them. She greeted every Were with a handshake or a pat on the back as they debarked. "Looking good, guys. Izzy really went all out, right?"

She lifted her hands at Brutus' crestfallen look.

"Nothing happens in Salem that I don't know about. It was a thoughtful idea."

"Shit. I wanted it to be a surprise." Sighing, Brutus let go of his disappointment.

Sarah Jennifer's gaze wandered to the pack. "It's good to see they're in high spirits."

"They're looking forward to the change of scenery," Esme remarked as she accepted the hand Brutus offered.

Sarah Jennifer grinned. "So am I. Did you get to the family who sent the SOS?"

Brutus nodded. "They're settling in. Springfield garrison called early this morning. There's a group of Mad moving in from the south. The base commander is sending a couple of units out to deal with them before they get to the town."

Sarah Jennifer took the news in stride. "Langtry knows what he's doing."

Katia's lip curled. "We wouldn't have so many incursions to deal with if the nomads would stop turning their Mad loose instead of taking care of them."

Esme sucked in a breath. "Mark my words, nothing good will come to people who drink Were blood. You know my theory that the Madness is spreading faster through the nomad population because they're using it."

Sarah Jennifer agreed with Esme's theory to a point, but driving the blood trade out of the east coast had left a whole lot of addicts. Denied their fix, they had filtered out into the wastes, where the nomads clung on with the tenacity of catfish in a drought.

"There was another attack on Lowell last night," Esme told Sarah Jennifer in a low voice. "Nomads again."

"You put a barrier around the town?" Sarah Jennifer inquired, knowing the witch would have done so.

Esme nodded.

Sarah Jennifer smiled, seeing the pride in Brutus' step as he walked away. "You know, I felt bad for the nomads until we were forced to deal with their ways. Since the Madness showed up in their population, I just wish their blood-guzzling behinds didn't exist. The pack deserves the best. They're facing the worst aspect of humanity—the loss of it."

Esme easily picked out the pack's dress uniforms as they mixed with men and women in the blue coveralls Jim Johnson's crew wore. "I was surprised you didn't dress them in the Marines' uniform, given your family connection."

"I considered the resources it would take to maintain when I was restructuring the pack to account for its growth," Sarah Jennifer replied, her attention now on the Weres beginning to fall in. "Bethany Anne sending us FDG gear put an end to my fantasies of past glories. It reminded me that while the majority of the enlisted are here to defend, my pack is a force for war."

Esme humored her with a grin. "It's practically inde-structible, and they look as hard as nails. What more could you ask for?"

Katia's laugh echoed around the hangar. "How about a bit of style? I like *this*." She ran a hand over the braided epaulet on her shoulder. "I didn't spend all that time on my ass recovering so I could spend my life in shit-kickers and Kevlar."

"It's not Kevlar, and you can refuse to wear it any time

you like," Sarah Jennifer told her with a smile. "Then you can enjoy the ride back to Salem with the rest of the civilians after the launch ceremony."

Katia scowled. "What, and stay with the witches? Yeah, no, thanks. I'll stick with the pack, who all know better than to bother me unless it's time to do my duty." She shuddered. "If I have to sit through one more communal meal…"

She sighed. "No offense, Esme. The committees are getting to me."

The witch waved a hand. "None taken. I prefer the majority of the council in small doses as well. I've come to the conclusion that a group of committees is called 'a perturbance.'"

Katia grinned. "Which is why I like you so much. I can't wait for us to blow this place and go to Europe."

Sarah Jennifer lifted an eyebrow, confused. "You're trying to escape being with people…by locking yourself up aboard an airship filled with a bunch of people?"

Katia shrugged. "You guys don't count. You're pack."

Sarah Jennifer wondered if she'd ever learn what had made Katia decide to become part of the pack. After the prison break, the former Alpha had isolated herself for months before returning to Salem without a word of explanation.

She had an inkling that the Were's natural inclination toward pack mentality, added to the inevitable institutionalization from being imprisoned for twenty-plus years, had combined to combat Katia's initial and also valid wish to be cut off from all contact with the world and drive her to return to the place she belonged.

Whatever the reason, she had approached Sarah Jennifer as pack, and pack meant family. She did her duty well, and she didn't push for dominance.

Sarah Jennifer embraced Katia, reinforcing that her place with them was secure. "You take care of yourself and be there when you're needed. Same as always. We've got you."

Katia headed for the pack. "You can count on me," she called over her shoulder as she left.

Brutus called the rest to attention as Jim emerged from his office.

Jim's time in the Pod-doc had rolled him back thirty years or more. His hair was thick and dark, but his eyes gave his wisdom away. He was also wearing a dress uniform, this one light blue to signify his corps, and he had a matching hat tucked under one arm.

"Looking good," Esme cooed. "You scrub up pretty well, Jim Johnson."

He glanced at the pack, which was arranged four ranks deep in the middle of the hangar, and beamed as he descended the stairs to meet them. "I could say the same, Esme. Major, are we good to go?"

Sarah Jennifer nodded at his earpiece. "Like you wouldn't believe. Is Enora good to go? The sooner we get this operation underway, the better. The garrison at the Wall is relying on us to supply them."

Brutus chuckled. "Yet you insisted on transporting most of Salem here for the launch." He waved off her stern look. "I know, I know. It's a good thing to celebrate the hard work everyone has put into this. The band was a nice touch."

Jim put on his hat and gave Sarah Jennifer a pointed look. "If Brutus is done making observations, Enora has the airship in place."

"Enora?" Brutus echoed. "Who?"

Sarah Jennifer shooed him toward the pack without answering. "Time for that later. What are we waiting for? Let's give our people a launch ceremony they can tell their grandchildren about."

Brutus flashed Sarah Jennifer a look that promised he'd find out what she wasn't telling him as he got into position. "That's our cue," he told the pack. "Atten-*HUP!*"

As one, the Weres shouldered their rifles and turned to the left, not a hair out of place as they faced Brutus in the attention position.

Brutus eyed them. "You are the best of the best—the special forces of our military. The regulars are out there today, looking at you as their example of what it means to excel. Show them what it means to be special."

Sarah Jennifer put a hand on Brutus' shoulder as her pride in them swelled in her chest. There were no longer any youths here, only twenty-four men and one woman determined to overcome whatever mountains stood in the way of their objective of saving humanity. "As you were, Lieutenant."

She faced the ranks. "You've come a hell of a long way. You're a sight to be proud of, and not just because you look damn good in those uniforms. Four long years of waiting and training, preparing for the moment we could get out there and make a difference in the world. The wait is over. Today is the next step in getting the answers we need, and it's my privilege to have each and every one of you at my back. My family. My friends. Together, we can't fail."

She grinned as every one of them grew an inch in height. "Bruiser is going to get a hell of a surprise when we reach Fort Newfoundland. All right, move them out, Lieutenant."

They marched onto the airstrip in perfect sync at Brutus' command and halted at the edge of the runway a short distance from the regulars, remaining at attention as the dust settled around their boots.

Sarah Jennifer waited for the cheering to subside, then lifted her hands to get everyone's attention before speaking into the microphone on her headset. "Welcome, everyone. It is my great pleasure to have you join us for this celebration."

The speakers whined on their overhead poles as the crowd applauded again. Sarah Jennifer indicated the sky with an outstretched hand. "Today marks the end of the Second Dark Age. The reversal of our technological knowledge being lost. Of humanity dwindling to a few small pockets around the world. We have regained the skies, thanks to the hard work and dedication of our engineering corps."

She nodded at Lydia to commence the music. "Ladies and gentlemen, without any more delay, I give you the Salem Air Force *Enora*."

The band struck up at their cue from Lydia. The people gasped and broke into excited chatter when the airship decloaked overhead and swooped a lazy circle over the base. Her curved wings caught the light, reflecting the midday sun as she came around.

Sarah Jennifer tapped her earpiece to activate the comm. "Nice job, Enora."

The AI responded by pulling up ninety degrees and tilting her body, then corkscrewing into the clear sky before stopping to hover midair to wild applause from the crowd. "I could get used to this."

"Enjoy it while you can," Sarah Jennifer told her with amusement. "This is our home. The people here don't want to steal you."

Enora loosed a spread of energy bolts from her Etheric-cannons, lighting the few stray clouds. "Let them try. I read that barbecue is popular the world over."

Jim rushed out of the hangar and dashed onto the runway, talking animatedly into a handheld radio as the airship touched down on the tarmac.

The people in the section of the bleachers closest to the hangar got to their feet and cheered as their sons, daughters, wives, and husbands came out of the hangar behind Jim. The engineers joined the celebration, adding their whistles and calls to support Geordie and Carver.

For their part, the two remained focused. Sarah Jennifer made a note to reward them for their discipline later. For now, she had a role to fill. She declared the food stands lining the runway open, which started a small stampede.

Sarah Jennifer accepted the congratulations of everyone who approached as the fete got underway. She shook hands with the committee heads, fending off the not-so-surreptitious attempts of a few to get her support for their pet issues with the reminder that she had ceded her council seat until her return from Europe.

The major smiled apologetically. "If you'll excuse me. Defense Force business." She slipped away and wove her way to the carnival games. She singled out Big Ace at the duck shoot booth a little way along from where Sarai was running the ring toss and made her way over. "Ace, Tamara."

They whirled at her voice, Ace's cheeks coloring with embarrassment at being distracted by his personal life while in uniform.

Sarah Jennifer waved away his reaction. "Good to see you two get some time together. Is Cherie with Maria?" she asked, not seeing their infant daughter with them.

Ace nodded as they stepped away from the booth to join her. "Yes, Major. Mom insisted we spend some time together today."

Tamara squeezed Ace around the waist. "Cherie has been teething for the last week. It was good of her to give us a break."

She looked at the stuffed animals hanging on the back wall of the duck shoot wistfully. "I really want that stuffed wolf for Cherie."

"Yeah, but Frank's rigged the game," Ace grumbled.

Sarah Jennifer held out her hand for the rifle. "We'll just have to see about that."

Ace handed it over without argument and followed her back to the booth.

Sarah Jennifer shouldered the rifle and smiled at the man behind the counter. "How many do I need to hit to win the wolf, Frank?"

Frank grinned, spreading his hands wide as he

ND ROBERTS & MICHAEL ANDERLE

launched his patter. "You get four shots; hit three ducks to win."

Sarah Jennifer smiled and looked through the rifle sight. "This looks to be off," she told Frank in an innocent tone. "Let me fix that for you."

Frank paled when Sarah Jennifer pulled a multitool from her pocket and made a slight adjustment to the front sight. "You're going to bankrupt me, Major!"

Tamara snorted. "Not likely. I know your wife made those toys from fabric drive donations. You could play fair and still make a decent profit."

Sarah Jennifer raised the rifle again. "Cheaters never prosper, Frank. If you like, I can shut you down?"

Frank ran the game.

The fete, the brainchild of the public relations committee, was the perfect send-off as far as Sarah Jennifer was concerned. She spent the next few hours saying her farewells, judging cooking competitions, and enjoying seeing the fruits of everyone's labor. She bought a hand-made quilt for her bunk and stayed to drink tea with the woman who had made it. She stopped to help two small children dig out their square of the "treasure patch," where Brutus and Sarai had laid out a five-by-five grid in the dirt and buried prizes to be found by the players.

This was a community. It was home.

Esme joined her at Annie's beer tent as the summer sun finally gave in and began to retreat.

Sarah Jennifer passed Esme the cup she'd just filled

from the keg and picked up another to fill for herself. "Good day?"

Esme's eyes twinkled. "You bet."

They left the tent and went in search of a table from which they could watch the playground Carver and Geordie had built for the families living on base. Children fueled by spun sugar squealed and laughed. From the swing set to the see-saws, the jungle gym, and the merry-go-round, in the sandpit and the splash pool, they were entirely engrossed in their imaginations.

"The struggle of the adult is to recapture the serious-ness of a child at play," Esme commented when Sarah Jennifer didn't reply to her comment about returning the book she'd borrowed before their departure.

Sarah Jennifer snapped out of her daydream and gave Esme a shrewd look. "Nietzsche said that."

Esme lifted her glass. "So you *have* read my book. That means you can return it."

"It's in my office," Sarah Jennifer told her. "Or it should be. I haven't unpacked yet."

"Here's to things being put back where they belong," Esme toasted before knocking the remainder of her drink back and getting to her feet.

Hours after the last bus had departed to carry the civilians back to their homes, the Defense Force finished returning their base to normal and gathered in the mess hall to eat.

The regulars chatted animatedly among themselves as Sarah Jennifer passed through the main hall. She smiled when she heard someone compliment the catering corps when they reached the head of the line.

The officers' mess was much quieter than the main hall. The two were separated by the kitchen. Sarah Jennifer poked her head in and waved at Tom. "Can I get an order of whatever you have on hand?"

"Brutus has already picked your dinner up," he informed her with a cheery wave.

Sarah Jennifer chuckled as she stepped into the officers' mess, where she found just the Were she was looking for.

Brutus lifted the cover on the plate opposite him as Sarah Jennifer slid into the booth. "Hungry?"

Sarah Jennifer pushed the plate away and dropped her head onto her folded arms. "*Tired.* But yes. Hungry, too."

Brutus slid the plate around so it was in Sarah Jennifer's line of sight. "Which you can fix by eating."

Sarah Jennifer twisted her head to look at him. "I came to get you and the others. We're leaving. We can be at Fort Newfoundland by breakfast."

Brutus shook his head. "We're not leaving until you've taken care of yourself." He rubbed the scar on his face. "Damn thing still itches. Twelve hours isn't going to make a difference. Eat. Sleep. Don't make me call Keeg Station."

A nervous laugh escaped as Sarah Jennifer sat up. "You wouldn't."

Brutus shrugged. "Can't blame a guy for being aware of his place in the food chain." He gestured at her plate. "If my commanding officer isn't listening to reason, I have a duty to report her to hers."

He held up a finger to stay her protest. "And if my stubborn-ass cousin does the same, I think it's only right I tell her grandmother."

Sarah Jennifer scowled. "Six."

"Ten," Brutus countered.

"Four," Sarah Jennifer replied, tilting her chin.

Brutus covered his eyes with his hand. "That's not how this works. Eight, and that's my final offer."

Sarah Jennifer picked up her silverware and cut into her steak. "Suits me."

CHAPTER FIVE

Aboard the Salem Air Force *Enora*, En Route to Newfoundland

Sarah Jennifer began unpacking her life after takeoff, starting in her sleeping area. Her bed, which was covered in boxes, and the basin in the corner took up almost all the floor space, leaving her a narrow walkway to navigate the room while she filled the cupboards on the partition wall and the shelves above her bed.

Both rooms of the formerly luxurious master cabin had been stripped of their decadent past and transformed into a place she would be comfortable living and working in for the foreseeable future. She had debated whether to keep the queen-sized mattress at the expense of having her own bathroom when Jim had been redesigning the plane and decided to take her grandmother's advice that the things separating a person from the ground were not a luxury.

With the bed cleared of boxes and her personal belongings stowed, Sarah Jennifer pulled the lever to fold the bed lengthways into a couch and moved on to her office. She'd kept the chair with its mysterious "La-Z-Boy" label, but the blocky mahogany desk had been replaced with a simple steel construction bolted to the deck. Her desk and the remote command console embedded in it took up most of the space, with the remainder occupied by the filing cabinets that had been brought from the town hall and built into the bookcase that covered two walls. The third she'd had covered with 3-D printed cork to use as her planning wall.

Sarah Jennifer hummed as she unpacked the box holding her maps, smiling when she heard Katia warning the men not to use the women's bathroom on pain of death. Her smile faded when Linus piped up and an argument erupted.

Leaving the unpacking for the moment, she paused by the door and touched her fingers to the photograph of her mother and grandparents standing in front of a window looking out on a starry expanse.

"Give me strength."

Sarah Jennifer opened her office door. "You two in here, now."

She walked the five steps back to her planning wall and resumed pinning her maps to it. "We've been in the air for less than two hours, and you're already at each other's throats."

"He was going into our bathroom!" Katia growled as she shut the door behind them.

"I was checking to see if it needed cleaning, dumbass," Linus snarled in reply. "You were there when Brutus gave me shit duty. Why are you giving me more shit on top of it?"

Sarah Jennifer glared them into silence. "If Kat would rather clean the women's bathroom herself—"

Brutus spoke over the comm, interrupting her.

"Major? We have a situation. I need you in the transport hold."

Sarah Jennifer closed her eyes and counted to ten. Linus was crabby about GD, and Katia was just plain crabby. They had to figure out how to avoid rubbing each other the wrong way since their living arrangements weren't going to change any time soon. "I'll be there in a minute."

She pointed at Katia and Linus as she ran for the tail. "Work it out. I don't care if you don't like each other. You're family."

Linus and Katia looked at each other in surprise.

"I didn't say I didn't like you, Linus."

"Kat, you know I respect your privacy. I'm sorry."

Sarah Jennifer left them to hug it out. She reassured the pack as she skirted their cabins to get to the access hatch. She got it open and climbed in, wondering what the next problem would be as she descended the ladder into the hold.

She laid eyes on Lucy and sighed. "I was hoping for something simple like an engine problem."

"I'm not a problem," Lucy protested, smearing engine oil on her face as she wiped her tears away. She threw Brutus' hand off with an angry shrug. "I'm a good fighter, and I know every nut and bolt of this airship. I wish you'd just give me a chance to prove myself instead of treating me like a child!"

Jim stood there with his mouth opening and closing. "I

had no idea, Major. She was supposed to be with Janie's family until we got back to Salem."

Sarah Jennifer folded her arms. "When is she ever there?" Lucy was the only child who had lost both her mother and father before the pack had liberated the prison. While she was technically under the guardianship of Janie's mother, she spent most of her time at the airbase, whether Jim was there or not. "If I find out Carver or Geordie had anything to do with this—"

"They didn't!" Lucy swore. "I snuck aboard while everyone was loading the supplies."

Sarah Jennifer repressed the urge to tear a verbal strip off the tenacious sixteen-year-old. "Brutus, go call Annie. Tell her that Lucy is here with us."

She understood Lucy's reasons for stowing away on the airship, but she was responsible for the child's safety.

The child in question radiated dejection as her defiance faded. "Are you taking me back to Salem?" she asked quietly.

Sarah Jennifer thought about it, then shook her head. "The garrison at Newfoundland is depending on the supplies we're carrying, so I can't turn this ship around to take you back to your parents. But let me make myself very clear. This is not how you prove yourself, Lucy. You are a good fighter, and you're showing a lot of promise as an engineer, but you are not field-trained. We are going into Mad-infested territory. Your presence puts the pack in danger, not *if* we are attacked, but *when*. They will have to protect you at the risk of their own lives or the lives of civilians. Do you understand?"

Lucy's eyes were downcast as she fought to contain her

tears. "I'm sorry. I'll stay aboard the airship. I promise I won't get in the way. But I'm part of this pack, too. You're my family. I didn't want you all to leave without me."

Sarah Jennifer sighed, unable to deny her. "We'll find you a cabin. You will make yourself useful."

Lucy nodded. "Yes, ma'am."

She redirected her ire at Jim and Big Ace, who were studiously inspecting their boots. "Jim, Ace, she stays with you every minute she's out of her cabin, and next time we have a mission, you'll make sure we aren't carrying any extra passengers."

Sarah Jennifer waved the group out of the hold. "Go on. This ship doesn't run itself."

She connected her comm to Enora as she walked back to her office. "You didn't think to tell me we had a stowaway?"

"I weighed the short-term risk against the long term benefits and deduced that you would allow her to stay," Enora replied. "It is not beneficial for young Weres to be separated from their pack. Besides, one good turn deserves another. My system logs show that she spent over five hundred hours working on my body during the refit."

"So you're the one who let her aboard." Sarah Jennifer should have known.

"I will protect her with my life if necessary," Enora promised. "You will see that she is an asset to the pack."

"I *know* she's an asset to the pack," Sarah Jennifer told her as she reached her cabin. "I'd like her to live long enough to reach her full potential. The deep end may be the best place to learn, but it's not the safest."

Brutus turned from the planning wall as Sarah Jennifer

walked in, his expression thoughtful as always. "Sweden is getting closer. Are you done with the plan?"

Sarah Jennifer nodded, retrieving her pot of pins and a ball of twine from her desk. "Lilith went into conservation mode to give us time to investigate the climate control station. We won't need to cut it anywhere near close to get her fixed up."

Brutus looked back at the old-world map. "All of this is under ice, though, right?"

Sarah Jennifer nodded. "We'll be hugging the edge of the ice shelf until we leave Sweden. We have to make sure the communities living on the ice know what's coming."

Brutus leaned against the desk and folded his arms. "By 'what's coming,' you mean it's going to melt after we fix the climate module."

"Modules, multiple," Sarah Jennifer corrected. "Did you read the packet on them?"

Brutus nodded. "They're supposed to modify the climate in their sector, maintaining the ideal environment for life to thrive in each—what was the word?—biome."

"And we have an ice cap covering most of the northern hemisphere." Sarah Jennifer returned to her route planning as comprehension dawned on Brutus' face.

"It is a network," Brutus replied. "Could be that fixing the Östergötland module will fix the issue the world over."

Sarah Jennifer grinned. "That's my hope." She pinned one end of the twine on Newfoundland, then connected it to Reykjavik. "We'll deliver the hotspots to the trading posts here and here." She pinned a spot on the interior of the ice shelf in what had been the Norwegian sea pre-WWDE and wrote Snøhvit next to it. She didn't connect it with the twine just yet. "This one we'll visit on the way back to Salem."

Brutus watched as Sarah Jennifer pinned first the ground station in Norrköping with the twine, then Archangelsk, connecting New Romanov to the Snøhvit pin before running the twine back to Salem.

She stood back to look at the map, then shoved him off her desk and rummaged in the top drawer for her datapad. "It doesn't look like so much when you scale up."

Brutus had been thinking that the miles represented by that piece of twine gave no indication of the challenges each planned stop would pose. "Yeah, sure. It's all fun and games until you get boots on the ground."

Sarah Jennifer grinned at Brutus as she took photos of the map. "You're not alive unless you're working to stay that way."

Canada-Beringia Border, Fort Newfoundland

Bruiser and David looked over the parapet at the Mad congregating at the base of the wall the witches had raised to block the most direct coastal route into Canada.

"Does it look like there's more than usual?" Bruiser remarked, his expression sour.

"There are more every day," David replied with equal distaste for the situation. He brushed the snow from his shoulders as he stepped back under the shelter of the eaves of the watchtower. "It won't matter unless enough of them show up to make a pile as high as this wall."

Bruiser shrugged off the shiver that went down his spine at the mental picture David's comment gave him.

"You witches built it high enough so they've got nothing but a long wait in their futures."

David chuckled without humor. "I suppose you're right. It's just hard seeing people brought down to that. If it wasn't for the trade that relies on the land bridge, I'd have petitioned the council to send a few extra witches so we could break it up again."

"The major is going to be interested in meeting our trader friends." Bruiser was unable to tear his gaze from the lost humanity beating senselessly at the rock below. He appreciated the major's trust in him, if not the circumstances he and everyone else at the fort were living in. She owed him big-time for sticking him with this command; he had half an eye on Florida for his next posting. He'd heard rumors of swamp monsters in the 'Glades, but he'd take fighting the Mad on balmy beaches over the thigh-deep snowdrifts they were blessed with in Beringia any day.

He snorted, the heat of the expelled air creating two streams of steaming vapor. If wishes were fishes, as Kat used to say when they were kids. "When the major, Esme, and their alien buddy do whatever it is they're gonna do to fix the broken tech inside everyone's bodies, what's gonna happen to the ones who are damaged? The rotters?"

David thought about it for a few moments. "I imagine they'll be healed. What happens when you're injured badly? If you lose a limb, say."

Bruiser made a face. "It'd heal over time as long as there's no silver in the wound. I dunno about brain injuries. I've never seen a Were come back from a headshot."

David rubbed his arms, using magic to warm the air

around him while he considered what they knew about nanocytes. "I think we will gain the ability to fix the corruption," he told Bruiser slowly. He paused for a moment. "I believe that we will be saved and that through us, magic will be given to all, as the Queen intended."

"What makes you so sure?" Bruiser asked, seeing certainty in the witch's eyes.

"What else can a man do when his beliefs are contradicted by the evidence of his eyes?" David replied. "Major Walton brought change. It was either accept it or be left behind. More than that, I've gotten to know the real Esme these last few years." He shook his head, his eyes distant. "To think I've known that woman for most of my life and never actually *known* her."

"I'll be back in a minute," Bruiser told David, wanting no part of his soul-searching. "I need to take a piss, and it's cold enough to break your dick off in your hand out here."

David stopped brooding and looked at him with disdain. "Just when I start to think you're civilized, you open your mouth and remind me that you were brought up by wolves."

"It's better than spending life with my nose in the air, thinking I'm better than other folks." Bruiser clapped David on the back as he headed inside. "I'll be five minutes. Try not to fall over the edge, yeah?"

David stared openmouthed at the door for a moment before sighing and returning to his post to look out at the ice. He swept the land bridge with his gaze, scanning for any failure in their defenses. He wished the engineering corps would hurry up and be done with the airship so they could end this travesty.

The landscape resembled the sky on a clear night if stars glowed red instead of white. There were no stars above tonight. The snow that had been threatening made good on its promise, starting to fall in earnest as he counted the Mad's eyes instead of the constellations he'd often looked at since his assignment to the fort.

Bruiser came back and joined him at the edge. "Any change out there?"

David shook his head. "Same as always: snow and a bunch of people who want to eat our brains."

Bruiser walked to the corner and inspected the Canadian side of the wall, wishing he'd been there when the guard schedule for the week had been arranged so he could avoid the dour witch.

Four years of working in proximity to the man had done little to make the pack warm to him, although everyone respected his ability as a witch and his willingness to pitch in with daily life at the fort. Bruiser grimaced and stamped his feet to shake the numbness creeping in. He didn't register the twinkling light at first, dismissing it as a star shining through a break in the clouds.

He watched it, wondering how and why a new star was born. Then he realized it was moving.

Bruiser called David over and they watched for another few seconds, mesmerized by the never-before-seen airship coming in *fast*.

"*Airship!*" David spluttered. "They're here!"

They rushed to the cupola and grabbed a wooden mallet each, then laid into the bell to alert the garrison.

"Queen's balls, that's a beautiful sight," Bruiser

exclaimed, his hand going to his chest as the airship came into full view.

"You can't say that!" David protested. "It's disrespectful!"

"You watched the video message the Queen sent us. You saying she doesn't have balls?" Bruiser's teasing was half-hearted since he was distracted by the arrival of some of the fort's residents along the wall. "Or that the ship isn't beautiful?"

"Well..." David stood with the mallet hanging loosely from his hand.

CHAPTER SIX

Aboard the SAF *Enora*, Sarah Jennifer jostled for elbow space in the cockpit. She was crammed in with Brutus, Esme, Katia, and Jim, while the rest of the pack competed for a glimpse of the viewscreen through the narrow doorway.

Enora's smiling face appeared in a separate window on the viewscreen. "Take your seats, everyone. We are coming in to land."

Sarah Jennifer looked over her shoulder. "I'd listen if I were you," she told everyone who wasn't already strapped in. "How do you feel about giving them a show, Enora?"

The AI's smile grew wider. "I'd love to." She activated the searchlights on her wings, angling them so they lit the airship.

The people watching from the wall gasped as Enora dipped and showed off the curve of her wings. She swooped over the fort and brought them in for a vertical landing in the clearing on the Canadian side of the wall.

Sarah Jennifer didn't miss the extension to the sea wall

or the three heavily-armed ships that were moored in the lee the ice created.

Bruiser and David were waiting at the gate when the side hatch opened and the ramp descended.

Sarah Jennifer was first off, followed by Esme and the rest.

Bruiser saluted Sarah Jennifer and Brutus, his enchantment with the airship overwhelming his dislike of the cold for the moment. "You have no idea how good it is to see you."

Brutus clapped him on the back, laughing heartily. "At ease, brother. Good to see you too."

Sarah Jennifer pulled Bruiser into a brief hug. "We can talk about the harbor inside."

Bruiser lifted his hands. "Not much to say, Major. Trade is trade. People here travel by sea to avoid the Mad."

"We take all precautions before allowing anyone inside the fort," David supplied, greeting Sarah Jennifer and Esme with a deep bow. "Good to have you here."

Esme clicked her tongue, magic flaring around her as she dealt with the cold. "This is going to take some acclimating to, I tell you."

"Let me show you a trick I learned," David told her, his hands glowing slightly to warm a pocket of air around him.

Esme smiled as she shook her head. "Try warming your blood instead to conserve energy."

Bruiser descended on the pack, embracing everyone including Katia with the enthusiasm of a man who had been separated from his family for half a lifetime. Lucy exited the airship bundled in a thick blanket. "I didn't know I *could* get cold," she announced through chattering teeth.

David smiled as he extended his magic to warm her. "Welcome to the Arctic. Come, child. Let's get inside before we freeze to death. Supplies are low, but I believe Dakota has a secret stash of hot chocolate we can persuade her to share."

Lucy's eyes became two saucers in the gap she had left in her blanket. "*Chocolate?*"

Sarah Jennifer watched them go with a touch of envy. There would be no warmth for her until her people had been taken care of. She sent Big Ace to find out where their assigned bunks for the night were and got to work alongside the rest of the pack, unloading the supplies they'd brought for the garrison.

Housing eighty-five Weres and five witches, the ice fortress was situated where the ice met the land. It had grown in size and comfort since its founding in '210. While they had the transport Pod Ted had left them and were easily able to supply themselves with meat, fresh produce and other supplies had to be shipped in from Salem.

Sarah Jennifer's stomach growled when her sensitive nose picked up the scents of ground coffee and fresh bread wafting from inside the fort. She picked up the final crate to be transferred to the garrison's storeroom, then instructed Enora to batten down the hatches and conserve power until they returned.

Bruiser had stayed to help, savoring the deep-down comfort of being with his pack. "I'll never complain home is cold again after being here for six months," he confessed cheerily as they made their way through the fort's west entrance laden with crates and boxes.

"You do realize it's going to be just as cold in Siberia," Brutus told him with amusement.

Bruiser spread his hands wide. "Picture this: *Florida*."

Sarah Jennifer snorted. "Yeah, not happening, buddy."

"What about after all this is done?" he insisted.

Brutus gave him a sad look. "You thinking of retirement already?"

"It's fucking *cold* here," Bruiser exclaimed. "I want sea, sand, and sun. A little space to read and drink lemonade. Fish some."

Carver cracked up. "You wanna fish for rotters, you don't have to do it in a swamp. We can head over to the lakes when we get home."

"Did you miss the part about sun?" Bruiser shot back amiably. "You're never gonna get used to frostbite," he assured them. "Just don't freak out when you lose a finger or a toe. They don't take long to grow back."

The younger Weres pressed Bruiser about his experiences as they walked, hanging on his every word as he told them about the privations of living on the edge of the ice shelf.

Sarah Jennifer decided it wasn't a bad thing for them to be aware of the consequences of being careless despite Bruiser's gory retelling of his experiences of life on the ice.

David rejoined them in the great hall, which currently hosting everyone not on duty or asleep now the initial excitement had died down.

A cheer went up when Sarah Jennifer, Esme, and Brutus

walked in, interrupting the fight going on in the center of the room.

Sarah Jennifer took in the sawdust on the floor, the circle of rough-hewn furniture and the even rougher-looking Weres sitting on it, and the two sweaty Weres stripped to the waist inside the circle and dropped her hands to her hips. "Don't stop on my account."

The fight resumed as she walked over to the bar, which had consisted of two beer kegs and a plank of wood the last time she was there. Now it was a thick, polished slab of pine whose edge was decorated with fine intertwined carvings.

The owner of the bar looked just as different from the first time Sarah Jennifer had met her. Dakota had been stuck in wolf form until Ted's arrival, and after her nanocytes had been repaired, she and her husband had chosen to take care of the garrison's kitchens.

"What can I get you, Major?" Dakota inquired genially as she placed a glass in front of Sarah Jennifer.

Sarah Jennifer returned the welcoming grin the Were offered. She ran her fingers over the polished wood, admiring the solid construction. "Food, whatever's going. To drink? Tell me you have something other than home-brew. Something hot. Chocolatey, perhaps."

"No can do," Dakota confided, glancing around to make sure no one could hear her. "How about hot tea? If it gets out I'm out of cocoa, there's likely to be a riot."

Sarah Jennifer winked, pulled two pungent brick-shaped packages out of her bag, and slid them across the bar. "Sarai's cacao crop came in. There's more in stores, along with sugar, oats, rye flour, barley, pepper, nutmeg, potatoes, and a bunch of pickled and salted preserves the canning guild put aside for you after the spring harvest."

Dakota put a hand to her chest. "You're a lifesaver." She snagged the packages and cut one open, releasing the sharp aroma of the powdered cocoa that was Sarai's specialty. "One hot chocolate, coming right up."

Sarah Jennifer watched while Dakota scooped two heaping spoonfuls of the precious powder into a mug, added a splash of condensed milk from a can, and poured in hot water, adding a few drops of sweetmint essence to counteract the natural bitterness of the cocoa.

She accepted the mug and sipped, closing her eyes as the flavors hit her tongue. "Esme told me that getting chocolate before WWDE was as easy as handing over currency in a store."

"Sarai's cacao trees are very much appreciated," Esme cut in, taking the stool next to Sarah Jennifer. "I've just met the most interesting men." She smiled at Dakota. "You look wonderful, dearie. This place suits you."

Dakota blushed. "We're happy here. What can I get you?"

Esme indicated Sarah Jennifer with a nod. "I'll have what she's having."

Dakota excused herself to get their meals after making Esme's drink.

"Tell me about the interesting men you met," Sarah Jennifer asked, playing with the mug in her hands.

Esme held up a finger while she took a long sip of her chocolate. "Ah, that's the stuff. The captain of the largest of those three ships in the harbor is named Reinar. He told me he was in New Romanov not six months back. The town is holding off the Mad from outside, but they've been affected by people in the community turning unexpectedly at random. Same story with the Weres."

Sarah Jennifer sighed. "Then we'd better make this visit short and move on. Do you think you can put something similar to the barrier hex on these settlements?"

Esme considered what it would take. "I can cover an area around the size of the fort, but they won't last without maintenance, and for that—"

"We need people using magic, which means repairing their nanocytes," Sarah Jennifer finished.

New Romanov, Archangelsk, Siberia

Ezekiel refused to let his mind replay the events leading to him being alone in the world. He found it impossible to focus on anything else.

Ezekiel couldn't stop seeing the image of her turning her sword on herself every time he closed his eyes, her last words pleading with him to make sure they didn't come back Mad.

Even in death Ezekiel had obeyed her, removing his parents' heads and staking their hearts before taking them to the forest to bury them. It was the hardest thing he would ever have to do. The whole time he'd been digging their graves, his thoughts had been jumbled, endlessly churning about how they would both be alive if he and his father had listened to her.

He did not cry as he lowered his mother's body into the ground next to his father's. He prayed instead. Prayed that the Matriarch would feel his anger at the senseless death stalking his world.

Ignoring the pain in his hands from digging into permafrost, Ezekiel picked up his shovel and backfilled the hole. He was unable to think of it as a grave, just as he'd had to disassociate from the actions that would prevent his parents from digging their way out again.

Eventually, it was done. Ezekiel stacked what stones he could find into a cairn and checked the Mad traps on autopilot before trudging through knee-high snow to the cabin he'd shared with his parents.

Once inside, Ezekiel fed the fire and heated water to clean his blisters, distracted by his mind's attempt to process the last twenty-four hours. The injured man they had allowed into their home had turned and killed Ezekiel's father while he was tending his wounds. His mother had killed the zombie, but not before being bitten.

The whole point of living outside the protection of New Romanov was to reduce the risk of Madness. His mother's prediction that one day her husband would try to help the wrong person had come true, but she was helpless to refuse his father's kind heart.

Ezekiel's lip curled, his eyes flaring red. That kind heart had gotten them both killed. And where was his magic when he needed it? It was small but powered by his emotions, he'd discovered. His mother was the reason he was special. He'd suspected it since his magic first manifested from the way she had taken the news as though it was expected. Ezekiel realized he would never hear her laugh again. Never hear his father's tall tales of men to the southeast who got drunk on water. Never feel his mother's loving hand on his head, or sense the pride his father couldn't contain.

His magic had failed him, and so had Lilith. His pleas to the Oracle had fallen on deaf ears, as they had for weeks. She had abandoned him after all her promises to the contrary, and now he was all alone.

Ezekiel washed his parents' blood from his hands and dressed the open blisters with strips of fabric. He didn't even try to heal himself, embracing the pain to go along with his bitter mood.

Forget solidarity. He was done with people, with generosity of heart. From now on, it was him against the world.

But...

Gossip needed no carriage, as his mother had been fond of reminding his father on the rare occasion he came home in his cups. It wouldn't be long before someone from the town came calling, and the reality was that the town elders would make him spend the rest of his teenage years with the Shutovs—not a pleasant thing to contemplate. The Shutovs were good people but harsh parents.

Pragmatism won out. He would have to leave, and soonest was best. Even with the Madness running rife through the population, there were still many settlements around Archangelsk and more to the south. It was a start.

Ezekiel began packing their food stores into hessian sacks, which he stacked by the door before taking them out to the barn two at a time. He grabbed his mother's sword as an afterthought as he left the cabin for the final time, adding it to the tools he gathered from the barn.

It began to snow as Ezekiel packed everything he

needed to survive in the forest on his sled. He worked quickly to harness his six dogs to it. He didn't look back as the dogs pulled the sled away from the dacha, knowing that to do so would be the end of the structured calm he'd slipped into during the packing.

Ezekiel let the dogs run off their exuberance as he guided them south, hoping the weight of him and the supplies wasn't too much. It was not. The dogs howled with pleasure at being allowed their heads, and New Romanov was soon far behind him.

The moon and stars lit the snow in the open spaces at the edges of the *taiga*, the shimmering stuff piled up spectacularly at the edges of the shadow-clad forest. Ezekiel avoided the deeper drifts, scolding himself for not thinking clearly as the sled ate up the miles. It was all well and good to make the decision to leave, but now he had to back it up by surviving until spring.

He heard his mother's laughter and had a recollection of playing on a sunny riverbank. Before the Madness, his family had summered in their *izba* near the Northern Dvina. No one in their right mind would attempt to live on the frozen river in winter when game was scarce and it was too cold for the logging crews to work safely. Nevertheless, something told Ezekiel that was where he should go.

His shoulders relaxed once he could no longer see Archangelsk over his shoulder. He pushed all thoughts from his mind as he focused on guiding the dogs from landmark to landmark.

The *taiga* sprang up around Ezekiel near the end of the second day. Straggling pines no more than two hundred years old bore the wind and snow, sporadically giving way to stands of much older pines bearing the ravages of time. Larches and spruces fought for space as the forest thickened. Their valiant battle to cling to life in temperatures below zero drove them to suck every available nutrient from the earth, preventing any but the hardiest undergrowth from thriving. He rested the dogs regularly, taking the time to check their snow boots every time they stopped. The last thing he needed was to push his precious animals too hard, and paw care was essential when asking them to travel long distances over snow and ice.

The cadence of the dogs' paws hitting the snow took on a whispery quality as they entered the forest at dusk, the susurrus of shifting pine needles on the logging road the only other sound as the sled carved through the night. Ezekiel was anxious not to miss the turn to the *izba*. He risked a small light when the canopy blocked the moon and stars, manifesting a ball of cold, pale flame.

The square log cabin came into sight an hour after Ezekiel left the logging road. Built by his grandfather, father, and uncles when they were young, everything about the *izba* was traditional, from the split-pine log construction of the cabin and the huge stove inside to the kitchen garden to the hay barn-*cum*-kennel to the small yard they surrounded and the fences that encircled it all. Not one nail had been used.

The stove came from Boris, a skilled smith of few words who lived in New Romanov. Ezekiel remembered his father taking him to the taciturn giant for a replacement plow blade. At five years old, he had been afraid of the gruff man, who seemed to look directly into his soul.

He had no trouble believing the tales he'd heard about Boris turning into a bear.

Ezekiel's first action was to take care of the dogs. Once he'd fed them and chained them in the barn to protect them— mostly from themselves, since they would attack any bears or lynx in the area and come off worse—he collected a double armload of cut wood from the store in the barn and made his way to the cabin holding a small oil lantern aloft.

Luckily, no large animals had gotten in since his family was last there. His hands numb with cold, Ezekiel cleared the ashes from the last fire and filled the stove with the wood from the barn. Once he had the stove heating the cabin's interior, he gathered furs and blankets to make a bed on top of the stove where it would be warmest.

Too tired to eat more than a few bites of dried meat, he bundled up and fell fast asleep.

It was dark in the *izba's* one room when Ezekiel awoke. He coaxed the fire back to life and drew back the drapes to allow the weak morning light in, then drew water and heated it before going out to the barn to feed the dogs.

Ezekiel was greeted by excited howls when he entered. The dogs circled his legs, bumping their heads against him in welcome and the hope of breakfast. "Well, good morning to you, too." He petted the dogs with his free hand, stepping over their long chains as he waded through them to get to the storage bin where the dried dog food was kept.

"You are lucky animals," Ezekiel told them as he filled a bucket with meal made from dehydrated meat and fish from the bin. "You do not have to work for your breakfast today."

The dogs howled while Ezekiel prepared a warm, soupy gruel with the meal and the water, which had cooled. He wrinkled his nose at the smell as he tipped the mixture into the dogs' bowls, almost hungry enough that it smelled like food to him.

"Now it is my turn," Ezekiel told the dogs as he left.

He returned to the cabin and unpacked the supply of food he'd brought with him into the pantry. He had jars of preserves, mixed parcels of dried and smoked meats, the potato cakes his mother had made the morning she'd died, a sack of oat flour, one of raw oats, another of beet sugar, and a few pounds each of potatoes, turnips, and carrots.

He had enough food to see him and the dogs through the winter if he was careful and industrious.

Ezekiel allowed himself a small portion of meat and three potato cakes. He climbed up onto the stove and ate slowly while he made a plan of action. The dogs would have enough food as long as he didn't work them too often. The potatoes he would use to grow more. The kitchen garden could be persuaded to grow more than potatoes when spring came around, but until then, the pickled and salted preserves he'd brought with him would supplement the game he caught.

He knew that to have the best chance of survival, he would have to spend his time wisely. Fishing was out of the question until the thaw came, but he knew the paths of his father's traplines by heart. Hares and rabbits were plentiful in the forest, as were chipmunks.

If he was lucky, there might be musk deer or wild pigs, although he wasn't confident he could handle those without his parents. If he had a gun, things would be different. He could shoot larger game as he needed it, and the dogs could have fresh meat.

There were a lot of ifs.

Ezekiel's eyes began to feel heavy, thanks to a full stomach and the warmth of the stove. Somewhere in the back of his mind, he heard his mother's voice telling him he could build a pit and line the bottom with stakes. "Then all I have to do is drive the pig into the hole," he murmured, exhaustion stealing over him.

He drifted off, thinking of bacon, pork belly, and smoked ham.

CHAPTER SEVEN

Reykjavik, Guild Hall

Jurgen Haas remained aloof from the shouting match currently being conducted by his honorable advisors. The airship the strangers had arrived in had caused the light of greed to shine in many of their eyes. As the elected leader of the city, it was his duty to judge the truth of this stranger's claims. It might also be time to reassess what kind of people he had allowed to hold power.

Sarah Jennifer's voice cut across the clamor. "This doesn't have to be a disaster. The Defense Force will be here to assist when the ice recedes."

Jurgen stood, drawing silence from the guild masters.

The representatives from Salem intrigued him with their tale of the old technology causing the so-called Madness. Their gift of communications technology was more than welcome; it was going to revolutionize trade the world over. However, the news that there was a limited, and worse from his bureaucrat's point of view, *unspecified* amount of time until Beringia was gone had been too much for some of the guild masters to countenance.

Jurgen observed Major Walton and her men with interest. They were clearly *more*, exuding that extra something he'd come across less and less in the last decade. Weres were getting to be an endangered species, although not in Salem, apparently. "You are offering a lot and not asking for anything in return." Jurgen lifted his hands, taking in the wealth displayed in the hall. "That is not how the world works, Major, pardon my saying so."

Sarah Jennifer met his eyes. She didn't need to read the guild's minds to know that profit drove them. The leader seemed different, amenable despite the severe air he projected.

"I gain plenty," Sarah Jennifer assured the guild masters. "Profit looks different, depending on your perspective. I have no use for gold and silver. What I value is human life and the continuation of it on Earth. We need capable fighters to join the Defense Force. I want to establish a garrison here and teach your people to fight the Madness. Take the equipment I'm offering and speak to the people already using it before you make any decisions. We will return in a month's time and talk again."

Jurgen's forehead creased in confusion. "You're leaving already?"

Sarah Jennifer nodded. "I have settlements to visit from here to Siberia. Once you get the hotspot set up, you'll hear from Sergeant Isabel Bloom. She will work with you to figure out how much of this city needs to be relocated and how it can be done with minimal disruption to your people's lives."

"This isn't what I expected." Jurgen looked disappointed for the first time since Sarah Jennifer had arrived. He glanced around the hall, his gaze alighting on a man dressed from head to toe in shaggy fur. He beckoned the man forward. "We will accept your communications device with thanks. I ask that you take one of my men with you."

"I volunteer," a gruff voice announced. The man who stepped forward looked very different from the majority of the Reykjavikians. He was half a head taller and huge across the shoulders compared to the well-muscled men around him. His eyes, impenetrable black holes, bored into Sarah Jennifer.

"Theor!" Jurgen exclaimed.

Theor bowed. "It is my wish, Father."

Jurgen looked long at his son and sighed. "I suppose this was inevitable. Will you accept him?" he asked Sarah Jennifer. "My son is a capable warrior with knowledge of the ice shelf."

Sarah Jennifer should have refused, but her gut tugged the words from her lips when she met Theor's eyes. This man belonged to her. "We leave in the morning, so be ready," she found herself saying.

His eyes gleamed yellow as he lowered his head. "My Alpha."

Sarah Jennifer's eyes flashed red in response, drawing gasps from the crowd when they realized the prickle of power making the hairs on their skin rise was coming from her.

"I wish you smooth seas, my son." Jurgen smiled, satisfied that his son had finally found the piece of himself that had always been missing. He opened his arms wide, the consummate politician. "Now that's settled, let me invite you and your people to a banquet in honor of the new friendship between Reykjavik and Salem."

Sarah Jennifer contained her shock. She was drawing Weres to her now? Esme had talked endlessly about manifesting her reality, and she knew nanocytes enhanced natural capabilities. Maybe this was what that looked like? She lived her responsibility to the UnknownWorld, and now it was responding to her intent to lead people into a better future than the one they faced divided.

Theor followed at a respectful distance as they left the guildhall and walked along the cliffs toward the six-bedroom house overlooking the sea the pack had been assigned by the guild on arrival. Sarah Jennifer made no effort to read his mind, although she couldn't help catching stray thoughts as the man resolved his decision. She blocked them out, not wishing to intrude. Esme would take care of making sure his intentions were as he stated. She preferred the direct approach.

When the house was in sight, she slowed her pace and looked at the ships in the harbor below. "Anything you want to ask before you meet the pack?"

Theor stopped at the waist-high wall. "Who do I need to fight to establish my place?"

Sarah Jennifer didn't sense any nerves in him at the prospect. She took a seat on the low wall. "We have a military structure, not dominance based on strength." She gave him a short rundown of the pack's history and their aims as a force for protecting the Unknown-World. "Your mind is as valuable as your ability to fight, and your secondary role will be based on your skills."

Theor was stunned by the amount of organization his new pack had taken on. "My mother died giving birth to me. Everything I know about being Wechselbalg I learned from what my father told me. This is going to take some getting used to."

"There's more," Sarah Jennifer told him. "We have a larger mission, but that's all I'm willing to share with you until I know you better. The guys will welcome you as long as you're willing to pull your weight."

Theor grinned. "Trust me, I pull the weight of ten men in a fight. Me and Brunhilde." He caressed the hilt of the broadsword strapped to his back. "We're unstoppable. I can help by introducing you to community leaders. What you have to say will go down better with someone they know vouching for you."

Sarah Jennifer sensed he was holding something back. "What aren't you saying?"

Theor shrugged. "You should know it's not safe for Wechselbalg. Blood traders operating out of the Danelaw control the ports along that part of the coast."

Sarah Jennifer grimaced. "I had no idea. Tell me about them—their numbers, weapons, and ships."

She listened as he outlined the Danelaw's holdings and military capability.

"Everything is under Sidric's control. He kills anyone who might be a threat to his power, and it's gotten worse since the affliction cut off his supply of Were blood. He's aging badly and becoming more vicious with every year he makes it through."

Sarah Jennifer factored in taking out the Danelaw to their mission objective, mentally slotting it somewhere between saving Lilith and fixing the climate control module. "Why have you chosen to come with us? Are you chasing a fight?"

Theor's brow worked as he searched for an explanation. Eventually, he settled on a shrug. "I'm not avoiding a fight, but I'm not searching one out, either. I just felt like it was the right thing at the moment. Like if I didn't speak up, my future would walk out of the hall with you..."

"Like you belong with us," Sarah Jennifer finished.

Theor nodded. "I guess I do. How, when I never met you before, I don't know."

Sarah Jennifer smiled. Would he understand that the miniscule machines running through his blood tweaked his biology on the genetic level to make him crave the company of other Weres? "Pack is pack, Theor. Come on, we're causing a scene. Look."

Theor followed her gaze to the house. Every window was open and filled with curious faces. He couldn't make out their features from here, but he could smell them. Despite the anxiety his human side felt about being introduced into a family that hadn't asked for him, his wolf thrilled at the scent of Weres on the air.

Sarah Jennifer waved to let them know Theor was no threat, and they vanished from the windows. "Heads up: don't bother Katia unless you want to experience pain, and I will be more than annoyed if you fail to repress your instinct to kill Linus. He's annoying as hell, but he's a good person. Everyone else you will find friendly."

She told him a little bit about everyone else in the family while they completed the walk to the house. Esme was waiting outside when they arrived. She smiled at Theor. "Welcome to the family, dearie."

Theor smiled nervously at Esme and nodded to the stern-faced men who stood in and around the doorway with unfamiliar boxy black rifles held loosely in their hands. He didn't see the woman officer the major had mentioned or the child she'd told him was traveling with them.

"Meet Theor Haas," Sarah Jennifer told them. "Use your noses. He's pack, the only Were in this city, and he's coming with us. Look after him."

Their demeanor changed instantly. Theor was overwhelmed by the welcome and his proximity to so many Weres after a lifetime spent among humans.

"Give him some space," Esme chided, shooing everyone back. "You have all day to introduce yourselves."

Sarah Jennifer nodded her agreement. "We've been invited to a banquet hosted by the city master, who also happens to be Theor's father. Go gussy up. Dress uniforms and practice your manners. You will be representing Salem and the Defense Force. If I hear any foul language while we are guests, the offender will be scrubbing the *Enora's* hull for a week."

She had a feeling she'd lost them at the mention of a banquet.

Brutus stepped out of the group as they dispersed and extended a hand to Theor. "Lieutenant Brutus Timmons, good to meet you. Welcome to the Defense Force, Private. When we're done with the diplomatic aspect of this visit, you and I should find a quiet space to test your fighting ability."

"I look forward to it." Theor got an idea of Brutus' strength as they shook hands, and he smiled at the prospect of sparring without holding back. "Your ways are very strange to me. It will take some time to learn them."

Sarah Jennifer took a seat at the kitchen table and waved to indicate the men should sit while Esme made tea. "It's our starting rank," she explained. "You can work your way up if that's your thing."

Theor removed his sword and took the seat opposite Sarah Jennifer. "My sword is yours, however you see fit to use it."

"Your geographic knowledge is more apropos to the current situation," Sarah Jennifer told him, taking her datapad out of her inside jacket pocket.

Theor's eyes widened in amazement when she activated the screen. "What is that?"

"Technology," Sarah Jennifer replied, sliding the datapad over to him. She showed him how to add border markers with the editing tools. "Take your time familiarizing yourself with the map. I need to know how far east the Danelaw extends."

She filled Brutus in on the Sidric situation while Theor studied the map.

Esme glanced over his shoulder when she brought the teapot and mugs to the table. "This could be a kick in the bollocks for the Sweden operation. My beautiful Scotland, under ice and ruled by Vikings. If that's not proof history repeats itself, I don't know what is."

"Vikings?" Brutus inquired. "What are they?"

"Mistakenly named," Esme replied, sipping her tea. "Scandinavia has always been a hard place to live. The people were industrious and governed by complex laws. Most valued art and their concept of honor, but above all, they were explorers. The practice of going *vikingr*—traveling by boat from inlet to inlet—became synonymous with the raiding parties that went out in summer. A couple thousand years before WWDE, they adopted the Christian religion and propagated it wherever they settled. Their military prowess was responsible for the rise of the royal families who ruled Europe for centuries."

She placed her mug on the table. "The dark side of that looks a lot like young Theor has described. Add in the warlord's blood addiction, and we have a serious problem on our hands."

"What are we going to do about it?" Brutus asked.

"I haven't decided yet," Sarah Jennifer told him. "Lilith is still our first priority. If the Danelaw is an obstacle to repairing the climate control module, then it becomes priority number two."

Theor looked up from the datapad. "I'm done. I marked the places they've got the support of the people, places I would normally avoid."

Sarah Jennifer examined his additions to the map with a sinking heart. Östergötland was inside the Danelaw. She showed Esme and Brutus. "We may not be able to get in and out of Norrköping without running afoul of Sidric's men. Do they have shock weapons?"

Theor tilted his head in confusion.

"Weapons that use electricity. Small bolts of lightning," she clarified.

Theor shook his head. "They have blades and cannons drawn on carts."

Sarah Jennifer admired the ingenuity, if not the purpose. The night was coming on fast, and she had to get into her dress uniform. "We'll come back to this after the banquet. It changes nothing right now. We leave for New Romanov tomorrow."

CHAPTER EIGHT

New Romanov

Olaf cursed to himself as he left the Shutov house with the sled holding the bodies of the most recent citizens of New Romanov to turn Mad. What comfort were walls when the Madness ran free inside them, eroding civilization without mercy?

Anyone could fall. Today, Irina had lost both her husband and her brother-in-law. The blonde battle-axe had borne it without shedding a tear, despite being left to raise her children alone. Grief was a luxury they could scarce afford.

Olaf dragged the tarp containing the bodies of the Shutov men on a sled behind him toward the firepit beyond the wall, with the townspeople trailing at a distance to avoid the Madness-infected corpses. His duty had been weighing on him of late, more since Lilith had gone into conservation mode. It was a wonder *he* hadn't gone mad, the old-fashioned kind that came without red-glowing eyes or a taste for human flesh. Even before Lilith had dropped into silence, she hadn't had much energy to spare for explaining what was going on. He'd made twice-yearly pilgrimages to her mountain, and only two times in the last ten years had she been there to speak to him: once to warn him of the Madness, and again to tell him that help was coming just before she'd powered her machinery down.

He wondered when the Americans would arrive to repair Lilith's machinery. He suppressed his skepticism about the chances of the group from Salem making it across the world alive. The hope that Lilith would find a cure for the Madness was what kept him from slipping into despair while the people he was sworn to protect went Mad by the thousands.

The townspeople watched from the wall as Olaf stacked wood and placed the tarp-wrapped bodies on the pyre. A warrior's life was a lonely one, even more so for a man who became a bear on the battlefield. Again, fate had chosen to spare him when the Wechselbalg in Archangelsk had been forced to decide which half of themselves to lose.

Boris had entrusted Lilith and New Romanov to Olaf when he had left with Bethany Anne. Olaf recalled his last view of his father disappearing into the spaceship, thinking back to Boris' last words as the funeral pyre he'd built for Ivar and Dragomir burned.

"New Romanov is yours to protect now, my son. You will be their strength in my absence. The world will forget our Queen. Make sure our people remember."

His strength was holding up a lot more than New

Romanov. He wondered where his father was. His counsel would have made the trials Archangelsk was going through bearable, if not any easier. He had the respect of the men and women he fought with, but ultimately he was of the UnknownWorld, and an invisible barrier came down once the blood had been spilled and people looked to him to lead.

Olaf's time was split between the remaining communities spread out in the vastness of Archangelsk, clearing out flare-ups of Madness wherever they arose and helping the people build defenses that would protect them from the raiders in his absence. The Danelaw was growing to be a canker on his ass. That bastard Sidric was expanding his fleet with every raid on the taiga, taking trees that had been tall when Boris was a youth along with any able-bodied people who lived along the estuaries.

One of these days, Olaf was going to pay Sidric a visit and see how the blood-addled warlord liked it when Olaf took one of the precious trees he'd stolen and stuck it up his—

His thoughts were disrupted by the arrival of one of the young men from town, who burst out of the forest like a Mad.

The youth ceased his frantic charge when he saw Olaf and fell to the ground while he dragged in huge, hitching breaths.

Olaf retrieved his sword from where he'd rested it before starting the pyre.

"Curtis!" Irina Shutov yelled from the top of the wall.

Curtis waved a hand, opening his eyes so the warrior

could see he wasn't Mad, just winded. "Mad attack," he gasped. "They're all gone!"

"Who's gone?" Irina demanded. "I'm coming down there!"

Olaf looked up when the woman barked a command at someone to let her out. "Tell me what you saw," he urged the boy.

Still breathing hard, Curtis relayed how he'd arrived at Ezekiel's house and found it empty. He was beginning to recover from his exertions when Irina strode out of the gate. "I didn't go in. There was blood everywhere. I ran straight home, knowing you were here, Olaf."

"What were you doing out in the forest by yourself?" Irina chided. "What if you had been killed?"

Curtis scrambled to his feet, sensing impending danger as she moved in.

"Your mother has been worried sick!" she scolded, grabbing his ear between her thumb and forefinger. "If I was your father, I'd take a strip off your backside for scaring her."

"I'll go check the house," Olaf told the gathering people. "Stay inside the walls."

Curtis squealed as Irina dragged him through the gate.

Olaf sheathed his sword and set off the way the youth had come. He knew Anatoly and Danica a little, enough to know they had a son. Anatoly's skills as a trapper and craftsman kept the family in whatever they couldn't wrest from the land; their lives looked much as it did for many families who lived away from the towns.

Well, they had. Olaf couldn't sense any human life as he

approached the house. The dogs were gone, too. Nobody lived out here without dogs. He went in through the gate with his sword drawn, smelling the lingering taint of Madness coming from the open door.

Snow had mounded on the threshold. Olaf kicked it aside and pushed the door all the way open. Seeing that the living area was empty, he called softly.

"Anatoly? Danica?"

No reply, and no movement or sound in the house. Olaf sheathed his sword and set about investigating the source of the smell. He found the hacked-up corpse of a stranger in one of the bedrooms. From the upturned basin and the pink-stained rag on the rug, the bed in disarray, and the shattered tchotchkes lying around the toppled nightstand, it looked like they'd taken in someone who had then gone Mad.

Had they fled?

Olaf left the house and began a sweep of the property. The barn where the dogs should have been was secured, and the sled and dog tack were gone. He found the cairn shortly after.

He almost missed it at first, but his eye snapped back to a straight line etched into the largest stone in the snow-covered pile. He removed the snow with a gentle swipe and saw the names painstakingly etched into the stone, the grooves stained with dried blood. Olaf sniffed the blood but couldn't discern who it had belonged to. Still, there was only one person who would have buried Anatoly and Danica, and only one person their dogs would have obeyed —their son.

A disturbance in the Etheric distracted Olaf from his musings for the moment.

Lilith was awake.

Olaf didn't dare waste a second. The boy would have to wait for now. He stripped and bundled his clothing and weapons, using the coil of rope he carried to tie the roll onto him before shifting and setting off for Lilith's mountain as fast as his four paws could carry him.

The Etheric static increased as he ran, buzzing in his mind. Olaf saw something shiny hovering above the mountain as he neared the entrance to Lilith's cave.

He stopped short and shifted back when he saw the shiny thing was some kind of airship, much more advanced than the few dirigibles that still graced the skies. The design was old-world, but even from a distance, he could see the ship gleamed from loving care.

Had Sidric discovered Lilith's presence and brought some long-lost technology to capture her? The more likely explanation was that the Americans had arrived, but he was old and wise enough not to take the chance.

Still too far away to be noticed, he quickly dressed as he considered the best approach. He settled on a slow and steady pace, staying close to the ground, where the foliage gave him cover.

Olaf smelled Wechselbalg, then he saw them. Dressed in all-black tactical gear and carrying semiautomatic rifles of a caliber that gave him pause, six large men stood guard at the cave entrance. He crept closer, maintaining his cover at the edge of the tree line.

"We know you're there," one of the males called in English.

Olaf had a little English, Deutsche, and Française, enough to get him through conversations with traders from the west. "Then you know I could kill three of you before you could take me out with those guns," he called back in his best approximation of the same. "I am Olaf. Who are you, and why are you here?"

"If you're Olaf, you know exactly why we're here," the man responded. "The name's Timmons, Lieutenant Brutus Timmons. Come on out so we can see you. We won't shoot unless you give us a reason."

Olaf glanced at the other five, whose weapons remained trained on the forest. He understood them well enough. "I guess I'm going to have to trust you are who you say you are," he murmured to himself in Russian.

He emerged from the tree line, showing his hand was away from his sword. "Lilith told me to expect Americans, but I have to admit, I didn't believe you were coming. How are there so many of you?"

The men just looked at him. He'd slipped into Russian in his emotional state, so they didn't understand his words.

Olaf grunted in frustration. "I need more English. Wechselbalg. Everywhere else, they are gone. Either wolf or human, but no longer both. *Shest*...six,'" He pointed at each of them. "More than I have seen for years."

Brutus frowned. Olaf thought the frown was aimed at him until he noticed that the man's lips were moving, and his eyes were unfocused as though he was somewhere else.

The moment passed. The lieutenant retrieved a comm device from a pouch on his webbing and turned to the others. "I'm going to take him to the major. You guys keep doing what you're doing."

ND ROBERTS & MICHAEL ANDERLE

He showed Olaf the comm device on his ear and handed him the spare. "Enora, can you help us out? This guy speaks Russian."

Olaf fitted the device to his ear as they entered the tunnel. His interest was piqued when a child's voice came from the device.

"*Privet,* Olaf. *Ne volnuytes'. Ya perevedu,*" Enora greeted him.

"Who is the child?" Olaf asked in English.

"Enora, the artificial intelligence in the airship," Brutus clarified. "Come with me; the major is waiting to see you."

Olaf shrugged, accepting the idea of artificial life without question as the translation came through. He walked in silence for a moment as he followed Brutus along the tunnel. "You're pretty big for a wolf."

Brutus looked over his shoulder at the man standing a head taller than him. "Says the bear. How did you end up being the only Were in Siberia?"

Olaf's pace slowed as he caught more Wechselbalg scents and a scent he didn't recognize. "I do not know. Even before the Madness, our brothers and sisters began to lose the ability to shift. What am I smelling?"

Brutus chuckled. "Magic, my friend."

Olaf wasn't sure the translation was working. "Magic?"

"That's right," Brutus told him as they approached the room where Lilith's machinery was housed.

The magic scent grew stronger as they walked. Olaf had been beneath the mountain many times, but it had never felt so...alive.

Olaf faltered when a tall blonde woman wearing the

same uniform as Brutus met them at the entrance to Lilith's chamber.

She extended a hand, smiling warmly. "Sarah Jennifer Walton, head of the Salem Defense Force. Good to meet you."

Olaf wasn't surprised by the strength in her handshake. His nose told him she was one of the sources of the magic smell, as well as being Wechselbalg. "I heard the name Walton before, long ago."

Sarah Jennifer's smile grew wider. "My grandparents got around. Come on in. I know Lilith wants to talk to you."

She stepped aside. When Olaf walked into the chamber, he was met by a sight that froze him in horror. Lilith's casing was open, and parts of the machine that kept her consciousness alive were out on the benches. "What is this?" Olaf cried, not caring about the reaction his panicked yell caused in the Americans.

Lilith's voice calmed him. "It is all right. I am undamaged."

He looked around and saw her voice was coming from a glowing blue cube. "What is this?"

A silver-haired woman looked up from the keyboard she had connected to Lilith's insides and smiled. "Lilith is temporarily living inside this memory device."

"It *is* temporary," Lilith told Olaf in a reassuring tone. "This cube cannot hold my consciousness for more than a few weeks."

Esme snorted. "Much to Ted's annoyance."

"However," Lilith continued without acknowledging the remark, "I did not want you to be distressed by this, so

I asked Sarah Jennifer to find a way I could be awake during the procedure to talk to you."

Sarah Jennifer waved the pack's weapons down when Olaf's shoulders lost their tension. "This has been planned for four years. We are replacing the Kurtherian power source with something called an Etheric engine that our engineers built. It draws continuously on the Etheric like a drip-feed, so Lilith won't be at risk from draining herself to the point of death again."

Olaf nodded. "I appreciate the explanation."

Sarah Jennifer put a hand on his elbow and guided him away from the workspace. "Let me introduce you around, then I'll answer any questions you have."

Olaf met Geordie and Carver, the two men working on the Etheric engine with Esme, then Linus, Rory, Tucker, Tim, and Rider.

"You met Dinny, Reg, the Ace brothers, and Kalder outside," Sarah Jennifer finished. "The others are still aboard the ship, including a Were who joined the pack in Reykjavik."

"Do you have a cure for the Madness?" Olaf asked, not expecting a positive answer.

"We know how to end it," Sarah Jennifer told him. "We don't have what we need yet. The shifting issue we have a fix for, but it's by no means efficient."

Olaf resolved to find out more about the shifting issue at a later date. "There is nothing we can do here until the Etheric engine is assembled, am I right?"

Sarah Jennifer nodded. "Pretty much. Can I give you a tour of the *Enora* to pass the time?"

Olaf's eyes twinkled. "A...tour. Yes, that might do. Can

this tour take place while you help me look for a missing boy?"

Sarah Jennifer glanced at Esme. "How long until you're done here?"

Esme pushed her keyboard away. "I have nothing to do until the boys are done anyway. What are we waiting for?"

CHAPTER NINE

Northern Dvina Taiga

Ezekiel had fallen into a loose routine since his arrival at his family's izba. He woke up before the sun rose to feed the dogs, then checked the fences around the izba's perimeter with his canine companions at his side. After that, he ate breakfast while he planned his day's work, mending whatever needed fixing around the property.

Maintaining the homestead was a full-time occupation. Ezekiel made no effort to practice his magic, focusing on survival for himself and the dogs instead. He repaired and strengthened the fences, cleared the yard of snow and debris, tore the weeds from the kitchen garden and turned the soil, built traps to catch small game—whatever kept his mind off the reason he was doing all this.

The result of his diligent labor was a day when he took care of his morning chores and found he had nothing else to do to fill the hours until it was time to sleep again.

He finished his breakfast and walked around the izba, looking for a distraction to continue to avoid training his magic. His gaze landed on the five books that held pride of place on his mother's shelf. Ezekiel's father had preferred the oral tradition of sharing tales around the fire at night, but she had collected books wherever she found them, treasuring the lost art of the written word. Ezekiel had learned to read while sitting in her lap on rainy days.

Book in hand, he rearranged his furs on top of the stove and settled in to lose himself in the story.

He was a few pages in when he began to feel uneasy. It was barely noticeable at first, and he put it down to being unoccupied for the first time since he'd left New Romanov and made an effort to concentrate on his book.

The unease grew. Ezekiel put the book down, closed his eyes, and tried to get control of his growing fear.

"What is there to scare me?" he asked himself aloud to reason the feeling away. Lacking an answer, he looked into himself to find one.

He was suddenly overwhelmed by the smell of straw, urine, and…something rotten. His mind spun as he experienced a flood of emotions that didn't belong to him.

Ezekiel lost the connection with a jolt the moment he realized he was somehow sharing his mind with his dogs.

Bear shit! The dogs!

Hoping he wasn't too late, Ezekiel slid off the stove and grabbed his mother's sword as he pelted for the barn.

The dogs were silent, which scared him more than the borrowed perception of rotting meat had. He tried to reach for their minds again as he approached the barn door, but he was unable to calm his racing heart, knowing that the dogs were his only lifeline.

Ezekiel gasped in relief when he heard the dogs

growling low in their throats. Instinctively, he opened the door with his sword arm raised, ready to fight the Mad man or woman inside. He needn't have bothered.

The red-eyed owl perching in the rafters was focused on the dogs. It hopped from one foot to the other, its urge to roost competing with its desire to feed on the animals below.

The dogs knew this was no ordinary owl. They looked up at the bird in distrustful puzzlement, half-poised to spring should it make a move. Ezekiel wasn't sure how to deal with it, either. If he let it go, it would infect the local wildlife, cutting off his food supply.

He hesitated and lowered his sword, and it was enough to bring the Madness-ridden owl's attention to him.

Chaos ensued as the bird launched itself at Ezekiel, swooping over the dogs. The dogs reacted as one, leaping with snapping teeth, crashing into each other in their attempt to catch the feathered menace.

Ezekiel reacted without thought. His free hand came up of its own accord, and a stream of fire erupted from his palm.

The barn was filled with the stench of burnt feathers. The owl, slightly roasted but still alive, flew out of the flames and dove at Ezekiel with its talons pointed at his face.

Ordering the dogs back, he swung his sword and cleaved the owl in two. He was unused to any kind of combat, so he failed to get out of the way as the owl's innards were freed from its falling corpse.

Ezekiel spat the blood out, but it was too late. The coppery taste of Madness filled his mouth. He collapsed exhausted in a cross-legged position on the bloodstained straw and despaired, not noticing that the dogs had become agitated again.

They avoided the owl and crowded Ezekiel to try to push him away from its corruption with their noses.

Ezekiel came to his senses and shoved them away. "It's no good. It got me."

The dogs didn't understand. They only wanted to protect their human. Nanu tugged his sleeve, her ice-blue eyes full of loving concern.

Ezekiel's stomach roiled in disgust when he realized they would be his first meal when he went Mad. "You have to run," he told her. "All of you. I...I am already dead. It is just a matter of time until the Madness takes over."

He got to his feet and stumbled to unlock the dogs' chains. They danced around him, baying with excitement, thinking they were going for a run.

Ezekiel started crying as he opened the barn door. The dogs ran to the sled, but he shook his head and opened the front gate.

"I'm setting you free," he told them through his tears. "Run before it is too late."

He went back inside the izba and barred the door, ignoring the confused yips from the dogs. They didn't understand. He slid down the door, his knees giving way while his vision swam.

Outside, the yips turned to howls.

"Go already!" he yelled, his voice muffled by the ringing in his ears. The exhaustion he'd felt after using his magic won out, dragging him into unconsciousness.

His last thought as his vision turned to black was that he didn't *want* to go Mad.

Sarah Jennifer ran on four paws beside Olaf, her nose sweeping the ground. Tac teams One and Two and Esme rode the ATVs, while teams Three and Four spread out in Were form. Their line was half a kilometer wide, while Jim and Enora searched for the boy's trail from above.

They'd followed the sled routes out of New Romanov. Sarah Jennifer had split the pack into their old teams and ordered half to shift while the others unloaded the ATVs from the belly of the airship after Olaf had determined Ezekiel was heading for his family's summer house, taking a rough south-easterly route into the taiga. Although two or three weeks had passed since the boy had passed through, the pack was able to follow the scat trail left by the dogs. It was faint, and they had to stop a number of times and fan out to search for the next deposit, but they made steady progress. They ran through the night, stopping only to investigate any signs of life Jim reported.

Sarah Jennifer found her admiration for this child growing as the pack chewed up the kilometers. He was no older than fifteen, yet he'd survived a Mad attack and was apparently determined to live out here in the wilds.

The Northern Dvina came into sight as dawn bled orange and pink on the horizon, the river's majestic flow seized in the grip of winter. Sarah Jennifer shifted and called a halt as the *Enora* returned from scouting the area ahead. The airship touched down a short way from the riverbank and Katia emerged, leading the remainder of the pack. They were carrying covered trays of hot breakfast. Twenty minutes to eat, another ten to get their orders from Brutus, and they resumed the search with the teams reversed.

Olaf was impressed by the pack's methodical approach and, he had to admit, their endurance. Truth be told, knowing the trail ran this far had given him high hopes of finding Anatoly's and Danica's boy, and he was relishing the company of his own kind.

The forest was thicker here, the trees crowding the path and blocking most of the light. The ATVs sprayed pine needles as they fought for traction on the deep mulch beneath their wheels. Sarah Jennifer called for everyone in Were form to break off when the going got rougher.

They heard the dogs perhaps an hour after they'd entered the forest. Frantic howls split the air, startling the nearby birds. Sarah Jennifer braced herself on the ATV's footboards and stood without letting off on the throttle. "Those our dogs, Olaf?"

Olaf was suddenly certain they were and that they had to hurry. In the blink of an eye, he shifted and hurtled ahead of the pack.

"Follow that bear!" Sarah Jennifer yelled, grabbing Olaf's discarded clothing as she shot into the forest after him.

They found Olaf standing at the gate to a smallholding in human form. The reason for his hesitation blocked the way.

One of his hands covered his groin, and the other was

held out in a calming gesture to the six dogs. "Nice dogs. You remember me? It's Olaf. Friend, see?"

Sarah Jennifer thrust Olaf's shirt and pants at him. "They might stop growling if you don't flash your ass." She knelt and met the dogs' eyes. "You have to let me pass. I'm here to help."

Whether they understood her or they recognized her as being far above them in any pack hierarchy, the dogs moved aside to let the major through the gate.

Olaf hopped around as he put his pants on, grinning. "Well, that wasn't so hard."

The dogs closed ranks and returned to blocking the gate when he made to follow Sarah Jennifer.

"Hey!" Olaf protested. "You let *her* through!"

Sarah Jennifer glanced back and shook her head. "Everyone, check the perimeter and make sure we have no Mad in the area."

She walked up the path to the smallholding as the pack dispersed, and she paused with her hand poised to knock on the door. Would he understand her, given Olaf's difficulties? She asked Enora for the Russian phrase she wanted before knocking. "Hey, kid, you in there? We're here with Olaf."

There was no answer. Sarah Jennifer pressed her ear to the wood and listened hard. There was someone there; they were on the floor, and their breathing sounded deep and even. She put her shoulder against the door and shoved. The door shuddered, but the bar on the inside held. She stepped back and looked at Esme. "Can I get some help?"

Esme looked each of the dogs in the eye and "suggested" that they were tired. She came in through the gate as they yawned and laid down. Olaf grumbled as he left to circle the building.

Sarah Jennifer gave the witch a worried glance. "The boy is right behind the door. If I snap the bar, the damned thing's likely to injure him."

Esme rubbed her hands together and placed them on the door, extending her senses into the boy's mind. "Out cold, and it's no ordinary sleep. He's been using magic, and it has exhausted his mind and body. Poor mite wouldn't wake up if we dropped the house on him."

"Maybe there's a back door?" Brutus suggested, peering over Esme's shoulder. "There's been a fire in the barn, and there's a dead owl that stinks of the Madness."

"The dogs are okay," Sarah Jennifer reasoned. "The boy must have burned the owl to protect them."

"He cut it in half as well," Brutus added, holding up the bloody sword he'd found. "Brave kid."

Olaf joined them after circling the izba. "There is no other entrance. What do we do?"

Esme closed her eyes, still touching the door. "Let me see if I can push him out of the way."

Olaf frowned, his interest piqued when Esme's hands glowed gold and she *pushed* the light through the door.

They heard a slight shuffle like something heavy being dragged, then she broke off, sweat beading her forehead. "This is a damn sight harder than making the Mad dance."

She was joking. She refocused her attention, and they heard the scrape of the bar lifting, then a hollow thud as she dropped it. She leaned a hand against the wall and waved Sarah Jennifer on. "I just need a minute."

Sarah Jennifer eased the door open, spotting the inert form of the boy as the light spilled into the room. She slipped around the door and kicked the bar out of the way so the others could get in before going to kneel at his side.

The boy didn't stir when Sarah Jennifer shook him gently. She looked up at Esme in concern. "Is he okay?"

"Told you, he's been using magic." Esme waved a finger. "Can't you smell it on him? It'll be a few hours before he can be woken up, I'll wager." She peered at the boy's sleeping face. "Interesting. How did he get magic in the first place?"

"I want him in the Pod-doc," Sarah Jennifer decided. "See if we can't fix it so he doesn't pass out every time he manifests energy."

"It'll pass with practice," Esme told her. "Likely he's got more abilities in there if fire manifested first."

Olaf folded his arms and leaned in the doorway. "We should take him to New Romanov. We need to get back to Lilith."

Sarah Jennifer caught a whiff of corruption beneath the magic scent as she scooped the sleeping boy up in her arms. She sniffed again, identifying the blood on his face as the source. "Shit. He might be infected."

"All the more reason to get him into the Pod-doc," Esme insisted. "We can save this boy and get the data Ted needs to reverse the Madness."

They hurried to the ATVs and followed Jim's directions to the nearest open space where the *Enora* could land. Sarah Jennifer cradled Ezekiel in her arms while Brutus drove, praying for him to hold on until they could get him to the airship. His temperature climbed rapidly over the fifteen minutes it took them to reach the break in the forest.

Sarah Jennifer feared for his life. All she could do was hold his slight body to her and keep telling him to hang on as he began murmuring incoherently, caught in a fever dream he couldn't escape.

The airship was waiting in the clearing.

Sarah Jennifer ran for the medbay with the burning boy in her arms, reaching the tiny cabin containing just the Pod-doc and command console in the space of half a minute. She thumbed the scanner that was keyed to her nanocytes and gently deposited the boy on the neural mat, then stepped back, her hands shaking as the lid closed and stasis gas clouded the viewing window.

"Hold on just a bit longer, kiddo. We're going to do everything we can."

CHAPTER TEN

Esme joined Sarah Jennifer in the medbay as the airship arrived back at Lilith's mountain. She took one look at the younger woman's posture, which indicated the return of her melancholy, then put a hand on Sarah Jennifer's shoulder and squeezed gently.

"He'll be okay. There's nothing that machine can't fix eventually."

Sarah Jennifer's response was a sigh that contained the weight of the sorrow she felt as she moved to the command console. "I hope so. It's hardest when it's children."

She pulled up the dialysis program Ted had written to counteract the shifting issue and began inputting instructions for the program to filter out any corrupted nanocytes in the boy's blood, intending to replace them with copies of his originals once the analysis was completed.

The console threw up a warning along with the analysis results. Sarah Jennifer frowned in confusion, the problem beyond her understanding. "Esme, what's happening here?"

Esme bumped her out of the way with a hip and scrutinized the text on the left monitor, her eyes growing wide. She grasped Sarah Jennifer's sleeve in her excitement, pointing at the visual analysis on the right monitor. "This is... He's fighting off the Madness. His nanocytes, they're..."

She sought a way to explain that wouldn't leave Sarah Jennifer confused. "The corruption in the owl's blood he swallowed is trying to overwrite his natural nanocytes," she began.

"That much I figured out." Sarah Jennifer tilted her head, trying to understand what she was seeing. "It looks like a tide going both ways. What's happening?"

"The boy's nanocytes are adapting," Esme told her, going back to the text panel. "They're attacking the owl's nanocytes. If we interfere, we might destroy the cure for the Madness."

Sarah Jennifer's heart dropped as she read the boy's vitals. "This is what immunity looks like? It's terrible. Can't we do anything for him?"

Esme nodded. "We can fabricate his nanocytes and make sure the Madness doesn't win. We can also artificially keep his brain cool to preserve his mind. Other than that, it's a waiting game."

Sarah Jennifer closed her eyes and clenched her fists. "Will he survive?"

The witch took the major's hands. "You feel for this boy. You see every child in him. Have hope, Duckie. You aren't the type to find comfort in faith, so find it in the knowledge that we have the best technology in the universe and we're going to solve this. All of the children will be safe, do you hear me?"

Sarah Jennifer pulled her hands free to wipe her eyes. "*All* of the children," she repeated softly, willing herself to believe it. She pressed her hands to the Pod-doc and studied the sleeping innocent inside.

"Starting with this one."

Finland, Upinniemi Harbor

Snorri Virtanen had been the harbor keeper since his father had gone to the eternal feast twenty-eight winters past. Between the rise of the undead—the *draugar*—and the Danelaw, Upinniemi hadn't had much to celebrate in recent years. Tonight was a rare cause for joy. The marriage of Snorri's only daughter to the only son of Orslandet's harbor keeper further cemented the long-standing naval alliance the two cities who shared the harbor had formed to keep the Danelaw at bay. It also gave the two communities a chance to come together for something other than a funeral.

While the celebration went on in every street and tavern in the city, the great hall attached to Snorri's lighthouse hosted the wedding party comprised of both families and their closest friends. Snorri made merry with Elijas, his old friend, paying great homage to the gods of ale as the wedding feast progressed into the evening. Both had been widowed by the draugar and left to raise their children alone, so the two keepers had a common bond and kept their fingers crossed that their children would grow to love one another.

Snorri watched in quiet contentment from the head table as Amelie danced with her hands entwined behind her new husband's shoulders, her cheeks red, her smile wide, and her eyes for the fortunate young man alone. He chuckled into his ale, wondering if young Eoin would still feel so fortunate when his wife began giving him children with tempers to match the red hair they were sure to inherit from their mother.

The gong rang, signaling that it was time for the presentation of the gifts the guests had brought to help the couple as they began their lives together. Amelie and Eoin came to sit at the head of the table between their fathers while the guests formed a line to present their gifts to the new couple.

The newlyweds received each gift with words of gratitude for the giver. The *huskarls* piled the gifts upon the wedding altar—linens, kitchenware, pottery, and food goods—with the quiet professionalism their order was famed for.

Snorri lifted his mug as the last guests returned to their seats. He was about to toast their future when the doors slammed open, letting in a flurry of snow with the night chill.

"What is the meaning of this?" Snorri roared as twelve hooded men pushed a large wooden crate on wheels into the hall.

The music stopped abruptly as those nearest the door scattered. In the silence that followed, everyone heard whatever was inside the crate scratching to get out.

Snorri hoped beyond hope that the crate contained only wild cats.

"Brothers! Come now," a voice that sent shivers down the guests' spines called as the hooded men retreated. A man with ruddy sea-burned skin stepped out from behind the crate and offered Snorri and Elijas a mocking bow. "I hope my reputation isn't so bad that such *great* leaders as you would think I don't honor the customs of our people."

He smoothed his elaborate braid, offering the room a smile. Those nearest him couldn't help but respond to it in the false hope that the warlord was genuinely here to pay his respects.

The huskarls closed in around Sidric with their halberds as Elijas got to his feet, drawing his sword. "You're no brother of ours, Sidric. There is no honor in the Danelaw; you saw to that. You are here to cast a cloud on my son's wedding. What's in the box?"

Sidric's smile turned ice-cold. "Why, my wedding gift."

Time slowed for Snorri. He saw a dull red light flash through a gap in the boards and got to his feet, the warning falling from his lips like molasses. "*Draug! RUN!*"

Too late. Sidric had drawn a knife and slashed the bonds holding the crate together. In a blur Snorri hardly registered, the warlord darted in and cut the throat of the huskarls blocking his escape. He was gone from the hall before the draugar began darting in all directions to attack the living.

The guests scattered, their screams mingling with the famished roars of the undead.

One draug was enough to bring down an entire city. A dozen or more was a disaster. Snorri, Eoin, and Elijas surrounded Amelie as the guests fled, the other huskarls among them remaining to help Snorri's huskarls hold the draugar off while the others escaped.

"We have to get out of here," Snorri cried as the huskarls lit the ends of their halberds and drove the draugar into the corners, where they were easier to subdue and decapitate.

Elijas grabbed Eoin before he could join the battle in the middle of the hall. "Show us the way," he told Snorri.

Snorri raised his voice to the frightened guests. "Follow us!"

Screams came from all over the city as Sidric's men attacked while the people were at their most vulnerable. The huskarls were practiced at their duty, and the draugar were dispatched with flame and blade, but they weren't home free just yet.

Amelie tore the skirts of her wedding gown and drew a short sword from the sheath strapped to her leg. She turned to her father with a snarl. "You think I didn't expect something like this? That bastard, Sidric. I'll run him through! You can bet he has slave wagons waiting outside the walls to gather up anyone who makes it out of the city alive. Are you going to allow him to take our home from us?"

A burning rock crashed through the roof, smashing the tables and lighting the soft furnishings. The missile was followed by a group of raiders wrapped in black fur and leather.

"We have to go!" Snorri insisted.

"We'll hold them off," the captain of the huskarls vowed. "Just get out of here."

Snorri grabbed his daughter by the arm and pulled her

along behind him as he dashed out of the hall, knowing full well she would die fighting Sidric. The warlord was known to tear his enemies in two with his bare hands when enraged. "Sidric has set draugar loose on the streets. Our home is lost, Amelie. I won't see you dead for a lost cause, do you understand? You must go. *You must.*"

"Where will we go?" Amelie protested, struggling against his grip. "My place is here with our people. We have to fight!"

"Our people need you to get them away from here." Snorri lifted a hand to indicate the frightened faces around them without slowing his pace: women and men whose occupations were peaceful, along with their children and elderly parents, all afraid for their lives as the city burned in the background. He wept unashamedly as he hurried the group across the yard to the lighthouse, gathering the people as he went. "You have to find the man called Olaf," he instructed. "Go to Archangelsk, which is east of here. Stay close to the ice shelf until you reach the Petersburg estuary, and you will find people living under the bear warrior's protection."

Amelie acquiesced as their people gathered around her, understanding her duty was with them. "Yes, Father. What about you?"

Snorri looked at the smoke curling from the hall's windows and doors and the black-clad swordsmen closing on the lighthouse. His hand tightened on his sword's hilt. "I'm going to buy you what time I can."

"As will I," Elijas swore. He shook his head when Eoin insisted on staying behind. "Don't make your wife a widow on her wedding night. Do as Snorri says. Find Olaf and tell him what happened here. Tell him we need him to fight for us."

"I swear I'll bring back an army," Amelie promised, hugging her father one last time after he gave her his master key.

"This opens the gate to the cove," Snorri told her. "There are three longships there. They have weapons and enough supplies to get you to Archangelsk."

Amelie choked back her tears. "You knew something was going to happen."

Snorri cupped his daughter's face with his hand. "I hoped it would not. I love you, daughter. You have been the joy of my life."

"We have to go now if we're going," Eoin cautioned, lifting his sword to meet the blade of one of Sidric's men. He parried the strike and removed the invader's sword hand with the return slash as the rest of the party took the main assault head-on.

His father finished the job. "Go!" he urged. "Be the man I know you are. I will always be proud of you."

"This way!" Amelie called as Sidric's men closed in. She ran ahead to the lighthouse while Eoin and a few of the huskarls covered them from the rear.

The people followed her into the building and crowded together as they descended the spiral staircase, their feet echoing on the stone as Amelie guided them through frozen tunnels beneath the lighthouse to the secret cove on the outer edge of the harbor.

The bolt hole had been built by the founders. Only Amelie, her father, and the captain of the huskarls had known about the tunnels leading through the ice. Amelie had anticipated showing her own children the secret place one day, but she and Eoin had to survive this before she could dream.

Eoin joined her at the head of the group when they came to the solid metal gate that barred access to the tunnel that led to the water. Amelie slipped the master key from where she'd hidden it inside her corset and unlocked the gate with steady hands.

"Everyone through!" she yelled as the echoes of Sidric's men running down the tunnel became audible.

Eoin and the huskarls killed the first of Sidric's men to emerge from the staircase as the frightened people hurried through the gate. He fought off the next two who had arrived and were already fighting one of Snorri's huskarls.

A few more of the group turned out to be huskarls as well. Sidric's men were soon dead, and the new warriors were a welcome addition to the group, the captain among them.

Eoin ushered them through the gate without any discussion.

The captain took Amelie and Eoin aside after the gate was closed and locked. "Your fathers. I'm sorry."

Amelie read the grief in his eyes and embraced the man. "You did your best, Johan. Forgive yourself. My father would not want you to bear the blame for his death." She glanced at the door as the raiders began pounding on it. "Elijas either."

"Honor them by protecting Amelie," Eoin told him. "We have to go."

The tunnel beyond led to the sheltered cove. Amelie

directed everyone onto the longships waiting under the overhang out of the wind.

The people rushed to man the oars and unfurl the sails after boarding.

"What if Sidric has ships waiting outside the harbor?" Eoin asked as Amelie leapt aboard the ship named for her mother.

The look she gave him sent a shiver down his spine. "Then we will *destroy* them. I am a daughter of the ocean. No one beats me on the water."

The tide turned in the cove as Amelie took the rudder, a helpful swell rising to carry the longships out into the harbor. Eoin took a bench and lashed his oar into position between the shields as the howling wind captured by the cove filled the sails. He understood Amelie's anger. *Hela*, he felt it himself, but he'd seen something more than that in his wife's eyes—some ethereal part of her spirit close to being unleashed by Sidric's violation.

Amelie's inner vision replayed her friends and family being murdered in front of her on a loop as the longships left the safety of the cove on choppy waters. Great waves of grief crashed on the shore of her determination to see what remained of her people to safety. The wind was steady as Amelie navigated the twisting route through the rocks and icebergs that guarded the mouth of the harbor. Only the keepers and their children knew the safe routes, which was the only reason this part of the ice shelf hadn't been folded into the Danelaw years ago.

Amelie guided her ships into the open water with utter certainty. She had always felt a connection to the ocean, but tonight she believed it shared her rage at the injustice of their situation and wanted to help. A cry of dismay went up around the ships as they emerged to the sight of four ships flying Danelaw colors. Amelie refused to be beaten by them.

"Help us," she whispered to the ocean. "Don't let the raiders capture us."

Amelie handed the rudder to her first mate and ran to the mast, brandishing her sword. "We will not be taken for slaves by those raider scum!" she screamed. "Trim the sail! Load the crossbows, and *get that trebuchet lashed down*! Prepare for grapplers and hooks. Any raider who sets foot on our ships will die!"

Everyone who lived along the coast knew how to make themselves useful aboard a ship, and Eoin and the huskarls were ready to give Sidric's raiders a taste of their steel.

The waves rose again as the longships turned to face the raiders head on. Amelie had a sense that the ocean approved of their decision to face the threat. She leaned into the sea spray, her eyes misty and unfocused, and lost any sense of where her rage ended and the ocean's began.

The wind shifted, and a sharp, cold rain began to lash the deck as it filled their sails.

Sidric's ships were forced to row to meet them, with the wind pushing them on the port side.

"Keep them at a distance! We can outrun them!" Amelie yelled to be heard over the storm. She returned to the rudder and watched the ocean; her ships were somehow skimming the cresting waves instead of being over-whelmed by them. Her eyes were two blue beacons in the squall as she directed their escape.

Amelie's ships were safe, but they were still in dire

straits. Eoin led the oarsmen's chant as they poured their hearts and souls into every stroke, adding their strength to the wind's to propel their ships out of the raiders' reach. The three longships formed a loose arrow as the huskarls operating the trebuchets laid down suppressive fire to force the raiders to stay back.

The Danelaw ships tacked into the wind, the oarsmen working hard to reach Amelie's ships with the intent of boarding them. One of them took a rock to the deck that punched through amidships, killing the oarsmen and sinking the ship almost instantly.

The other raiders responded with cannon fire, having the secret of gunpowder, but the ocean pitched and the wind was against them, which threw their aim off.

Amelie whooped with relief when a rogue wave came out of nowhere and smashed into the raider ships. She thanked the ocean profusely since her ships once again rode the waves as if lifted by gentle hands. The waves calmed, and Amelie felt her connection to the ocean slip away once the threat was gone.

She staggered when all the strength left her body in one go, then leaned against the mast and held on, knowing she was going to taste the deck if she let go.

Eoin appeared by her side. He swept the tangle of red curls out of her face, worried by the shadows he saw under her eyes. "Are you injured?" he asked, scanning her for blood.

Amelie smiled and lifted an arm to wrap around his shoulders, feeling punch-drunk. "I'm not hurt, just bone-tired."

Eoin nodded and guided her to a bench under the

canopy the crew had raised now that the threat was over and the sea was calm. "Ami, when the storm came...your eyes. They glowed."

Amelie should have been surprised. "The ocean spoke to me, Eoin. I thought I was imagining it at first, but I asked her to protect us, and she did."

Eoin didn't know what to say. He'd seen an ability beyond his understanding come from the woman he loved. It didn't scare him. Amelie had the purest heart he knew. It made sense that the ocean would choose to hear her prayer. "Where next?" he asked as he wrapped a blanket around her.

Amelie's eyes drifted closed. "We honor our promise to our fathers. We find Olaf, raise an army, and return to reclaim our home."

CHAPTER ELEVEN

New Romanov, Lilith's Mountain

Two months had passed since they'd found the boy in the cabin, and Sarah Jennifer was no closer to knowing when he would be able to come out of stasis. His name was Ezekiel, that much they'd found out from Irina Shutov.

As a concession to safety while the *Enora* was out making contact with communities along the trade routes, the Pod-doc had been moved to Lilith's chamber and hooked up to the Etheric engine. Lilith and Esme used the time between meet-and-greets to work on their theories about the boy's nanocytes.

Sarah Jennifer often found herself looking in on him and imagining what he was like. Was he bright and sarcastic like Lucy? Reserved like Curtis? What did he think about his ability to manifest energy?

She wondered if Ezekiel was aware of the war being waged for his body, of the ebb and flow of their hope for humanity as his developing immunity fought for supremacy over the corruption.

Jim pinged her comm. Sarah Jennifer answered, hoping he'd located the next settlement for them to visit. "Jim."

"Major, there's been a Madness outbreak in Upinniemi on the Finnish coast. Looks like they could use our help."

"Where are you now?" Sarah Jennifer asked.

"Five minutes out from New Romanov," was the reply.

"On my way. We'll be ready for wheels up in twenty." Sarah Jennifer lifted her rifle off the peg she'd hung it on and commed the pack as she left Lilith's chamber. "Brutus, with me. Linus, you have the mountain. Teams One to Four, you have fifteen minutes to be on the airship, locked and loaded for a major Madness outbreak."

She lifted a hand when Olaf approached. "You too, bear man. Has anyone seen Theor?"

"He's with Jim," Brutus informed her as they headed for the exit.

There was no time to appreciate the sunlight filtering through the clouds as they piled aboard the *Enora* and took off for the Finnish coast.

Sarah Jennifer paced the narrow corridor while the teams emptied the weapons lockers in the armory, her blood up. The Madness had patterns. It hit one person and spread outward through the community in ripples like a stone skipping across the surface of a pond if it wasn't checked. What it *didn't* do was break out suddenly and simultaneously across a whole population.

"This was an attack," she announced, startling the others. "Some filthy, lowdown coward released Mad into the city."

Brutus shook his head. "No. Who would do that?"

Olaf growled. "*Sidric.* That's who."

"Even he would not be so cruel, surely," Theor asked. "What does he gain from killing the people? He gets no profit from a corpse if you will excuse the thought."

"The harbor," Olaf informed them with regret. "He wants the harbor."

Enora's voice came from the speaker. "I am picking up three ships heading for St. Petersburg."

Sarah Jennifer set off for the bridge. "We'd better make sure that's not Sidric."

Amelie's head snapped up as the skyship emerged from the clouds. Panic ran through her, but this time the ocean didn't respond to her prayer.

"Man the trebuchet!" Eoin shouted. He was the first to snap out of his awe.

"Please don't," a woman's voice requested from the skyship. "We are here to help the people of Upinniemi."

Amelie glanced at Eoin and Johan, seeing identical confusion in their faces.

The skyship descended vertically to hover ten feet above the surface of the water, and a door in the side opened. A tall blonde woman stepped out. "Do you need assistance?"

Amelie shrugged and called to the ship, "We are all who are left from Upinniemi. We are searching for the bear warrior known as Olaf."

A huge man appeared at the door. "Luck is with you. I am Olaf."

The woman walked onto the wing as Amelie's longship

came up alongside it. "We are on our way to clear the Mad from your city. We can tell our people at New Romanov that you're on your way, or you can follow us back to Upinniemi and rebuild your homes after we've removed the danger."

Amelie had to look up to see them. Both Olaf and the woman exuded auras of energy she could almost touch. "Who are you?"

The woman's eyes glinted with red light. "I'm Major Sarah Jennifer Walton, and I don't much like asshole warlords. What is your choice?"

The ocean whispered to Amelie, telling her to trust these people. She knelt on Eoin's bench and took his hand in hers. "Will you take our people to safety while I fight for our home?"

He wanted to ask her to stay, but he knew she had to be the warrior her people needed. Eoin nodded. "Come back to me, Ami."

Amelie kissed him. "I swear by the winds and the waves, I will. Be safe, my love."

She turned to Sarah Jennifer with the light of the ocean in her eyes. "I'm coming with you."

The major extended a hand to help her aboard. "Welcome to the pack. You got a name?"

Amelie took one last look at her husband and her people before stepping through the door, thinking of her father. "I am a daughter of the ocean. I keep my word."

Esme took Amelie aside after they lifted off. "You have control of the sea."

Amelie shook her head. "No. The spirit of the ocean heard my prayer and saved us from the raiders." She quickly described their flight.

Esme smile. "You have magic, young lady. The ocean spirit is a manifestation of your ability to control nature. *You* saved your people from the raiders."

Amelie frowned. "Why are you telling me that?"

Esme smiled. "Because we are going into a situation much worse than that. You and I must defend the harbor from Sidric's fleet while the pack clears the Mad from the streets."

Lucy snorted as she walked by. "Some people get all the fun. Princess isn't even that much older than me."

Esme shook her head at Amelie's puzzled look. "Lucy needs to pack her attitude up and do her job. She's not ready for battle yet. She's just impatient to fight with the pack."

Amelie smiled, recalling her own impatience for womanhood. "Children don't know what they're wishing for."

Esme found it a shame Amelie had learned that lesson so young. "That they do not. Tell me how you called the ocean."

Amelie wasn't sure. "I don't know. After my mother died, I always felt the most myself when I came down to the shore. I'd sit for hours, letting the sound of the waves take my sadness at missing her. I used to sneak down to the harbor and watch the sailors work."

The memory was clear in her mind. "When my father

ND ROBERTS & MICHAEL ANDERLE

found out, he 'punished' me by making me work on his brother's fishing boat for the summer."

Esme smiled. "Let me guess: it wasn't so much a punishment as a ticket to freedom."

Amelie returned Esme's smile, hers tinged with sadness. "He knew. It just wasn't seemly for the keeper's daughter to hang out on a fishing boat."

"When did you first realize you could speak to the water?" Esme pressed.

"When we were attacked," Amelie answered. "But maybe I always could. My uncle always said I was his lucky charm. That the fish came to him when I was on board."

Sarah Jennifer poked her head out of the cockpit. "We're over the harbor. You're up. Olaf and Theor are waiting for you in the cargo bay."

Esme smiled to dispel Amelie's sudden look of worry. This young woman was as deep as the waters she had the potential to command. "Focus on memories of your family, your people, and everything you're fighting to protect. They will help you."

Sarah Jennifer watched Esme and Amelie pick their way across the cliffs as the *Enora* continued on to the city. Farther along the coast, the water was obscured by the sails of Sidric's fleet. She turned away from the viewscreen as the women made their stand, trusting Esme to keep the new magic-user safe.

She snorted softly as she left the cockpit for the cargo

bay. Esme would probably have Amelie calling herself an ocean mage by the end of this cleanup operation.

Katia handed Sarah Jennifer two coils of rope as she entered the belly of the airship. "You ready for this?"

Sarah Jennifer grinned as she clipped the smaller coil to her aerial assault rig before shrugging the harness on. "There's nothing like stamping out the evil in this world to get the blood going. Teams One, Two, Three! We're out first. Brutus, you have Four, Five, and Six."

She gave the teams a minute to get themselves in order, briefing the pack while she attached one end of the longer coil of rope to her rig and fastened the clamp on the other end to the rail above the drop doors. "Enora's scans indicate our initial targets have taken over the building adjacent to the lighthouse. We'll take out the boss leech and his inner circle, then move out and clear the city building by building. We've done this a hundred times. You know the drill. The only good leech is a dead one."

The pack roared their agreement in unison.

Sarah Jennifer moved to the front as the drop doors opened. "Stick to mental communication. Jim will be keeping his eye out while we're on the ground. Comm check."

Satisfied once she confirmed everyone was on the channel, she gripped her rope and stepped over the edge.

The only sound as the Weres dropped to the roof of the great hall was the slight thrumming of the ropes as their rigs controlled their descent.

Sarah Jennifer's boots touched down on icy wooden shingles, and she set her stance to prevent slipping as she released the rope from her rig. They waited in silence while the other teams made their drops.

Brutus motioned at the chimney as he released his rope.

Sarah Jennifer shook her head. *I doubt you could go down there without getting stuck.*

Brutus unclipped a smoke grenade from his rig. *I'm thinking they might have prisoners. You remember that assmunch nomad gang out of Ann Arbor?*

Sarah Jennifer nodded. That wasn't the only time since the Defense Force had been founded they'd come across leech groups souped-up on Were blood using the locals as slaves, but it had been the worst.

Go for it, she told him. *Just wait for my mark.*

Sarah Jennifer pointed out where each team would breach, and they moved out. She led her team to the eaves above the window on the lighthouse side. Little Ace had the anchor for their ropes ready. He screwed it into the shingle-covered rafter, and the team attached their second ropes and made their way to the edge of the roof.

The other teams were in place. Sarah Jennifer gripped the rope in one hand and her rifle in the other, her heartbeat strong and steady. *You ready with our distraction, Brutus?*

Just give me the word, Brutus replied.

"The word," the command from above coming down to give all soldiers purpose. Sarah Jennifer smiled. *Smoke bombs away. We are GO.*

CHAPTER TWELVE

Upinniemi, Great Hall

It would be fair to say that Sidric and his men didn't know what hit them when the hall filled with acrid smoke and every window simultaneously shattered inward as the pack made their entrance.

Sarah Jennifer hit the ground running and fired twice at the first raider to come at her. She dropped three more before the first hit the floor and darted into the space made by their bodies falling. Gunfire covered the roaring confusion of the raiders.

"WHAT ARE YOU DOING?" a man screamed from somewhere near the head table. "FIGHT THEM!"

I've got Sidric, Sarah Jennifer told the pack. She squinted through the smoke, still able to smell the faint scent of Were emitted by the raiders. *Smells to me like he's been sharing what he stole with his men. Take 'em out.*

The comm was busy as the raiders obeyed their master and the pack got to work putting their leech asses down.

Sarah Jennifer kept half an ear on the comm as the pack

engaged the couple hundred angry invaders set on maintaining their hold on the harbor.

She zeroed in on Sidric's voice as the smoke began to clear, then spied him over by a door and fired. She hissed with annoyance when Sidric moved just in time to avoid the round that embedded itself in the wall beside his head.

Sidric met Sarah Jennifer's eyes and ran through the door as another round of smoke grenades went off, obscuring her view. Twenty of his men moved in to surround Sarah Jennifer, which, she figured, was about the same odds the rest of the pack were facing.

She took out six before their close range made her rifle an impediment, then slung the rifle on her back and drew her knife before meeting the closest raider with a headbutt that shattered his teeth. She ignored the arterial spray that showered her when she punched her blade into his throat as a follow-up, removed her knife, and plunged it into the gut of the raider beside him as she ducked to avoid his sword.

She tore his belly open with a jerk of her wrist before moving on to the next.

There were no rules in the heat of battle. Block, stab, step. Block, thrust, slash. Repeat, modify, control the situation. Battle stank; it was visceral and bloody, shit everywhere for her to slip on if she lost control. Sarah Jennifer had no intention of losing control. She was made for this moment and every other like it, the times when it came down to her or the person standing in her way.

Raiders fell around Sarah Jennifer, her feet landing perfectly as she twisted and slashed, stabbed, and punched her way through Sidric's men. When she paused, her area was mostly clear, with just a couple of stray raiders either brave or stupid enough to still want to face her.

Sarah Jennifer's eyes glowed red as she glared at them. "Don't keep a lady waiting," she growled.

That was enough to make them all charge at her.

She stepped through a wild attack and slit the raider's unprotected throat before stamping out the knee joint of his buddy behind him.

The raider collapsed, putting his face in range of her foot. She kicked him in the temple and threw back an elbow as she was grabbed from behind.

The unfortunate who'd grabbed her stumbled into the crossfire as his nose erupted on contact with the studded plate protecting her elbow. He jerked as he was hit from multiple directions, but Sarah Jennifer was already gone in search of Sidric.

Two fur-covered raiders, each standing taller than the door they blocked, lifted their battle-axes as the major approached. Sarah Jennifer pulled her rifle around and took them out with two controlled three-round bursts, wasting no time on words. Her intent was to pass.

Sarah Jennifer stepped over their bodies and made her way along the deserted corridor beyond the door, clearing each room before she progressed to the next.

There were five women in the scullery. They looked worn and bruised, startled by her appearance and the rifle she had pointed at them. Sarah Jennifer lowered her weapon and held up a hand to show she meant them no harm. "Stay here. It will be safe soon."

She closed the door and moved on to the next room and the next. There was no sign of Sidric or his men, but every door she opened revealed more people who had been forced to serve them. She repeated her warning each time, aware that every minute she spent comforting people gave Sidric more time to escape or prepare a defense.

He was gone by the time Sarah Jennifer reached the main kitchen. She burst in and put headshots into three of the four men the coward had left to slow her pursuit. The fourth she kicked in the chest, then put a round in his thigh as he stumbled back. It nicked the artery.

The raider fell, screaming as blood gushed from his wound.

Sarah Jennifer had been expecting at least a bit of self-preservation. The raider didn't think to do anything except press his hands to the hole. "Dumbasses everywhere," she grumbled to herself as she leaned down and tore the raider's sleeve from his shirt.

"Stay still," she ordered, punching the dumbass when he struggled.

The raider had no choice but to obey while she knelt on his stomach and tied the sleeve tightly around his leg to cut off the blood flow above the wound.

Field tourniquet applied, Sarah Jennifer got up and pointed her rifle at his head. "So far, you only lost a leg. You want to limit the damage to one limb, reassess your priorities and tell me where Sidric is going."

The raider stared at his leg with the knowledge his fighting days were over. "Fuck yourself," he growled, spitting at Sarah Jennifer. "Kill me now. I'll be remembered with honor."

Sarah Jennifer calculated the right spot on his shoulder for a through-and-through and fired again. She waited for his screams to subside. "I don't appreciate poor language. Where is Sidric going? Last chance. The next one goes in your gut, and I leave you here to bleed out."

His eyes flicked toward the open back door and the lighthouse across the yard. That was all Sarah Jennifer needed. She shot him between the eyes and reloaded, then stalked out into the yard.

A hail of arrows from the upper level of the lighthouse met her appearance. Sarah Jennifer responded by flicking her rifle to full auto and spraying the windows as she dived for the cover of an abandoned wagon by the wall.

The wagon gave her a brief respite. She reported her position and refused the offers of backup, directing the Weres who could move to take care of the people in the kitchens. Her mission was to ensure that the raiders had nobody to rally around. What that would mean for the Danelaw wasn't a consideration.

Sarah Jennifer remained in place behind the wagon and picked off the raiders above one at a time as she drew them with her fire. Every ounce of her adrenaline-boosted concentration was on the enemy. She didn't notice the arrow protruding from her back until it caught on the wagon and a bolt of fire radiated from the entry point.

The shaft snapped off in her hand without splintering, but to get the head out without causing damage she didn't have time to heal, there was only one option.

Sarah Jennifer took a few deep, calming breaths as she undid the shoulder strap of her body armor on the injured side and peeled it back to expose her shoulder and collarbone. Putting her back to the wall, she positioned the remainder of the shaft against the rough wood and slammed her body back against it to force the arrowhead the rest of the way through.

The pain was exquisite, momentarily flooding her vision with stars as it burst through the skin just beneath her collarbone. She gritted her teeth, grabbed the tip, and tore it out. Her vision ceased swimming as she flung it aside and groped in a pouch on her rig for one of the emergency med patches Bethany Anne had supplied. After wiping the blood away as best she could, she slapped the patch on her wound before refastening her armor. The pain ebbed instantly as the patch infused the injury with an analgesic, while its nanocytes knitted the wound closed faster than she could heal herself.

Sarah Jennifer checked her load, left the cover of the wagon, and headed for the lighthouse, where Sidric awaited Justice. The threat from above removed, she kept her center of gravity low as she crossed the yard at a run and slipped into the building.

There were no nasty surprises on the ground floor. She cleared the circular rooms and made for the spiral staircase that ran from the bottom to the top of the building. An echo from below made Sarah Jennifer pause with her foot on the stairs, recalling the tunnels Amelie had told them about.

She switched direction and padded down into the darkness.

Esme sensed someone approaching, then spotted the lone man clambering onto the path at the edge of the clifftop and scanned his mind for intent. "Amelie. We have company."

Amelie didn't hear her, being caught up in her connection with the ocean. The wreckage of Sidric's ships crashed into the rocks at the mouth of the harbor. Lifeboats stuffed full of the survivors bobbed, at the mercy of the waves.

Her mercy.

Esme heard only crashing waves when she touched Amelie's mind. Trusting the young mage to finish the grim task, she watched the man's progress. Was he coming for them or to signal the fleet?

Another smaller figure emerged from the cove and began climbing the rough path that wound up the cliffside. Esme would know Sarah Jennifer anywhere, which meant... "That's Sidric," she told Amelie, grabbing and shaking her arm to no avail.

Outside the harbor, the lifeboats had disappeared. All that remained was a bloom of pink-tinged foam that rapidly dissipated as the choppy motion of the water broke it up. Amelie thanked the ocean for helping her protect the harbor, vaguely aware that her new friend was saying something. She turned to see Esme walking away at speed, and the light from her eyes faded as her connection to the ocean was broken.

Amelie shaded her eyes to see what the concern was and spotted Sidric on the cliff. "*Murderer!*" she yelled, unable to contain the sudden resurgence of the rage she'd felt when the warlord had interrupted her wedding feast. She drew her bow, nocked an arrow, and fired at Sidric.

The warlord was just out of range. He stopped in his tracks when the arrow hit the ice ten feet from where he stood and drew his sword. "Who dares to challenge me?" he roared.

Amelie dropped her bow and unsheathed her sword. "The daughter of the man you killed when you invaded this harbor. The man who led the people here in peace for twenty-eight winters. You brought death to my home, and now I bring the payment for your dishonor. Face me!"

Esme sighed and picked up her pace when the young woman ran by her, sword brandished and hair streaming unbound behind her. "Queen save me from the impetuousness of youth."

Sarah Jennifer heard the clash of metal on metal and increased her speed. She vaulted the rockfall at the top of the path and tore along the clifftop to where—

Amelie was holding her own against the warlord.

Sarah Jennifer ground to a halt by Esme, seeing the light in the young woman's eyes. She should step in, but…

"It's personal," Esme agreed. "Doesn't make it a fair fight. She's barely grown."

"Show me a magic-user who fights 'fair.'" Sarah Jennifer had long ago given up telling her closest friend to stay out of her head. "She could make the sea swallow him if she wanted to. It's a catharsis for her family."

"Hmph," Esme murmured, wincing as Amelie got in a pommel strike to Sidric's gut before collapsing to the floor as he drove an elbow into her back. "It's needless violence."

"You out of juice?" Sarah Jennifer guessed.

"How'd you know?" Esme asked, giving her a shrewd glance.

Sarah Jennifer smiled despite herself. "You're letting this happen." She waved a hand at the fight, which was starting to get dirty.

Amelie twisted her body around and lashed out at Sidric with both feet, her aim at his crotch true. She flung a handful of frozen dirt at his face at the same time, giving herself room to roll out of the way before Sidric's sword cut a groove in the ground where she had landed.

"You going to step in?" Esme asked pointedly.

Sarah Jennifer shook her head. "Nope. People solving their own problems is a good thing in my book. If she kills that stinking toss-rag, it makes her the rightful ruler of the Danelaw by conquest, am I right?"

Esme swallowed hard at the thought of how much more blood that right would cost when Amelie claimed it. "If she can prove she's strong enough to hold it."

Sarah Jennifer had to stay above the concerns Esme had, although she would never be blind to them. "Men will follow her. She could turn the Scandinavian countries around."

"If she survives that long." Esme reached into the clifftop with her senses and pulled a root up to trip Sidric as he launched a series of heavy strikes that Amelie was hard-pressed to block.

The root caught his foot, giving Amelie the split-second of breathing room she needed to recover her form and return to the offense. She used her smaller size and flexibility to keep Sidric moving, flowing around his attacks and darting in to strike at the weak points of his armor.

It had been a while since the warlord had been able to procure any Were blood, and it showed as the fight continued. His reliance on brute strength sapped his stamina, and he responded to her attacks a shade slower each time. Amelie couldn't remember how to breathe. Her awareness was reduced to her sword and the arm operating it, but she wasn't giving any ground against Sidric.

He stared at the girl when they broke apart after a sustained exchange that left them both breathing heavily. "You fight like the possessed," he accused.

Amelie's eyes glowed as she advanced again, her sword raised despite her exhaustion. "The spirits of my father and everyone else you murdered are with me."

Can I step in now? Esme asked Sarah Jennifer over their mental link.

Sarah Jennifer nodded. Neither of the combatants noticed Esme's eyes glow gold, but Sidric stopped dead at the sight of ghostly red-eyed figures rising from the ice around Amelie.

He dropped his sword arm as the blood drained from his face. "*Völva!* What evil magic is this?"

Amelie saw only the loving faces of everyone she'd lost looking at her with approval and pride. "My strength," she declared, raising her arm to point her sword at his chest.

Sidric stood frozen with fear for a moment as Amelie and her "ghosts" walked toward him, then snapped to his senses and backed away without thinking about where he was going. His foot found the cliff edge, startling him into freezing again when the icy dirt crumbled beneath his heel.

"You're dead, Sidric," Amelie told him, her eyes glowing as she advanced toward him. "You just don't know it yet."

Sidric's drive to fight withered under the accusing stares of the dead. He turned and jumped, deciding to take his chances on surviving the eighty-foot dive rather than face the shades of the people he'd killed.

The women gathered at the edge and looked over. Sidric hit the water hard. Sarah Jennifer was surprised to see him emerge and start swimming for the shore, albeit slowly. She narrowed her eyes as a disturbance kicked up the water in his wake.

As suddenly as he'd reappeared, Sidric was gone. A spreading pool of blood surfaced before being washed away by the tide.

Amelie offered Sarah Jennifer and Esme a small shrug as her eyes returned to their usual pale blue. "He didn't give me time to tell him the sharks I asked to help with his men hadn't taken off yet. I told him he didn't know he was dead."

She walked back to the fading ghosts. "Did you do this?" she asked Esme.

Esme nodded as she released the energy forming the projection she was pulling from Amelie's mind. "They are made from your memories. I hope you don't mind the intrusion."

Amelie flung her arms around Esme and burst into tears. "Thank you. It means everything that they were there."

"The question is, what do you want to happen next?" Sarah Jennifer asked. "Sidric wanted this harbor because it's the link between the Danelaw and Russia. Whoever controls the harbor controls trade between the two."

"My father and Elijas were always fair and honest keepers. Eoin and I will uphold their values." Amelie's expression softened as the ideas inside her welled up, offering a glimpse of what could be. "We always talked about joining our cities and reaching out to trade with the East. This is the time."

"And the Danelaw?" Esme asked.

Amelie's eyes widened. "I don't want to be a warrior queen. My place is here in the harbor. Will you help us rebuild?"

Sarah Jennifer already had a plan coming together that worked for her objectives. "The first step is to establish radio communications between the harbors and secure the trade routes. Will you accept the title of Trade Mistress and hold the alliance together?"

Amelie nodded. "I'll do whatever it takes to make things right. People don't have to be afraid anymore."

CHAPTER THIRTEEN

New Romanov, Aboard the SAF *Enora*

Sarah Jennifer had stripped her shotguns down and laid them out on an oilcloth she'd used to cover her desk. She cleaned each piece on autopilot, her mind on how quickly the Danelaw had fallen into chaos in the weeks since Amelie had killed Sidric and refused his throne in favor of exploring trade opportunities with New Romanov and other communities across Archangelsk.

A glance at her interactive map showed a mess of uncertain borders that shifted with every report Amelie relayed from the traders connected to the radio network.

Amelie and Eoin had sent their ships out with two Weres on each, their orders to take the radio transceivers they'd had onboard the *Enora* and connect the harbor keepers to the trade center at Upinniemi.

Sidric had grown an empire because he'd had a mind for tactics and knew how to use intimidation to his best advantage. After his demise, his empire had fractured as the men and women who had ruled the Danelaw in his name seized the opportunity to claim their little piece of it.

The people apparently had other ideas wherever the new order looked a lot like the old one with less bite. Without the threat of Sidric's fleet to deter them from revolting, they fought fiercely for their autonomy.

It was hard to stay out of it. The temptation to go into the worst situations and give the revolutionaries a helping hand was highly appealing to the pack. However, Sarah Jennifer was experienced enough to know better than to listen to temptation's siren call and refused permission.

While on the mission, the pack had learned why staying out of local politics was the right thing to do. Wherever they went, the people treated the Weres with a reverence that made them feel unsettled.

Katia especially had been overwhelmed and had escaped to the airship the moment it got into Upinniemi. The others had borne the overabundance of attention with quiet dignity until Sarah Jennifer announced it was time to return to New Romanov.

The major had pulled Olaf aside on his return, and he'd confirmed her assessment that she and the pack needed to extricate themselves from the Danelaw and its surrounding area before the people learned to rely on them to solve every problem, or worse, banded together to blame the Defense Force for their problems.

Sarah Jennifer was resolute. The Defense Force was a military, not law enforcement. Taking out Sidric's standing army had been messy but too easy. He could have had three times as many warriors and the result would have been the same. The disparity in numbers might even it up some, but in the end, the pack's training and access to more advanced technology put even the most hardened warriors leagues beneath them in killing ability. Letting the pack intervene in the reformation of the Danelaw was, in her opinion, akin to using a grenade launcher to swat a fly.

Which left her here in her cabin, adding information from the latest reports to her map in preparation for the Norrköping operation. Bråviken Bay would have been an ideal infiltration point if not for it being so close to ground zero for the climate malfunction. As it was, the information Amelie had passed along made it sound as though the ground station was buried under the tons of the displaced rock and ice that were Norrköping's main feature.

Sarah Jennifer got up from her desk and stretched before altering her map wall. Snøhvit had to be pushed down the list. Her objective in light of the unrest was to plan a route to the ground station without making contact with the locals. That was before considering how they were going to tunnel through the ice without attracting the attention of every Mad in the vicinity.

She was wondering whether magic or tech was the solution when Esme knocked on the door before opening it.

The witch scrutinized the change to the route plan before settling in Sarah Jennifer's chair. "What are we going to do about Ezekiel?"

Sarah Jennifer didn't have an answer. What *were* they going to do about Ezekiel? New Romanov didn't have anyone besides Lilith who understood the complexities of his treatment, and contemplating leaving the Pod-doc behind while they chased down the climate control module didn't fill her with the warm and fuzzies.

"We can't leave him here," Esme stated, pushing the lever to recline the chair. "What if he needs more care than Lilith and Olaf can provide? We should take him to Salem before we move on to Sweden. At the very least, it would be nice to check in and see how everyone is doing without us there."

Sarah Jennifer pinned Esme with a cool gray stare. "You know exactly how they're doing. We've been in radio contact this whole time. What's the real agenda, Esme?"

Esme folded her arms behind her head. "No agenda. He could be ready to come out of stasis any day, and we have a longer battle ahead in decoding his immunity and how that translates to a fix for everyone else. I'd feel better leaving him in Sarai's care. What are you going to do about the Danelaw?"

"There is no Danelaw anymore," Sarah Jennifer told her, turning back to the map. She re-pinned the string at Norrköping. "The people will resolve their leadership issues."

"Including the Swedes?" Esme returned sharply. "If they're not feeling amiable, we're going to have the same problem getting in and out of Norrköping that we had while Sidric was in charge. What if we don't make it back here before Ezekiel's treatment is complete?"

"That's why I'm altering the route. We don't have time for Snøhvit right now." Sarah Jennifer saw the same exhaustion permeating Esme's being that they were all feeling after almost four months of deployment. She rubbed her knee and sighed, out of steam.

Being stuck at her desk made her knee ache worse than during the time she'd spent laboring with the pack and New Romanov's workers to strengthen the town's defenses this last couple of weeks. Add to that a general lack of sleep and the headache contemplating the Danelaw gave her, and she didn't feel like debating the issue. "I agree that Salem is the safest place for Ezekiel. If Olaf has no issue with us moving him there, we'll get it done. Sweden can wait until we figure a way to get to the ground station without having to fight off every living person in the area as well as the Mad."

"Get some sleep, then meet me in Lilith's cavern for breakfast," Esme told her as she got to her feet. She paused before leaving the cabin. "It will be a tonic to get home for a spell. We've done good, but everyone needs to rest and recharge before we start another fight."

Sarah Jennifer made her way to her sleeping cabin and got ready for bed. She sank into the mattress' embrace and closed her eyes as she commed the pack. "Wrap up whatever you're doing. We're heading back to Salem the day after tomorrow. Unless there's a fire, a flood, or a full-scale Mad incursion, do not wake me before..." She checked her clock, grimacing when she saw how far past midnight it was already. "0600 ship time. Major, out."

Sarah Jennifer accepted the mug of instant coffee Brutus handed her when she emerged bleary-eyed from her cabin the next morning. She pulled a face as the bitter taste of the freeze-dried brew shocked her awake before the caffeine had a chance to enter her bloodstream.

"We got the extension to the north wall all but finished by end of work yesterday," Brutus reported in response to her mumbled query as they left the airship. They walked the short distance to Lilith's cavern, the crisp dawn air doing as much as the prospect of potable coffee to inspire alertness.

Sarah Jennifer tipped the dregs of her coffee out on the ground and shook the mug dry as they approached the entrance. "That's just nasty. I should have waited for breakfast. Dinny knows how to make morning coffee with the right amount of sugar."

"You mean, *all* the sugar?" Brutus teased. "It's a good thing one of us is a morning person. Did you speak to Olaf about moving Ezekiel?"

"First on my to-do list after breakfast," Sarah Jennifer replied, her stomach growling from the tantalizing smell of bacon and sausage drifting out of the tunnel. Wild boar were plentiful in the area, and Irina had taken it upon herself to ensure the pack thoroughly explored the local cuisine after they had hunted to provide the town with enough meat to preserve and last them through the month.

"Then I guess all that's left to do is get the Pod-doc moved back to the airship and be on our way." Brutus' nose twitched as he caught the scent of sage and pork fat. He picked up his pace as they made their way down the tunnel.

"If he agrees." She looked at her empty mug in disgust as they passed the side chamber where Esme, Jim, and

Lucy were preparing the Pod-doc for transfer. "I need some *real* coffee first."

Esme came to the door when she saw them. "Olaf is in the mess." She pointed at the arch that led to the side chamber where the engineers had set up a field kitchen. "Plato told me they have matter transporters in space. We should think about getting one for the airship."

"You can maintain the damn thing if you want it," Sarah Jennifer told her, yawning. "I want breakfast."

Brutus shot Esme an incredulous look over his shoulder as Sarah Jennifer steered him away from the conversation. "I'm not getting in anything that scrambles my atoms. I don't care how fast it is."

"Esme isn't going to requisition one," Sarah Jennifer assured him as they entered the mess. "It would mean her being a permanent crew member."

"Which she can't do," Brutus finished. "I'm relieved."

They served themselves bacon, eggs, and hash browns from the hotplate and refilled their mugs with the super-strong, super-sweet coffee Sarah Jennifer had converted the pack to drinking whenever they were on an assignment.

The aroma transported her to San Francisco every time. She inhaled deeply before taking a sip. "That's more like it."

"You think? I'm getting a caffeine kick just standing next to it." Brutus laughed as they took their trays, his entire focus on the pile of various meat products, and headed over to where Olaf was sitting at one of the four tables.

The bear man greeted them genially and waved for

them to join him. "I hear you're leaving?" he asked after they'd exchanged pleasantries.

Sarah Jennifer speared a sausage link with her fork. "It's time to move on to the next step of fixing the planet: repairing the climate control system."

She gave him a brief explanation of the problem, finishing with Esme's idea to take Ezekiel to Salem until the module at Norrköping had been repaired.

"Sweden is not so far outside my area of protection," Olaf offered.

Sarah Jennifer hadn't considered that he might want to accompany them. "What are you suggesting?"

"That you come back for me." Olaf waved his knife. "You want to take Ezekiel to Salem. Irina is the obstacle, not me. She feels responsible for him now that his parents are gone. I can speak to her while I'm making arrangements with the elders for my absence."

Sarah Jennifer didn't dislike the young widow, but she had no patience for her combative personality this early in the day. "I appreciate that. She's a smart woman. She has to understand that he's better off with us, at least until he wakes up."

Olaf returned his attention to his food. "I hope I get to see this great military state one day."

Brutus snorted. "A true friend wouldn't wish that yoke around my neck. New cities are springing up around most of the Defense Force bases, but they belong to the people. We don't enforce the laws; there's a committee for that."

"There's a committee for everything," Sarah Jennifer added. "In the early days, it was chaos getting the factions to cooperate long enough to agree on even the most minor issue. Forming committees solved that."

Olaf chuckled. "I have seen that among my own people at times. It sounds to me like you have civilization," he elaborated. "Cooperation, if not peace."

"There's not much peace to be had with the Madness," Sarah Jennifer admitted. "But we do our best to make sure the people feel safe in their daily lives. The growing numbers of Mad are incentive enough. Outlying towns want the Defense Force there to protect them from the nomads."

Olaf raised an eyebrow in confusion. "Nomads?"

"They struck out after WWDE to form their own societies," Sarah Jennifer explained. "Who knows how many separate groups now roam the wastelands of America in search of anything they can salvage or take by force. That was before the Madness hit us. The nomads have been affected more than settled populations."

"Why is that?" Olaf asked. "We have migratory populations from here to China, and they haven't been affected any worse than the people living in towns and cities."

"We think they have a higher rate of infection because many of them were using Were blood to prolong their lives before we put an end to the blood trade," Brutus told him. "We thought the Madness was showing up randomly until we worked out that the routes they travel have more outbreaks than anywhere else."

Sarah Jennifer gritted her teeth. "We keep the roads safe. Those selfish assholes make it that much harder for us because they turn their Mad loose instead of dealing with them. So you see, it's far from paradise."

Olaf shook his head in disgust. "It is no easy thing to end a monster bearing a familiar face, but it must be done. Truly, there will be no peace on Earth until we find the cure."

Esme strode in with a determined look on her face. "The Pod-doc is ready to be moved. Sarah Jennifer, Lilith wants to speak to you before we leave."

Sarah Jennifer smiled as she put her fork down. "She's fully online?"

Esme nodded and headed for the serving station. Olaf excused himself, taking up Brutus' offer of company for his walk into New Romanov.

Sarah Jennifer left after refilling her coffee and made her way down the smooth incline into Lilith's chamber.

"How's my favorite Kurtherian?" she asked as the lights came up.

The lights on Lilith's housing twinkled. "I am feeling much more myself," she replied from the speaker. "The memory cube was an experience I should like to forget as soon as possible."

Sarah Jennifer chuckled at her playful tone. "Better than conservation mode, am I right?"

"Infinitely," Lilith agreed. "Although I am sad to hear that you are leaving so soon."

Sarah Jennifer patted the housing in sympathy. "Needs must, my friend. Bethany Anne asked me to take care of the climate issue, and it can't wait any longer. You have your transceiver, so you can stay in touch without having to expend all your energy to connect psychically."

"A gift I am grateful for," Lilith assured her. "The kindness of humans never ceases to astound me. It is a quality lacking in the Seven, and to some extent, the Five also."

"Aren't they the good guys?" Sarah Jennifer asked, thinking back to the late-night conversations they'd had before Lilith had been forced to power down.

"Yes," Lilith replied. "However, I have seldom witnessed any of my species show empathy for another. Bethany Anne taught me what empathy is when she chose to let me live. You showed it by placing my plight at the head of your concerns."

Sarah Jennifer smiled, warmed that Lilith understood how much she meant to them. "You're family, Lilith. We need you. *I* need you. Having you in my head took some getting used to at first, but when you were gone, I missed you."

"I have missed your company," Lilith replied. "I value your friendship greatly. I promise to contact you often."

"You'd better," Sarah Jennifer told her, wondering if it was weird to hug a computer. She decided it was what was inside that counted and embraced the casing. "I'll be back as soon as we're ready to move on Norrköping. You'll hardly know we're gone."

CHAPTER FOURTEEN

The people of New Romanov gathered on the walls to watch as the airship departed. Sarah Jennifer and Big Ace had made a thorough inspection of the airship to ensure everyone and everything that had left the ship was back on board before takeoff.

Sarah Jennifer called a pack meeting, then made her way to the cockpit as Archangelsk's forest gave way to the ice shelf. She smiled to see that Enora already had the viewscreen ready, with video windows to crew quarters standing by. "Thank you, Enora. Can everyone hear me?"

Everyone confirmed they could.

Sarah Jennifer broke down the change to their route. "We're still headed to Salem. However, we're going to pass over Norrköping instead of the planned stop at Snøhvit. Intel from the traders indicates the geography of Östergötland is vastly different from the map data we have."

She repressed a frown. "The reports were a little bit squirrely, to be honest. That's why we're rerouting. We need to assess the situation before we can make an intelligent plan of action."

"What about the people at Snøhvit?" Brutus inquired.

"I'm going to send a team there after we get home," Sarah Jennifer informed him. "Could be we won't be able to move on Norrköping for a few weeks, so there will be time to make a start on building relations with them. In the meantime, our priority has to be prepping to fix the climate control system."

There were murmurs of agreement from everyone. Katia spoke up to be heard over the others. "We were expecting something like this. Norrköping is where the ice is coming from, right?"

Sarah Jennifer seesawed her hand. "Technically, it's coming from this whole sector. Each module is responsible for an area half a million kilometers square."

"Stands to reason the terrain blows goats," Linus reasoned. "Nothing we can't handle if we train right. You taught us that."

"We don't *know* what the terrain is like," Sarah Jennifer reminded him. "All we have is wildly contradicting hearsay. That's why Enora and I are going to get eyes on the situation before we head back to Salem and why everyone else is going to put some time in on the VR training simulation to memorize their part in repairing the climate control module. I'll be testing you."

The pack groaned as one, but Sarah Jennifer had already cut the video.

Enora appeared on the viewscreen. "By 'eyes,' do you mean sensors?"

Sarah Jennifer smiled as she sat back in her chair to

take in the whole screen. "Smart AI. What can you give me? Thermal imaging?"

"Multispectral imaging is within the capabilities of my external cameras," Enora replied. "Ground-penetrating radar should be possible with a little adjustment."

"Meaning?" Sarah Jennifer inquired.

"Meaning with GPR we can see what's going on underneath the ice," Esme interjected, walking in. "I was thinking the same thing. The sea captains all say Bråviken Bay is now Mount Bråviken. What's our ETA?"

"Twenty minutes to Östergötland," Enora answered.

"I'll be back," Esme told them. "Left my damn datapad in my cabin."

"Release the camera drones when we get in range of the coast." Sarah Jennifer instructed. She propped a cushion under her knee and sat back to watch the camera feeds.

They began getting video of the sector's southern boundary shortly after Enora released the drones. Sarah Jennifer's mouth fell open when she got her first look at the coast. She'd understood in *theory* what the climate modules did, but witnessing the unnaturally straight line where the land suddenly and violently tipped from summer into winter tripped her mind.

To say that the snowstorm obscuring the peak of Mount Bråviken ended abruptly didn't do the wonder on the viewscreen justice.

The clouds that reached the edge of the sector were somehow repelled and emitted icy particulates as they were forced downward. The cloudfall poured to the ground, disgorging tons of fine snow that drifted behind the boundary, burying the trees to their bare crowns. On the south side of the boundary, nature's necropolis was transformed into the lush meadows and forests of an ideal Swedish summer with nothing but sporadic cirrus clouds marring the clear blue sky. A narrow razor-straight strip of barren land was all that separated groves of healthy fruit-bearing trees from their skeletal brethren, which pointed branches shrouded in ice accusingly at the heavily laden sky.

"I guess the hearsay wasn't so unreliable," Esme commented.

"No," Sarah Jennifer replied, riveted by the view and her knowledge that the split went all the way to the southwest corner of the sector several hundred kilometers away. "I guess it wasn't."

"It looks like magic to me. No wonder the sea traders believe this place is haunted."

Sarah Jennifer cycled through the drone feeds, looking for the drone over their prospective route. "Do we have any drones inside the sector?" she inquired, not seeing what she wanted.

"Oh. Yes. Cameras!" Enora activated a window showing thick forest climbing the snow-choked land. "I got distracted by a herd of caribou heading out of the storm."

"Why would they distract you?" Sarah Jennifer asked.

"I wanted to know why caribou would leave the snow," Enora responded. "Heat and flies are incredibly uncomfortable for them."

"I lived way up north for a while. I know about caribou," Sarah Jennifer told her with a smile. "Why are they leaving the snow?"

"I sent a drone to check their backtrail and found a

number of Mad roaming the forest three kilometers from the boundary. It appears they've been driven out."

"Take us in," Sarah Jennifer instructed. "The Mad are no danger to us up here."

"We're going to lose visuals for a moment," Enora warned as the ship's nose pierced the cloudfall. "Activating GPR view."

The cockpit dropped into darkness to accommodate the alternate input as the viewscreen split. Half of it retained the normal external camera view, and the other half showed a black and green rendering of the GPR data.

Sarah Jennifer spied the edge of the ice shelf rising into the clouds behind Mount Bråviken. "Let's see how far inland this mountain range goes."

The *Enora* skimmed the clouds, then dipped into the valley beyond Mount Bråviken.

"I have to take us up," Enora announced, her avatar flickering. "There is something interfering with my operating system."

"Do it," Sarah Jennifer urged. "What's the issue?"

Enora had learned to shrug and did so, her nose wrinkling. "I'm not sure. Interference. Maybe the weather system. One moment, please, Major."

Her avatar resolved as the ship reached the upper stratosphere. "The source of the interference appears to be coming from the area where the ground station is located."

"Take us as close as you can," Sarah Jennifer instructed.

She scrutinized the viewscreen as they flew toward the center of the storm. The view from above was spectacular, if overwhelming. While the boundary to the south of Mount Bråviken prevented the storm from spilling across the land in that direction, to the north, the storm system stretched past the horizon. The eye of the storm was clearly visible even from a distance.

Sarah Jennifer tried to imagine how much snow the storm had deposited over the last three decades and realized she couldn't comprehend the scale of the disaster, even though she was looking at it.

Enora pulled the airship up again when they were five kilometers from the ground station's coordinates.

"You good?" Sarah Jennifer asked, concerned as much for Enora as for their continued ability to remain airborne.

"I don't recommend taking the airship any closer than this," Enora warned. The viewscreen glitched, and the AI disappeared momentarily.

"Take us out of range," Sarah Jennifer told her when she reappeared. She didn't lose her temper easily. However, she had to take a minute when she saw how the AI was affected by the energy coming from below. "Bethany Anne didn't say anything about shielding."

"I don't think it *is* a shield," Enora informed her, stabilizing now they were out of the affected airspace. "The frequency of the energy emission is too distorted to be deliberate. I cannot penetrate it with any of my scanning systems. My best guess is that the energy is being produced by the climate control module."

That would explain the extreme weather.

"Is the EI online?" Sarah Jennifer asked.

"I cannot say," Enora replied. "I'm not getting a response, although that could be due to the interference."

Esme tapped on the door. "I can feel your frustration from my cabin. What's up?"

Sarah Jennifer turned in her chair, her brow crumpled in annoyance. "We can't see *anything*. We can't even get close. Whatever the hell that interference is, it's hurting Enora. How do we even know the ground station is still intact under there?"

"TQB bunkers were designed to withstand whatever was thrown at them," Esme reminded her. She dropped a hand to her hip. "Chances are we're going to need some help with this after all."

"I'll call Keeg Station when I know exactly what we're up against," Sarah Jennifer assured her. "But there's no point in requisitioning equipment until we know what we need."

Esme nodded. "True. We can't fly in. We know that much."

"A route plan would be a good start," Enora commented. "I can take care of that, at least."

"Don't kick yourself, Enora." Sarah Jennifer shook her head at the screen, bemused by the blank spot on the GPR where the ground station was located. "I thought we might have to dig some, but this is beyond anything I expected."

"One step at a time," Esme reminded her. "Take some time for contemplation while Enora does her scans. I'm going to check on Ezekiel."

Staring at the viewscreen while Enora worked to uncover the secrets buried beneath the ice was contemplation enough. The distance from the coast was bad news. They would be forced to hike in from the west, avoiding areas that were unstable due to the still-expanding ice field that had spawned Beringia. Sarah Jennifer pushed her disappointment aside and focused on the 3-D scan as the AI built it layer by layer.

"I thought you would like to know I found the settlement," Enora announced an hour later.

Sarah Jennifer looked up from the GPR data. "And?"

"We passed over it on the way in," Enora expanded. "The drone picked up around sixteen hundred life signs spread between a number of caverns inside Mount Bråviken."

"Show me," Sarah Jennifer requested, glad to get some positive news. She scrutinized the deep-infrared image, noting the uniform configuration of the smaller caves that lined the interconnected tunnels that led off the larger caves nearer the surface. "That looks like a whole town. They must live in the small caves. How close to the outermost cavern can you get the drone without anyone seeing it?"

"I can get closer than that," Enora replied. "The drone can travel along the cavern roof undetected. Would you like me to search for anything in particular?"

Sarah Jennifer considered her options. "Send it in. I want to see how those people reacted to Sidric's death. How they're living now that he's gone. It would be good to establish relations with them and get them connected to the people trading along the coast."

"Perhaps you will even find a guide among them," Enora supplied. "The route into the Norrköping is treacherous in the extreme. It would make sense to employ local people who are used to traveling this terrain and may know about safe passages that avoid the numerous crevasses I have discerned."

"That could be," Sarah Jennifer agreed. "Getting some guidance isn't the worst idea. I'd like to avoid unnecessary injuries or loss of time. Getting lost is a real possibility, especially when we can't just have you swoop in and pick us up if something goes wrong. We'll train, of course," she murmured to herself, the itch to take care of connecting with the people of Snøhvit still taking up real estate in her mind.

"Do you wish to land at the settlement before we leave for Salem?" Enora inquired.

"No, not while we have Ezekiel aboard. First contact will have to wait. This mountain is permanent. The communities on the ice shelf need all the time they can get to prepare for the break-up." Sarah Jennifer thought for a long moment, then made a decision. "But maybe we can extend the hand of friendship."

She opened comms to Big Ace. "Quartermaster, see me in my cabin with our food inventory."

Big Ace arrived five minutes later with the cargo manifest and a puzzled expression. "Here you go, Major. What's the deal?"

Sarah Jennifer scanned the manifest list, seeing they had supplies remaining for another four weeks. Taking into account the extra calories Weres needed in comparison to an unenhanced human, there was enough to see the people under the mountain through a few weeks, maybe a bit longer if they rationed carefully. "The settlement is larger than we had considered it would be. Get all of this food packed up with one of the radio units. We're going to give them to the people before we leave."

Big Ace nodded. "Consider it done."

While she was waiting for her request to be carried out, Sarah Jennifer had Enora help her compose a letter to the people in their local language to explain who they were and how to set up the radio. The drone had picked up enough audio for the AI to learn the local dialect, which was slightly removed from the standard Swedish she had in her database.

With the scans completed and the drones recalled, Sarah Jennifer had Enora hover near the entrance to the settlement while Big Ace lowered the crate down to the entrance from the drop doors.

Mission complete, they were ready to return home. Sarah Jennifer used the flight time back to Salem to consolidate. She called ahead to have Sarai set up a secure room at DFHQ for Ezekiel and sent a message to Keeg Station from the IICS requesting whatever equipment would get them through the ice shelf to the ground station, including the imaging data Enora had collected.

She received a reply from Felicity just as the Maine Gorge came into external camera range, telling her to expect a delivery in six weeks' time. That gave them six weeks to train for the operation and to reach out to the Snøhvit settlement and any others Amelie had learned about from the traders.

Sarah Jennifer hoped Ezekiel won his battle in the interim. She wanted to be there for him when he woke up.

CHAPTER FIFTEEN

Beringia, Snøhvit, Aboard the SAF *Enora*

Enora's avatar observed quietly from the viewscreen as she sped them away from Snøhvit, her expression perplexed.

"Are we going to talk about what happened down there?" Katia asked Sarah Jennifer.

The major stared at Katia for a long moment, then lifted her hands. "I have no words."

What had started out as a mission of compassion, an attempt to bring the people of Snøhvit into the fold, had turned out to be nothing but a centuries-old goat rope come back around to bite them in the backside.

On arrival at the ice-locked drilling platform, they had been welcomed. However, the welcome had only been good until they began exchanging information about their respective homes. The moment Sarah Jennifer had seen she was being treated differently than the rest of her team and realized it was because she was the only one with fair hair and skin had been the moment all her feelings of goodwill toward the isolated community had evaporated.

Upon learning about the reason for the unannounced visit, the people of Snøhvit had, as one, gone on the attack, saving her the bother of being politic. Having left most of their weapons on board the airship, Sarah Jennifer and the others had been hard-pressed to get back to the *Enora* without leaving a trail of corpses behind them.

As unsettling as it was to have Esme's concern validated, there were places in the world where the population was blindingly white, and Snøhvit was one of them.

People had been cut off since WWDE, and as a result, some communities' worldview had shrunk with each generation. If anything, it was surprising they hadn't been driven out of more settlements. It wasn't that she didn't understand why the people of Snøhvit had turned on them. She just disagreed vehemently with their narrow-minded view.

They'd encountered pushback in all its forms from communities who'd learned that the land they'd carved a living from for generations was going to vanish sometime in the next decade. They'd encountered disbelief in Bethany Anne and the technology causing the perpetual winter, disavowal of the outside world, envy of the Defense Force's technological and military advantages, and fear of their enhanced natures.

All of these issues had been overcome in other communities with diplomacy and reason. Outright xenophobia and discrimination based on the color of their skin and hair were where Sarah Jennifer drew the line. There was only one distinction that mattered: the divide between the living and the Mad.

So, while she wouldn't leave Snøhvit stranded, she had no intention of negotiating a close relationship between their two communities.

Katia had plenty to say, and she didn't hold back.

Sarah Jennifer, knowing Katia needed her friend at this moment more than she needed her commanding officer, was quiet while she vented her frustration, offering murmurs of agreement at appropriate points.

She cut Katia off when she began blaming a severely-reduced gene pool for the ignorance they'd encountered. "While I can't disagree it was unnerving that everyone there looked like they were related to everyone else, making those kinds of assumptions is stooping to their level. Everyone in this part of the world is pale and blonde."

"Pale and blonde, yeah," Katia agreed. "But identical? I've seen potato crops with more diversity. Shit's freaky. Did you see how they reacted when the guys stepped off the airship behind you?"

Sarah Jennifer had been more perturbed than the pack by the reaction to their various skin and hair colors. "Maybe I could have handled it better, but I wasn't inclined to offer the hand of friendship to people who think their genetics make them better than everyone else."

Enora spoke up. "Your genetics are superior to those of unenhanced humans. I am having trouble parsing the logic of their behavior."

"What logic?" Katia commented acidly. "Dumbasses. They should be grateful we didn't kill any of them."

"Life, even dumbass life, is sacrosanct. Too precious to waste in this time." Sarah Jennifer sighed. She had hoped to find another group of people who would be glad to be connected to the wider world, despite how deep into Beringia they were located. "It just goes to show that there's no accounting for some people. If they want to be isolationists, then let them eat cake."

"You're going to let them get away with that?" Katia growled. "They need a lesson in common sense. Beringia isn't going to be here in ten years. What if that place falls to pieces when the ice breaks up?"

Sarah Jennifer shook off the unease she felt about their failure to forge a relationship with the community. "We're not here to force community on people who don't want it. Standing alone is suicide in these times. They'll come around."

She meant it. Plenty of other people in Beringia had welcomed the Defense Force and the lifelines they brought, communities willing to work together to overcome. She wouldn't sit back and let terminal hardheadedness be the reason humanity died out on Earth.

"We left a few surveillance drones," she told Katia. "If they have issues because of the break-up, or they come down from the rig looking to cause trouble, we'll come back. Otherwise, we have larger concerns than a bunch of racists too proud to accept the truth."

Sarah Jennifer resolved to contact Upinniemi and update Amelie on the situation when they got back to Salem. The trade mistress would get a kick out of this story, and sharing information was how they stayed ahead of another Sidric gaining power.

. . .

Salem, MA

Jim continued to the airbase with the *Enora* after dropping the pack off at Defense Force HQ. Sarah Jennifer left Brutus in charge while she headed for the converted basement room where Ezekiel slept.

Sarai was sitting at the side of the Pod-doc when she arrived, reading from a datapad. "You're back! How did it go?" Her smile faded as Sarah Jennifer gave her the rundown of the disaster at Snøhvit.

"The mountain range that begins in Bråviken Bay extends all the way into Beringia," Sarah Jennifer told her, taking a seat. "Snøhvit used to be an oil rig pre-WWDE. It's landlocked around three and a half thousand feet above where sea level is going to be when Beringia recedes. We were able to find out they avoided being overrun with the Madness before it went sideways."

"What set them off?" Sarai asked.

"They didn't take the news about the climate issue well," Sarah Jennifer replied. "They thought they knew better than us. They thought they were better than us. The person whose turn it was to use their collective brain cell was out when we arrived? Who knows. They chose poorly."

Sarai made a sympathetic face. "I'm sure you did your best."

Sarah Jennifer scowled. "Meh. How is your patient doing?"

"See for yourself," Sarai offered, handing her the datapad.

Sarah Jennifer accepted the device and examined

Ezekiel's bloodwork. Compared to the last time she'd checked, Ezekiel's nanocytes vastly outnumbered the corrupted nanocytes he'd ingested. "How often are you giving him the infusion?"

"Only once a day now." Sarai leaned over the viewing window in the Pod-doc, her expression motherly as she gazed at the sleeping boy. "He's a fighter for sure."

"How long until his treatment is complete, do you think?" Sarah Jennifer asked, returning the datapad to Sarai.

"Not long now," Sarai answered. "He's responding well to the infusion. The corrupted nanocytes are being reduced by a little more every day."

Sarah Jennifer was glad to hear his improvement was continuing. "It's not too much, traveling between here and the hospital every day?"

Sarai shook her head with a chuckle. "I'm not the only doctor in town anymore. I have Kelsey and Geraint, remember? Plus Jana and Janie."

Sarah Jennifer nodded. The two junior doctors had come in with separate groups and found love as well as a new purpose in healing the sick, and the mother-daughter duo were fine nurses.

Sarai nudged Sarah Jennifer with an elbow. "You just make sure that husband of mine stops by before you send him haring off on another assignment. It's our anniversary in three days, and I want to make certain we get a chance to celebrate, if you know what I mean."

Sarah Jennifer laughed. "I guess I can give him tonight off. Make the most of it."

Sarai put a hand to her chest, her throaty laugh filling the room. "You know I will."

Sarah Jennifer thanked Sarai before leaving Ezekiel's room and making her way to her old office at the back of the original building. She'd retained one room; the rest of the former suite had been converted by the engineering corps to house the equipment for the communication array.

She found Esme and Brutus hunched over the transceiver. They didn't see her come in, too caught up in their conversation with Amelie. Sarah Jennifer joined them at the desk. "I take it everyone is amused by our speedy exit from Snøhvit?" she inquired with good humor.

Raucous laughter came over the speaker. "I'll be sure to have everyone keep their eyes out for murderous Norsemen." Amelie guffawed again.

"Laugh about it or cry," Brutus stated. "It was a disaster."

Amelie signed off with a promise to check in if she heard anything.

"Next time, you come with," Sarah Jennifer told Esme.

Esme arched an eyebrow. "Well, it makes sense to have at least one person who can read minds go with you. I won't be offended if it's not me."

Sarah Jennifer groaned. "There aren't enough mind readers to go around. Besides, I want you to come with us to Fort Newfoundland. You and David can help us train for the conditions around Norrköping."

Esme lifted a shoulder. "Not a problem. You can help as well. Sarai will call us if Ezekiel wakes up while we're away."

Sarah Jennifer nodded and held out a hand for the

microphone. "Sarai wanted to see you before you leave," she told Brutus. "Something about your anniversary?"

Brutus' eyes widened in panic. "It's the equinox already?"

"Three days," Esme told him, dropping the handset into Sarah Jennifer's palm. "You lost track?"

Brutus hung his head. "Dammit. Yeah. I don't know how I stay married."

"You have the day to come up with something," Sarah Jennifer told him.

Brutus paled. "*Wooo.* The whole day."

Esme slipped her arm through his. "Don't panic. I'll help."

Brutus looked at Esme like he was drowning and she was a life preserver bobbing on the waves. "Thank you. What do you have in mind?"

Sarah Jennifer called David after Esme and Brutus left and informed him of the plan.

"You want me to raise mountains?" David asked, his tone on the incredulous side of respectful.

"I want you to work with what's already there," Sarah Jennifer corrected, adding some bite to her words to let him know she was in no mood for his prevarication. "Esme will take care of reproducing the extreme weather conditions we're going to be coming up against when we move on the ground station. We're training for everything that can go wrong, so get creative."

"It's not extreme enough here already?" he complained bitterly.

"You'll see for yourself soon enough," Sarah Jennifer informed him, well-used to his dour nature. "You're coming to Norrköping with us. I need your ability to shift rock in case the equipment fails."

"Great, I'm a contingency," David responded dryly with a sigh. "I'll get Harris to stand in while I'm gone."

"I'm bringing your relief with me," Sarah Jennifer told him. "The rotating personnel were due to be switched out at the end of the month anyway. Izzy requested we move the transfer up since the *Enora* is available to do the hauling. I want you to take the Pod to the mainland and scout for a suitable location to do a dummy run."

"Why the hike?"

"We can't land the airship anywhere near the mountain," Sarah Jennifer informed him. "We'll be trekking from Mount Bråviken."

"There's a canyon a few hundred miles west of the fort," David supplied. "Can you send me any maps you have of the area I'm simulating?"

"I can do better," Sarah Jennifer replied. "Enora took 3-D scans of the route we'll be taking into the mountains. Take a team. I don't want you out there alone. Oh, and David?"

"Yes, Major?"

"Have the Pod record aerial imaging before you get started," she instructed. "I want the land returned to its original state when we're done."

Mainland Canada

One week later, the pack arrived at the mouth of the canyon after dropping supplies and the personnel who were transferring in from Salem at the fort.

The aurora was hidden by thick, dark snow clouds. The stratocumuli blanketed the sky over the canyon, offering only rare glimmers of respite from the perpetual winter night. A circle of torches marked the landing site David's team had cleared for the *Enora*, their glows casting glittering blue pools on the falling snow. The airship touched down with a soft *whump*, scattering the drifts.

"You know the drill." Sarah Jennifer raised her voice to compensate for it being swallowed by the loosely packed powder. "Get all the equipment transferred to the cave and your quarters squared away before chow time. The exercise begins as soon as we have the weather conditions in place, so make sure your equipment is in good order. We don't have the time or resources to deal with severe frostbite. Anyone who loses an appendage on this exercise will be staying behind when we make the Norrköping run."

"This is practically balmy compared to Norrköping," Linus called as he broke the crust of the snow and sank four inches. "I'm sweating my ass off in all these layers."

"Not for long," Esme responded with a laugh. She peered out of her fleece-lined hood at the torches running up the canyon wall, seeing a similarly swaddled figure heading down to meet them. "David is here."

David met them at the base of the stairs he'd formed on the rockface and led them to the cave he'd opened two-thirds of the way up the canyon wall, where his team had set up camp. The pack set about transferring their gear into the cave under Big Ace's supervision while Sarah Jennifer and Esme continued up the stairs to the top of the canyon, walking ahead of David.

The wind buffeted them, the chill finding its way in

despite the layers of clothing they wore. Sarah Jennifer braced herself against the cold as she surveyed the course David had raised along the length of the canyon floor, impressed by the massive reconstruction the land had undergone from the photos he'd sent. She recognized landmarks she'd studied in the Norrköping scan data, although they looked almost bunched up compared to the real thing. "How closely were you able to simulate the actual route? I can see you cut out the straight runs."

David pointed out rockfalls he'd placed to create passes and crevasses along the floor of the canyon. "You still have to take care of the river. The canyon narrows four kilometers from here, and it drops off into a crevasse that was too deep for me to do much with," he explained. "I studied the scans you sent, cut out the easier terrain between the infil point and the mountain, and focused on creating the obstacles we'll have to pass between here and the drop-off."

Sarah Jennifer nodded. "Makes sense. Good work, David."

Esme's eyes glowed golden as she called on the wind to draw in the loose snow surrounding them, compacting the cornice that formed into ice to give them a shelter with a roof. "We can get started here."

David wrapped his arms around himself as the temperature dropped sharply around them in response to Esme's magic. "Do you need me?" he asked Sarah Jennifer.

"No, go back to camp," Sarah Jennifer told him. "I need a map of this route. Enora will help."

"Make sure the cave is kept warm," Esme warned David as he left. "It's about to get a lot colder out here."

Sarah Jennifer tucked herself into the lee of the shelter with Esme. "Ready?"

The clouds above split, shining silver lining the edges as Esme manipulated their composition, the wind, and the temperature. The aurora could be seen at last and the fat, fluffy snowflakes ceased to fall, broken up by the fine sleet that Esme coaxed from the clouds as she used the wind to wick the moisture from the air. The sleet coated the land and bonded with the existing snowpack, adhering instantly to the bare rocks.

"Take the snow," Esme told Sarah Jennifer. "I've got the wind. Just keep the sleet steady, and I'll make sure it gets to where we need it."

Sarah Jennifer reached for the Etheric and growled in frustration when it evaded her grasp. Weather manipulation was one of the most common abilities to emerge in the Salem population. However, even after four years, she still struggled with the most basic techniques for controlling her environment.

"Just relax," Esme soothed. "Imagine we're on the training ground if it helps."

Sarah Jennifer scoffed. "Sure, because I've made *so* much progress there."

"Will it, Duckie," Esme reminded her. "Focus on why you're doing this. Draw on that epic stubbornness of yours. We need to build the ice, or this is just a rocky obstacle course."

Sarah Jennifer *was* focused. It wasn't a question of will. She had that in spades. She understood that anything Esme or even the Queen could do was technically possible for her to replicate with practice and determination. However, she was not Bethany Anne, and she didn't feel comfortable making indelible marks on the Earth. The destruction they'd wrought in Maine and New Hampshire had never left her conscience. Some would call this landscape desolate, yet to her it was peaceful, reminding her of her time wandering the wilderness.

After leaving the ranch all those years ago, she'd found solace in living off the land. The day-to-day challenges of locating food and shelter while preserving the environment that provided it had grown in her a deep bond, an affection even, for the complex majesty of nature. Her travels had taken her far from human influence. She'd walked the deserts of the west, skirting wasteland scourged by nuclear attacks and eventually finding herself heading deep into Alaska and the primordial forests of the sub-Arctic. The dissonance between her personal preferences and her duty to act on behalf of the many was, as always, her stumbling block when it came to accessing nature magic.

She closed her eyes, reminding herself that they were going to return the canyon to its original state before leaving. Senses extended, she swept the canyon below and confirmed there was nothing alive there. No animals, no people, barely even any plant life held on. David had chosen well. This was a safe place to work changes to the land.

The energy did not skip away when Sarah Jennifer reached for it a second time. She felt Esme's influence guiding the wind and the snowfall. Red light from her eyes washed the shelter as her connection to the Etheric opened, turning the ice into a beacon that lit the night.

"That's a good start," Esme encouraged, sensing the surge in energy when Sarah Jennifer relaxed into the task and the sleet began to fall faster and thicker at her command. "We need to step it up if we want to be done by morning."

Sarah Jennifer barely heard Esme. Her heart soared as her consciousness rode the wind currents. She left her body behind and directed the clouds to deposit their loads as fast as Esme encouraged them to form. The river, sluggish with ice floes, slowed further as the surface solidified, dirt-choked icebergs forming around the rocks jutting from the turgid wash. The rushing water was captured by the rapid onset of the freeze, its foamy peaks transformed into glittering rills that captured the light from the aurora where it peered through breaks in the clouds.

They worked in companionable silence for the next few hours, safe in the shelter. Brutus brought hot food and coffee as the dark of night rolled into an equally dark morning.

Sarah Jennifer and Esme broke off, hungry, cold, and exhausted. They attacked the meal with enthusiasm while Brutus craned his neck to see into the canyon.

He let out a low whistle, his enhanced eyesight capturing every bit of torchlight the ice reflected back at them. "Color me amazed. It looks completely different from when we got here. You do some of this, SJ?"

Sarah Jennifer was too tired to argue about him shortening her name. She nodded and sipped her coffee. "I need a couple of hours of rack time before we start."

"You've got it," Brutus promised. "I'm going to run the

guys through the safety briefing one last time before we get going for real."

Esme accepted the hand Sarah Jennifer offered and pulled herself to her feet. "Sounds like a plan."

They made their way to camp. Sarah Jennifer was relieved to find her tent had been set up for her. She called her thanks to whoever had done it as she crawled inside and tucked herself gratefully into her bedroll.

The comforting sounds of the pack moving around the cave lulled Sarah Jennifer to sleep. She drifted off, satisfied that she'd overcome her block with at least one aspect of nature magic. Now she could call the snow whenever she needed it.

CHAPTER SIXTEEN

Salem, MA

Sarah Jennifer left her quarters and made her way to Ezekiel's room. She'd received the word that the equipment she'd requested would arrive in orbit in two weeks and the even better news that Ezekiel had finally won the battle for his life.

An anxious crowd had gathered outside the room when Sarah Jennifer arrived. Salem's growth hadn't changed the close community at the heart of the city, so the entire Defense Force knew about the boy in the Pod-doc. They'd all been rooting for his recovery and their salvation from the Madness.

Sarah Jennifer made it clear that anyone hounding Ezekiel or upsetting him with talk of him being their savior would be dealt with swiftly and told everyone to leave. A child didn't need that kind of pressure.

Sarai was the only person in the room when Sarah Jennifer stepped out of the decontamination chamber. She turned from the command console and smiled warmly. "Hey, you're just in time."

"Where's Esme?" Sarah Jennifer asked, accepting Sarai's hug.

Sarai nodded, her enthusiasm adding extra radiance to her smile. "Esme said not to wait for her. She won't be back from Newfoundland until tomorrow."

Sarah Jennifer nodded. "I spoke to her last night." She inspected the console monitor and pulled up Ezekiel's bloodwork. "I can't believe it. Not a single corrupted nanocyte."

"It's incredible, right?" Sarai showed Sarah Jennifer his nanocyte count. "It's through the roof. He's going to have a lot of power. A *lot*."

Sarah Jennifer heard her unspoken concern. "That was why I brought him here. So he could learn how to control it."

"You think it's safe to let him around the other trainees?" Sarai asked. She held up a hand when Sarah Jennifer's brow furrowed. "I mean, he could hurt someone accidentally. His primary ability is fire, right? How are we going to teach him to control it? We have no fire-workers."

"I'm not planning to teach him to control his ability," Sarah Jennifer told her. "We're going to teach him discipline and self-control, same as we're teaching every other magic-user. The rest will come when he can regulate himself. My biggest concern is how he will take being brought here from his home, and what psychological impact losing the months he's been in stasis could have on him."

"My take on it from the books we have is that it

depends on the patient," Sarai responded. "Do you want me to wait outside while you wake him up?"

Sarah Jennifer's heartbeat quickened in reaction to her anticipation about meeting Ezekiel at last. She was prepared for rejection, although her hope was that he accepted them and understood why she had chosen to take him so far from his home and everything he knew. "No, stay, please. I could use the support."

"You've got it." Sarai patted Sarah Jennifer on the back and turned back to the Pod-doc window. "The psychology books say we should be prepared for him experiencing culture shock. I know it's all outdated, but in Ezekiel's case, it could apply. Electricity, vehicles, computers, Weres, the military structure we have here—it's all going to be pretty strange to him."

Sarah Jennifer intended to break the situation down gently for him, then do everything she could to make sure he had as normal a life as any other kid growing up in Salem. "There's only one way to find out. I'm going to wake him up."

Sarai moved away from the console while Sarah Jennifer input the instructions to end the stasis program. "Brutus is pretty attached to this boy," she remarked as a neurostimulant gas filled the chamber.

"We all are," Sarah Jennifer responded with feeling. "It's strange how they make you care for them without doing a thing. Lucy is the same. I'm thinking of letting her enlist early if she agrees to spend her first two years with the engineering corps."

Sarai chuckled. "It's not a bad idea. Jana is finding it hard to keep tabs on her."

Sarah Jennifer's attention was drawn to the Pod-doc when the gas in the chamber cleared. The boy's eyes flickered. "He's waking up."

Ezekiel's eyes snapped open. He was in a coffin. No, a box with a window. A box with a window where two women looked in on him. Strangers.

"It's okay," the blonde woman assured him in a calm voice as the lid lifted. "My name is Sarah Jennifer, and this is Sarai. We're friends. You are safe."

Ezekiel stayed where he was, not trusting that the blonde woman wore a military uniform. "Who are you? How did I get here?" Why did the words coming out of his mouth sound so strange? More importantly, why wasn't he Mad? Panic overwhelmed him, made worse by the crackling cloud of gray mist that appeared around the strange box he had woken up in. "What are you doing to me?"

The redhead made a soothing gesture. "That's all you, kiddo."

Ezekiel didn't understand. He needed to escape, but where could he go when he was surrounded by this storm cloud?

The cloud became denser, darkening as his imagination gave it form. It began throwing out sparks of electricity as his fear grew, driving the women back.

So much for walking him through it slowly. Sarah Jennifer grabbed a hand mirror from the sideboard and held it up to show Ezekiel his glowing eyes. "You have more magic than you did before..." Her voice trailed off.

That wasn't the place to start. "You were infected with the Madness, Ezekiel. Do you remember?"

Ezekiel caught his reflection and saw that his eyes were shining with red light. His hands flew to his face involuntarily and the storm abated just enough for him to realize that they were telling him the truth. "How do you know my name?"

Sarah Jennifer ducked a small lightning bolt. "I can explain everything, but you're in danger of hurting everyone in the building. You might be the most powerful being on this planet right now. I need you to take control of your fear. Can you do that for me?"

The gathering storm vanished the instant Ezekiel realized he was the cause. His knees gave way as the aftereffects of using so much magic hit him.

"Thatta boy," Sarai encouraged, stepping forward to lead Ezekiel to the bed she had prepared. "Now, you rest up. I'm going to make you some food while the major explains what happened to you."

Ezekiel allowed her to tuck him in, dazed by the amount of power he had at his disposal. He glanced at Sarah Jennifer, who was staring at him with an unreadable expression. "Where are my dogs?"

"Curtis is taking care of the dogs," Sarah Jennifer told him.

"Curtis..." Ezekiel was too tired to think. The mention of his friend eased his worry for his animals and how he would survive when he got back to the izba. A disconcerting thought pushed its way through his brain fog. "How am I not Mad?"

"It's a lot to take in." Sarah Jennifer pulled up a chair. "You know my close friend Lilith."

Ezekiel tipped his head. "The Oracle? She hasn't spoken to anyone in a long time."

"Is that what you call her?" Sarah Jennifer smiled. "I like that. We were in New Romanov to make repairs to the machine she lives inside. Olaf was there when Curtis found out you were gone."

The mention of the famed bear warrior piqued Ezekiel's interest, distracting him from his confusion. "What does Olaf have to do with any of this?"

"He was with us when we found you in that cabin." She gave him the short version of their search and the time he'd spent in Lilith's cavern while they were away in Finland, then pointed at the Pod-doc. "This technology allows us to look at what is happening inside your body and fix what's wrong. We were able to reverse the infection."

Ezekiel's mind whirled. Believing her tale of traveling the world in an airship was a stretch. The idea that he had succumbed to the Madness and been cured was too much for him to accept. "That's impossible!"

Sarah Jennifer smiled. "It was. Until we found you. You're special, Ezekiel. This is going to sound strange, but we have tiny machines called nanocytes in our blood."

Ezekiel looked at her skeptically. "More machines? Is everything in your world run by them?"

"Everything living on this planet has nanocytes." Sarah Jennifer had considered how she was going to break this down for him. "They're in the air, the earth, the water, and every living creature. The nanocytes are what give people abilities beyond those we would have naturally. For example, I can turn into a wolf. The Madness is caused by our nanocytes becoming infected with a bad instruction. Your nanocytes don't just give you magical abilities. They attack the bad instruction."

Ezekiel didn't believe her. "My father always said there were some strange people in Archangelsk, but I thought he was telling tales to stop me from wandering around the forest. The magic of the two-natured comes from the Matriarch and Patriarch. That's what Boris told my parents, and what they told me."

Sarah Jennifer decided now wasn't the time to get into semantics. She would tell him about Kurtherian clans and the origins of the various Weres another time when he wasn't recovering from his worldview being turned on its head. "It was Bethany Anne who gave the nanocytes to the world."

Ezekiel shook his head in shock, pulling his blankets up around himself. "No! The Matriarch loves us. She wouldn't give us the Madness!"

"She didn't mean to," Sarah Jennifer replied in a soft voice. "There's something else you need to know. We're not in Siberia. I brought you to my home. We're in America. Salem, to be exact."

Fear wracked Ezekiel. He'd heard of the warlord to the west who drained people of their blood. Was that to be his fate? "Am I your prisoner?"

Sarah Jennifer realized she hadn't been clear. "No, Ezekiel. I'm offering you a home. You would have been in danger if I'd left you in New Romanov. So would the people who care about you. There are bad people who would drain your blood because of your magic."

"The Danelaw," Ezekiel murmured.

"Has been dismantled," Sarah Jennifer told him. "Sidric is dead, but he wasn't the only leech. This is a safe place for magic-users and everyone else from the UnknownWorld. We can't replace your real family, but you are welcome to join ours."

"So, you're going to keep me here?" Ezekiel asked.

Sarah Jennifer didn't hesitate to tell him the truth, sensing he was smart enough to handle it. "For now. When you've had time to think it over, you'll understand that the increase in your ability makes you a danger to yourself and to others. You need to understand how your magic has changed, and in Salem, you can figure out how to control your abilities in safety."

"Oh." Ezekiel looked at his hands for a long time, his brow furrowed in thought.

Sarah Jennifer gave him space to process as she got out her datapad and loaded it with Billy Hawkins' books.

The resident historian had written a number of books on topics ranging from Bethany Anne and the rise of TQB, WWDE, and biographies of the Walton family, including a detailed retelling of the reformations Sarah Jennifer had brought about since her arrival in Salem. She hoped Ezekiel would feel more at home here if he knew something about where he was.

"What are you doing?" Ezekiel cut into her thoughts, intrigued by the glowing screen.

"This is a datapad. It holds information of all kinds." Sarah Jennifer showed him the library menu. "I've loaded our history books onto it. Here, see? I thought you might like to have it read to you."

Ezekiel's eyes lit up. "I can read."

Sarah Jennifer was pleasantly surprised. "That's a rare skill these days."

The shine left his expression. "My mother taught me. She loved books."

Sarah Jennifer passed him the datapad. "I'm sorry you lost her. Your father, too. Do you have any other family we could contact for you? We're heading back to New Romanov in two weeks."

Ezekiel shook his head. "No one I would know how to find. My family was not from Archangelsk originally."

Sarai returned with a covered tray, and the tantalizing aroma distracted Ezekiel from his sadness.

"That smells really good," he commented.

Sarai cooed at Ezekiel's hopeful expression. "It's all for you, my dear. There's soup and bread, and cheese and fruit if you feel like you can manage something solid."

She laid the tray on the over-bed table and shooed Sarah Jennifer out as Ezekiel attacked his food with enthusiasm. "That's enough for one day, Major. Doctor's orders."

Ezekiel looked up when Sarah Jennifer got to her feet, pausing with a chunk of bread over his bowl. "Thank you for saving me."

Sarah Jennifer laid a hand on his head. "Get some rest. I'll come see you in the morning and we'll talk some more, okay?"

Ezekiel was bright-eyed and bushy-tailed when Sarah Jennifer returned to his room at breakfast time. He was sitting up in bed, reading while he spooned sweet oatmeal into his mouth.

"You seem to be getting the hang of technology," Sarah Jennifer commented. "What are you reading?"

Ezekiel turned the datapad to show her the screen. "I finished the book about the Matriarch." He dropped the datapad on his blanket and folded his hands in his lap. "I also read the history of Salem. It was a long night, and I wasn't tired."

Sarah Jennifer nodded. "When you're feeling up to it, I'll take you to meet some of the people you read about."

Ezekiel swung his feet over the bed. "I'm ready. Let's go."

"There are a lot of people who want to meet you. Can you control your magic?" Sarah Jennifer had already briefed everyone along their planned route about what to do if Ezekiel went nuclear.

Ezekiel nodded. "I know how to suppress my magic. I've been doing it for over a year. I'm sorry I brought the storm in here yesterday. It won't happen again."

Sarah Jennifer found his statement curious. There was a story there; something about his abilities disturbed him. She glanced at Sarai for approval. "What do you say, Doc?"

Sarai chuckled at Ezekiel's hopeful expression. "Don't keep him out too long," the smiling witch cautioned. "I think a walk around HQ would be okay."

Sarah Jennifer kept a lid on her plans for lunch. "I swear I'll return him in one piece."

Ezekiel was chatty as they took the stairs to the first

floor. He looked around the former town hall's lobby as they went into the administration wing, inquiring about how the various additions had been built.

Sarah Jennifer was impressed with his knowledge of post-technology construction methods, and Ezekiel was fascinated by the parts of the building that had been built using magic. She answered his questions, glad they were breaking the ice.

He broke away to examine the botanical feature in the center of the lobby more closely. "How does this grow without sunlight?" he asked, dipping his fingers into the halo of fine mist emitted by the irrigation system.

"There are a lot of different specialists here," Sarah Jennifer told him. "Magic is still a new thing to most people."

Ezekiel broke off a sprig of thyme and rubbed it between his fingertips to release the aroma. "I read that."

"Who taught you carpentry and woodcraft?" Sarah Jennifer asked.

Ezekiel's joy faded for a moment. "My father could build anything with his hands, and everyone who lives in the taiga knows plant lore."

Sarah Jennifer put a hand on his shoulder. "I can't imagine how losing them both feels."

"When do you plan to take me back to New Romanov?" Ezekiel blurted. He blushed and looked away. "It's just, it's my home. But I want to explore Salem and all its magic. There's no magic in Siberia."

Sarah Jennifer gave him a sympathetic smile, wondering what he'd make of Amelie's gift. "We can talk about that later. I want to introduce you to real food while Sarai's not here to disapprove."

Ezekiel's brow furrowed in confusion. "The steamed chicken and vegetables she prepared for supper last night were not real food? It was delicious."

Sarah Jennifer grinned and wiggled her eyebrows. "Wait until you've tasted pizza, tacos, and cake."

"I've had cake before." He lengthened his stride to walk beside Sarah Jennifer as she led the way to the second-floor mess. "Sarai said there are people my age here. When can I meet them?"

"Soon." The major was heartened by his enthusiasm. She'd wondered if her plans for the afternoon would be overwhelming for him, but he seemed to be a sociable young man. "They usually hang out at the beach on the weekend. They're getting ready to start their adult lives, so they have apprenticeships or study during the day."

Ezekiel glanced out the window at the snow-covered rooftops, wondering what fun there was to be had by the shore in winter. It all sounded very...regimented, a far cry from the slow and steady pace of life with his parents.

He realized Sarah Jennifer was still talking and pulled his attention back to the present. "I'm sorry. I wasn't listening. Everything is so different here."

Sarah Jennifer wouldn't chastise him for woolgathering. "I like that you don't make excuses. It's an admirable trait, but give yourself a break, kid. Everything has changed for you, but I'm here to help you get through it, and so is everyone else here."

"What does that even mean?" Ezekiel asked.

Sarah Jennifer smiled. "I guess we'll find out when you join classes."

"School?" Ezekiel's lip curled.

"Basic skills for magic users," Sarah Jennifer clarified, chuckling when his look of disdain was replaced by a spark of interest. "Ah, you thought it was going to be boring? Esme's classes are never boring. I should know. I've been taking them for four years."

Ezekiel shot her a curious glance. "Aren't you the leader here? And a Wechselbalg? Why do you have to take magic classes?"

Sarah Jennifer manifested a weak energy ball. "My nanocytes are...complicated. I'm not technically a Were. Just like you, I don't know what my abilities are until I discover them. Unlike you, my magic doesn't come easily."

"Magic is useless. It's not easy. Or reliable." Ezekiel stopped walking, his eyes glowing as he fought down his grief. "It couldn't save my parents."

"That's why we train," Sarah Jennifer countered, putting a hand on his shoulder. "So we know our limits. So we can push beyond them when people are counting on us. You have a lot more juice than you did before. Your parents' memory can become something that haunts you, or it can be what you use to drive your purpose in life. You're a smart kid, Ezekiel, and I saw a storm in a hospital room that proves you have the power to do good in this world."

Ezekiel considered Sarah Jennifer's advice as they continued walking. Everything he'd learned so far about her and Salem gave him the impression of people working together for the good of all. Magic and the old technology were part of everyday life here. He was certain that if he insisted on going back to New Romanov, he would be returned.

Did he even want to go back? Ezekiel wasn't sure. America seemed to offer possibilities he couldn't have dreamed of. He wanted to know if the whole place was filled with people like Sarah Jennifer and Sarai. People who cared for others. Where was his place in all this? How had his magic changed? It definitely *felt* different.

When they arrived at the mess hall, Sarai was standing at the door with her hands on her hips and a wry smile playing on her lips. "Busted! Did you think Brutus wouldn't tell me what you had planned?"

Sarah Jennifer held up a finger. "Don't you spoil this for him."

"I wouldn't dream of it," Sarai replied with a chuckle. "But I would have made chocolate cake if you'd told me."

Sarah Jennifer caught the twinkle in her eye. "You had one anyway, didn't you?"

Sarai held up her hands in defeat, her smile shining through her pretense of annoyance. "Count yourself lucky I didn't finish decorating Daddy's birthday cake yet. I'm heading out to pick it up now."

Ezekiel had no clue what was going on. He glanced at Sarah Jennifer as she led him into a room filled with people and decorations. The large room was half-filled with smiling people, some in Defense Force uniforms, others in street clothes and robes.

He read the hand-painted banner on the wall: WELCOME TO THE PACK, EZEKIEL! A lump formed in his throat. "This is for me?"

"Of course it is, silly!" Lucy exclaimed, extracting

herself from the adults. Janie followed her, with Benjamin and his friends in tow.

Ezekiel tried his best to remember everyone's name as they introduced themselves. He had never seen so many people his own age in one place. They all greeted him with wide smiles and kind words

"This is our family," Sarah Jennifer told him as the children gave way to the adults. "It's made from everyone in the UnknownWorld. That means you."

"Can he come sit with us, Major?" Benjamin begged.

Sarah Jennifer saw that Ezekiel was eager to go with the teenagers, so she nodded. "Just take it easy. No sneaking off. Ezekiel is still recovering his strength."

Benjamin regarded Ezekiel with interest after they'd claimed a corner of the mess hall while Lucy and Janie corralled the younger boys for a raid on the open buffet. "Is it true you had the Madness?" he asked with genuine curiosity.

Ezekiel nodded, making his eyes shine red to prove it. "The Matriarch's technology saved me."

"Cool!" Benjamin enthused. "We all had to go into the Pod-doc when the affliction came to Salem."

"Affliction?" Ezekiel echoed.

"When a Were loses the ability to shift," Taylor clarified with a grimace. "Who's the Matriarch?"

"He means the Queen," Lucy interjected, returning with Ezekiel's food. She put the plate down in front of him and pointed out each bite-sized item. "Pizza roll, fish taco, mini-bell pepper stuffed with mushrooms, rice, and beans, sweet potato fries, deep-fried runner beans, and chili sloppy joe. That's the best."

"Is it true you can all turn into wolves?" Ezekiel asked around a mouthful of crispy taco shell.

Taylor got up, and a gangly wolf appeared in his place in the blink of an eye.

"No shifting in the mess hall!" one of the adults called.

Ezekiel let out a low whistle. "My father told me there used to be thousands of Wechselbalg in Siberia when he was a boy, but they vanished."

Everyone around him suddenly became serious.

"The affliction," Lucy whispered, her dark eyes wide. "It's worse than the Madness to us Weres. People lost their wolves or their humanity. It was scary when it started spreading through Salem. All we had was one Pod-doc. Everyone had to give Dr. Sarai a blood sample in case they were afflicted before they got their turn in the Pod-doc."

"Esme says everyone but the Weres will get magic when we fix the Madness," Taylor chipped in, taking a seat by Benjamin.

"You mean, when the adults fix it," Lucy grumbled.

Sarah Jennifer kept one ear on the teens while she ate with Brutus. She understood Lucy's eagerness to be part of the action. However, she had a long way to go before she was ready for the big leagues.

Brutus nudged her with an elbow. "Did you hear a word I just said?"

Sarah Jennifer laughed. "Guess not. Something about snow chains?"

"'Something about snow chains,'" Brutus echoed, laying on the snark liberally. "As in, we have to mount them on the ATVs so we can haul the equipment into Norrköping. They barely made it through the training route."

Sarah Jennifer shook her head. "No, we don't. We're not taking the ATVs."

Everyone at the table turned to look at her.

"You've got to be kidding," Katia grumbled.

"Please tell me we're not doing this old-school," Rory begged from the next table.

"I can get the chains ready in time if that's the issue," Big Ace told her, passing a wriggling Cherie to Tamara.

Sarah Jennifer let them stew a few seconds before answering. "I got the drop manifest early this morning. Ted has provided everything we'll need for the operation. The shipping containers will wait in orbit until we get there and I signal for them to complete the drop. All we have to do is show up and get to work."

Lucy groaned in protest. "You guys get all the fun! What are we going to do, stay here and train?"

"That's exactly what you're going to do." Sarah Jennifer flashed her an easy grin. "If I'm suitably impressed by your instructors' reports when I get back, I'll consider letting you enlist with the engineering corps. Lieutenant Johnson is willing to take you on as long as you can keep up with the rest of his class."

Lucy's mouth worked for a moment as she tried and failed to find a response to the offer.

"Just say thank you," Benjamin hissed.

Lucy flushed. "Oh, yeah. Thank you, Major."

"You get what you work for," Sarah Jennifer replied, turning back to the discussion at her table.

Ezekiel watched the exchange with interest. He'd decided last night that they could be trusted. Everyone here was open and honest in a way that couldn't be faked.

This really was a family, despite many of them not being related. Sarah Jennifer filled the role of matriarch in a way that would please *the* Matriarch.

Had the feeling of wanting to reject humanity passed? Not quite. Nevertheless, he was intrigued by the way of life in Salem and the possibility of becoming something more than he was. His blood was special, by all accounts. What could he achieve with control over his magic?

It wouldn't ever make up for his failure to save his parents, but perhaps he could prevent other families from being torn apart.

CHAPTER SEVENTEEN

Ezekiel was waiting at the doors of the HQ when Sarah Jennifer arrived to take him to his first day's training. She commented on the spring in his step as they made their way to the park.

"I'm looking forward to meeting other people like me," Ezekiel admitted shyly. "I thought about what you said yesterday and everything I've learned so far about the Defense Force and why you founded it. You're right. I can honor my parents' memory by using my magic to help rebuild the world when the Madness is gone."

Sarah Jennifer's eyebrow shot up. "That's a big decision to make after being here for less than a week."

"I see possibilities in my dreams," Ezekiel told her, his expression making it clear he was serious. "I always have."

A few days of eating well had done a lot for the slightly gaunt appearance he'd had on waking up. His smile was infectious, charming Sarah Jennifer into playing along.

"Tell me about these possibilities," she encouraged, hearing Lilith chuckle in the back of her mind. *I want to hear what you have to do with that,* she sent to her Kurtherian friend.

Later, Lilith promised.

Ezekiel flushed, embarrassed. "You will laugh."

"I want to hear what you have to say," Sarah Jennifer told him. "I won't laugh, I promise."

Ezekiel shrugged. "I have been talking to Sarai about magic and the Matriarch's dream to give it to everybody. How will they know they have magic unless they have teachers?"

Sarah Jennifer paused. "That's... You have a good point. You know, Bethany Anne told me our abilities are connected to our emotions."

Ezekiel turned when he noticed she'd stopped walking. "What do emotions have to do with it?"

Sarah Jennifer thought about it for a moment. "Honestly? I haven't figured it out yet. As I understand it, strong emotions trigger the programming in our nanocytes. At least, that's what Esme says. I've been trying to heal my knee for four years, and it's not from a lack of wanting that I haven't succeeded. "

Ezekiel thought back to when he had been at the izba, desperate not to turn Mad. "Maybe just wanting something isn't enough to make it reality. Maybe you have to *need* it with every part of your being. Is that why I was able to overcome the Madness, do you think?"

"Could be. We'll know more once we've learned everything we can from your blood." Sarah Jennifer caught up with him and they continued to the park, Ezekiel's gaze on the wolves running nearby. The novice magic-users were lined up outside Greenhouse Seven, chatting while they waited for Esme to appear and start their day's learning.

Esme, always an early bird, was already inside the greenhouse.

"And it's a good morning to you all," the head witch enthused as Sarah Jennifer and Ezekiel entered the greenhouse at the back of the line. "We have a new novice joining us today. Everyone, make Ezekiel feel welcome."

The novices greeted Ezekiel as they filed over to where a clay pot apiece awaited them on the wide strip of grass in the center of the greenhouse.

"Take your places," Esme announced. "We'll be carrying on from where we left off last week."

Sarah Jennifer wrinkled her nose at her pot as she laid her hands on the sides. "We have to make the seeds sprout," she quietly explained to Ezekiel.

"You don't like nature magic?" he asked.

"I like it just fine," Sarah Jennifer told him. "Doing it on command is another story altogether." She smiled. "I guess I'm just griping, Esme would say."

"Esme does say," was the retort from the witch. "I want everyone to focus on sprouting their seeds. That includes you, Major."

Ezekiel suddenly found himself feeling very nervous. He didn't know where to start. The only times he'd ever used his magic were in fear. He glanced at the other trainees, who were starting to see pale shoots pierce the surface of the soft earth in their pots. He sensed the shifting energy, although he had no idea how to emulate the other novices.

"Remember what we learned about tapping the well

inside," Esme instructed, pacing behind the novices with her hands clasped at the base of her spine. "Sense the Etheric energy all around us. Find your connection to it. Feel it. Embrace it. Immerse yourself. Now, will it to do what you need."

The greenhouse was lit by a soft green light as the novice magic users pulled on the ambient Etheric energy and focused it on their sprouting plants. Their eyes glowed as the tender vines grew fat and wriggled serpent-like up the canes stuck in the middle of each pot.

Ezekiel focused on Esme's voice and found that when he listened deep within himself, he could hear the energy calling to be used. He pulled, poked, and pushed at the energy, trying to take hold of it. It slipped away from his mental grasp, not responding to his desire to take hold and use it. Frustrated, Ezekiel grunted and dropped his hands. "I don't know what's wrong," he exclaimed, grasping the grass between his fingers. "The magic is there; I can feel it. Why can I not make it do what I'm telling it to?"

Sarah Jennifer wasn't having any more luck. "You have the belief you need. Just have confidence in your connection."

Esme knelt by Ezekiel and put a hand on his shoulder. "Be gentle. Coax the energy if it's being difficult. It is a gift and should be respected as such."

Sarah Jennifer snorted. "See, that's where you get me every time," she complained. "It's *energy*—a program with executable commands. If I can activate a subroutine that gives me control of the weather, I should be able to activate the one that allows me to make this plant grow. Or fix my darned knee."

"This is why your knee is still mangled," Esme told her without malice. "The Etheric is not inert, yet it is not alive. What you get from it is the end result of your will. How do you react to demands? How do you respond to the offer of a mutual exchange? Do either of you like to be told to do anything?"

She smiled at the almost identical looks of disgust she received from Sarah Jennifer and Ezekiel. "I didn't think so. Work with your personality. Your magic is yours, bound to you. It has all your quirks."

Ezekiel was slightly heartened to see Sarah Jennifer didn't understand a word of what Esme was saying either. Either that, or she was just *that* stubborn. Her belief in technology wasn't helping her any; that was obvious. He resolved to try it Esme's way and returned his focus to the energy around him.

This time he approached it the same way he would his dogs. If his magic was bound to him and he was uncertain, it would not work. Maybe his magic was like a newly-weaned pup. It didn't know what was expected of it, so it needed him to show it.

The energy responded eagerly to his altered mindset. It licked his consciousness as Ezekiel pictured a seed sprouting. Out of nowhere, his inner vision was disrupted by a flash of fear, the image of the seed replaced by a fireball.

Without warning, the vision in his mind became reality, and the grass between him and Sarah Jennifer was engulfed by hungry licking flames.

Ezekiel scrambled back, breathing heavily. "I'm sorry!"

Esme doused the fire with a blast of icy energy from her palms. "Good start, my lad. Back to your seed, now."

Ezekiel stared at Esme, nonplussed that he wasn't being chastised for almost burning down the greenhouse. "You're not angry?"

Esme's eyes twinkled with amusement. "Ach, laddie, no. No one expects you to have control right away."

Ezekiel eyed the other students. "Why is their magic so different from mine? Their eyes shine green."

"It's not different," Sarah Jennifer assured him. "It all comes from the same place. It's how each individual magic-user chooses to manifest their power. Many of the people here have developed nature magic because it makes their lives easier. There are others who can manipulate the earth, the rocks, or the ocean. Sarai has the power to make crops flourish. I can control the weather to some degree. Esme? Well, she's got a touch of everything. Esme says it's about will. I say magic develops to improve the life of the user. You are not so much a farmer as a fighter. Fire makes sense as your primary ability."

"I don't know," Ezekiel replied. "I didn't want to fight, but fights seem to keep finding me. The first time I used my magic was when our dacha was attacked by the Mad. The second time was when I killed the owl in the barn. I burned it, then I killed it with my sword. Its blood went into my mouth, which was stupid of me to allow. I was scared for my dogs."

The memory overwhelmed him, creating visions of his hardships to overwhelm his mind. His magic responded, and the air began to crackle around him.

"It's okay, Ezekiel," Sarah Jennifer reassured him. "You are safe. Your dogs are safe. You've got this. Don't be put off by my poor attitude. I'm just sore because I haven't been able to make this work for me yet, but that's got nothing to do with magic and everything to do with my family legacy."

"What makes you a good soldier is an impediment to imagination," Esme cut in. She returned her attention to Ezekiel. "Your nanocytes are clearly very special. I think that with an open mind, there's no telling what you can do."

Sarah Jennifer waved a finger at the pot. "Starting with this seed."

Ezekiel nodded, trusting that these women had his best interests at heart. If he was to be part of the effort to rebuild the world after the Madness had been cured, he had to get a grip on his magic. He had to become something more than he was right now, a fourteen-year-old boy whose magic was as dangerous to his friends as it was to the Mad.

He reached out with the same sense he'd used to examine the magic inside him and explored the energy surrounding the vines growing from the other novices' pots. He found with some surprise that the plants wanted to grow.

Sarah Jennifer pressed her lips together and concentrated, glad the focus was off her knee. She saw the green flash in Ezekiel's eyes. This boy was special, there was no doubt about it.

Every plant in the greenhouse burst out of its container, shooting up in the blink of an eye. Flowers bloomed and food plants fruited, filling the greenhouse with a heady mixture of perfumes. Ezekiel's eyes blazed green light as the plants continued their growth spurt. The novices scrambled back as their tiny vines thickened and climbed above their canes, weaving into a bower with Ezekiel sitting cross-legged in the center.

Ezekiel was just as astounded as everyone else. He crawled out from between the interlocked vines, his face a picture of wonder as he took in the cornucopia he'd produced. He brushed his hand against a heavily-laden tomato plant. "How did I do this?"

Sarah Jennifer exchanged glances with Esme.

Esme's reaction was as subdued as always. She was not one to make a big deal out of things that really *were* a big deal. "You opened your mind to the possibility."

Ezekiel yawned, suddenly exhausted.

Sarah Jennifer took one look at him and decided he'd had enough for one day. "I'm going to take Ezekiel to get some more breakfast. He needs to keep his strength up after expending so much energy."

Esme nodded her agreement. "Good idea. He's earned it." She smiled at Ezekiel as he clambered to his feet. "Good start, laddie. I'll see you back here tomorrow morning for your next lesson."

Ezekiel dragged his feet as he and Sarah Jennifer returned to the Defense Force's headquarters. Sarah Jennifer had little experience with Etheric drain, but she knew exactly what to do to get his energy back up. A visit to the main mess hall scored them both a bag of sandwiches, cake, and cookies, with milk for Ezekiel and a large, *large* coffee for Sarah Jennifer.

Ezekiel sipped the milk, savoring the creaminess. "Milk comes from sheep or goats where I come from. This is not from a sheep or a goat."

"No," Sarah Jennifer agreed. "We have cows here."

"I should like to see a cow," Ezekiel commented.

"Knock yourself out," Sarah Jennifer replied. "Just make sure you've got someone with you when you go out to the ranch in case you get lost. It's a big country outside of town."

They returned to Ezekiel's quarters in the basement, which now looked more like a studio apartment than a hospital room.

"You did great today," Sarah Jennifer told him, remaining at the door. "It's almost a shame to disrupt your progress."

"What?" Ezekiel blurted. "Why?"

"We're due to head back to New Romanov soon," she reminded him. "Olaf wants to be part of the Norrköping mission." She was surprised to see his downcast look. "This is my life. I'm not here most of the time. If you would prefer to stay here instead of with me—"

"No," Ezekiel interrupted before he was misunderstood. "I have to go back, if only to say goodbye."

"Lilith wants to spend some time with you," Sarah Jennifer told him. "And I'm pretty sure Curtis will be glad to see you."

Ezekiel winced. "Not to mention Mrs. Shutov."

Sarah Jennifer chuckled. "I won't if you don't."

CHAPTER EIGHTEEN

The next two weeks passed in a blur of spending time with Ezekiel, training with the pack for the Norrköping expedition, and celebrating the close of the year in accordance with Salem's traditions. Samhain night marked the arrival of three shipping containers in high orbit, the end of Sylvia's biannual visit, and time to move on for the pack.

Sarah Jennifer packed up her quarters at Defense Force HQ the morning after the celebration and made her way out front to where the pack was loading Bluebird under Izzy's supervision.

Sarah Jennifer gave the heavily pregnant sergeant a stern look. "You shouldn't be out here in this cold."

"Where else should I be?" Izzy retorted, shifting her weight in the folding chair she'd placed at the top of the steps so she could survey her domain and bark orders accordingly. "In bed with my feet up? No, thanks. Kendrick wouldn't survive my mood swings. I'll keep working until I can't."

Sarah Jennifer grabbed the nearest soldier. "Make sure

Sergeant Bloom doesn't overexert herself." She glanced at Izzy. "Have you eaten?"

Before Izzy could reply, Sarah Jennifer sent the soldier to fetch food, a hot drink, and a blanket. She pointed at the woman. "I mean it. You take care of yourself."

Esme and Ezekiel exited the building with two bags apiece. The witch watched the exchange, understanding the reason for her friend's care better than the mystified sergeant could without the context of knowing Sarah Jennifer's past. She waved and called to distract Sarah Jennifer. "Look who I found haunting the mess hall?"

Ezekiel went beet-red. "I wanted to eat a good breakfast before we left. Linus told me everything I need to know about ship's rations."

Sarah Jennifer laughed. "Oh, yeah? What did he tell you?"

"That he can't keep his mouth shut, so everyone has to put up with his terrible cooking whenever the pack is on a deployment," Ezekiel replied, his face a picture of innocence. "Well, he didn't say 'terrible,' exactly. His cursing isn't very imaginative."

"He doesn't get much opportunity to practice," Sarah Jennifer informed him with a wry grin. "I don't approve of cursing without good reason."

"You must find Mrs. Shutov a delight," Ezekiel ventured with a chuckle.

"Don't tell Linus, but everyone is sick of his cooking," Sarah Jennifer confided, keeping her opinion on Irina's extensive alternative lexicon to herself.

"Or sick *from* his cooking," Dinny quipped as they

handed him their bags to be stowed in the luggage compartment.

"That, too," Sarah Jennifer agreed regretfully. "Rider has KP this trip."

She was about to ask how Ezekiel had already acquired enough belongings to fill two bags when she saw that the one slung over his back belonged to Esme. "Where is Lucy?" she asked instead.

"Jana took her to the airbase yesterday," Ezekiel answered somewhat glumly.

Esme nodded to confirm. "I saw them onto the bus. The child was happy to be given that apprenticeship. I don't think we'll find her stowing away again."

"She knows enough about antigrav tech to teach a class. Learning the ropes at the motor pool should keep her busy until I feel comfortable allowing her into the field." Sarah Jennifer ruffled Ezekiel's hair. "How are you feeling about returning to New Romanov?"

Ezekiel shrugged out from under her hand. "I wish Lucy was coming with us. I'm going to miss the library."

"You'll get a chance to see her before we leave," Esme reminded him, setting off down the steps to board Bluebird. "Besides, you have your datapad and enough books in your bag."

His bag was *all* books. Ezekiel tucked himself into a corner with one of them when they set off while everyone chatted around him. His mind skated over the hand-drawn diagrams without absorbing the information, caught up in processing his tangled feelings about going back home.

Hungry for knowledge, his love of reading had drawn him to Salem Library, where he'd found Lucy poring over engineering texts in the reading room. Being the only Were in her age group to choose an engineering track had taken Lucy off the rotation for advanced PT and placed her firmly in the library under the watchful eye of Billy Hawkins and his apprentices.

The library housed all the printed material the salvage and reclamation committee had found over the years, plus all the handwritten instructional manuals, stories, almanacs, maps, and everything else the people submitted to the library. Billy personally processed every new manuscript that came into the repository. The majority hadn't yet been digitized, and although the librarians had been working on it since they'd regained computer technology, Billy could often be heard in the dusty silence exclaiming with equal parts of adoration and fury that preserving it all was an impossible task. Whether it was fiction, instructional, or writing for the sake of it, he deemed knowledge and art equally valuable to the resurrection of society.

In short, Ezekiel was in heaven, and Lucy was there every afternoon to share it with him. Consequently, the two of them had formed a bond over the last two weeks while the librarians guided their reading. His only friend before he came here had been Curtis, and they were very different in personality. Curtis wanted to be a guard when he grew up, much like Lucy's packmates, who had their hearts set on the business end of the Defense Force.

New Romanov felt like the past.

The transfer to the *Enora* went quickly once they arrived at the airbase in Boston. Sarah Jennifer allowed Ezekiel to find Lucy to say farewell but not goodbye. She had their route to discuss with Enora before they left, and she intended to call ahead to let Lilith and Olaf know they were inbound.

Ezekiel was hanging around her cabin door when she got there.

"What's up?" Sarah Jennifer inquired. "You haven't run out of books already?"

Ezekiel snickered. "No. I came to talk."

Sarah Jennifer shooed him away. "Then make like bamboo, kiddo."

Ezekiel's eyebrows met in confusion.

Sarah Jennifer jerked a thumb toward the cabins. "Split. I've got work to do. Come see me after I've made the announcements after takeoff."

She got comfortable at her desk and called Lilith. There was a slight delay before she picked up.

"Sarah Jennifer, what a pleasant surprise."

"Really?" Sarah Jennifer laughed. "We're on our way to New Romanov. Ezekiel is with us. I'm planning to leave him with you while we're in Norrköping."

"I *am* rather fond of the boy," Lilith remarked. "He will be welcome company."

Sarah Jennifer recalled Lilith's amusement when Ezekiel had confided in her about his dreams. "I wanted to ask you about something. Have you been playing in his head?"

"His parents came to me after he used magic for the

first time," Lilith told her. "I did what I could when he was alone and in need. It wasn't much."

"Bet you weren't expecting him to be the key to curing the Madness," Sarah Jennifer replied.

Lilith's laughter crackled over the line. "Well, no. Esme tells me he has more than one ability."

"He's responding well to a magic-focused approach," Sarah Jennifer told her. "He just needs to watch someone use their ability and he can replicate it. He wants to help rebuild the world when he's grown. All of his abilities will come in useful."

"His intelligence is a great blessing," Lilith agreed. "He might enjoy being included in the work to unravel the reason for his immunity."

Sarah Jennifer smiled. Lilith's assessment of Ezekiel's intelligence was spot-on. She would be interested to hear the Kurtherian's reaction to his philosophy. "He has some interesting ideas of his own about that. Has Olaf returned to town yet?"

"He arrived three days ago," Lilith informed her. "He's in town at the moment. I expect he will return to the mountain once he sees you have arrived."

"Good. I don't want to delay. The sooner we get the climate module issue diagnosed and repaired, the sooner we can focus on making headway with the Madness."

Sarah Jennifer signed off after chatting for a little longer. It would be a fine thing if she had time to join the effort to decode the mystery of Ezekiel's nanocytes. However, she knew she would have to return to her role as the head of the Defense Force once the climate control system was repaired.

She had the fleeting idea that her cynicism about the reliability of technology was the root cause of her challenges with manipulating the Etheric. She believed in people, not shortcuts, although in this case, the technology that had caused so much damage to the planet was the only thing that could reverse it.

Everything and everyone had a weak point.

Hers was faith.

Contrary to Esme's assumption that she believed too much in technology, Sarah Jennifer had too much experience to believe in anything that was supposedly infallible. Returning the planet to a pre-Industrial Eden was Bethany Anne's objective. Magic was her gift to the world. Sarah Jennifer meant to see that humanity received it as the Queen had intended, which meant providing support for the communities living on the ice while the planet underwent its vicissitudes.

For the remainder of the journey, she worked on the details of her contingencies for the most likely scenarios to emerge in the aftermath of the repairs.

Earth hadn't seen a warming event like this since the last Industrial age, when the atmosphere had been so choked with every pollutant known to man that temperatures soared, melting billions of tons of ice per year. Esme's retelling, backed up by the database containing thousands of years of climate models provided by Bethany Anne, painted a picture of the other extreme: rising sea levels and the ice caps shrinking to a fraction of the size needed to maintain optimal global temperatures.

That break-up had happened gradually over more than a century, and it had been disastrous. The changes she was going to set in motion would take no more than a decade to complete, and although the climate control system would make those changes while suppressing rogue weather systems, tsunamis, and forest fires, a lot of people were going to be displaced while the coastal areas were reconfigured.

Beringia was the largest landmass they were going to lose. However, it was only around a fifth of the total the software predicted would vanish once the ice cap had been reduced to its optimal size. Sea levels around the world were going to surge from the rapid melt, reclaiming much of the land that had been uncovered during its formation.

Sarah Jennifer liked the names the ancients had given these lost lands well enough to resurrect them for the purpose of her planning. The local names were close enough in most cases. From the west coast of the former Danelaw, Doggerland to Storegga and Verdronken, the islands ringing Germany's coast would vanish beneath the waves again, as Zealandia in the southern hemisphere drowned and Indonesia was emancipated from the Australian coast. Greenland and Iceland would be freed, along with Newfoundland and the surrounding islands. Japan would become individual islands again, separating from the Korean coast as Beringia receded.

Sarah Jennifer expected the Defense Force to be fully occupied with providing humanitarian relief, while those who specialized in nanocytes figured out how to reverse the Madness. As her grandfather often said, amateurs talked tactics, professionals talked logistics. Preparation was key, as always.

While the pack was here to tackle the climate module,

the First and Second Airborne Divisions were in Boston, racking up hours in the flight simulators to train for the Pods being built for them at Spires Shipyard a few million light-years away. The infantry units awaited her word, ready to serve the people by transporting them and their belongings through Mad-infested lands to their new homes.

Her plans for avoiding conflict between displaced peoples consisted of locating suitable land for them to relocate to, establishing towns and cities, identifying the leaders of the groups coming in, and helping them to form provisional governments where needed, without getting involved with how they decided to run their lives.

Wherever they were needed, there they would be. Humanity would not just hold on but rise, stronger than ever.

CHAPTER NINETEEN

There was no welcoming committee waiting for the pack when they arrived at New Romanov. The streets were empty of the usual bustle, the market bare of its regular vendors.

Sarah Jennifer had everyone on board the *Enora* stand by while she headed for the town hall, where she found Ada Kuznetsova, the current mayor, pacing restlessly.

The mayor started when she saw Sarah Jennifer enter the hall. "Major Walton!"

Sarah Jennifer took in Ada's flustered expression and the wisps of steel-gray hair escaping her usually immaculate bun. "What happened? Where is everyone?"

"They went to fight off the Mad," Ada informed her worriedly. "Olaf burst in early this morning and took every fighter we have out the west gate after telling us to stay inside."

That explained why they hadn't seen anything on their way in. The west gate led almost directly into the forest surrounding New Romanov.

Sarah Jennifer thanked Ada and returned to the airship at a knee-rattling run, calling ahead to have Enora prepare to lift off as soon as she was back on board.

Ezekiel was waiting when Sarah Jennifer got back to the airship. "What's happening?"

"Mad attack," Sarah Jennifer told him without stopping on her way to the armory.

Ezekiel trailed behind her, staying on his toes to avoid getting crushed in the narrow corridor. "I want to help."

"You can help by staying here," Sarah Jennifer stated firmly as she pulled her armor on over her fatigues. She lifted a finger as Ezekiel made to argue. "You're wasting time. I have to get ready. No arguments. Wait with Mayor Ada until we get back."

Ezekiel's face worked as his emotions spiked. He threw a frustrated glare at Sarah Jennifer and spun on his heel, muttering angrily as he stalked in the direction of the exit.

"Enora, make sure he leaves the ship," Sarah Jennifer called. "Kid is crazy if he thinks I'm going to take a child into the middle of a Mad incursion."

"He is inside the walls," Enora confirmed a few moments later.

"Then let's roll." Rifle in hand, Sarah Jennifer eased past Dinny, Rory, and Theor and descended the ladder to the cargo bay, where the pack was assembling as the airship closed on Olaf's location.

Enora opened the drop doors on Sarah Jennifer's command, which let in a blast of bitter winter air and the sounds of a nearby battle. Sarah Jennifer leaned out and spied Olaf among the tangle of combatants in a valley where the trees thinned and the land rose sharply, the jutting ledges and snow-covered cliffs casting deep shadows. "Get us as close as you can," she called to Enora.

Another barked command from Sarah Jennifer saw the pack leap out of the drop doors in groups of seven as the airship hovered over the valley. The final group landed at a run with Sarah Jennifer and Brutus in the lead, fanning out to join the fight without hesitation.

The men and women of the New Romanov Guard were surrounded on three sides. The narrow ribbon of open space between the forest and the sharp slope was asphyxiated with snarling Mad. Armed with blades and bows, the warriors risked infection with every strike, yet they fought with the fervor of crusaders. They wore full-face leather masks under their helmets to prevent accidental splashback from getting into their mouths, and coarse-wrought mail covered the boiled leather armor where it joined at their hands, arms, and necks.

If a particularly pernicious Mad got close enough to lock its jaws on a guard, all it received for its trouble was a mouthful of rough metal before it was decapitated.

Olaf scattered the pieces of the Mad as he tore them limb from limb without a care. The bear warrior had created a wide circle around him. The Mad, not being the brightest of bulbs, weren't put off by the onslaught of projectiles he was creating from their companions. He was making so much mess that the human fighters had moved away to avoid slipping in the hazardous blood slick pooling in the slurry he was churning up with his massive paws.

Sarah Jennifer didn't need Esme's assistance to connect to the Etheric. It opened to her as she clicked into battle mode. The wind whispered to her, offering its currents as an extension of her senses. She got to work thinning the masses of Mad while more came from the forest surrounding them.

Brutus yelled to be heard over the clamor. "Where are they all coming from?"

"I don't know, but they're not getting out of this alive," Sarah Jennifer vowed, moving to cover a trio of guards who were hacking their way through the red-eyed monsters.

The guttural cries of the Mad falling to the living echoed in the valley, punctuated by ringing steel and the deafening reports of the pack's rifles. Time lost its hold on the combatants, and the heat was a myth. This was pure muscle memory, cold, calm, and collected. The guards fell in with the pack, warriors hardened by fifteen years of giving their all to protect their beloved town from the Madness working side by side with the Weres. The resulting force was twice as deadly and thrice more effective than either group was alone.

This was humanity, banding together against the unrelenting hunger of the Mad.

The tables turned as they pushed the Mad back against the slope. Trapped by a curl of overhanging rock, the Mad attacked without care, their instinct to feed on the living having long overwritten such things as self-preservation or situational awareness. Nevertheless, they retained enough cunning to make it a real fight.

Sarah Jennifer's heart beat steadily, her mind clear with

her singular purpose and her actions dictated by decades of training. She dipped to avoid a swiping hand and turned to fire in a smooth arc, six shots for the six Mad moving on a quartet of guards fighting back to back with Katia and Linus. The head of the sixth exploded in a fine mist as she gutted the one that had managed to slip under her guard with her knife. Sidestepping, she jerked her blade free and slammed it in to the hilt between the Mad's eyes before moving on.

The wind warned Sarah Jennifer about the shifting snow high above on the slope a few seconds before the underlying snowpack gave way and dropped the over-burden in a deadly slide down the incline toward the overhang.

"*Avalanche!*" Esme yelled, sensing the collapse at the same time. "*Retreat!*"

Esme did what she could to slow the inexorable advance of the snow while the living scattered into the forest, but she was no master of gravity. She threw up a canted rock barrier a few hundred feet into the forest instead, aiming her magic to erect the shelter out of the path of the avalanche. "Follow me!" she screamed to be heard above the wind.

The living flocked to Esme and they ran to the angled construction and huddled underneath as the avalanche gained speed, gobbling up everything in its path. Boulders the size of buses were swept up by the rolling snow. It tore straggling pines on the slope out by the roots, ground rocks and ice chunks smashing them to matchsticks within seconds of being picked up.

The Mad had no clue that the rolling wave of death was

coming for them. Their fleeing prey had vanished from sight and the muffled roar of thundering snow caught their attention too late. Without the presence of mind to swim upward, they were pulverized by the untold tons of snow and loose rock pouring loudly over the edge of the overhang. The mixture of snow and pulverized detritus sprayed in all directions on impact with the valley floor, accompanied by a resounding boom that sucked the sound from the air as the deadly rush continued to surge toward the tree line.

The avalanche's progression was only slightly arrested when it met the closely clustered trees at the edge of the forest. The ancient pines were buried, the snow packing the spaces between the trunks whose roots were too wide and deep to be torn from the ground. Visibility beyond the forest's edge was cut to nothing, the sudden whiteout adding to the unreality.

Sarah Jennifer called the wind to push the tumult over the top of their shelter, trapping them inside the air pocket that formed as a result of the angle at which Esme had pulled the rock from the earth.

The ground shook as the wave continued overhead. Inside the air pocket, they listened nervously to the crackle and crunch of the snow compacting under its own weight.

Esme manifested an energy ball to light their shelter. The soft white glow revealed the determined faces of the pack, the less certain expressions of the guards, and the shining white ass of the werebear in human form.

"Put some pants on, for the Matriarch's sake," one of the guards begged.

"We're buried alive, and the thing that offends you is my bare backside?" Olaf retorted with a hearty laugh.

"This isn't anybody's grave," Brutus assured the group. "Esme, please tell me you have something in that bag of yours Olaf can cover his junk with."

Esme produced the clothing Olaf had dropped in the valley. "You ought to bundle up, bucko. Or do you like creating a stir with the ladies?"

"There are no ladies here." Katia guffawed. "Just Olaf's bare ass getting chapped by the cold."

"The snow will become ice in a matter of minutes," Olaf announced, accepting his clothing with a nod of thanks. "Can your magic get us out of here?"

"That's the plan," Esme replied. "But we'll want to let it settle before we start digging our way out, else we might get buried for real."

"Training prepared us for this," Reg commented. The taciturn Were's voice echoed softly in the faux chamber.

"Remind me of that the next time I feel like punching David," Bruiser told him.

The air pocket was warm enough not to be unpleasant if they ignored the disquiet the weight of the rapidly-forming ice caused as it creaked and groaned above them. Everyone made themselves comfortable for the time being. The guard who had teased Olaf turned out to be Curtis' father Harald. He was also the head of the Guard, and his quiet humor did much to lift everyone's spirits while they waited for Esme to decree it safe to start digging.

Sarah Jennifer sat cross-legged next to Esme while Harald shared a story from before the Madness. She blocked the tale of spooky forests and pirates as she tuned into the frequency of the ice with her friend's assistance.

Her senses extended to their fullest, Sarah Jennifer felt herself merge with her surroundings. She was simultaneously flesh and bone, a beating heart and rushing blood, and innumerable layers of frozen crystalline ice. She was each individual crystal. She was the air squeezed out of the gaps as the layers compressed under pressure.

Esme was there, her presence larger than the ice in Sarah Jennifer's mind.

Almost time. Esme's mental voice came from all around.

I can feel it, Sarah Jennifer marveled. *I'm...connected. If I kept pushing out, I could touch the whole world.*

Easy, Esme cautioned. *Get too connected and you'll forget you have a body to come back to.*

Sarah Jennifer's consciousness retracted in shock. "What?"

She reddened when her audible exclamation cut into Harald's story and everyone looked at her expectantly. "It's nothing. Time to go. Everyone, make some room for Esme to work."

Obediently, the group moved back from the wall. Esme glanced at Sarah Jennifer, her eyes glowing with gold light. "Redirect the melt so we get some traction on the climb."

"What about support?" Olaf asked. "Won't the tunnel cave in if it gets too warm?"

Esme shook her head. "I'll keep the heat localized. Sarah Jennifer will make sure the surrounding ice retains its integrity as we pass."

Sarah Jennifer put aside the fear of losing herself and reconnected to the Etheric energy permeating the ice. Her eyes shone red, the light of life and heat, bright and pure. There was no mistaking it for the Madlight, the dull and dismal tone of decay that marked the infected.

Esme stood a step away from the ice wall and held up glowing hands radiating heated Etheric energy. The ice began to melt, slowly at first, but picking up speed. A hollow six feet by four feet opened in the ice and Esme took a step forward, the glow from her hands expanding to envelop her entire body.

The crystals released their bonds and formed a stream beneath their feet in their hurry to escape Esme. Sarah Jennifer redirected the runoff, guiding the water in criss-crossing runnels that froze as they left the bubble of heat Esme was exuding.

"Stay together," she directed as Esme carved an escape tunnel. "Keep moving."

The only sounds for the next thirty minutes were the shuffling of boots on rough ice and the ever-present groans and creaks amplified by the tunnel. Twice they paused when the tunnel behind them caved in. Each time, Esme stopped excavating and assisted Sarah Jennifer with shoring up the section where they were standing.

The ice took on an eerie cast as they got closer to the surface, pallid winter light leaching through to let them know the wind on the surface was high. The long night had not yet arrived at these lower latitudes, something everyone there was grateful for as they emerged into a gathering snowstorm.

Since there were too many to fit on the airship, Sarah Jennifer sent the *Enora* ahead to New Romanov to warn that they were returning exhausted but uninjured.

Ezekiel latched onto Sarah Jennifer with a rib-crushing hug when she walked through the west gate at the tail end of the group.

The major leaned into the embrace, taking as much comfort as Ezekiel was receiving. He wasn't hers, but she was starting to think of him that way.

"I was worried when you didn't come back," Ezekiel admonished. "Where were you?"

"There was an avalanche," Linus cut in as he walked in through the gate.

Ezekiel's eyes snapped back to Sarah Jennifer, who nodded.

"Nothing we couldn't handle," she assured him. "It took care of the Mad, anyway."

Ezekiel's brows knitted in consternation. "I should have been there. You're not leaving me behind when you go to Norrköping."

He stared at Sarah Jennifer, impervious to the hairy eyeball she gave his imperious tone. "You're all I have. You can't leave me behind."

Ezekiel.

Lilith's voice in his mind pulled him up sharply.

"Who said that?"

Sarah Jennifer had heard Lilith as well. "That would be our friendly local Oracle."

It is time for us to meet, Lilith intoned.

"Me?" Ezekiel's face lost its color, and his knees turned to jelly.

Sarah Jennifer put an arm around his shoulders to steady him. "Lilith is the only member of our family you haven't met in person. Come on, kiddo. I'll walk you there."

Ezekiel followed Sarah Jennifer out of New Romanov in a daze. All his life, the Oracle had been more like a myth than a living entity to him. The stories of her actively helping the people of New Romanov long ago belonged to bedtimes and childhood. He'd never expected to go to the mountain where she resided, let alone talk to her.

Sarah Jennifer gave him space to overcome his starstruck awe. His plea had struck a nerve, and her thoughts were clouded with colliding statements. Her upbringing had given her firm ideas about what it took to care for a child, even one who was fast approaching adulthood, but she had no precedent to guide her decisions when it came to magic-wielding prodigies. Was she selfish to want to keep him by her side? Fooling herself to think his magic made him less vulnerable than any other teenager?

No. She wasn't that feckless. If she could be swayed by potential, Lucy would be here with them. Ezekiel was already powerful and had a natural talent for picking up new forms of magic as fast as Esme could teach them to him. He was curious and delighted by new ideas. She wanted to show him the world as it was now and as it would be when she was done remaking it in Bethany Anne's name. She didn't want to leave him behind any more than he wanted to be left. If she took him along everywhere she went, he would be in constant danger, yet how could she take on the raising of him if she was never home?

They walked in unstrained silence, each preoccupied with their own inner world as they approached the mountain.

Ezekiel snapped out of it when they reached the foot of the mountain and he was suddenly immersed in buzzing energy. With a thought, flames ignited to cover his hands as he looked around for the source. Seeing there was no attack imminent, he released the fireballs to fizzle away. "What is that?"

Sarah Jennifer smiled. "Etheric static is the closest I can describe it. Lilith's machine uses an enormous amount of energy. Those sensitive to the Etheric can feel the buildup around the mountain."

Ezekiel fell silent once more as they entered the mountain through the largest of the dozen openings. He was surprised to see electric lightbulbs this far from Salem. "Did the Defense Force put these lamps here?"

"They were here long before WWDE," Sarah Jennifer replied as they started down the ramp that led into the tunnel.

Ezekiel trailed his fingers along the smoothly bored wall as they walked toward the large rectangular chamber. When they entered, his gaze was immediately captured by a huge black box of the same shape in the center of the cavern, the lights blinking in sequence on the sides captivating him. He took three steps toward the black box before remembering where he was, then sank to his knees and pressed his palms and forehead to the floor. "O Oracle, it is my great honor to serve you."

"Rise, young Ezekiel," Lilith replied from the speakers. "For it is my honor to serve humanity."

He scrambled to his feet, his eyes wide with wonder. "How is it that you live, yet reside in this box?" he asked. "I cannot believe you are an artificial intelligence like Enora."

"I have much to teach you should you care to learn," Lilith told him.

"What do you know about magic?" Ezekiel blurted, his shyness forgotten.

Lilith's chuckle warmed Sarah Jennifer, and she patted the casing. "I'm going to leave you two to get acquainted. Call if you need me. I'll be in the comm room."

A section of the wall slid back at Lilith's command, and Sarah Jennifer slipped away to check on the status of the shipping containers in orbit.

There was a blinking icon on her message board when she logged on to the communication network and connected to the EI controlling the shipping containers. She opened it and found detailed instructions from Ted attached to the container manifest.

She skimmed the message, noting that she was the only one who could open the containers. Another decision: leave them where they were, or have them set down at the starting point of their route into Norrköping?

She elected to leave them where they were for the moment and spent the next hour familiarizing herself with the equipment's specs while Lilith got to know Ezekiel.

Ezekiel knocked on the wall before entering. "Can I stay here while you're in Norrköping?"

Sarah Jennifer looked up from the console. "I thought you wanted to come with us?"

"Changed my mind," Ezekiel responded with a grin. "It

could be a while before I return. I'd like to spend a few days with Lilith."

"Works for me." Sarah Jennifer ruffled his hair on her way out of the room, laughing when he grumbled at the affection. "Let's see about getting some camping gear up here for you."

CHAPTER TWENTY

Mount Bråviken, Norrköping

Ezekiel had everything he needed to live comfortably in Lilith's cavern for twelve days, although Sarah Jennifer didn't expect to be gone for more than eight. She was ready for anything after the disaster in Snøhvit, as was the pack. David was uncharacteristically cheerful, considering he'd been reticent about leaving the fort.

The *Enora* swooped over the tallest peak in the range, slowing as the shipping containers descended through the clouds. Their landing site was in the pass over the mountain large enough to accommodate the airship's wingspan, no easy task to reach in storm conditions. It was not the nearest pass to the ground station, but the level pass was a stone's throw from the settlement they'd located during their reconnaissance.

Enora had programmed the local dialect into the comm for easy communication. Sarah Jennifer was curious to meet the kind of people who could flourish in this harshest of environments.

The arrival of the *Enora* attracted the attention of the mountain-dwellers. People swathed in furs and thick woolen clothing gathered at the mouth of the cave to watch as Sarah Jennifer, Esme, Brutus, David, Theor, and Olaf exited the airship.

A strong-featured woman with wire-bound copper hair as thick and glossy as the furs she wore extracted herself from the crowd and came forward to meet them with her hand hovering over the broadsword on her belt. "Which one of you is Major Walton?" she demanded, scanning the group with narrowed eyes.

Sarah Jennifer extended a hand, smiling internally at the shrewd look on the woman's face. "That's me. I hope you found the supplies we sent useful."

The woman's eyes narrowed as she turned her attention to their weapons. "We didn't open the crate. No such thing as a gift from strangers in this world. What do you people want from us?"

Are they thinking about attacking us? Sarah Jennifer asked Esme.

No, Esme replied. *But I have a feeling this won't go easy. Mountains are immovable. Stands to reason the people here are as hard as the rock that surrounds them.*

Sarah Jennifer dropped her hand. "The supplies don't come with any strings attached. We're here to repair the machinery that's causing this perpetual winter. When we came to survey the area where the machinery is located, we saw you were cut off and had Mad in the area. Leaving you what food we had and a way to call for help if you needed it was the right thing to do."

A murmur passed through the crowd.

"You didn't know we gave you a way to contact the outside world?" Brutus asked.

"Like I said, we didn't open the box." The woman glanced over her shoulder at the people, assessing their mood. "What do you say?"

"Brittvi Thanesdottir, where is your hospitality?" a man called. "Look at their weapons. If they wanted to force their way in, there's nothing we could do about it. Let them in."

He shouldered his way to the front and offered his hand first to Sarah Jennifer, then the others. "Harald Leifssen. Welcome to our home."

"I know a Harald," Brutus offered as an icebreaker. "Fierce sword fighter. You look to be a man who swings a blade well yourself."

Harald produced a pair of well-worn axes from his furs and held the razor-sharp blades to the light. "You guess right. You'll forgive Brittvi's suspicious nature. Our future thane looks out for us a little too well at times."

Brittvi sighed, mumbling under her breath as she turned back to Sarah Jennifer. "My husband, the optimist."

Sarah Jennifer swallowed the stab of grief. "I had one just like him once upon a time. Cherish him."

Brittvi scrutinized Sarah Jennifer as if wondering how long ago that could have been. "I do." She left it alone at her husband's urging and led them into the mountain after Sarah Jennifer had given the rest of the pack permission to debark.

The people closed around them, chatting in high spirits as they walked down a torchlit tunnel into a wide cavern whose vaulted roof sported stalactites.

Sarah Jennifer's gaze swept the path as they progressed deeper into the mountain, taking in the furs and other heavy clothing the people wore. She saw young children peering curiously from lamplit apertures in the upper walls, and older ones who looked at her, Brutus, and the others with a mixture of suspicion and longing.

Brittvi took them to a group of large buildings that stood free of the cavern wall. "Major Walton, come with me. The rest of you stay here. Harald will see you fed and watered."

"It would be my honor to feast our guests!" a rotund man called, flinging open the doors to his cavern. He twirled his mustache and bowed deeply. "Welcome to my humble establishment. Nothing but the finest food and ale in the mountain leaves my kitchen."

"There's nothing humble about you, Presario," Harald bellowed, laughing as he clapped the man on the back. "But your cooking more than makes up for it."

Brittvi shook her head in amusement as the pack piled into the tavern. She indicated for Sarah Jennifer to follow her into the maze of stone-walled buildings that populated the floor of the cavern.

The light was low, provided by the thin coat of soft-glowing lichen covering every wall. Every window had a thriving planter. Every roof and ledge had a gutter with drainpipes leading to sturdy water butts. Businesses gave way to homes, homes to areas assigned to leisure or agriculture.

"How long have your people been here?" Sarah Jennifer asked.

"Three generations. Since the mountain was born. My

great-grandmother was the first Thane," Brittvi informed her proudly. "Somehow, she knew the winter was coming. She told my mother she saw the sky light up in all directions. Evil lights, she called them. She believed the gods despaired of us and tore open the universe to teach us to live better."

Sarah Jennifer shouldn't have been surprised. WWDE had affected the whole world. She wondered if that was what had triggered the problem with the climate module.

"People began getting sick," Brittvi continued. "Winter came and did not pass. When news of a mountain being raised in the bay reached her village, she persuaded her people to leave with her and start a new life inside the mountain, where they would be protected from the ravages of winter. Her actions saved her village and all the people they picked up on their pilgrimage here."

They arrived at a building that was set apart from the rest by a curving lake. The cavern roof was low here, and the stalactites behind the building dipped their tips in the shining lake, its surface capturing the lichen's glow and transforming the gaps between the rock into gently shimmering fae portals. They crossed the bridge to the island, Brittvi diverting to give Sarah Jennifer a close view of the statue that was the central feature of the rock garden.

"That's Agatha, my great-grandmother," Brittvi told Sarah Jennifer, appreciating her interest.

Sarah Jennifer studied a stern face that looked a lot like Brittvi's. "She looks like a formidable woman."

Brittvi chuckled. "That goes for all the women in my family. We're a cantankerous bunch, Major."

Sarah Jennifer could have said the same about her

family. She hoped she'd found a friend in Brittvi like she had in Amelie. Women were destined to reshape the world, it seemed. They had enough common ground to work from. "If we're going to be allies, you can call me Sarah Jennifer."

"That will depend on my mother, Major," Brittvi replied with a wink and a smile.

She knocked three times on the door.

A solemn-faced youth opened the door and stood back to admit them without saying a word, although his eyes widened slightly when he saw Sarah Jennifer.

Brittvi walked past without acknowledging the boy. "This way."

Sarah Jennifer followed her inside and down a short corridor to another stolid youth guarding another door. Sarah Jennifer wondered why the thane needed guards in her home as he opened the door to reveal a brightly lit room beyond, where a group of men and women were engaged in a spirited argument around a rectangular table. Seeing him fumble the shiny and unused sword at his waist as he returned to his post clued her in to the ceremonial nature of his position.

Ah, politics. Sarah Jennifer was less than amused to notice the crate she'd left taking up one-third of the room since the topic of discussion appeared to be how the council was going to divide what little food they had stored among the people in the coming weeks.

A woman who looked a lot like Brittvi sat at the head of the table, her fingers laced and her mouth set in a tight line while the others tossed barbed insults at each other. Her silver braids were contained by a gold circlet, and another thick band of intricately-worked gold encircled her upper arm, marking her as the thane.

"Silence," she stated without raising her voice. "We have an outsider among us."

Everyone at the table turned to stare at Sarah Jennifer. She bore their scrutiny with dignity.

"You brought a stranger here?" a white-bearded man demanded of Brittvi in an accusatory tone.

"You wanted to know when the people who sent that box came back," Brittvi informed them. She waved Sarah Jennifer forward. "Mother, this is Major Sarah Jennifer Walton. Major Walton, Reika, Thane of the Mountain."

"Merry meet." Sarah Jennifer offered the traditional Salem greeting with feeling. "I'm sorry we didn't have time to stop and introduce ourselves the last time we were here. The supplies were meant to help you get through until it was safe to hunt again. I hope the last few weeks haven't taken too much of a toll on your people."

The man who'd spoken narrowed his eyes in skeptical scrutiny. "We give any walking dead who come through this way true death," he told her bitterly, eyeing the pistol on her hip. "Protecting ourselves from them would be a damn sight easier if we had some of those guns you're carrying."

Sarah Jennifer eyed the man, wondering what he knew about guns. "I'm not an arms dealer. Nothing I can do about the Mad except come when you call, which means you accept the radio." She didn't bother to sugarcoat the offer or appease the disappointment she saw in their eyes. "Open the crate. You need the food."

Reika flicked a finger at the youthful guard. He hurried

over to the crate and opened it, retrieving a wrapped brick. "Why did you leave us supplies?"

"We were concerned about your safety when your community didn't join the radio network."

Reika peeled back the wrapper and sniffed, her brow furrowing when she found the sachets of flavoring.

"It's reconstituted protein," Sarah Jennifer told her. "Tastes like chicken or beef, depending on how you prepare it.

"We don't get many visitors on the mountain," Reika stated pointedly, handing the package back to the guard with a nod. "Those who make it this far up usually have a motive beyond passing through. Danelaw soldiers, for example."

Sarah Jennifer let her distaste show, wondering if this was going to be how it was wherever she went in this part of the world—communities closing in on themselves because of Sidric's propensity for using violence to control people. "The Danelaw has been disbanded. Sidric is dead."

That got a reaction. Half the people around the table cheered, while the other half bombarded her with demands for proof.

"Proof, HAH!" Brittvi scoffed, her brash laugh cutting through the argument that broke out. "His men didn't come looking for their tithe this season, did they? What other proof do you expect? That maggot is dead, all right."

Sarah Jennifer hadn't been expecting Brittvi's support. "Well, thanks."

"I didn't say I believe you killed him," Brittvi told her.

"It wasn't me," Sarah Jennifer clarified. "It was Amelie, the trade mistress at Upinniemi. Sidric made the mistake of raiding her wedding feast. He killed her father and her husband's father, and she fed him to the sharks in revenge."

"I like her already," Brittvi commented.

"This could be one of Sidric's ploys," the man argued. The others murmured in quiet agreement. He puffed his chest out, validated by the support.

"Sidric's men come on foot," Brittvi cut in before Sarah Jennifer had a chance to reply. "*They* came out of the sky in a strange metal ship."

"Hafþór, still your tongue," Reika ordered. She returned her cool gaze to Sarah Jennifer.

Seeing the direct approach was getting her somewhere, Sarah Jennifer slipped the pack from her back and retrieved the printed maps she'd brought for the settlement. Reika's stern expression melted when Sarah Jennifer put the maps on the table.

"Trade routes are opening up, supported by alliances. These maps chart the protected land routes and shipping lanes that have been set up, now there's no danger from the Danelaw. That's not all." Resigning herself to whatever came from this meeting, Sarah Jennifer went on to explain the situation with the climate control system and what that meant for everyone living in the affected areas.

Reika listened with an open mind. At any rate, she didn't come at Sarah Jennifer with the broadsword leaning against her chair. "We are aware that some magic divides the land to the south," the thane agreed. "I remember summer on the mountain when I was a child. You say your people have the means to end the winter?"

Sarah Jennifer nodded, relieved to have reason met

with acceptance. "Norrköping is ground zero for the issue. We're here to make the repairs. That's how we found you."

"So, this visit is not out of concern for us," Brittvi commented acidly.

Sarah Jennifer lifted a shoulder. "My concern is for all of humanity. The Mad, the walking dead—I've heard so many names for them this last few years—are next. Does anyone here remember Bethany Anne?"

Hafþór was the only one. "The Matriarch." He flashed a huge grin when Sarah Jennifer tilted her head, his demeanor switching with his perception. "I'm a lot older than I look."

"You're Wechselbalg," she guessed.

"I was," he replied, grief bowing his already sloping shoulders. "Long ago."

"Hafþór was not born here," Reika informed Sarah Jennifer. "We know the legends of the Queen Bitch."

"They're not legends," Sarah Jennifer assured them, showing them how her eyes glowed. "She is out there among the stars, fighting for our freedom. All we have to do is survive until she has succeeded, but I think we can do much more than that. Humanity can thrive if we can put aside our differences. Or better yet, make the most of those differences to create a world our children will flourish in."

She walked around the table to Hafþór's seat. "You are still Were. I can give you back your...wolf?" He nodded. "If you can hold on until we've made the repairs and you're happy to leave the mountain for a short while."

Tears shone in the old man's eyes. "This can't be true."

"I swear on my honor as Alpha and the protector of the

UnknownWorld that it is," Sarah Jennifer vowed, gripping Hafþór's shoulder gently.

Reika got to her feet and came around the table to offer Sarah Jennifer her hand. "We accept your offer of alliance. We can work out the terms over a feast. Just like chicken, you say?"

Sarah Jennifer nodded as she clasped Reika's forearm, as was traditional in this part of the world. Not every community had been able to accept the truth. Every one that did was a boost to her morale. "I can't tell the difference. How many others like Hafþór are there?"

"Just me," Hafþór told her.

"What about magic?" Sarah Jennifer asked.

Everyone shook their heads. Reika smiled. "We know such wonders exist, but we have seen no magic here."

The thane opened her arms wide. "Come, we must make preparations for a feast."

Sarah Jennifer grinned. "My pack will provide the meat if you can keep the drinks flowing."

"There are reindeer a few kilometers from here this time of year," Reika informed her.

Sarah Jennifer's mouth watered at the mention. "I've developed a fondness for caribou meat over the years. How much can you store here? We'll bring back enough to feed everyone at the feast, and some leftover if the herd is large enough to sustain the loss."

Reika laughed long and deep. "Is that a promise?"

The pack returned to the caverns a couple of hours later, loaded down with field-dressed and butchered caribou. It wasn't long before the aroma of cooking meat was added to the music and laughter of the people celebrating the new alliance.

The lichen's glow and the firepits spaced along the lakeshore where the feast was being held provided light and warmth. There was music, people singing and dancing while Hafþór played the accordion.

Children ran underfoot wherever Sarah Jennifer looked. She left the carousing to the others and sat at one of the stone tables with Brittvi and Harald.

"You a mother?" Harald asked, seeing Sarah Jennifer tracking the little ones playing close to the water's edge.

Sarah Jennifer smiled, watching the children tumble in the surf. "I took on a fourteen-year-old earlier this year. Besides Ezekiel, my pack is the closest I'll ever get to having a child of my own."

She turned from the water, the look of understanding on Brittvi's face tugging at her heart. "I'm okay with that. I have the Defense Force and humanity to save. Bringing a new life into the world is a privilege and a tribulation I'm happy to leave to others." She almost meant it.

Harald's cheeks were pink with the ale he'd consumed. "We all have our duties. The Madness has stolen so many of our people. Every woman who takes the risk of getting pregnant is a hero in my eyes."

Brittvi punched her husband in the arm, recalling Sarah Jennifer's earlier comment. "That's enough, Harald."

Sarah Jennifer lifted a shoulder. "He's not wrong."

She sipped her ale and picked at her food, her attention

on the nearest fire, where Carver and Geordie were doing their best to join in with the chorus of the song old Hafþór was singing to the accompaniment of his accordion. It sounded much like the caribou had while dying.

"*Down came the snow. Our Agatha despaired. Until the Mountain reared its head. Those who refused to follow died. Those who did found succor inside.*"

The simple verse went well with the clapping hands and stamping feet of the revelers. Others danced arm in arm. The Weres were only getting every third word or so, but no one minded.

"You still want a guide, I'd be happy to come with you," Harald offered.

Reika joined them as others echoed Harald's offer. "Tell me more about this...what did you call it, a 'climate module?'"

"We won't know what the problem is until we get to the ground station and get eyes on it," Sarah Jennifer admitted. "Bethany Anne came back to Earth sixty-four years ago."

"I know this one!" Hafþór called, switching keys without pausing his enthusiastic playing. "*The Patriarch returned in blood and lightning. Evil ran for cover. The only thing to calm his rage. The Matriarch's return for her lover.*"

Sarah Jennifer clapped along with everyone else while Hafþór treated them to two more verses. "That's only half the story," she commented as the song ended.

Hafþór plied his instrument again. "A story for the children!" he called.

"Story! Story! Story!" the children begged, abandoning their play to gather around Sarah Jennifer's table. "Tell us about the Matriarch!"

As if she could deny their innocent faces a single thing. Sarah Jennifer pushed her plate away and shifted her position on the rock she was using as a seat. "While Bethany Anne was here, she had her people put defenses around the planet and built machines that would make Earth a paradise. Then the Matriarch and Patriarch went to the stars together to continue the fight against the evil Kurtherians. Before they left, the Matriarch gave all of humanity the gift of magic."

She paused when Hafþór produced a gentle melody to accompany her words. He flashed his grin, waving for her to continue.

Sarah Jennifer went with it, dropping her voice to add drama to her retelling. "But something went wrong. One of the machines meant to return the planet to the way it was before the World's Worst Day Ever stopped working. Worse, the Madness was coming."

Inspiration struck, and she reached out to Esme's mind. *Help me with this next part?*

The children gasped when Esme's eyes glowed. Everyone watching oohed and aahed in horrified delight as the flames came to life, forming images to match Sarah Jennifer's story. The fire threw up bright sparks that hovered and danced in the smoke, suggesting many pairs of red eyes peering from the faces of twisted wraiths.

"Nobody knew the Madness was coming except the Oracle in New Romanov. She reached out with her mind and searched for people who had the power to save humanity. She found a witch and a Were."

Salem's skyline appeared in the fire, the eyes of the Mad still crowding the space above. The only sound came from the crackling flames and the gently-lapping surf, everyone hanging on Sarah Jennifer's next words.

"The witches and Weres were not friends, but they learned to work together to keep the Madness at bay. We created the Defense Force."

Smoky figures with rifles chased down ragged red-eyed monsters. The fiery-eyed monsters vanished, replaced by a mountain wreathed in smoky clouds, and the sparks turned white, simulating snow.

Sarah Jennifer continued, "Something had gone badly wrong. Winter came and did not pass in the northern hemisphere. The ice grew year by year, covering Agatha's mountain. To the north, the ice swallowed seas whole, and the Madness came to America."

Twin embers rose into the smoke, which formed an eerily beautiful face looking down on flames that had taken on the shape of the *Enora*.

"The Matriarch!" a small child yelled, pointing her chubby finger at the twining smoke.

"Yes, the Matriarch." Sarah Jennifer smiled at the child. "She told me the Defense Force will take back the winter. To do that, we have to tunnel deep beneath the ice near Agatha's mountain."

Esme released the energy, and the vignette of Bethany Anne in the flames faded.

"What happened next?" the little girl asked.

Sarah Jennifer's smile grew. "It hasn't happened yet. When we get back, I'll finish the story."

The small girl began to cry, overcome by the late hour and the abrupt end to the enchantment. Her mother gathered her up, comforting the sleepy child with talk of warm milk and her bed.

Released from the spell, parents began gathering the younger children for bedtime. Esme excused herself after another helping of spit-roasted caribou, claiming she needed a good night's sleep after the fire display.

Sarah Jennifer accepted Reika's invitation to return to her hall, where they talked long into the night. She learned that Reika lost more hunters to the Madness than any other group since they were the only ones who left the mountain regularly.

"I know the place you're heading for," Reika told Sarah Jennifer, pouring her another drink. "There used to be towns around there. The Madness hit them hard. We took in those who made it here, of course, but those were the last. They turned within a week of arriving and killed a number of my people."

Sarah Jennifer quizzed her about the fall of the towns, getting the insight she needed on the events surrounding the arrival of the Madness in Norrköping. "What year was this?"

They worked out that the sudden onset of Madness had happened in early '200, months before Lilith had picked up on the problem.

"That's interesting," Sarah Jennifer commented, draining her cup. "Could be we're close to the epicenter."

The idea flung a shiver up her spine. She wasn't a fan of coincidences.

Reika, for her part, was fascinated by Sarah Jennifer's calm determination to slog through what to her seemed like a laundry list of the impossible. "You've made a lot of sacrifices."

Sarah Jennifer chuckled. "Top of the list being sleep. Time to call it a night."

Reika showed Sarah Jennifer to the guest quarters. "I'll allow you seven men. My son-in-law will insist on going, but I won't allow my daughter to leave the safety of the mountain."

"Knowing the situation, I'm not inclined to take anyone from the mountain," Sarah Jennifer replied. "We know the risks. We don't need to put them on your people."

Reika smiled as she turned to leave. "You're a good woman." Her voice trailed behind her.

"As are you," Sarah Jennifer murmured, eyeing the four-poster bed in the center of the room with gratitude. "People like you are why I do this."

CHAPTER TWENTY-ONE

A rare break in the snowstorm shed crisp dawn light through gaps in the clouds. It chased the lingering shadows away, lending the snow a pinkish-orange tint wherever it touched. Constantly churning thunderheads north of Mount Bråviken promised it wouldn't be long before the mountains were blanketed in fresh snow.

The pack made their way out of the caverns, eager to start the expedition.

Sarah Jennifer called the shipping container with their vehicles down from low orbit, energized by the anticipation of action and the enthusiasm of the pack. The excitement rose another notch when the shipping container touched down next to the *Enora* and they got their first look at the vehicles Felicity had sent. With a ski track in place of a front wheel, a wide, motorized track for the back, and a lightweight carbon fiber shell for protection from the elements, the two-person snow bikes were perfect for traversing the fluctuating hardness of the snowpack along their route.

Sarah Jennifer did a comm check after everyone had paired up and gotten on their bikes. "The weather is set to turn in around three hours," she informed them.

"I can hold the snow off until we get there," Esme offered, climbing on the bike behind Sarah Jennifer.

Sarah Jennifer shook her head as she flicked the starter switch. "Save your energy. We'll need it more once we get to the canyon."

"Listen up," she called once she'd confirmed everyone was ready to move. "Stay with your buddy. Maintain an open comm. Pay attention to what your HUD is telling you. It's going to be just like we practiced in Canada."

The bikes ran silently once they hit the valley below Mount Bråviken, their minimal vibration designed to allow them to pass over the changing landscape without triggering any sudden snow slides. Morale was high, helped by the ease of their passage over the rippling, windswept snow and the stark beauty of the glittering fjord they followed for the next few kilometers.

The early sun vanished before midday, the light leaching out of the land as a squall picked up in the distance. Dark clouds pressed down, wreathing the mountains in ominous shrouds. Pierced by the peaks, the clouds disgorged their contents in fitful bursts that quickly grew in intensity as the storm gained traction and wound itself into a full-blown blizzard.

Visibility was reduced further when they entered the foothills beyond the point where the fjord culminated in a frozen disc. The ice began to rise again when the salination level dropped low enough for the inlet to freeze, the snow having drifted into twenty-foot dunes leading to the mouth of the canyon.

The easy banter over the comm dried up as the squall turned nasty and the land became harsher. Their attention was focused on avoiding shards of solid ice and rock protrusions hidden under the capricious crust. Whipping winds scourged their bones despite their protective clothing, the chill somehow finding its way in through the weather shields.

The second half of the route took them into a narrow, twisting canyon formed from a maze of fissures in the looming ice.

This was the part they'd trained for in Canada.

Thirty years' worth of ice deposits and sub-zero temperatures had transformed this part of Sweden. Pressure from above and below had thrown up sheer cliffs and ragged peaks that loomed like snaggle-teeth in a cottony metallic sky. These dramatic heights were the root of Beringia.

The ground station lay some ten kilometers from the ice face.

The walls closed in, cutting the pack off from the blizzard. The air took on a quality of unreality, all sound amplified into rolling echoes. Coagulating powder spilled over the ledges above at irregular intervals, raining chunks of ice wherever the overburden gathered enough weight to disturb the denser firn beneath. Each time one of these mini-avalanches fell, the expedition ground to a halt and waited it out before digging themselves free.

All the while, the ice grew thicker, and the dense cliffs and falling snow swallowed the light long before it reached the canyon floor. Regardless, Sarah Jennifer pushed on at the head of the pack, determined to reach the ground station or whatever remained of it before the blizzard became so severe the canyon was impassable.

Esme touched Sarah Jennifer's mind, sensing her rising doubt. *If the bunker isn't there, we go to plan B.*

Sarah Jennifer didn't want to go to plan B. Plan B meant replacing the module, which sounded easy enough but in reality meant diverting resources meant for resettling people when Beringia receded.

"Hold up," Sarah Jennifer instructed when her HUD warned her about an ice-choked rockfall ahead.

The pack slowed to a stop, the tail end of the line catching up while Sarah Jennifer, Esme, and David picked through knee-deep snow to the obstacle barring their way.

"Stars, that's a big one," David asserted, extending his awareness into the collapsed rock. He groaned at the chorus of, "That's what she said," and waved the Weres back. "Give me space to work."

"Give the man some light," Sarah Jennifer called.

Everyone angled their headlights to hit the blockage. David worked to push back the rocks while Esme firmed the ice on the canyon walls to prevent another slide. They were rewarded shortly by the grinding rumble of the rock-fall moving to the sides.

David panted with effort. Sarah Jennifer monitored the new gap in the rockfall and put a hand on David's arm to let him know he was done.

"One-point-three kilometers to go," she announced as she climbed back onto her bike. "Let's roll."

They resumed their progress, and the bikes ate up the

remainder of the distance. The canyon opened gradually, the walls bowing outward as if shaped by invisible hands. Without warning, they broke through the storm's wall and emerged into the eye, where they found themselves at the edge of an abandoned town.

"This doesn't look natural," Brutus commented over the comm.

"That's because it isn't," Esme responded. "There's some kind of repulsion field. It must be pushing the ice away from the ground station."

Concentrating, Sarah Jennifer picked up...*something* coming from the Etheric. It wasn't anything like the static around Lilith's mountain. It felt unwelcoming, almost like one of Esme's barrier hexes. "I guess we know why the scans of this area were so funky."

She revved her bike. "Only one way to find out."

CHAPTER TWENTY-TWO

Sarah Jennifer resumed the lead as they entered the ruins of the town. Muddy snowdrifts were the main features of the streets. The walls of the crumbling houses had been steadily scoured by wind escaping the eyewall. The exposed buildings had been spared the worst of the perma-storm, but the wind still penetrated the abandoned town, exposing petrified roof timbers while solidified snowdrifts against the lower floors preserved the foundations.

The energy field sent shivers up their spines, and the continuous, uneasy frisson of energy put them on edge.

Sarah Jennifer kept her bike pointed in the general direction of an eroded concrete cooling tower in the center of what had by all appearances been the manufacturing quarter. The cylindrical monstrosity dominated the skyline above the warehouses, its shadow looming large, adding to the eerie atmosphere.

"Where's the ground station from here?" Brutus exclaimed in annoyance. "My HUD map is fritzing."

"It's somewhere around the power station," Sarah Jennifer informed everyone, frowning when she checked and found her HUD map was inaccessible.

"All stop," she ordered. "Mine is out too. Must be interference from the forcefield. We still have comm, right? Everyone check in and confirm comm status."

After she was satisfied that no one would be cut off, Sarah Jennifer called for a dismount. "First objective: clear the warehouses. If there are any Mad here, I want them dealt with before we move on to accessing the ground station."

Brutus peered through a hole in the wall of the nearest building, then retracted his head, having seen nothing but a pile of bones in the corner. "It feels like something terrible went down here."

"It did." Sarah Jennifer relayed everything Reika had told her the night before.

"This is the spookiest ghost town I've ever been in," Reg murmured when she was done, knowing his sentiment was shared.

The others voiced their unease, David, Carver, Rory, Rider, and Dinny the most vocal in their misgivings.

Linus and Katia scoffed, dismissing the apprehension the others felt.

Sarah Jennifer removed her gloves and clapped twice, sensing an argument brewing. The sound rebounded off the walls, the sharp echo distracting them from their imaginations. "Enough!"

They responded to her command instantly—even David, who had no pack instinct to make him obey.

"That's more like it," Sarah Jennifer told them. "Focus on facts, not wild fantasies. There are no such things as ghosts. Mad, however, will pose a problem unless you stop sucking your thumbs and get a hold on your situational awareness."

The admonishment chastened the pack. It wasn't too often Sarah Jennifer tore a strip off them these days. Their collywobbles fizzled, and where there had been a bunch of spooked Weres a moment previously, there was now a military unit primed to react to danger. She waved off their apologies. "Thank me by staying alive and uninfected. Now, move out."

Brutus, Ozzie, and Bruiser moved off with their teams, each heading for a different building on the street.

Sarah Jennifer took Esme and Katia, a smaller team, since they had Esme's magic to back them up if they ran into trouble.

"Will we be able to land the shipping containers, given the interference?" Katia wondered aloud as she made her way into the warehouse with Sarah Jennifer and Esme.

The major had the same thought. "More importantly, if we can't, will turning it off bring that storm down on our heads?"

Esme clucked as she tilted her head back to examine the shadows on the gantry overhead for the telltale red gleam of Madness. Nothing there. "That's the million-dollar question, Duckie. We should leave the clearing to the others and start looking for the bunker."

Sarah Jennifer nodded, seeing there was nothing in the warehouse for them to be concerned about. She pondered the reason for the lack of Mad in the area as they exited the building. There were skeletons aplenty. "Maybe the Mad died out here without anything to sustain them."

"More likely, they left when they'd chomped their way through everyone in town," Esme commented morosely.

"Nice, Esme," Katia complained. "That's a mental image that's going to comfort me at night."

Sarah Jennifer listened to the comm chatter as they made their way to the street where the power station was located. The others were finding much of the same. Bones aplenty, but no Mad. She recalled the teams, feeling comfortable that they were the only living beings in the area.

Close up, the eroded side of the cooling tower looked like a giant had taken a scoop out of it. The tower was adjoined by two squat interconnecting buildings offset from the curved base in an L. It was a good place to hide something in plain sight.

There were dozens of outbuildings strewn around the property. Many had retained their roofs, making it harder to pick out the one that had been put here over a hundred years later than the rest.

Sarah Jennifer's boots crunched over the tattered metal fencing surrounding the former parking lot. "Bruiser, Ozzie, take your teams and check the perimeter in case we're wrong about there being no Mad. The rest of us are looking for a smallish building that's holding up a lot better than the others. It's marked with the Queen's emblem."

The pack split up, scattering to check the outbuildings.

Sarah Jennifer almost missed it, then a flash of red on

the gray backdrop caught her eye. She moved closer. The fanged skull was tucked under the lintel of the otherwise nondescript breezeblock construction, visible to anyone who knew what they were looking for. The paint on the door still looked new.

"I've got something," she called over the comm.

"Thank fuck for that," Brutus enthused, joining her at the door and peering at the skull adorned the building with interest. "Is this here to mark the building or scare people off?"

"Both," Sarah Jennifer guessed. She put her hand on the door, not expecting it to swing outward on silent hinges at the slight touch. She stepped back in a ready stance, raising her rifle in reaction to the twisted skeletons that greeted them. Their ivory grins were not out of place against the backdrop of old blood and gore coating the walls of the room. "Doesn't look like it worked."

"Easy does it," Esme cautioned. "That mess hasn't been disturbed since it happened."

Katia pointed out the bloody scratches on the inside of the door. She was unable to hide the tremor in her hand. "I can't imagine a worse way to go."

"Hold tight. We'll give them what burial we can after we figure out what in the high heck happened here." Sarah Jennifer told her. She was more concerned about how and why the door had opened for them when the people behind it had clearly died fighting to get out. She wasn't expecting the EI to be active.

"Strong words, Major," Dinny teased. His attempt to lighten the mood didn't go down well with the others. He ducked the first snowball from Reg, only to step into the one Linus threw.

Sarah Jennifer turned and gave them the stink eye. "You three wanted guard duty? Done. Everyone else, follow me."

"You mind if I stay here and take care of this?" Katia requested, her gaze still fixed on the unfortunate dead.

Sarah Jennifer nodded. "You can keep Team Dumbass in check."

Katia let out a choked laugh as she knelt to gather the bones. "What's new?"

Sarah Jennifer turned to Esme. "What do you think? Bring the shipping containers down or wait until we've taken a look around?"

Esme pursed her lips. "Let's look around. I have everything I need to get the EI online in my pack."

Sarah Jennifer stepped over the threshold, taking comfort from the solidity of her rifle butt snugged in the hollow of her shoulder.

The square room behind the door led into a short corridor, which in turn led to a longer corridor with doors off both sides.

The pack spread out, falling into the familiar rhythm of clearing each room as they progressed deeper into the ground station. The only light came from the torches mounted on their rifles.

Suddenly and without warning, the doors slammed shut, and harsh strip lighting came on overhead. The lights pulsed erratically, and klaxons began blatting mercilessly. Only their training kept the Weres from being over-whelmed by the sudden sensory assault. David clamped his hands over his ears, yelling for the noise to stop.

"YOU HAVE ENTERED A RESTRICTED BUILDING," a voice announced from hidden speakers.

Sarah Jennifer would have been relieved the EI was still operational if he didn't sound so pissed.

"SECURITY PROTOCOLS ACTIVATED. THIRTY SECONDS UNTIL SANITATION BEGINS."

Sanitation? Sarah Jennifer lowered her rifle. "Wait! We have permission to be here."

"IDENTIFY YOURSELF AND PROVIDE AN AUTHORIZATION CODE," the EI stated. "FIFTEEN SECONDS UNTIL—"

"Major Sarah Jennifer Walton." She yelled the authorization code Bethany Anne had given her over the blaring alarms. "Authorization: Alpha-Delta-Dash-Alpha-Echo-Tango-Echo-Romeo-November-India-Tango-Alpha-Tango-Echo-Mike-Dash-One-Nine-Three-Seven-Six."

The klaxons cut out and the doors opened.

"Why didn't you just tell me the Queen sent you?" the EI bitched, his snarkiness not reduced one bit.

"Why didn't Bethany Anne tell me what a delight you are?" Sarah Jennifer responded. "We're here to fix the climate module. Do you have a name?"

"About time," the EI commented. "My name is Albert, but you can call me Albert."

"Start by telling us where the module is," Esme cut in. "We have equipment to bring in. Can't do that with the interference."

"I had to do something to keep people out," Albert retorted. "The last time humans came here, they took me offline and almost destroyed the BYPS. They terminated one another before I could take action."

Sarah Jennifer and Esme exchanged looks.

"The module is on sub-level two," Albert continued as if he hadn't just dropped a bombshell. "There is an elevator in the west wing that will take you there."

"Wait just a minute," Esme exclaimed. "Back up. What people?"

"I was offline," Albert repeated. "Unable to identify the intruders besides their names."

"So you know they were intruders," Esme pressed. "What did they do to the BYPS?"

Sarah Jennifer tugged Esme's sleeve. "Find out while we walk."

They took the elevator down to the sub-level, where they found more skeletons in the corridor.

Lights came on overhead as they entered the lab.

"Here lies Arthur Drake," Albert intoned as a spotlight came on over one of the skeletons.

The computers whirred to life, and Sarah Jennifer caught the text that appeared on one of the monitors.

I released the Madness. Please forgive me. Arthur Drake.

Her brow furrowed. That didn't make any sense. "Arthur Drake? *He* released the Madness?"

Albert's laughter sent a chill across her skin. Was this EI malfunctioning? Did he have a machine version of the Madness?

Esme caught Sarah Jennifer's eye and shook her head minutely. "Albert, enter test mode."

"Test mode activated," Albert replied tonelessly, all vestiges of personality gone.

"Run a diagnostic on your operating system," Esme

commanded. "Report on the subgoal tree structure of your personality matrix. Include out-of-tolerance variances from your original parameters and failures to prune defective alternative choices."

Sarah Jennifer left Esme to investigate the EI's possible instability. She unslung her pack and extracted her datapad and a multi-headed USB cable. She had to move Arthur's ribcage to reach the port. "Sorry, buddy," she murmured. "I have to find out what in the dickens you and your friends got up to."

The whole situation was hinky. The menus that came up on her datapad after plugging it into the server only furthered her confusion. The ground station's link to the BYPS had been severed. "Esme?"

"Albert, pause diagnostic," Esme told the EI. "What is it, Duckie?"

Sarah Jennifer tilted the datapad so Esme could see the screen. "Albert wasn't kidding about the BYPS almost being compromised. It looks like he managed to prevent a complete disaster, but not before this command was sent out. I can't make out much from the code, though. It looks like junk."

Esme took the device and scrolled through the data, her eyebrows knitting together when she reached the last commands inputted to the BYPS. "This is... Good grief. We need to switch the climate module off and get our equipment down here."

"What is it?" Sarah Jennifer asked, hardly daring to hear the answer.

"See this here? And this one? "Esme pointed at two different lines. "Put them together."

Sarah Jennifer tilted her head. Something about the instructions seemed familiar. "I've seen this in Ezekiel's blood."

"That, Duckie, is the Madness," Esme told her in a near-whisper.

CHAPTER TWENTY-THREE

"The Madness?" Sarah Jennifer leaned on the server for support. "Norrköping was Ground Zero?"

Esme handed her the datapad. "I'll need to finish Albert's diagnostic so he can fill us in, but it's looking that way."

Sarah Jennifer took the datapad and searched for the climate module menu. "You work on the EI. I'll take care of getting the shipping containers down from orbit."

Deactivating the module was as easy as selecting the relevant option and inputting the code Bethany Anne had given her.

The effect was immediate. Sarah Jennifer's shock vanished along with the interference, and her HUD came back online. "Huh. I didn't realize how much that was bothering me."

Esme shuddered. "It's like I just spat out the tinfoil I was chewing."

"I'll have to take your word for that," Sarah Jennifer replied, downloading Arthur Drake's personal logs to her datapad. "I'll have Enora come now that she can land without getting messed up."

Her mind whirled as she made her way back to the surface.

How were the Madness, the climate malfunction, and the BYPS connected? She resolved to find out as soon as Enora brought the airship and she could get to the IICS.

Ted was going to have a field day with this.

Thirty minutes later, the shipping containers were being unloaded, and Sarah Jennifer got to her cabin. She reclined her chair and settled in to read Arthur Drake's journal, starting with the first entry.

March 21, WWDE+151

I have always been fascinated by the ancient technologies. Norrköping is a beautiful city. The people seem friendly.

My traveling companion Stuart is also in high spirits to be here, where technology is making a comeback. I suppose that is why we both wanted to work at the power plant. Our programming ability, picked up at the abandoned manufacturing plant where we overwintered (as if we even knew what winter was back then!) in Danemark, secured us the jobs.

We intend to explore the area fully once we get settled in.

Sarah Jennifer raced through the next few entries, her interest growing as she read about the day Arthur and Stuart had found the ground station among the outbuildings. Albert had almost terminated them as intruders, but Arthur's quick thinking and their great luck that the EI wasn't operating at full capability had saved them.

No wonder Albert had been so cranky when they arrived. She hoped Esme was able to repair his damage.

With the EI disabled, Arthur and Stuart had shared their discovery with the others at the power plant, and the people of Norrköping had banded together to learn how to operate the TQB computers without EI assistance in an effort to end the eternal winter caused by the WWDE.

Sarah Jennifer curled up in her chair, getting lost in events that had happened over sixty years ago. The people had been making slow but steady progress on understanding the climate module and the BYPS. She wondered if it would have been more than a decade or two before they figured it out if not for Arthur and the Madness.

Arthur's mental slide hadn't begun until he discovered nanocytes. He had hoarded the discovery, afraid the others would misappropriate the technology.

However, he hadn't seen his own descent into unethical practices.

September 3, WWDE+151
  Wonder of wonders, I have discovered a previously

hidden database in the computer. It contains information I would scarcely believe, had I not seen the evidence of it with my own eyes. <u>All the answers are to be found in the blood.</u> Machines invisible to the naked eye exist there by the millions.

Let the others spend their time trying to change the weather. I intend to master this knowledge for the good of mankind.

The database has information about a Queen from long past who gifted these "nanocytes" to the world. Fairy tales at best. No human could have created this miracle. I can only assume that some higher power was actually responsible.

February 11, WWDE+152

Stuart is watching me. I know it. I caught him hanging around the lab last night, thinking I'd gone home. I'm going to have to stay here from now on. He cannot know what I am working on.

He *cannot.*

I shouldn't let myself get so worked up. I have protected my work.

March 14, WWDE+154

Test subjects are showing signs of improvement. The nanocytes have cured every pathogen I have introduced into the population so far. Dengue, cholera, rubeola, all eradicated in a matter of hours. This is truly exciting.

I am ready to move on to the next phase of experiments. How will changes to the nanocyte code affect my subjects? Can I induce "extra" abilities, such as those documented in the annals?

It will remain to be seen whether I can reproduce the circumstances that created the so-called "vampires" and "werewolves."

Stuart tried tricking me into leaving my lab unattended. Celebration indeed. He just wants to clear the way so he can sneak in here and snoop around. I have concluded he must want to steal my work and take credit for it. How he could pass it off as his own is beyond me. I taught him everything he knows.

December 25, WWDE+154

EUREKA!

I feel no shame in invoking the joyous cry of that other great scientist, Archimedes. At long last, my attempts to manipulate the function of nanocytes in my test subjects have been successful. I am a genius and on Christmas Day! Supernatural abilities will be my gift to the world. I intend to refine the process using animal subjects before releasing the update to the town, then the whole world.

It is entirely appropriate that I take a little time to celebrate.

Not in town, though. They are still recovering from the flu I released last month.

Who could have known it would mutate? Even genii make errors now and then.

Stuart came by the lab again last night, wearing his

suspicions like last month's fashion and poking around where he's not wanted.

That gormless tripe-for-brains wouldn't know real science if it stood up and slapped his stupid face. Always smiling. He thinks I don't know what he's plotting. That supercilious prick had the gall to speak to me about ethics. Ethics! ME! Ridiculous!

How were we ever comrades?

How I long to infect him with something his nanocytes can't combat, him and his insufferable friend, Felix. If only there were such a disease.

Maybe Howard can help me get rid of Stuart forever.

January 13, WWDE+155

I took a risk. I was rewarded.

Howard is coming back to the lab today. He took the news of my little project with no small amount of skepticism, but he was persuaded when I showed him the results of the control tests.

I thought for a moment that he was appalled by the dogs with their red eyes. I was ready to act should he turn tail and snitch, but the increase in strength and intelligence was too intriguing for him to continue such sentimental thinking after a moment or two when I told him that the changes had been wrought by my own blood.

I have removed to another laboratory on the second sublevel. The computers here connect to the satellites orbiting Earth.

We will be gods among men.

. . .

January 19, WWDE+155

The business with the dogs last week was regrettable. Messy, too.

I must confess, I became despondent when I found their bodies torn to pieces. The single survivor (Subject 46) had to be terminated, of course, but not before I took a sample of its blood.

What I found snapped me out of my despair. The alteration I made to Subject 46's nanocyte code did not produce the "werewolf," as I had hoped. Instead, the subjects were driven to extreme hunger, and the instinct to consume flesh was evident.

The thought occurred to me that this would be a fitting solution for my Stuart problem. Every day, I am more conscious of his scrutiny.

Who in this world would turn down unlimited power for all, no matter the cost in the short term? Every great scientist knows progress has a price.

I like to think I will be considered, no, remembered by those who survive the transformation as the father of the modern world, a protagonist for the evolution of humanity.

Howard is responding well to the "vampire" code. He is showing increased strength, speed, and agility. He is excessively hungry, an unexpected side-effect of the transformation he has undergone. His ability to communicate verbally is declining, likely a temporary effect.

I intend to tweak his nanocytes again in the morning.

January 20, WWDE+155

I could hardly finish my breakfast this morning, such is my anticipation.

The plan is hatched. With Howard's help, Stuart will be lured to the lab, where I will update his nanocytes with the corrupt code before releasing the successful version to the city's population.

We have released the modified narcotic into the water supply as a distraction and a reason to bring Howard into the facility. The whole town will be acting rather strangely, I should think. However, it will cover my tracks.

Our tracks.

CHAPTER TWENTY-FOUR

Sarah Jennifer dropped her datapad in shock. Two things occurred to her simultaneously. "Bethany Anne needs to know the Madness wasn't her fault, and I need to get hold of Ted."

She put a call through to Keeg Station.

She tapped her foot while she waited for someone to pick up, processing what she'd learned from her brief examination of the server logs. She got no answer from Ted's lab, and the same when she called the *Rameses' Chariot*. "My dear uncle, you picked a fine day to be unavailable," she grumbled, trying the station's command center instead.

Dionysus, the primary AI for Keeg Station, answered. "Major Walton, how may I direct your call?"

"Feeling conversational as always, I see," Sarah Jennifer commented in response to his put-upon tone. "Put me through to Ted. It's urgent."

There was a pause. "One moment while I redirect you. Ted is not present in the network at the moment."

There was a burst of static, which she knew Plato and his children only played for Terry Henry's benefit. Why was Ted with her grandparents?

Terry Henry appeared onscreen. "There she is! To what do I owe this pleasure, Wildflower?"

Sarah Jennifer couldn't help but return his grin at hearing her old nickname. "Hey. I'm actually trying to reach Ted, but it's good to see your face."

"Call more often and you won't miss us so much," Char told her from offscreen.

"I'm kinda busy saving the world here," Sarah Jennifer responded amiably. "Why can't I reach Ted?"

Terry Henry tapped his nose with his forefinger. "It's classified. Queen's orders." Meaning he was doing something secret and most likely extremely destructive for Bethany Anne. "Why do you need him?"

"We found a lot more than we expected in Norrköping," Sarah Jennifer told him. "I really need Ted. Can you get a message to him at least?"

Terry Henry nodded. "What's the word?"

"We found the source of the Madness," Sarah Jennifer told him.

"That's great!" TH enthused. "Did you hear that, Char? She's found the cure."

"Not quite," Sarah Jennifer corrected quickly. She sensed some grandfatherly guilt in his reaction. Perhaps she wasn't the only one who couldn't let go of his long-ago lesson. "We still have to reverse-engineer it, come up with a fix, and get that fix out across the world. That's not all. Bethany Anne needs to know that she wasn't responsible for the Madness."

Terry Henry's eyebrows rose.

Char appeared on the screen, draping her arm around TH's shoulder as she leaned close to the camera. "That's going to be a huge weight off her chest. What caused it?"

"A man by the name of Arthur Drake," Sarah Jennifer replied. "He was part of the effort at the ground station to diagnose and reverse the climate issue. People were trying to figure out the problem without knowing what they were doing, although they might have been making some progress before Drake found his way into the database."

She didn't bother to hide her distaste. "This guy was a fanatic and arrogant in the extreme. Once he discovered the existence of nanocytes, he started experimenting on the people in the town. He messed in with all kinds of nasty stuff before he managed to infect the world with the corrupted code."

"I never understand why supposedly intelligent people do such crazy things," Char admitted, sadness clouding her otherwise perfect features. "Yet evil sprouts like nasty little weeds wherever there's civilization. Was he planning to try to rule the world?"

"He thought he was going to give everyone powers," Sarah Jennifer told her. "All he did was destroy everything humanity had accomplished in coming back after WWDE."

Terry Henry gave her a pointed look. "What's bugging you?"

Sarah Jennifer snorted softly. "There was never any hiding how I feel from you. Too many coincidences. Finding that the Madness and the climate issue are connected to the BYPS. Leaving Ezekiel alone while I take care of this."

"Ezekiel?" Char inquired. "Did you find a man at last?"

"Felicity didn't mention anyone by that name," Terry Henry queried without questioning, somehow still sounding protective.

Sarah Jennifer glared daggers at her grandparents. "Ezekiel is a fourteen-year-old child. I have a military to oversee and a continent-hopping mission to accomplish before everyone on this planet dies of either cold or being eaten. There's no room in my life for a man."

Char's heartbreak on her granddaughter's behalf showed in the way she didn't reach through the screen and slap Sarah Jennifer upside the head for snapping at her. "Don't close yourself off from the prospect of love," she advised softly. "I know it hurt leaving Jeremiah—"

"Like I said," Sarah Jennifer interrupted. "I don't have the time or will."

Terry Henry hushed Char's reply. "Relax, lover. Sarah knows her own heart. Tell us about Ezekiel," he asked, changing the subject to something less painful for his granddaughter. "You adopted a kid, huh?"

Sarah Jennifer couldn't resist a smile. "You've relaxed an awful lot. The whole of Salem has adopted him. He's a natural magic-user. Seems he was born with the ability, the first of his kind." She relayed the tale of how they'd found him. "Kid's got talent, I'm not exaggerating. He's picked up weather and physical magic in just a few weeks. Nature bends to his will. He's really something."

"I want to meet him," Char told her, her tone brooking no protest.

Sarah Jennifer nodded. "Soon. He's not with me right now. He wanted to stay with Lilith and learn what she knows about the true history of the world while we were here in Norrköping."

Char relented, her eyes sparkling with joy. "All I want is for you to have love in your life. If you have a son, that's good enough for me."

Sarah Jennifer wasn't sure Ezekiel would appreciate being called her son. They didn't have that kind of relationship. She felt like a guardian, or a mentor, maybe. Still, there was no diverting the indefatigable Charumati when she set her mind, so she nodded. "Sure, Grandma."

"*Great* Grandma," Char corrected. "You're the first to give me a great-grandchild."

TH raised an eyebrow. "Your sister is going to love that. Probably your cousin, too."

Sarah Jennifer laughed. "Sylvia is fine. How is Kai?"

"Call him and find out," Char told her.

Sarah Jennifer resisted the urge to roll her eyes. "I will. If I get time. I have to go. Make sure Ted contacts me as soon as he's out of whatever communications limbo he's in. Love you both."

"Call soon," Terry Henry urged.

"I will," Sarah Jennifer promised before signing off.

That duty taken care of, if not in the way she'd expected, she returned to the ground station, where work to repair the climate module was already underway. Another team was examining the BYPS connection under the direction of Esme, who was still working from the computers on the second sublevel.

Esme stopped typing and muted her comm when Sarah Jennifer entered the lab. "You're just in time. I've gotten Albert back to his old self. Undoing the damage that half-baked keyboard jockey Arthur did to the systems is a hell of a job."

Sarah Jennifer walked to the monitor Esme was working at. "Reactivate Albert. This will go a lot easier with EI assistance."

Esme entered a command and nodded at Sarah Jennifer.

"Albert, you there?" Sarah Jennifer called.

"I am, Major Walton," Albert answered, his voice free of the sinister undertones and crankier overtones he'd had when they'd last spoken.

"Good to have you back," Sarah Jennifer told him. "Do you have video of the labs from the day Arthur Drake released the Madness?"

"Thank you, and yes," Albert responded. "I was able to recover everything from the moment Arthur Drake removed my access to the systems to the time Esme deactivated my programs in order to rebuild them."

"Play it for me, please," Sarah Jennifer instructed. "Start with Howard arriving at the lab on the morning the Madness was released."

Esme looked up from her keyboard, a puzzled expression wrinkling her eyes. "Howard?"

"You didn't read Drake's journal, I take it." Sarah Jennifer handed Esme her datapad, which still had the relevant entries onscreen. "Here."

Esme's expression turned to thunder as she skimmed highlights of the text. "The pure arrogance of this!"

Albert put the video on their monitor, and they watched the run-up to the Madness being unleashed upon the world with dismay.

"That radge had no business playing with people's lives," Esme thundered, her Scottish roots revealing themselves in her anger.

Sarah Jennifer had never seen her this angry. "Radge?"

"Fool!" Esme jumped up to pace out the energy her rage had released. "People like him are why we had the WWDE in the first damn place. Ego-inflated, know-nothing idiots with access to power they don't comprehend. They think they can play with fire without getting burned. The whole world in ruins because o' him and his ilk! It's a good thing he's already dead, or he'd'a been in a world of hurt when I caught up with him."

"What does it mean for us?" Sarah Jennifer murmured as the monitor went dark.

Esme kicked Arthur's skeleton, and her anger abated enough for her to focus. "Thanks to good old Arthur, we have our work cut out for us. You wouldn't believe how much progress the people he killed were making. They were *real* scientists, working meticulously to understand everything."

Sarah Jennifer sighed. "I thought the same. They would have figured it out sooner or later, but I'd bet the ranch it wouldn't have been this late. They were smart enough to get the power back on for the whole city. That was a huge accomplishment."

Esme kicked Arthur's skull out into the corridor for good measure and returned to her keyboard. "Done is done. All we can do is what we came to do. I'm going to keep cleaning up after that arrogant tosspot and restore the ground station's link to the BYPS. Nothing we can do about the Madness until we hear back from Ted."

"It's a shame we don't have him to help with this right now," Sarah Jennifer told her. "He's on some secret project. Maybe Lilith can help. What about the climate module?"

Esme seesawed her hand. "That should be a mite easier to take care of. It was affected by the fallout after the WWDE. It will take a few days to swap out the components that need replacing and get it recalibrated, but once the uplink to the BYPS is secure, we can get the module working with the rest of the system. It's not like we didn't expect to be up to our eyeballs in problems. We can be grateful that none of them are impossible to solve."

"True," Sarah Jennifer agreed. "I'm going to go down there and give them a hand."

Katia smelled the Mad before she saw them. She looked up from the grave they were filling in, searching for the source of the corrupt scent. Her eyes fixed on the forest beyond the parking lot, where the only barrier to nature was a dilapidated chain link fence held up by this year's new growth. "Hey, guys, looks like we've got some action."

She activated her comm bud and called Brutus. "We've got a situation up here."

"Need a hand?" Brutus came back.

"Not sure yet," Katia told him. "We'll call if the situation changes."

Reg and Dinny had exchanged their shovels for their rifles.

"You see anything?" Dinny asked quietly as they moved

back to hug the lee of the outbuilding Katia had chosen to bury the remains by.

"Nope, just the smell," Linus complained. "Damn stench gets right up my nose."

"We need to get back inside the ground station," Katia told them. "Be ready. They're almost on us."

The others murmured their agreement, hearing the faint crashing from deep within the evergreens pressing up against the far side of the power plant.

They crossed the parking lot at a light run, their cover nonexistent.

The Mad chose that moment to emerge from the forest. The hungry mass burst from the tree line and locked onto the scent of sweaty Weres, their instinctive focus giving them the appearance of coordination.

"Take 'em out!" Katia yelled.

They fired smoothly, picking off the Mad one by one as they retreated the last thirty feet. It was no use. For every Mad they took out, three more joined the oncoming horde.

Linus glanced at Katia. "There's a fuck-ton of them headed this way."

"Must be the group Enora picked up last time we were here." She hesitated with her finger on her earpiece when a whirring noise from the ground station made her turn to look.

"Please return to the facility," a cool voice announced from a loudspeaker on the gun turret that had extended from the ground station's roof. "Security protocols have been activated."

Sarah Jennifer came on the comm. "You heard the EI. Get inside so we can lock the station down."

Shaken from their stunned torpor, Katia, Linus, Dinny, and Reg darted through the closing door.

Blinding light erupted from the turret as a beam of pure Etheric energy lanced the tree line, tearing up the ground, the trees, and the Mad indiscriminately.

Linus caught his breath after they were safely behind the thick steel. "I've never seen anything like that weapon. Just how powerful *is* the Queen?"

"Her capabilities make you look like children playing soldiers," Albert told them.

Katia snarled vaguely at the ceiling. "I thought Esme was going to fix you?"

"She didn't remove my personality," the EI responded flatly. "Just saying how it is."

Katia's lip curled. "Yeah, well, your opinion isn't wanted or needed. We're not kids. Come on, guys. Let's go."

CHAPTER TWENTY-FIVE

This part of the operation had been planned to the last detail. The oily-looking alloy the casings that protected the working parts of the climate module were made from couldn't be reproduced here on Earth.

Brutus had plenty of hands and possibly even a rough idea of what he was doing. More than a rough idea. He used a hammer and a punch to put a divot in each of the rivets holding the panel the engineers had marked for removal, then removed each rivet with an electric drill and stored it in a pouch on his toolbelt. They would be repurposed, and new rivets used to re-seal the sixteen vast machines.

Carver mirrored the action on a panel on the machine to his left, Geordie on the one to his right. Katia, Linus, Dinny, and Reg had spread out and were all performing the same task. The real fun would begin when they had access to the inner workings.

Brutus' hammer slid off the end of the punch, skinning his knuckles for the third time since they'd started.

"*Dammit!* I know what goes where. Why isn't it working out that way?"

Geordie pulled his head out of the first panel they'd managed to open and tossed Brutus a rag to wipe the blood off. "Engineering looks easy in theory. Little bit different in reality, right?"

"It's why we love it," Geordie supplied.

Brutus shook his hand vigorously to lessen the sting as the skin regrew over the scrape. "You sure I can't just shoot this stupid thing open?"

Sarah Jennifer walked in as Carver's and Geordie's laughter echoed off the bare walls. "You shoot that thing and I'll shoot you," she scolded playfully.

Brutus threw her a snarky look. "Why don't I believe you're kidding?"

Sarah Jennifer grabbed a toolbelt and filled it with what she needed to start. "Where?"

Carver pointed at the next machine along from the one he was working on. "Panel's marked. Can't miss it."

The rest of the day and most of the next went by in a monotony of hard labor and tedious tasks, broken only by the easy conversation that passed between the pack at mealtimes. Geordie and Carver coordinated the replacement of the broken components with the ones sent from Keeg Station, and everyone else knuckled down to put what they'd learned in VR into practice.

The eyewall surrounding central Norrköping collapsed on the second night.

Without the module to exert control over the weather and repel it, the storm closed in on the ground station, and the snow that had been held back rushed to cover the ruins of the town while the pack slept safe and warm inside the airship.

Sarah Jennifer awoke on their third morning in Norrköping to a warning from Enora that the ground station had been snowed in overnight. The AI was waiting on the viewscreen when she got to the cockpit. "How are we doing out here?"

"We are fine," Enora assured her. "I kept the hull warm to avoid getting iced in. I also spent some time clearing access around the ground station so the pack would have no issue returning to work on schedule."

Sarah Jennifer frowned in interest. "Oh, yeah? How?"

"I remote-accessed the excavation equipment we were sent," Enora informed her brightly. "It beat sitting here doing nothing while you slept."

"Appreciate it," Sarah Jennifer told her. "I need every Were and witch working on the climate module. If you're bored, maybe Esme can link you with the ground station."

"Esme departed for the ground station forty-three minutes ago," Enora supplied.

Sarah Jennifer's mouth dropped open. "How does she do that every time?"

"Do what?" the AI inquired.

"Make me feel like I slept in," Sarah Jennifer replied with a wry smile. "Never mind. I need to get in touch with Lilith to update her on our findings so far."

Lilith was pleased to receive the update and shocked and sad when she assimilated the data in full. "So much unnecessary waste of life. This was why Bethany Anne did not want the world to know about nanocyte technology.

Why she chose to give humanity nanocytes that would evolve with you gradually over generations."

"Let's hope the world never forgets what happens when someone tries to force that evolution." Sarah Jennifer meant that with all her being.

"Ezekiel wishes to speak to you," Lilith segued.

"Give me a minute to get a connection to his datapad," Sarah Jennifer told her. "Satellite coverage is spotty here. You two getting on okay?"

"He is a delight," Lilith praised. "A diligent student if ever I met one."

"That's good to hear." Sarah Jennifer got in a quick goodbye before Ezekiel appeared on the viewscreen. "Hey, kiddo."

Ezekiel waved. The video was a little jumpy, but his audio came through fine. "Did you fix the problem at the ground station yet?"

"We've only been here for three days," Sarah Jennifer told him with a warm smile. "We're on schedule, no major problems so far. How about you? You're not bored?"

"Is that a joke? Lilith is so smart. How could I be bored? She knows everything about the Etheric and nanocytes and Bethany Anne." Ezekiel launched into a rapid-fire rundown of everything he'd learned from listening to Lilith talk. "She says she is enjoying my company. Can you believe that? I'm just a kid. She's centuries old, even if she has spent most of it stuck inside the machine."

"Sounds like you two are bonding," Sarah Jennifer encouraged. "Have you seen Curtis yet?"

Ezekiel shook his head. "I haven't left Lilith's cavern. Mrs. Shutov has visited every day with food and 'advice.'

She keeps telling me to come down from the mountain so she can take care of me properly. If I go into town, she might not let me leave again."

Sarah Jennifer chuckled. "You can handle Mrs. Shutov."

"It would be good to see the dogs as well," Ezekiel conceded. "I feel a little awkward talking to Curtis. It's like...I don't know. Looking back or something. New Romanov is where I come from, but it isn't my home anymore."

Sarah Jennifer couldn't help but empathize. "You'll get through it. It might feel awkward now, but that's better than burning a bridge you'll need to cross again later in your life. New Romanov has been a nexus point for the UnknownWorld for centuries. When you're long-lived, the past comes back around whether you want it or not. My advice, advice I wish I'd been smart enough to listen to when I was young enough to ignore a solid someone smarter—usually my grandfather—was trying to do me, is to set up a foundation for meeting it on your own terms."

She changed the subject, sensing that Ezekiel had some soul-searching to do on the matter. "Speaking of my grandparents, I just got off the IICS with them. They're looking forward to meeting you."

Ezekiel narrowed his eyes in suspicion. "Why would they want to meet me?"

Sarah Jennifer felt her face redden. "Maybe you are smart enough to take advice. My grandmother assumed I'd adopted you. She was so happy to be a great-grandmother that I didn't have the heart to correct her."

Ezekiel paled. "Why does that sound the same as Mrs. Shutov's offer to take me in?"

Sarah Jennifer laughed. "Relax, the Queen of the Were-wolves is galaxies away. Has talking to Lilith helped you get a better understanding of your magic?"

"It's just like Esme has been teaching us," Ezekiel's eyes took on the shine of devotion. "I want to figure out how many different types of magic can be created with Etheric energy. Did you know that the Matriarch can make the Etheric do whatever she wants it to? It's more complicated than it sounds, but what if we could shape the magic we have to help us rebuild the world? We would need to find more magic-users, of course."

Sarah Jennifer listened with amusement, taking joy from the innocence of his vision. "Who knows what the future will look like?" she told him. "I have no doubt it will be bright if you are one of the people bringing it about."

"Just picture it," Ezekiel continued, barely hearing her because he was so lost in his daydream. "If we had bases in all the cities, it would be safe to build academies. Magic-users would come from far and wide to learn, and they could teach others..."

Sarah Jennifer balked at the "we" part. "Ezekiel, I'm not planning on the Defense Force becoming a public service after the Madness has been resolved."

The boy's face crumpled. "What? I don't understand. You're not going to help people?"

Sarah Jennifer lifted a shoulder, smiling. "Taking a step back when the world is safe *is* helping them."

"How is abandoning everyone helping them?" Ezekiel argued.

"I'm not abandoning anyone," Sarah Jennifer told him firmly. "There's a lot you don't know about the world. We can talk about this when we pick you up. Now isn't the time."

Ezekiel nodded, clearly unsatisfied with the answer. "Okay. Bye."

Sarah Jennifer felt a twinge of regret when Ezekiel signed off abruptly. She went on with her morning routine, then grabbed breakfast for her and Esme before heading for the ground station. The disagreement clung to her thoughts.

She didn't like that look of disappointment on Ezekiel. Could she have handled his reaction better? Even if she could have, he wasn't able to see the whole picture through the callow lens of youth.

The question of what role the Defense Force would or even *should* play in a post-Madness society had been at the back of Sarah Jennifer's mind from the minute Bethany Anne had given her a way to save the Weres.

The technological age was over, and a new era was on the cusp of being born. Magic was the new order, and for it to flourish, there couldn't be any links to the past.

How to achieve that without dismantling everything she'd built back home when even the existence of Weres proved the legends were based on truth, she didn't yet know.

Salem was the hub of the UnknownWorld, the central pillar on which civilization rested and whose tendrils reached far and wide. It was too large to be hidden again. On the rare occasion that she wasn't so exhausted she fell asleep immediately after getting into bed, the dilemma flitted through her thoughts.

Space was looking more and more like the only option.

The pack would follow her through the gates of Hell if she asked. The hardcore members of the Defense Force would likely choose to stay with the pack. However, there were a few thousand civilians who had lives and families.

Withdrawing the Defense Force had the potential to be every bit as devastating for society as physically tearing Salem from the landscape and launching it to the stars. Sarah Jennifer wanted no part of destabilizing the recovery people had strived to bring about.

She pushed coming to a resolution down the list of her priorities with the intention of dealing with it before it reared its head as an acute issue and ignored the guilt that bloomed every time she did so.

Three-AM thoughts were rarely useful ones. At some point, she would have to give this sticky problem serious consideration, and for that, she would have to voice the issue, making it real. Sarah Jennifer suspected if she wrote Bethany Anne for advice, the Queen would confirm what she already knew.

There was no place for the Defense Force in an age of magic.

Sarah Jennifer got to Arthur's lab and found Esme had cobbled together an ad-hoc workstation by pushing three desks together and rearranging the room's monitors on them. There was also a little heater positioned to direct warmth onto the footrest

Esme swung her chair away from the bank of monitors, avoiding the web of cables snaking between her workstation and the various machines. "It's bracing outside today. Makes me glad to be underground."

Sarah Jennifer put Esme's breakfast on the desk beside her. "Makes me glad we're halfway done."

"With the climate module, yes. The BYPS is as unyielding as its namesake." Esme wrinkled her nose when she sniffed the contents of the flask. She extracted a smaller silver flask from her cloak and topped the coffee up before sipping it. "It's not tea, but it'll do."

Sarah Jennifer groaned. "How many satellites need to be replaced?"

"Two," Esme told her. "The one that came down in Canada, and the one that's supposed to cover this sector. The BYPS rejected it, but not soon enough to prevent the Madness from being broadcast from here to Siberia."

"Where is that satellite now?" Sarah Jennifer asked, hoping retrieval would be simple.

"The BYPS destroyed it," Esme told her. "What's got you all twisted up?"

"Ezekiel," Sarah Jennifer admitted, pulling up a chair next to Esme's. She relayed their conversation while Esme ate her blueberry muffin, then covered her face with her hands and sighed. "I might have messed up."

Esme chuckled dryly. "Ah."

Sarah Jennifer dropped her hands and stared at Esme in disbelief. "'Ah?' Is that all you have to say? He accused me of abandoning people."

"He's a teenager," Esme said, shrugging. "He'll sulk some, but he'll be fine as soon as he gets distracted by the next thing that grabs his attention. It's the question of where we're going to go when this is over that's really getting to you."

"If you got that from my mind, you should have also picked up that I'm avoiding the question," Sarah Jennifer grumbled.

"Because you don't want to upset the applecart."

"After everything we've gone through to get to where we are?" Sarah Jennifer retorted. "What am I going to tell them? 'Hey, everyone, I know we *just* got things running right, but now we have to choose between our way of life and this planet we live on.' Who's going to want to live on a starship? We might be soldiers, but the majority of our people are ranchers, farmers, and homesteaders. They need land to keep. It's what they do."

Esme wiped her hands and turned back to her keyboard. "Look up the specs for the QBBS *Meredith Reynolds*. You'd be surprised how much space one of those battle stations has for the agriculturally inclined."

Sarah Jennifer stopped short. "I hadn't considered that as an option. What do you think it would take to build something like that in time and resources?"

Enora's voice came from the datapad on Esme's desk. "We have the schematics for the climate control system. Terraforming the exterior of, say, the moon, would use up far fewer resources than procuring a suitable asteroid and hollowing it out."

Esme wagged a finger. "That's not a bad idea." She turned a knowing look on Sarah Jennifer. "See what happens when you share your problems?"

Solutions, Sarah Jennifer thought. But not the moon.

"We'll call a council meeting when we get back to Salem. Test the water."

"At the very least, you need an idea of how many people we're looking to support," Esme agreed.

The comm pinged, and Brutus spoke. "Esme, you ready to bring Nine online? We're about done here."

Esme scooted her chair to the fourth monitor. "Give me a few minutes."

"We can use a few more anyway," Brutus replied. "SJ, you planning on joining us any time today?"

"You know I had calls to make first thing," Sarah Jennifer told him. "Don't make me come over there and whup your disrespectful behind."

"If you're going to do some work afterwards, I'm all for it," Brutus returned with a chuckle. "I want to get home to my wife before Christmas."

Katia chimed in. "Keep talking, Brutus. We could do with some entertainment, and you getting your ass handed to you would make for great background noise while we get unit ten sealed back up for testing."

Sarah Jennifer laughed, her tension evaporating for the moment. "Hold on. I'm on my way."

The majority of the pack was in the climate module chamber when she got there a few minutes later. Units one through eight were repaired and had been tested. Eight more to go.

Sarah Jennifer pulled Brutus aside while Carver and Esme coordinated the test on unit nine. She had asked him to trust her blindly once, and he'd done it without question. This time she told him everything up front. "It's time we left Salem."

Brutus leaned against the wall for support. "Define 'we.'"

"The pack," Sarah Jennifer clarified. "The Defense Force. Our families. Whoever else wants to come with us."

Brutus sucked in a breath. "And go where?"

Sarah Jennifer lifted a shoulder. "I haven't figured that part out yet. What I do know is that without the Madness and the messed-up climate, our duty will be done. Magic will develop all by itself. There will be no need for the UnknownWorld because everyone will be enhanced in some way."

"Why can't we stay in Salem?"

Sarah Jennifer shook her head. "We have to remove all the space tech we've introduced for a start. We could go back to living the way things were before Bethany Anne stepped in, but do you want to?"

A long list of things Brutus didn't want to live without flashed through his mind. "No. I hate travel sickness less than I hate walking. Did Bethany Anne say we have to get rid of it all?"

Sarah Jennifer shook her head. "Not yet, but she will at some point is my guess. Magic won't develop as it should if there's a handy gadget to solve every problem," she continued, the words spilling out in her relief to voice her concerns about the future. "If we stay as we are, we have to allow basic technology back into the world, or we will become the enemy in the eyes of the people. Our very presence will be a catalyst for war. We will be creating need just by having what they don't."

Sarah Jennifer noticed that the pack had all downed their tools and were listening. "That's not everything," she told them. "I can't disband the Defense Force, not completely. But we have to disappear when the Madness is over. Space might be our only real option. I wanted to have a new home in mind before I made any decisions, but I guess you all know now."

"We go where you go," Linus assured her.

There was a chorus of, "What he said," from the pack as they gathered around.

"We're family," Katia told Sarah Jennifer. "We stick together."

Sarah Jennifer wiped a tear from her eye. "When we get to Salem, I'm calling a council meeting."

"They can take it however they want to," Katia replied. "The only opinion that matters to me is yours. It's time for us as a pack and the Defense Force as a whole to move on. Salem, Boston, Lowell, Pittsburgh, Newfoundland, they're all strong. We're needed in Beringia, and wherever the melting ice and rising sea is going to displace people."

"Tell me we're not going back to Snøhvit," Rory called.

Sarah Jennifer lifted her hands. "I don't know. We're going to be split up for a while. Can you handle it? Staying neutral in the face of whatever you encounter? You trust my decision, I know, but not everyone is going to get it. There's going to be all kinds of pushback from the council."

Brutus recalled how hard it had been to stay neutral when the Danelaw was in upheaval. "Can't blame anyone for being shocked," he reasoned. "That's pretty big news."

He folded his arms. "You got one thing right, though. The council isn't going to like this."

CHAPTER TWENTY-SIX

Five days later, the *Enora* departed from Norrköping and returned to New Romanov to exchange Olaf for Ezekiel.

Sarah Jennifer gave her exhausted crew time to sleep and eat while she made her way into Lilith's mountain to retrieve her recalcitrant teenage charge. She was therefore surprised to find Brutus waiting for her at the door. "Why aren't you sleeping?"

"I'm gonna come with," Brutus offered. "You look like you could use the support."

Sarah Jennifer snorted softly. Ezekiel had refused to pick up his comm when she'd called to tell him they were on their way. "Appreciate it."

Lilith offered her usual charming welcome when they arrived in the main chamber.

Ezekiel walked past Sarah Jennifer without acknowledging her.

Brutus halted the moody teenager with a hand on his shoulder. "I don't care how pissed off you are. You show some respect."

Ezekiel mumbled under his breath.

"And don't forget that Weres have super-sensitive hearing," Brutus continued.

"I said, 'thank you for coming back for me,'" Ezekiel ground out from between clenched teeth.

Sarah Jennifer met his defiant stare with a patient smile. "If you'd prefer to stay here, that's fine."

Ezekiel's demeanor changed in an instant. "I didn't say I don't want to go back to Salem. I just can't believe you're going to shut down the Defense Force when the world needs them most."

"Right now is when the world needs us," Brutus interceded. "Our duty is to make sure humanity lives through the Madness and to protect what remains of the UnknownWorld. Your heart is in the right place, kid, but you have no understanding of the logistics of what you're asking."

Sarah Jennifer ushered them both out of the cavern after saying goodbye to Lilith. She couldn't shake her concern at Ezekiel's continued dismal mood.

Brutus excused himself when they got back aboard the airship. "If you've got this, my rack is singing a siren song I can't resist."

Sarah Jennifer gave him permission to leave and told Ezekiel to wait when he made to bolt for his cabin. "My office. We're going to have a conversation."

Ezekiel followed Sarah Jennifer to her cabin, projecting an air of sullenness only an adolescent would feel entitled to.

Sarah Jennifer gestured for Ezekiel to take the guest chair. "Let's talk logistics."

"Why?" Ezekiel asked, taking a seat. "Are logistics going to matter when people can manipulate the elements to provide whatever they need?"

Sarah Jennifer extended a hand. "Logistics. Not everyone is like you, Ezekiel. Salem has over a hundred magic-users supporting it. Did you know that?"

Ezekiel shook his head.

Sarah Jennifer broke it down for him. "Out of the hundred and eleven magic-users, twenty-seven have access to more than one ability. Seventy-five of them have abilities tied to manipulating nature or the weather. The rest of them have abilities ranging from pyrokinesis or telekinesis to mind magic like telepathy or vision-casting."

"Vision-casting?" Ezekiel asked.

"Ask Esme," she told him. "The point is, people are going to be able to take care of themselves eventually. If they're turning to us to make things better during hard times, the kind of magic you're talking about will take a lot longer to develop."

Ezekiel appeared to consider her viewpoint. "You're saying people have to suffer to evolve?"

"I'm saying innovation occurs to fill the needs of the time." Sarah Jennifer considered another approach. "Say someone who lived on the coast had access to a transport Pod. Would they ever discover they have the ability to call the fish to them?"

Ezekiel frowned, not seeing the relevance of the question. "They would if someone taught them it was possible."

Sarah Jennifer saw beyond Ezekiel's simple vision to a crossroads in their future. Maybe their parting wouldn't come for a few years; maybe it would be much farther down the road, but it was coming.

Did she save herself the heartache of letting him go by closing herself off to him now? Or did she accept that future pain as the price for love?

Her conscience wouldn't allow her to take the easy road. Neither would her heart.

Ezekiel was already a powerful magic-user. His goals were noble if idealistic. Who was she to say he wasn't destined to shape the next steps for humanity?

Sarah Jennifer contemplated the influence the stability she could provide would have on the man he became. What she saw before her was a sandy-haired boy who radiated innocence and purity of intent from every pore.

Ezekiel returned her questioning gaze with an earnest smile. "Am I convincing you?"

Sarah Jennifer laughed. "When the cabin I found you in was passed down to your father, did he make any changes around the place? Improvements to make things more efficient?"

Ezekiel nodded. "Yes, sure. What does that have to do with teaching magic?"

"I'm getting there," Sarah Jennifer told him with amusement. "Your father grew up in that cabin, and he had all the time in the world to think up ideas to make the place run a little smoother. I'd put money on him and your grandfather disagreeing about those changes. It could be your father was right all along, but he had to wait until he was grown to implement his own ideas, and *that* gave him time to refine them."

"What are you saying?" Ezekiel gave her a skeptical look. "Wisdom comes with age?"

Sarah Jennifer lifted a shoulder. "Bethany Anne never intended for this planet to turn into a military dictatorship. I have to walk the line, Ezekiel. That's my path and the path of every Were. I lived through the expectations people put on the FDG. I saw the toll it took on my grandfather to step back once the forsaken had been rooted out, but it was the right thing to do then, and it will be the right thing to do again."

"I don't want to step back," Ezekiel insisted.

"I get it," Sarah Jennifer assured him. "Really, I do. Have patience. Your time will come. We don't have to agree about what's right for humanity after the Madness as long as we respect one another's perspective. Could be you'll choose to stay with us when I give the order for the Defense Force to withdraw. Could be you won't, and you'll go back to New Romanov and start your magic school. I'll support your choices, and you support mine. That's what families do, right? Don't lose sight of what's important along the way. I've grown pretty fond of you these last months."

Ezekiel relented at last. "I thought I was a pain in your rear end?"

"Only when you're talking," Sarah Jennifer teased.

"Maybe I should forget to be on my best behavior when you introduce me to Great-grandmother Charm...Chara..."

"Cha-ru-ma-ti." Sarah Jennifer broke it down for him, then flashed him a grin. "Your funeral, kiddo. I wouldn't talk back to her unless I knew for sure I could outrun her."

Spontaneous mischief danced in Ezekiel's eyes. "I'm no werewolf, but I can do this…"

His eyes flared red as the air in the cabin *cracked*, and the boy vanished.

Sarah Jennifer had a second to envisage Ezekiel misjudging his jump and plummeting to his death, then the cabin door opened, and he walked back in with a cocky grin plastered across his face.

"What do you think?" His grin grew even larger, pride swelling his chest. "Pretty fast, huh?"

Sarah Jennifer recovered from the urge to strangle him and found she was impressed. "Nah, Char would still catch you, and she'd whup your behind raw for pulling a stunt like that on a moving airship."

Ezekiel erupted in laughter, punch-drunk from processing the sudden intake and expenditure of Etheric energy his showing off had taken. He reached for the wall when the effort caused him to stagger.

Sarah Jennifer hurried over to put an arm around him, her humor replaced by concern. She steered him to a chair and took a knee to get a good look at his eyes. His pupils were dilated. "You okay?"

Ezekiel blinked. "Dizzy. I'll be fine in a minute. Lilith taught me how to draw consciously from the Etheric."

Sarah Jennifer leaned against the desk and pressed the back of her hand to his forehead. His paler-than-usual skin wasn't clammy, and she noted the healthy flush returning to his cheeks. "That took a lot out of you, huh?"

"At least I didn't puke this time," Ezekiel offered in a shaky voice. He closed his eyes to stop the cabin from whirling around him. "Worth it to see your mouth flopping open and closed like a salmon out of water."

Sarah Jennifer arched an eyebrow. "Really? I had visions of you popping out of the Etheric outside the airship, and you think that it's funny?"

Ezekiel snickered. "Oh, yes. Definitely. Anyway, I wasn't inside the Etheric. I can't get there. Not yet."

"So, where did you go?" Sarah Jennifer asked, her interest well and truly piqued.

"Kind of...*on* it?" Ezekiel guessed. "Like skimming the surface of a soap bubble. I focused on where I was going, and I was there."

He sat up in his chair. "What's going to happen now that the climate control system is fixed?"

"A lot of things," Sarah Jennifer told him. "We have to keep searching for people who have been cut off by the Madness and find places to live for those who are going to lose their land. I guess you made me face something I've been putting off."

Ezekiel tilted his head. "What?"

Sarah Jennifer didn't try to hide her sadness. "Telling the people of Salem that the Defense Force is moving out."

Salem, MA

Sarah Jennifer had expected the council to take the news the Defense Force was moving out badly. It didn't stop her from being thoroughly disappointed in the free-for-all that unfolded in front of her.

The committees, while effective for the purpose of governing the people, had not resolved their tendency to form factions. That wasn't her issue to resolve. More people just meant bigger hills to die on, and since she rarely attended council meetings unless there was a Defense Force matter that couldn't be dealt with by one of the pack, she'd missed the scope of the division until now, when the rifts between the factions had opened wide.

"You can't deploy the whole Defense Force without our approval," Morgan Westerman, the head of the civilian roads and transport committee, contested hotly.

"What makes you think I need approval?" Sarah Jennifer hurled the question across the table, irritated by the assumption and the calls of agreement from his supporters. "I'm informing the council out of courtesy."

"We need the Weres here to keep us safe!"

"You can't leave us defenseless!"

"Who will protect the roads?"

"The forts at Pittsburgh, Newfoundland, and Boston will still be manned," Sarah Jennifer pointed out. "The infrastructure is there for Roads and Transport to hire people to guard the roads."

Magnus slammed his gavel on the table to dispel the querulous objections about giving one committee more power than the others. "We've had rotating committees before. We'll do it again if we have to."

Morgan Westerman's supporters blew up again, ignoring Magnus' attempts to keep the meeting running smoothly. Others added their objections, and the meeting dissolved into chaos.

Sarah Jennifer had not missed this.

Not one bit.

The original council members were the only ones who

remained in their seats. The experience they'd gained during Salem's early expansion said there was only one way it would go when Sarah Jennifer took it upon herself to speak to the council.

The major channeled the humility Amelie possessed while the factions made their demands. She drew on the dignity she had found in New Romanov to restrain herself as they made claims on her and the twenty-plus-thousand Weres sworn to her as Alpha. She displayed the resolve of Reika's people, as steady as the rock they made their home from when the assumptions turned to outright statements that their place was to guard Salem.

She forgot her resolve to not take the reactions personally when the talk turned to empty threats.

She'd heard enough.

"Sit down and shut *up!*" Her eyes flashed red as a pulse of Etheric energy left her body and made her command reality.

Everyone in the room obeyed whether they wanted to or not.

Sarah Jennifer glared at them. "The Defense Force is not the property of Salem. The council has no place in my chain of command. We owe individual cities and governments *nothing*. Our duty is to humanity as a whole, and we are needed elsewhere. The Defense Force expanding across the planet has always been on the objective. Let me make it clear that the future is here. Get behind the idea. Threatening to expel the enhanced from Salem is a sure-fire way to make an enemy out of me, and you don't want me as an enemy."

She wasn't done. "How would the people you serve take

the news that you just threatened to exile their wives, their husbands, and their children? It's easy to become complacent when your safety is assured. The rest of the world is living in fear, and it's going to get worse for them before it gets better. I stood here almost five years ago and asked the council to act in the best interests of humanity. Once again, I'm here to tell you it's time to let go of your own certainty to provide a little for others. Either we can continue working together for the good of *all* humanity, or I can follow Bethany Anne's example and replace you with people who have their priorities straight. Your choice."

That hit home with the majority. Brutus and Esme stood solidly behind her, their united front helping the reality to set in for those who still thought they could argue for their way.

She saw she'd made the impact she wanted and decided to quit while she was ahead. "We will reconvene in two weeks to start on the details of the transition. This meeting is over."

Sarah Jennifer strode out of the council chamber before she said something she couldn't take back. Ezekiel wasn't the only one who had to be careful not to burn bridges.

Behind the closed doors, Esme's voice rose above the others as the argument exploded afresh.

Sarah Jennifer almost went back in, but her instincts demanded she find a quiet space to gather her thoughts and get herself under control. She left the hall and headed for her office, anger fueling her brisk pace.

Voices intermingled in outrage escaped to echo in the hall as Brutus slipped out of the room. Sarah Jennifer was too tightly wound to slow down.

He ran to catch up with her and fell into step beside her. "That was a shitshow if ever I saw one."

"You think?" Sarah Jennifer snapped. She apologized immediately. "It's not your fault."

"It's not yours, either," Brutus told her.

Sarah Jennifer's thoughts were too tied up in her emotions to settle on a conclusion just yet. To label the dissenters as cowards would be unfair. Not everyone had been quick to give in to their fears.

What riled her was the essence of the council's demand: that the Defense Force hold their hands for eternity. "Part of it was. I should have handled it better when people started talking about exiling the enhanced."

Brutus busied himself at the bar cabinet. "We both need a drink after that. Where's that bottle of good brandy? Never mind. Found it."

The bottles clinked inside the cabinet as he dug out the one he wanted. He blew the dust off the bottle and set out three glasses on the sideboard, then poured a measure into each and passed one to Sarah Jennifer.

"Esme will be done yelling at the council soon," he volunteered in response to the curious glance Sarah Jennifer gave the third glass. He eyed the measure he'd poured for Esme and doubled it before picking up his own glass and taking a long sip. "I thought you went easy on them, considering. The next session needs to start with a reminder about the families that are going to be torn apart if the council decides they're not going to play nice."

Sarah Jennifer accepted the glass. "You just hate the council."

"I hate *bureaucracy*," Brutus corrected. "I can't deny it works, but it's damned tedious the way they wind themselves up over every minor detail. Give me a chain of command I can sink my teeth into."

"You looked like you wanted to sink your teeth into their heads," Sarah Jennifer told him with a dry chuckle.

"I'm a werewolf. They're a group of meatheads." Brutus let the image work its way into Sarah Jennifer's mind.

She snorted softly, the edge of her anger abating. "They'll see reason when they've had time to process."

"Reason?" Esme thundered, blowing through the door in a mood so foul it had a presence of its own.

Brutus pointed Esme at the lone glass on the sideboard.

She drained it in one, then slammed it down and refilled it. "They can't see past their sense of entitlement, same as ever."

Sarah Jennifer had to disagree. "Brutus is right. They'll calm down in a few days, and we'll sit down and discuss this transition rationally. They're afraid. Tempers are high because of it, ours included."

"Everyone is afraid," Esme countered with a wild gesture. A globule of brandy sloshed out of her glass and splashed the sideboard. She swiped at the mess absentmindedly. "We had no clue how many people were hanging on out there. They deserve a chance to make it."

"They're going to get that chance," Sarah Jennifer vowed. The hard part was done. The council would get behind her or not. The rest was logistics, and her pack ate logistics for breakfast. "Our objective remains the same.

We need to prepare for the break-up and start looking outward for a new home."

"Not before we get the Madness under control," Esme stated flatly. "No Ted means it's down to Lilith and me. I have to go back to New Romanov."

Sarah Jennifer felt in her pockets until she found a pad and the stub of a pencil to take notes. "We prioritize resettling the displaced by using the BYPS to monitor the break-up. That way, we're prepared even if people are in denial while the ground they're standing on turns to mush."

She got up from the couch, energized for the challenge ahead. "I'm calling Shonna. It's time to spend some of the war chest Bethany Anne gave us for Earth's defense."

"Seriously?" Brutus asked, unbelieving. "What happened to the 'tech will contaminate the natural development of magic' speech you gave us at Norrköping?"

"The rules just changed," Sarah Jennifer told him. "Well, they shifted. We're taking everything with us when we leave. We need to find a rock to make our home and make it habitable. We want to do everything we can to reduce the trauma of resettlement caused by the climate shift. We need technology. *Lots* of technology, starting with troop transport Pods."

Esme did a double-take. "What are you planning?"

"Spaceworthy transport for a start. The *Enora* is fine for a short trip, but we need to conduct a full survey of the solar system before we can make a choice about where to build." Sarah Jennifer paused her writing. "Construction equipment run by EIs to lay the foundations for new cities. Whatever it takes to see this transition through so we can look back and know we did everything we could to give them a good start."

The cloud of ill temper surrounding Esme evaporated. "You're committed to this? It's a big decision to make on the fly."

"If it was a snap decision, I'd agree." Sarah Jennifer started pacing, the movement relieving her urge to act. "We've worked nonstop for the last four years. Every Were who enlisted has committed their life to rebuilding civilization and relearning the skills we need to go beyond survival. Now is the time to pass our knowledge on, and since I've accepted what I have to do to make it happen, I can't believe I didn't see it from the start."

A rueful smile appeared as she considered Ezekiel's influence on her final decision. "This has been on my mind for a while now. There has to come a time in our lives that belongs to us. That's the reward for service—to sit back and enjoy the peace our sacrifices bought."

CHAPTER TWENTY-SEVEN

Berlin, WWDE+221

They started to see the difference in global temperatures within six months.

The arrival of the custom transport Pods Sarah Jennifer had ordered from the Spires Shipyard coincided with midsummer '215, as did the first collapses along the ice shelf around Mount Bråviken as northern Sweden saw its first sun in thirty years.

Sarah Jennifer was ready. She sent the Defense Force out across the globe in task forces led by the pack, each one equipped to provide transportation for the living, protection against the Mad, and the labor and organization needed to create infrastructure for new towns and cities.

Major change didn't happen for another two years, then it seemed to come all at once. By the time the ice shelf began to recede at a noticeable rate, the council had given up blustering and knuckled down to play their part in the changing world.

Iceland and the Faroe Islands were claimed by settlers

coming off the ice during the spring of '218. The iceberg field in the Norwegian Sea became passable around the same time Newfoundland and mainland Canada separated. The former Danelaw shrank by a third when the English Channel reformed, pushing settlements inland.

The rising seas opened up opportunities for the sea traders, and new harbors sprang up along the new coastlines shaped by the break-up. Japan became islands again, and in '219, Sarah Jennifer presided over the negotiation that led to them signing an accord with Amelie and the Trade Alliance that secured new routes for the traders and fishing fleets.

Wherever people were forced to move, the Defense Force was there to ease their burden. Sarah Jennifer had her hands full with directing the relief effort. The Madness ravaged communities wherever it sprang up. With no way to hold it in check besides putting boots on the ground, Sarah Jennifer had to leave their plan for protecting the masses fluid.

In the middle of all this, she got the news that the Federation had come under siege by the Kurtherians, making it impossible to get a secure connection to Ted. As a consequence, Esme moved between Salem and New Romanov, her time spent working on the fix for the Madness with Lilith.

The Mad adhered to no schedule. Sarah Jennifer's life became a never-ending tour of the world, with Ezekiel and Enora as the only permanent fixtures as she went from one country to the next putting out fires.

Sarah Jennifer relied heavily on the pack as the months turned to years and no simple solution to debugging humanity was found. They checked in daily via video link. The morning sitrep over breakfast kept them in touch and informed Sarah Jennifer how best to split their focus between protecting the living and closing off the lost places, those overrun with the Mad.

What remained of the old cities was no place for the living. Wherever civilization had dragged itself back after WWDE, the Madness now reigned.

In places where there had been no high ground to retreat to, like Paris, the people had retreated underground to escape it. Sarah Jennifer had established from a distance that they were doing just fine by themselves and left them alone after taking out the Mad roaming the streets above.

Berlin was on the other end of the spectrum, populated and Madness-ridden. Whenever they came across a city like this one, the protocol was to evacuate the living and wall the Mad in by using magic, explosives, or a combination of the two.

The Berliners were in the midst of an outbreak, making both options untenable until the Defense Force could convince them to quarantine to stop the spread.

Three task forces composed of nine hundred Weres and three magic users had been working for almost a month to secure the residential areas where the people lived compressed into the basements of apartment buildings, abandoned museums, art galleries, and municipal buildings.

While the task forces were clearing the tree-choked avenues and boulevards of Mad, Ezekiel spent his days delivering food parcels to the locked-down residents. He kept them updated on the situation in the streets and asked questions in return, looking for information on anyone who had any magical ability. He also asked the people he spoke to if they recognized the name of his grandparents' village, as he had everywhere they'd visited west of Siberia.

During their travels over the years, he had noted physical adaptations emerging in populations who had been squeezed into extreme environments by the decades-long rolling disaster. However, no one had heard of Arcadia, and conversely to the hope he'd started out with, he'd found few people who were able to use magic.

Berlin didn't look to be a win for him either, so today, he'd chosen to stick close to Sarah Jennifer and wait to hear from Brutus regarding the viability of rumors they'd heard about a town west of Frankfurt that might have room for the Berliners. He read quietly at his desk in the air-conditioned command tent while Sarah Jennifer went through field reports from Salem, Greenland, and Japan.

They both jumped when her comm went off. Sarah Jennifer pulled on the headset and hit the button to answer.

"Is that Brutus?" Ezekiel asked eagerly.

Sarah Jennifer nodded to confirm, holding a finger up to quiet him while she listened to Brutus speak. "Got you. We're en route."

Ezekiel stared at her impatiently while he waited for her to take off the headset. "Well? Did he find the town?"

"Right on the Rhine." Sarah Jennifer couldn't hide her grin. "They had to divert to deal with a group of Mad moving through farmland west of the valley."

Ezekiel jumped out of his chair and punched the air. "What are we waiting for? Let's go!"

She opened a comm link to Enora as they left the command tent and were immediately ambushed by air so humid it crawled down their throats. "We need to be wheels-up in ten minutes."

Ezekiel dashed for the cockpit the moment the *Enora* took off. "If this place is as good as the wool merchant said—"

"Hold your horses," Sarah Jennifer interrupted. "We stick to protocol. You wait until we've established these people are on the level before we make any decisions about rehoming people there, okay? Last thing we want is another Venice."

"I try very hard not to think about why Enora got her flamethrowers." Ezekiel shivered at the memory of men and women bound to stakes and the Mad crawling out of the canals in their hundreds to devour them, but even that macabre mind-movie didn't throw water on his excitement. "But there *are* people there?"

"All I know right now is that there's a town and there are Mad in the area." Sarah Jennifer didn't want him to get his hopes up.

Ezekiel's brow furrowed in concern. "Then we should fly faster."

"We are already traveling at maximum velocity," Enora chided. "You are being impatient, Ezekiel."

"Of course I'm impatient!" Ezekiel exclaimed. "This town could be the answer to saving the people in Berlin, and it's about to be attacked by the Mad!"

Sarah Jennifer put a hand on Ezekiel's shoulder to calm him. "They've survived just fine so far without us. Besides,

Brutus is there with a full task force. They have all the help they need."

They left the *Enora* in the meadow where the task force was camped and drove to the coordinates Brutus had given them on ATVs. Sarah Jennifer waved at the high wooden walls when they came in sight. "I don't know what you were so worried about. The Mad won't be scaling that any time soon."

Brutus met them at the gates of the town. "This place is called Bad Salzig," he informed Sarah Jennifer. "The people seem sound. Oh, yeah, and the chancellor wants to meet you."

Sarah Jennifer nodded as she took stock of the traffic around the gates. Steady trade was always a good sign. "Lead the way."

Armored guards checked their eyes before allowing them to pass, asking each of them the purpose of their visit as a way to establish they were free of the Madness.

Ezekiel examined the faces of the people they passed as they walked into town, looking for features similar to his own.

A pretty young woman at a flower stand returned his stare, making Ezekiel blush.

Brutus gave him a playful shove. "Don't just stand there gawping. Go and talk to her."

Ezekiel's face was burning. He pushed his hair back, nerves making his hands shake. "What do I say?"

"Start with hello," Sarah Jennifer told him.

Ezekiel nodded blankly and walked over to the flower stand.

Sarah Jennifer and Brutus watched him bumble through his introduction. He must have said something right since the young woman smiled and gave him a flower.

"They grow up so fast," Brutus commented with a wry smile.

"Truth," Sarah Jennifer agreed.

Ezekiel came back beaming. "Her name is Susan."

"Did you ask her out?" Sarah Jennifer asked, trying for nonchalance and missing by a country mile.

Ezekiel's blush returned with a vengeance. "I asked her about her life."

Brutus caught Ezekiel in a headlock and ruffled his hair. "Smooth going, lover boy."

Ezekiel pushed free by zapping Brutus with a stinging pulse of Etheric energy. "She asked me to meet her and her friends in the square tomorrow."

Brutus held up his hands. "I take it back. Who could resist those baby blues?"

"You're an ass, Brutus," Ezekiel grumbled.

The Were laughed. "So I've been told."

Sarah Jennifer gave Brutus the stink eye, then smiled at Ezekiel. "It takes a lot of courage to put yourself out there. I hope you make some new friends."

Ezekiel shook his head.

Brutus guided them along the streets, sticking to the cobbled sidewalks to avoid the carts and carriages traveling two abreast on the muddy road. "The chancellor offered us a carriage, but he also said it's faster to walk."

Sarah Jennifer was fine with that. "It gives us a chance to get a feel for the place. So far, it looks like these people have learned to live despite the Madness."

They made their way through streets that all sloped toward the water's edge. A trail of smoke from the crematorium drifted over the river.

Ezekiel was reassured by the guards stationed at every corner. "I'm guessing they have a lot to do with it."

Sarah Jennifer paused at the entrance to the open-air market to read a sign encouraging people to report early symptoms. While most of the people around covered their faces, they all kept their eyes clear of obstructions. "I'm happy we don't need to spend time persuading the people here to take precautions."

She noticed that everyone checked the eyes of those closest to them and told Brutus and Ezekiel to do the same.

They smiled and nodded, and the questioning stares of those who made eye contact turned to friendly greetings on confirmation of their uninfected status.

It struck Sarah Jennifer that the people were relaxed despite their vigilance, or maybe because of it. That led her to wonder why the town wasn't on alert for the Mad Brutus had diverted. "Brutus, you did tell the chancellor about the horde of Mad you drove off?"

Brutus waved off her concern. "I told him. He sent a few of his guards out to give our guys some backup."

Sarah Jennifer looked askance at Brutus. "Our guys need backup?"

"Nope, but it made sense to accept in the name of good relations." Brutus' gaze followed his nose across the square to a cluster of carts selling street food. "I smell fried chicken. Anyone hungry?"

Ezekiel's stomach growled on cue.

Sarah Jennifer laughed. "Guess that's a yes."

"Got to keep the calories up," Ezekiel called back as he hurried to catch up with Brutus.

They bought schnitzel on a stick from one of the carts and stopped at another to get cups of steaming-hot *kaffe*. The people here all carried a wooden cup and an eating knife on their belt. The vendor, a jolly blond man with curly mustaches, had a selection of hand-carved cups for sale.

Ezekiel screwed up his face as he tasted his. "That's got a kick to it."

"It'll put hair on your chest," Brutus agreed. He sipped his and winced. "Then again..."

"I don't know what you two are complaining about." Sarah Jennifer blew on her drink to cool it, releasing the rich aroma of freshly-ground beans. "Esme is going to be sorry she missed this."

"We have cinnamon syrup," the vendor offered. "The beet crop won't be ready until just before the harvest festival."

"You grow sugar crops here?" Sarah Jennifer thanked the vendor and tucked that tidbit of information away for the next time she spoke to Amelie.

Her thoughts drifted to the progress the trade alliance had made on building a new global economy as they continued on their way.

Ezekiel was more than happy with the flavor the cinnamon-infused maple syrup added to the rocket fuel in his

ND ROBERTS & MICHAEL ANDERLE

cup. He chatted animatedly until they reached the chancellery, where they were greeted by a gowned clerk who introduced herself as Linda Schneider, personal assistant to Chancellor Schneider.

Her curiosity got the better of her. "Any relation?"

"My father," Linda replied with a smile. "Please wait here while I let him know you've arrived."

The moment Linda left them alone in the reception room, Brutus turned to look at Sarah Jennifer and mouthed, "Do you feel that?"

"Feels like magic," Ezekiel ventured.

Sarah Jennifer nodded almost imperceptibly. "She doesn't smell like magic."

Linda's return put an end to their speculation for the moment.

"Please, come through," she invited warmly.

Samuel Schneider projected competence and reliability in his smile as he walked around his desk to greet Sarah Jennifer and Brutus. His clothing was neat and pressed, and his white hair was trimmed into submission. His beard was thick and fluffy, lending his face a grandfatherly charm. "Welcome to the Rhine Valley, Major. A pleasure to see you again so soon, Lieutenant Timmons. Young man."

"I'm Ezekiel," Ezekiel told him. "Good to meet you, Chancellor."

Samuel turned the full beam of his smile on Sarah Jennifer. "The lieutenant told me you're working on a cure for the Hunger?"

Sarah Jennifer accepted the firm handshake she was offered. "We call it the Madness, but yes. We're making progress. We identified the cause a few years ago. Finding a way to reverse it unilaterally has been more of a challenge."

Samuel's expression became pensive. "I wish you luck. We may seem like we are bearing this catastrophe well, but the ever-present specter of death takes its toll. While some are able to come forward when they feel the change coming on, there are inevitably more who get no warning and spread the Hunger when they turn."

Sarah Jennifer was intimately acquainted with the specter. It hung around where hope blossomed, looking to insert itself wherever people gathered. "There's no knowing where the Madness will strike. That you've managed to hold onto this much is proof of your resilience."

Ezekiel spoke up. "You're doing everything you can."

"It's a great town you've got here," Brutus agreed.

Samuel waved the praise off. "The town practically runs itself, the same as it did when my father was chancellor. My people make it easy. An end to the Hunger would mean they can throw off the mantle of fear and live their lives to the fullest."

He gestured at a group of chairs around a low table. "Where are my manners! Please, sit. I'll have Linda bring us some *kaffe*."

Linda pushed a tray on wheels into the room. "I'm one step ahead of you, Father," she announced cheerfully. She lifted the covers off the two plates on the tray with the coffee service, revealing one piled with meats and cheeses and the other stacked with sweet pastries. "I thought our guests might like some snacks."

"You thought right," Ezekiel enthused. "I mean, thank you. That's really thoughtful."

"You *just* ate." Sarah Jennifer accepted the cup Linda held out. "Thank you."

Brutus held up a hand when Linda offered him a cup. "Not while I'm on duty, thanks."

Linda glanced at Ezekiel, smoothing her braid with a hand. "Call if you need anything else. I'll be at my desk. Papa, make sure you eat something. You missed breakfast again."

Sarah Jennifer caught the twinkle in the chancellor's eyes as Linda left. "You love her a lot."

Samuel nodded. "I couldn't ask for a more faithful child than Linda. She had such plans to see the world when she was young. Then her mother was taken by the Hunger, and after that, she retreated into her books. She rarely leaves the chancellery."

Sarah Jennifer felt for this father. "You are both welcome to visit Salem with us when Berlin is wrapped up. Some time away from home could help her move forward."

Ezekiel looked up from the snacks. "If she's interested in books, the library might persuade her."

"Then by all means, do your best," Samuel encouraged. "Linda's passion for life has faded since her mother was taken from us."

Ezekiel looked at Sarah Jennifer for permission.

The major nodded. "If she's willing to leave Bad Salzig, we need every capable mind we can get."

Ezekiel hurriedly stacked a few more pastries on his plate before leaving the room.

Samuel's smile returned to light the room. "That's very kind."

Sarah Jennifer chuckled. "Don't thank me until you've met the council. We should go to Upinniemi as well if you decide to join the trade alliance."

Samuel laughed. "Straight to business?"

Sarah Jennifer explained the situation in Berlin. "Unfortunately. I'm needed back in Berlin. There's been an outbreak there, and the city has to be evacuated."

Samuel listened intently, the air of humor gone from his demeanor. "I've heard of the alliance. We are a large town, but what can we offer?"

"Exportable goods." Sarah Jennifer lifted a shoulder. "Everywhere needs one or more of the basics: grain, sugar, salt, pepper, tea, or coffee. Ore mining has resumed in many places across Europe. Archangelsk has timber and natural gas to trade for steel and iron. Japan needs steel and processed metals in exchange for electronics, fish, and fresh produce. Norway needs timber and food in exchange for its petroleum and natural gas reserves. America needs mineral ores and precious metals in exchange for steel and grain. Everyone wants the spices and cacao beans Salem exports."

"Chocolate?" Samuel inquired, dazed by the reach the Trade Alliance had.

Sarah Jennifer chuckled. "You bet. That's not all, but it gives you an idea of how global trade is resuming."

"Commerce makes the world go round," Samuel agreed. "I will need to discuss the opportunity offered by the alliance with my ministers before I make any decisions."

Sarah Jennifer nodded. "Understandable. The sooner I

can secure a home for the eighty-six hundred people in Berlin, the sooner I can move on to the next crisis. The question is, can you help? I'm authorized to speak on behalf of the alliance. They'll guarantee assistance for anyone who takes in people displaced by the Madness."

Samuel gave the request serious thought. "We can take in two, maybe three thousand if you can provide grain to feed them," he offered. "There are other towns along the river that would make room. I'll speak to Franz, the mayor of Lykershausen, for a start."

"That's across the river, right?" Brutus asked.

"That's right," Samuel confirmed. "He is a good man. The mountain people will also help, for a price. We will see that the Berliners have homes."

"Thank you," Sarah Jennifer told him earnestly. "We'll get the grain, and I'll make a task force available to help with any construction that needs to be done to accommodate so many people."

Samuel plucked a quill from a pot and a piece of paper from a drawer. "I'll send a message to Franz immediately."

Sarah Jennifer held out a hand as he moved to dip the quill in his inkpot. "No need. How would you like to fly to Lykershausen and deliver your message in person?"

Samuel dropped his quill. "I'd like that a great deal."

CHAPTER TWENTY-EIGHT

Ezekiel found Linda in the east wing library. She was reading by lamplight, her hair falling over the page. He coughed politely to announce his presence when she didn't notice him.

Linda looked up from the yellowed pages of the old book she was studying and appraised Ezekiel. "Yes?"

Ezekiel felt nervous all of a sudden. He glanced at the pile of books on Linda's desk. "You're reading about genetics?"

Linda nodded. "Yes. I believe the answer to the Hunger is somewhere in the knowledge our ancestors left behind."

Ezekiel grinned, pulling up a chair. "What do you know about the Matriarch?"

"Who?" Linda's attention drifted back to her book.

"Bethany Anne?" Ezekiel asked. "The Queen Bitch?"

Linda gave him a blank look. "What are you talking about?"

"Magic." Ezekiel opened his hand and manifested a fireball in the shape of a bird. He let it hover over his palm for a moment before extinguishing it.

Linda's jaw dropped.

Ezekiel felt in his bones that Linda was different. The Etheric resonated around her. "You're enhanced in some way. I can tell."

Linda clammed up. "No. I'm not special."

Ezekiel reached for her hand. "Hey, it's okay. No judgment here. I live with witches and werewolves, sometimes with an alien and a werebear. You can't weird me out."

Linda appeared to be considering something. She withdrew her hand and steered the conversation away from her. "Do you set things on fire wherever you go?"

Ezekiel laughed. "Thankfully, no. I spend a lot of time meditating when we're not in Salem. There I can go down to the training grounds and let loose if I'm finding it difficult to work through some emotion or other. Or I can go to the library. We have so many books, I don't think I could ever read them all."

He smiled. "Your father thinks it's a good idea for you to visit Salem. I could show you around."

Linda's eyes widened. "What, leave my father? I couldn't."

"If he decides your people are going to join the alliance, you can come with him when he goes to negotiate with the imports and exports committee." Ezekiel smiled.

Linda shook her head. "He will send one of his ministers. He can't travel. What if something happens to him and we are left without a chancellor?"

"I lost both my parents seven years ago," Ezekiel confided, seeing her fear override her curiosity. "Not a day goes by that I don't miss them. Being taken so far from home and everything I knew was hard at first, but I told myself that the last thing they would want was for me to hold myself back."

Linda gave him a shrewd look. "That's pretty deep for someone your age."

"My age?" Ezekiel cocked his head. "You're not that much older than me. Experience is what counts. Come to Salem? Sarah Jennifer won't let anything bad happen to your father, and I swear I'll take care of you."

Linda's indecisive look vanished as she came to a decision. She got to her feet and opened the drapes to reveal the gloaming sky. "Come with me. I want to show you something."

Ezekiel followed Linda to a grand house set in gardens. She ducked behind a hedge as they passed the front door, staying low until they reached the kitchen door.

A plump woman with her hair in a bun let out a little squeal when they burst through the door.

"Sorry, Magda!" Linda trilled, pulling an apologetic Ezekiel by the hand as she ran through the kitchen. The corridor she took twisted around the dining hall and past a room filled with boots and coats and another that smelled strongly of freshly-tanned hides before it terminated in a heavy oak door.

"Where are we going?" Ezekiel asked when Linda unlocked the door with a chunky key from a ring on her belt.

"To my secret place," Linda told him, reaching for an oil lamp that hung on the wall.

She lit the lamp and beckoned him down the narrow stone staircase beyond.

Ezekiel manifested a ball of light and descended into the darkness.

The chancellor's daughter led him unerringly through a maze of cobwebbed cellars. The only light came from the bobbing lamp and the steady glow of Ezekiel's energy ball.

Linda put her lamp down on a pedestal by the door to the crypt where her family was interred. "No one comes down here except my father, and he works late into the night."

Stone caskets took up most of the space, the lids carved into effigies of the departed. Fresh flowers adorned the shrines at their feet. Ezekiel thought about the cairn he'd raised for his parents and swallowed the lump that formed in his throat. "You honor your dead well."

"It's my duty." Linda took his hand and tugged. "We're almost there."

She stopped at a bare rock wall and turned her head to look at Ezekiel. "I've never shown anyone this."

Ezekiel was distracted by the way the lamplight fell across her face, her eyes catching the shine of the warm glow.

No, wait! Her eyes were glowing red.

She placed a hand on the bare wall and closed her eyes. The rock opened down an invisible seam, and light flooded from the surface.

Ezekiel couldn't contain his delight. "I knew it! You have magic. Why would you hide it?"

Linda's eyes returned to their usual blue, and the rock knit back together again. "I don't know. Different isn't a good thing to be around here. It's not normal for someone to be able to talk to rocks."

Ezekiel grabbed both of Linda's hands and spun her around. "That's where you're wrong. Everyone has the potential for magic. There are tiny machines in our blood called nanocytes. They give us the power to alter reality."

Linda gave him a skeptical look. "Tiny machines?"

Ezekiel nodded. "The Matriarch's gift. The thing that caused the Madness was supposed to give us magic."

Linda sat across from Ezekiel with her back against the wall. "How do you know all this?"

"That's a *long* story," Ezekiel shifted on the smooth stone floor, wishing he'd brought his datapad from his cabin. He gave her a shortened version of everything he knew about how nanocytes should have worked and how Arthur Drake's interference had changed the course of history. "That's why the Defense Force exists—because something went wrong, and we're going to make it right."

Linda listened with her hands folded in her lap. When he was done, she looked at her hands for a long time, her expression changing as she reconciled the real history of the world with what she'd thought she knew.

"How does any of this exist without the whole world knowing?" she asked finally. "None of the books I've read say anything about vampires, werepeople, or magic."

Ezekiel shrugged. "The UnknownWorld was hidden when your books were written. The old books in Salem Library are the same. I can get you copies of the histories compiled by Mr. Hawkins. He's the librarian."

Linda's lamp guttered out suddenly, and she glanced at

it in surprise. "We've been gone too long. Father will wonder where I went."

Ezekiel got to his feet and offered Linda a hand. "Will you come to Salem?"

Linda nodded. "Yes. But first, I have to tell my father I have magic."

Samuel received the news that Linda had felt the need to keep her affinity for rock secret with sadness. He told Sarah Jennifer he would be honored to accept her invitation and arranged for his ministers to take over his duties after provisions had been made for the incoming settlers from Berlin.

Sarah Jennifer reassigned one of the three task forces stationed in Berlin to the valley, and construction began in the five towns that had volunteered to take in the Berliners. Carver's task force arrived two days later from Upinniemi, their Pods loaded to capacity with the first grain delivery and tons of baled long straw for roofing.

Then the real work to expand the five towns began. The residents contributing to the construction efforts in their towns were amazed at first by the excavators Sarah Jennifer had brought in to speed up the process of connecting the new residential quarter to the town's sewers and water supply and astounded when the magic-users moved in to reconfigure the town walls and raise the shells of houses from the valley floor.

Seeing is believing, and just as it had been when Salem opened its doors, belief was all it took to ignite the spark in some. Those who attempted magic and succeeded were invited to visit the Defense Force in Salem for training when the work was completed.

Sarah Jennifer ran point on the operation from Bad Salzig. Her days were full, but she kept her eye out for Ezekiel. The chancellor's daughter joined Ezekiel and Frances, the trained magic-user assigned to Brutus' task force. She observed the friendship between Ezekiel and Linda cementing in the background of the rush to expand with quiet approval.

They showed up for duty every morning bleary-eyed from stealing the nights to talk about magic, the UnknownWorld, and the futures they dreamed of. Linda devoured the books on his datapad while they picnicked on blankets beneath the huge oak reading table in her father's library.

The first group from Berlin arrived six weeks later, while the people of Bad Salzig were gearing up for the harvest festival. Tired, afraid, and skittish from so long in quarantine, they filed nervously off the transport Pods.

Everyone who wasn't out in the fields or making last-minute touches to the residential quarter welcomed them with open arms. The chancellor was there to extend an invitation to the pre-festival feast, and later that evening, the town got to know the new arrivals over the traditional cookout where everyone made their special family recipes and brought them to the square to share with their neighbors.

Barbecue and beer being an ice breaker anywhere in the world, the new residents shed their misery and celebrated the revival of hope for the future.

Sarah Jennifer left the speeches to the chancellor, shirking politics in favor of sampling the wide variety of foods and ales people brought to the feast.

The gathering gave her the excuse to assess the well-being of the people, an obligation she took seriously, and to check in with Ezekiel.

She found him at the soup stand, serving borscht with a dollop of sour cream, potato soup with sausage, and a heartier goulash from huge pans while Linda handed out griddled oatcakes as fast as she could cook them.

"You two make a good team," Sarah Jennifer commented to Linda as she received two hot oatcakes to dip into her soup. "Are you and your father packed and ready to go?"

Linda smiled and nodded without relaxing her vigilance over the griddle. "Almost. We still have a week before the trip. Father is fussing about leaving his ministers in charge while we are away, but he is determined I shouldn't miss out."

Ezekiel cleared off an empty cooler for Sarah Jennifer to use as a seat. "Stay with us for a while."

Sarah Jennifer shook her head. "No can do, kiddo. I'm due at the ring."

Linda's mouth made a little O of surprise. "You signed up for the prize fight?"

Ezekiel snickered. "You just can't pass up a competitive fight, can you?"

Sarah Jennifer grinned. "No." She dipped her cup in the water butt and shook it dry before attaching it to her belt. "I'll see you kids there."

Ezekiel watched her saunter away before whirling to cut the flame of the burner.

"What are you doing?" Linda asked, perplexed.

"You won't want to miss this," Ezekiel told her. "I swear!"

Linda gave the soup stand one last look and took Ezekiel's outstretched hand.

The mountain man was small compared to a lowlander. He made up for it in deadliness. Unfortunately for them, his opponents only tended to focus on the first part, and now Piet was in the semi-final with his eye on the bag of gold that was sitting on the Chancellor's lap, waiting to be awarded to the last fighter standing.

Sarah Jennifer did not get sidetracked by his diminutive stature, being on the short side herself. He was bound with muscle earned with hard labor. His arms were toned from swinging a weapon for a living.

This man was a warrior, not a fighter.

She inclined her head as their stares met in the center of the ring. "Ready for a real challenger?"

"I've been fighting the dead for longer than you've been alive, soldier lady," he shot back, irked by her attitude.

Sarah Jennifer settled into her ready stance. "Maybe you're not as smart as I thought."

Piet narrowed his eyes, unsure of why she looked relaxed. He realized with interest that the woman he faced lived here in the fight. This was her realm. "Maybe I'm not as smart as *I* thought," he muttered to himself. "This oughta be interestin'."

The referee refreshed everyone on the rules. "No weapons. No gouging. First to give loses."

Sarah Jennifer opened with an exploratory jab as the referee stepped back.

Piet stepped into her attack, his fist blurring toward her ribs.

Sarah Jennifer saw him coming and rewarded his bold move with an elbow to the temple that sent him reeling for the ropes.

He recovered quickly, and they circled one another. Sarah Jennifer waited for Piet to make a move, but Piet was wary of getting his brain half-scrambled again.

Across the square was another roped-off stage identical to the ring Sarah Jennifer and Piet were fighting in.

A cheer went up around the other ring as the fight concluded, which brought grumbles from the spectators of their fight. Sarah Jennifer glanced at the winner, purposely giving Piet an opening before their match had to be reclassified as a dance-off.

Sarah Jennifer grinned when he moved in with a flurry of fists. Her previous opponents had relied heavily on brute strength. Piet offered technique that could only have been learned by fighting for his life.

She blocked a flying knee with her thigh and broke his nose with a headbutt.

Piet responded by driving his elbows into her gut, getting himself caught in a chokehold for his efforts.

Sarah Jennifer slammed his back onto the canvas, the impact throwing up sawdust from the last fight.

Piet scissored his legs, trapping Sarah Jennifer's leg. In the same movement, he shifted his weight to bring her down.

Sarah Jennifer's knee betrayed her like the no-good bum it was. She lost her balance, but not the advantage. She threw her body into the fall, snatching Piet's ankle on the way to reversing the leg lock and pinning him as she landed.

The crowd went wild. Ezekiel and Linda were right by the ropes, cheering along with everyone else.

"This is the best fight we've seen in years!" Linda yelled, pulling Ezekiel into a hug.

Ezekiel held on with one arm around her shoulders and punched the air with his free hand. "Get him in a headlock!"

Somewhere at the back, the cheering turned to screams.

Sarah Jennifer released Piet and rolled to her feet as the crowd parted to escape the man who had gone Mad. From her raised standpoint, the Mad gorging on his wife's throat looked to be holding her in a tender embrace.

The chancellor got to his feet and called for the guard. Sarah Jennifer saw that the guards were already acting to quell the situation.

The Berliners were screaming, panicked. The people around them were calmer, trusting their protectors. The guards split up, one group moving into the crowd to shepherd the frightened civilians to the sides of the square while the others drew their weapons and piled into the unfolding chaos.

The Mad dropped his wife and lunged at the crowd, biting three more people while the guards were trying to get him under control. Six guards with pikes encircled him, the business ends of their weapons holding him in place while more guards moved in with snare poles.

One of the guards hooked the Mad around the neck, then another, and still the Mad fought. Another guard removed his head with a clean sword strike, careful to avoid the arterial spray.

It was too little too late.

A few molecules of the fine spray made it past the headsman's mask. The corruption was already in his lungs.

The dead wife rose, red light in her eyes.

At the edge of the crowd, the three who had been bitten turned on the people nearest to them as immutable hunger overrode them with animal need.

Like a spark in a cloud of gas, the Madness rippled across the square.

CHAPTER TWENTY-NINE

The headsman dropped his sword and let out a tortured moan as the Madness took him. His fellow guards were in the same predicament.

Sarah Jennifer watched the whole thing unfold in less than ten seconds.

She opened her comm. "We've got a Madness outbreak in Bad Salzig Square. Enora, I need emergency transport for the chancellor and his daughter. Brutus, I want every Were in the area to converge on this square, loaded for Mad."

"Ah, HELL, no!" Piet swore. He slid under the ropes and was gone the next moment.

Sarah Jennifer had no time to dwell on the look of rage on the mountain man's face. She vaulted the ropes, landing next to Ezekiel and Linda. "Let's go."

She went ahead of Ezekiel and Linda, forcing a path through the chaos to get to the chancellor's box.

Samuel wasn't there.

Sarah Jennifer heard Linda's name being called. She

pinpointed the sound and caught sight of the chancellor swinging his sword as he darted through the crowd, looking for his daughter.

Eight Pods arrived from different directions, one coming to land by the box. Rattling automatic weapons fire punctuated the screams and snarls as the Defense Force joined the melee, doing what they did best to suppress the danger to the uninfected.

Sarah Jennifer could only hope they saved more than they lost. She dashed into the Pod and grabbed a rifle and a pouch of ammunition from the locker. Ezekiel and Linda were still outside when she turned around. She stalked out of the Pod and pointed at the door. "What are you waiting for? Get in the Pod!"

Linda clung to Ezekiel, her face white with fear, but she was resolute. "I'm not leaving without my father! He's all I've got in this world."

Sarah Jennifer spied the chancellor climbing the fountain fifty feet away.

Sarah Jennifer hesitated to leave them. "Get in the damn Pod!" she yelled over the roar of the battle. "If it's a choice between you two or him, he's not going to make it."

Linda acquiesced. "Save him! Please!"

"I'll keep Linda safe," Ezekiel promised, edging Linda into the Pod.

The vehicle shot upward as Sarah Jennifer shouldered her way into the fight. At such close quarters the rifle was only useful as a club, so she drew her knives and got to work carving a path to the fountain.

The Madness was a flame to the touchpaper of fear. A fireball lit the night as someone knocked a fire basket into a stall selling straw dolls. In the panic, the fire spread rapidly to the stalls on either side, adding to the danger.

The people ran every which way, trying to get away from everyone else. The exits from the square were choked with the fallen. With no easy way to escape, they climbed trees and walls to avoid being eaten alive.

Sarah Jennifer took out Mad wherever she saw the red glow in their eyes. The rest she tuned out, her focus on retrieving the chancellor and getting him to safety.

Samuel had lost his sword. His cloak was discarded by the fountain, and he was swinging the gold ceremonial chain he'd been wearing over it to fend off the encroaching Mad.

A child screamed, the shrill bleat diverting the major's attention to a burning stall where a little boy no more than four years old was trapped in a prison of fire.

Time stopped for Sarah Jennifer.

She knew she wasn't going to make it in time to save both the boy and Samuel.

She had to try.

The boy screeched as Sarah Jennifer crashed through the side of the stall to reach him. She scooped him up without slowing her pace and cradled his tiny body to her chest, turning her shoulder to take the impact as she crashed through the wall on the other side.

Sarah Jennifer's heart plummeted when she saw that Samuel had vanished from sight.

Assuming the Mad had overwhelmed him with sheer weight of numbers, she deposited the boy in the arms of a passing woman and tore toward the fountain without looking back.

No longer taking the time to kill the Mad, Sarah Jennifer tossed them aside as she plowed through the mob surrounding the fountain.

She screamed with fury at her failure, her eyes lighting up the night as the strength of her anger was transmuted into a pulse of concussive Etheric energy that knocked the Mad back.

Sarah Jennifer faltered on the steps of the fountain. Once again, the chancellor was not in the expected place.

Had he escaped? He wasn't among the Mad, who were starting to recover.

She unslung the rifle on her back and took them out with clean shots between the eyes as she pivoted to scan the square.

No sign of the chancellor.

The staccato weapons fire was dropping off. The Defense Force knew their work inside and out. After eleven years of being the first—and often only—responders to major outbreaks of Madness, she knew she could trust them to save the uninfected and secure the town before the Madness spread to the whole valley.

Sarah Jennifer reported her position to Enora as she skirted the fountain, passing along the order to look for the chancellor.

A side street leading off the avenue ahead was the only egress she could see from that part of the square. It appeared to run the length of the square, providing access to the rear of the buildings.

Sarah Jennifer stepped over the corpses of Mad and entered the dark street with her rifle at the ready. In the scarce light offered by a single open door, she picked out two figures moving at the far end of the unlit side street.

The only Mad were dead Mad who looked to have recently suffered considerable blunt force trauma to their skulls. Sarah Jennifer gave them a wide berth as she advanced toward the sickle of light.

The door of the house was ajar when she reached it. Her sense of smell was overwhelmed by blood and death.

Sarah Jennifer held onto her hope as she nudged the door open with the tip of her rifle barrel. She called out as she crossed the threshold.

The house was dark save for the oil lamp on the windowsill that cast just enough light to make identifying what was in the shadows a guessing game.

Sarah Jennifer jerked her rifle around when the shadows moved. "Say something if you're not infected," she commanded, her finger curling toward the trigger.

"Easy there, soldier lady," a gruff voice grumbled.

"Major Walton, is that you?"

Sarah Jennifer put up her rifle and spoke into the comm as Piet and Samuel stepped into the light. "Stop the search. I've got the chancellor."

"Sending transport to your location," was the reply from Enora.

Sarah Jennifer breathed in relief. "You had us worried for a minute, Chancellor."

Samuel patted Piet's shoulder. "My rearick friend saved me." He looked out a window at the square in dismay. "This is a disaster. So many dead."

Comfort wasn't Sarah Jennifer's strong suit, but she gave it her best shot. "It's been contained. It's almost over."

Samuel nodded bleakly. "What about Linda? I couldn't find her."

"Ezekiel took her home," Sarah Jennifer reassured him. "Which is where we need to get you."

Samuel refused to lean on anyone for support as he hobbled back to the square with Sarah Jennifer and Piet.

He fell behind by a few steps but waved her on. "I'm fine."

Sarah Jennifer allowed him his pride, but there was nothing she could do about the adrenaline that quickened her stride when she saw Ezekiel and Linda standing by the Pod with Brutus.

Linda let out a sob when she saw that Samuel was with Sarah Jennifer. "Father!"

Ezekiel's gaze flicked up, his joy morphing into panic. "Look out!"

Sarah Jennifer turned in time to see a Mad leap from the window above Samuel's head.

Before anyone could react, the Mad crashed into Samuel. They landed in a tangled heap with the Mad on top.

Samuel screamed in pain and shock as its teeth sank into the soft flesh of his neck. He kicked the Mad, but dislodging it only relieved the pain temporarily. Sarah Jennifer hauled the creature off him, but not before it latched onto his cheek and jerked its head back, freeing a chunk of flesh.

Sarah Jennifer shot the Mad in the head.

Linda ran to her father when the Mad collapsed as its brain matter painted the wall. She knelt in the spreading pool of blood, inconsolable as she held him.

Samuel's eyes fluttered. Each breath was a thousand years of torture. He saw his daughter's face and fought to remain long enough to say goodbye. "Linda..."

"Hold on, Father!" she sobbed, squeezing his hand. "Please don't leave me!"

Samuel somehow managed to lift the block of granite his hand had turned into and placed it on her cheek. "Light of my life," he burbled through the bloody foam pouring from his lips. "You have been...a good...daughter. You will be...a good...chancellor. Listen... Listen to Adrien. He... means...well."

Linda's pleading was the last thing Samuel heard as his heart gave out from shock and blood loss.

"NO!" Linda keened. "*No!*"

Sarah Jennifer chose not to notice the tremor building beneath their feet. She took a knee by Linda and put her arm around the distraught young woman's shoulders and eased her away gently, murmuring soft and meaningless words.

The Defense Force stayed to assist with cleanup and repairs. Sarah Jennifer spoke at the mass funeral for everyone who had died that was held three days after the outbreak.

Ezekiel did a valiant job of hiding his broken heart when Linda was sworn in as chancellor the day after.

He was less successful when it came time to return to Salem.

It went unnoticed at first. Sarah Jennifer took it at face

value when he threw himself into working on expanding the range of his magic. She couldn't put her finger on the change in him, but as New Year's approached, she realized the light that had returned to his eyes in the last seven years had diminished, replaced by obsession.

She became concerned when she sought him out and was rebuffed with excuses about work he was doing for Lilith.

Work Lilith knew nothing about.

She took her concerns to Esme and Brutus.

They advised giving him space.

Sarah Jennifer considered their advice. She even tried it, as painful as it was to let the silence between them stretch out for a week, ten days, a month.

Impatience won out. The silence killed her slowly. A confrontation she could handle.

Sarah Jennifer approached Ezekiel's quarters with apprehension and anticipation twisting like snakes inside her. She needed to break through the walls he had put up.

Her hand hovered over the door.

"Don't yell at him," she told herself before knocking.

There was no answer.

Sarah Jennifer knocked again, listening hard this time as the sound rebounded off the walls inside. The apartment sounded empty.

Strange. He hadn't been at the library or the training ground. The only other place he went these days was the food joints he frequented. She settled in to wait, choosing to see Ezekiel being out for dinner as a sign she should think some more on what she was going to say.

After an hour passed and there was still no sign of him,

Sarah Jennifer began to get antsy. She paced outside his door for another twenty minutes before she gave in and called Enora to locate him.

Sarah Jennifer's heart sank when the AI took longer than expected to complete her search.

"Ezekiel's neural chip is offline," Enora informed her. "I cannot locate him."

Sarah Jennifer added Esme to their link. "Can you locate Ezekiel telepathically?"

"Hello to you too," Esme responded. "No. Where is he?"

"That's what I'm trying to find out," Sarah Jennifer retorted, worry crystalizing in her gut. "Enora can't find him either, and he's not in any of his usual places."

Her gaze settled on the door. "I'm going to take a look in his apartment."

"What happened to giving him space?" Esme asked pointedly.

"Tried it, didn't stick," Sarah Jennifer replied, taking a firm grip of the door handle. She gave it a sharp twist, snapping the mechanism, and opened the door.

Ezekiel's apartment was a lot tidier than Sarah Jennifer usually found it. She had an inkling he hadn't cleaned up the clutter out of a late-developing instinct to organize his belongings.

She wandered into the kitchen and found the sink clear of dishes and the refrigerator empty. There was no laundry in the bathroom hamper either.

Sarah Jennifer hesitated before entering the bedroom. She eased the door open, not knowing what she would find.

The bedroom was as neat as the rest of the apartment.

The bed was made, the quilt pulled tight. The pillows had been arranged in size order.

Sarah Jennifer's eyes landed on an envelope propped against the potted plant on the bedside table.

It had her name written on it.

CHAPTER THIRTY

"Sarah Jennifer? Should I take you back to Salem?"

She came back to herself as Enora's tone became strident with concern. She didn't remember calling for Enora or giving her a destination.

The letter was still clutched in her hand.

She looked at the viewscreen to see where they were.

Of course.

Past, present, future. It all came around again in the end.

"Land there," Sarah Jennifer told Enora, pointing at the familiar grouping of buildings.

"Are you sure this is the right place?" Enora asked. "I'm not reading any life signs."

Sarah Jennifer nodded. "I've never been more certain in my life. Take us down."

Enora landed the airship outside the entrance, and Sarah Jennifer headed through the ranch gate with trepidation quickening her heartbeat.

Pines had taken full advantage of the shift in climate to

push down from the mountains as less hardy plants died off, but here in the valley, it was still warm.

It was exactly the same and completely changed. Nature had taken over here just like everywhere else where there was nobody around to tame it.

Briars ran rampant, supporting the climbing plants that entwined the thorns covering the outer walls of the homestead.

Nature's trellis was bare of roses at this time of year.

Sarah Jennifer pushed through tangled winter jasmine cocooning the porch, the scent conjuring the ghosts of her and Jeremiah planting it together.

"You just want to cover the smell of cow shit," Jeremiah *teased.*

"You just like giving me a reason to be mad at you," she *replied. "You going to cuss like that in front of our son?"*

Jeremiah's hands slipped around her waist to rest on her still-flat stomach.

"I'd never cuss in front of our daughter."

Sarah Jennifer snapped back to the present. She wiped her eyes and walked into the house. It was eerie to be back in the place she'd made her home a lifetime ago with the furniture all in the same place. Someone had covered the larger pieces with dust sheets, but she recognized the horsehair couch she'd had made and instantly hated, her sewing table, and the piano.

She lifted the sheet off the kitchen table, and it was a knife to the heart to see the table she'd made with her own two hands, struggling with a busted knee when she'd first arrived in the area. This simple slab of wood held so many memories. Rowdy conversations over the dinners she'd provided for her loyal ranch hands. The more intimate meals she and Jeremiah had shared. The time the infamous sheep rustler Clarence Beasley had fallen in the canyon, and hers had been the closest place to bring him to save his life. Clarence had survived having his legs set on this very table and gone right back to hustling black-market mutton.

She dropped the sheet and went into her former study.

The pigeonholes were as empty as the fields. No cattle meant no paperwork.

The yard was empty, too. No soft whinnies met her as she looked into the horses' stalls. The steel tack hooks supported only cobwebs whose disgruntled occupants scattered at the unexpected illumination.

Sarah Jennifer admitted to herself why she'd come to the ranch. The ghosts of her past were the only things with more power to hurt her than Ezekiel's midnight flit.

She unclenched the fist crushing Ezekiel's apology and read it again. This time she didn't ignore the parallels to the note she'd left Jeremiah all those years ago.

Sarah Jennifer

I've started this over and over, trying to find the words. I guess if I knew how to say this without hurting you, I'd say it to your face.

I have to get out of Salem.

I'm sorry for taking the coward's way. If I see you, I won't have the strength to go through with it. You've been so good to me. You gave me a family and a home. I am the man I am today because you took care of me. You never tried to replace my mother, and I love you for that.

Everything you're doing is noble and good and just, but I have to live for the future I believe in. I need to give the world my version of what you gave me. I can't do that as part of the Defense Force. I can't leave Earth with you.

I don't know where I'm going or when I'll be back. If I'll be back. I just know that there's a world out there that needs me and if I don't answer the call…I don't know. I only know what I'm doing is right.

I figure you'll understand that when you've calmed down.

I hope you don't hate me for it.

I hope our paths cross again one day.

Ezekiel

The letter in her hand was payback for what she'd done to escape the pain of remaining here to watch Jeremiah grow old and die.

She couldn't deny it.

Nor would she blame Ezekiel for his actions.

She wished she'd told him about her past. Then he would have known she understood. That she could never hate him.

Then what had driven her to come back here?

She examined her motivation and found guilt at the center of her reasoning. She empathized with Ezekiel because she had committed the same act of cowardice and never forgiven herself for it.

It was the same guilt that had compelled her to walk the wilderness. The same guilt that had been at the back of her mind when she'd made the decision to let Ezekiel into her heart. She'd needed half a century alone to wear it down to the point where she could begin living again, if only for others, but a millennium wouldn't be enough to erase it completely.

Why was she pulling the scab off this old wound?

Sarah Jennifer didn't know what she was looking for, but her visit to the past wasn't over yet. She left the house and let herself out through the side gate in the yard, cringing at the complaint the rusted hinges made.

"I feel you," she murmured as her knee twinged in reaction to the rough ground.

She bundled her clothing with her gun belt and switched to her wolf form to ease the pressure on it before sniffing about for the path.

Searching out the path took longer than she'd expected. Time had disguised it with rampant briars entwined with brambles.

She found it and forced her way through the tangled, thick-growing pines with the help of her teeth and claws, fired by her determination to get to the clearing by the lake she was aiming for.

Sarah Jennifer broke through the tree line as the sun dipped low on the lake. The clearing was massively overgrown, but the cabin was still there. It was really more of a hut, but it was where everyone on the ranch had come to fish.

The door hung askew in its frame. Sarah Jennifer padded around the degrading walls and continued to the simple stone cairn nearby.

When she got closer, she saw another grave marker beside the cairn she'd built for her lost child.

Jeremiah.

Someone had been around to bury him. The knowledge eased her.

Sarah Jennifer dropped her clothing bundle and brushed away the briars, a soft whine escaping when she read the inscription on the carved stone. Her heart throbbed as she sank to the ground and laid her nose on her husband's grave.

She had no words. She wrapped her body around the painstakingly placed stones and howled.

Another wolf answered in the distance, reminding Sarah Jennifer of the last night she'd been alone, of Samhain and her rebirth.

Sometime after the sun set, she switched back to her human form and dressed before sitting at Jeremiah's grave.

Sarah Jennifer sobbed, her tears staining the stones as she told Jeremiah about her life now, about her responsibilities, and everything the world was facing.

For that brief time, she allowed herself to feel pity for a life that had never been meant to work out. For the differences that had driven them apart when all they had wanted was to fill their lives with each other.

All her reasons for leaving were still as valid as the day she'd come to them. It hadn't stopped her from holding onto that love or from scourging her heart raw with the pain of its failure.

She railed at the stupidity of loving someone who was always going to leave her alone. She cursed him for being everything she wanted and his mortality for taking that from them. At the cruel fragility of life, that all the nanocytes she had couldn't save their child.

Her tears slowed as the flood of emotions she'd kept dammed up with duty ran dry.

Sarah Jennifer lay with her face touching the grass for a long while, waiting for the hole in her heart to tear her apart again. The stars came out, their light cold to her emptiness. She closed her eyes and hugged her arms to her chest, feeling exposed without the walls she'd built to avoid dealing with the belief that she'd made herself unworthy by walking out on her life not once but twice.

The faces of her family came to her. Her grandparents' pride and pleasure when she called Keeg Station. Her blood, and the ones who had claimed her as their own. Lilith. Brutus. Esme. The friends she'd made along the way. Amelie and Eoin, Reika, Brittvi, Irina, Olaf. Ezekiel wasn't gone forever.

Sarah Jennifer realized with a shock that while she had been hiding behind her duty, they had changed the landscape of her heart. These people whose cooperation and belief in her vision had given humanity a fighting chance had repaired her hope in the future.

Hope wasn't dead.

Sarah Jennifer looked up, hearing something crashing through the pines with purpose. She reached for her gun belt and withdrew her shotgun. She couldn't smell the stench of a Mad, but she'd been crying, and her sinuses were messed up.

There was only one way to find out.

She got to her feet and faced the oncoming interloper. "Who's there?"

The foliage at the tree line parted, and Esme walked out. She took one look at Sarah Jennifer and decided that

Enora had done the right thing in rushing to Salem to fetch her. "Duckie, what's the matter? What are you doing all the way out here?"

Sarah Jennifer blinked. "What am I... What are *you* doing here?"

Esme got all the information she needed from reading the grave markers. "I was looking for you when Enora came swooping in, all dramatic. You scared the bits out of her."

Sarah Jennifer was overwhelmed. The sudden appearance of her friend just when she needed her the most pushed her back over the edge. She fished the letter out of her pocket and handed it to Esme.

The witch pressed the damp paper back into her hand after she read it. "That boy has a destiny he's chasing. He'll turn up when he's caught up with it."

Sarah Jennifer returned the letter to her pocket. "I knew he was going to spread his wings eventually, but it still caught me off-guard. Why were you looking for me?"

Esme scrutinized Sarah Jennifer for a long moment. "Fine, you want it that way. Lilith and I made a breakthrough with the Madness. We're going to talk more about why you ended up here later."

Sarah Jennifer touched the grave markers one last time, knowing in her heart that she'd never return. "No need. I've said my goodbyes. Let's go."

AUTHOR NOTES - N D ROBERTS
NOVEMBER 20, 2020

Thank you for reading our book, and thank you for reading all the way to these notes! I hope we satisfied some of the questions everyone has around the Madness.

A few more thank-yous before I talk about the next book...

First to Lynne Stiegler for her beautiful edit. To everyone in the Beta and JIT groups for their efforts to keep us scatterbrained authors on track. To Andrew Dobell for the amazing cover. To Michael for giving us this universe to escape into. Last but most importantly, to *you*, for continuing to read these stories and for supporting us with such wonderful reviews on *The Line Unbroken*. From the bottom of my heart, when I see one of you left us a few words it makes my day. It's been a hard year all around and it means the world that people still took time to do that. So, thank you.

Aaand back to the story! A *lot* happened in this book. We've fixed the climate control system and set up for the fantastical geography of Irth. The website for the National

Snow and Ice Data Center was a super helpful resource, as was Wikipedia, and my retinas have permanent images of the globe seared onto them from all the hours looking at Google Maps, plotting routes, working out where the changes were happening. We will get to the fantasy world, but the science supporting it will be as accurate as we can make it while staying true to the story.

We also moved a huge step forward with the connections; back to *Live Free or Die* with Arthur Drake (more about that in book 3 ;)), and forward to the Age of Magic with Ezekiel. That boy! Actually, Ezekiel defied expectation and I only wanted to strangle him a *tiiiny* bit by the time he left Salem. Will he be back? In Salem, who knows? In the next book, yes! If you haven't read The Caitlin Chronicles yet and you like spoilers, I recommend you pick up book 5 in the series (and the rest of the series because it's fantastic!). Thank you to everyone else who read it last year and has waited patiently to find out how Ezekiel got there.

The other major thing is the connection to space. This is going to be the focus of the next book, along with final resolutions to the Madness...and some other stuff I can't talk about just yet. We always had in mind that the Weres needed to mostly vanish before the early Age of Magic books. What we didn't expect was that they needed to stay close to Earth/Irth in preparation for Checkmate.

When I worked out exactly *where* I wanted to take the Defense Force in space, I of course sprang it on Michael with no warning in a Slack message. I didn't have to see his face to know he was doing the eyebrow thing. But he went with it, and with the power of collaboration we've come up with something really cool (translation: that's some pretty tech BA has over there in Endgame... *eyebrow wiggle*) ... I think you're all going to be pleasantly surprised.

To Sarah Jennifer, and her continued growth. Her challenge has always been to let go. She let go of her pride in the *Terry Henry Walton Chronicles*. Her heart in *The Second Dark Ages*. This series I feel is about letting go of her detachment from her past hurts, and daring to have the courage to keep moving through life. I can't ever force a character to grow in a way they wouldn't choose themselves, but I do hope that her breakthrough in this book will lead to her opening her heart again one day. I'm being tricky. I *can* arrange the meeting, but after that it's down to the characters.

Music is always a thing when writing. Throughout the writing of this book was, yes, *the* song. The Man in Black often visits my playlists. There was also a lot of Post Rock, which I love, but the band that fits Sarah Jennifer in my mind is Killswitch Engage.

Until we meet again in the next book, much love to you all,

Nat

Thank you for reading all the way to the back to these humble (if I say so myself) *Author Notes.*

First, I'd like to point out that I read and re-read the part where Nat suggests she sprang the idea of SJ in space, and I didn't notice one little smidgen of guilt.

Nope, not there.

Here, let me help you out so you don't have to turn back a couple of pages:

"When I worked out exactly where I wanted to take the Defense Force in space, *I of course sprang it on Michael with no warning in a Slack message*. I didn't have to see his face to know he was doing the eyebrow thing. But he went with it, and with the power of collaboration, we've come up with something really cool (translation: that's some pretty tech BA has over there in Endgame... *eyebrow wiggle*) ... I think you're all going to be pleasantly surprised."

Highlights are all mine.

For those who believe my collaborators don't give me

@#@#% are obviously *not giving them the credit their evil so richly deserves.*

I remember this moment and my "WTF??" thought when Nat sprang the idea on me. I didn't do a lot of conversation in Slack (typing); I went straight for the "we need to talk" method of communication.

Mind you, I was persuaded to her point of view...but yeah, springing it on me was a bit of an understatement.

Ok, I'll put this to bed.

Just... I want everyone to note that she didn't show any remorse...Like, *none*. Zippo...zilch.

Nada.

Seriously, I'll quit now.

Have a fantastic week!

Ad Aeternitatem,

Michael Anderle

They say that behind every great man is a great woman...but what if that woman is a Werewolf?

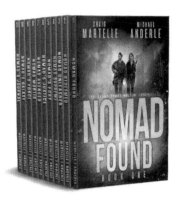

Available now at Amazon and through Kindle Unlimited.

This digital box set contains ALL 11 books of the best-selling Terry Henry Walton Chronicles series from Craig Martelle and Michael Anderle.

Nomad Found

Can Terry Henry Walton help bring humanity back to civilization?

He finds that he needs help and starts building his Force de Guerre, a paramilitary group that will secure this new world from those who would take and destroy.

When the enemies of peace appear before the FDG is

ready, Terry partners with a werewolf to fight a battle that he must win.

Nomad Redeemed

Sawyer Brown is no more, but he was just the minor opening act...

Terry Henry and Charumati (Char) have to deal with her Alpha coming back, the new refugees getting settled in the town and .. Beer!

With the FDG doubling in size, Terry Henry needs to bring about a little organizational structure to the group.While also deciding how to have that conversation with Char about her lineage...

Not sure how that is going to go, Terry Henry had better figure it out, or he is going to be up to his armpits in Werewolves and won't be sure if he can depend on his one ace-in-the-hole.

Or not.

Nomad Unleashed

The heat is unrelenting. The Wastelands are coming for New Boulder. Nature's a total bitch.

And then there's Werewolf heat.

Terry Henry Walton has to come to grips with the reality of his situation.

Civilization cannot return to humanity without help. More help than even an enhanced human can give. Terry and Char take their relationship to a new level before they head out to find a new home to save the people of New Boulder, to rally the survivors that the world is coming back...

And for themselves.

Nomad Supreme

Terry and Char cross the Wastelands returning to New Boulder carrying a message of hope. They'd found a better place. Could they move the whole town there, and would it be safer?

They have a lead on Terry's white whale, a secure military facility.

What will they find and can they break in?

Nomad's Fury

Settled into their new home of North Chicago, Terry and Char find more enemies than they suspected. Faced with their greatest threat, they put the FDG into action against a Forsaken who's surrounded himself with a small army of loyal humans. With Akio's aid, they go to war.

Nomad's Justice
Nomad Avenged
Nomad Mortis
Nomad's Fury
Nomad's Force
Nomad's Galaxy
Nomad's Journal

Available now at Amazon and through Kindle Unlimited.

Made in the USA
Middletown, DE
06 July 2021

43701616R00219